I0565678

Fear

And Other Stories from the Pulps

Fear

And Other Stories from the Pulps

ACHMED ABDULLAH

INTRODUCTION BY
DARRELL SCHWEITZER

WILDSIDE PRESS

FEAR AND OTHER STORIES FROM THE PULPS

Copyright © 2005 by Wildside Press.
All rights reserved.

"Introduction" copyright © 2004 by Wildside Press. "The Charmed Life" originally appeared in *All-Story Weekly*, September 22, 1917. "Framed at the Benefactor's Club" originally appeared in *Detective Story Magazine,* April 16, 1921. "The Yellow Wife" originally appeared in *Munsey's Magazine*, July 1919. "Bismallah!" originally appeared in *Argosy-Allstory Weekly*, June 11, 1921. "Light" originally appeared in *All-Story Weekly*, May 18, 1918. "A Yarkand Survey" originally appeared in *The Argosy*, July 20, 1918. "Fear" originally appeared in *Detective Story Magazine*, February 4, 1919.

For more information, contact the publisher at
www.wildsidepress.com

Contents

Introduction

ACHMED ABDULLAH. There was a time when his name was synony-mous with romantic, exotic adventure. The byline of Achmed Abdullah appeared on numerous magazine stories and books. His English style was excellent, even poetic, but with a voice of authenticity that suggested that maybe this writer was an Arab or some other "Oriental." All the better, in an era in which Lawrence of Arabia was one of the first media celebrities and Rudolph Valentino's portrayal of *The Sheik* played to every woman's daydreams.

The truth is more complicated and even more exotic. Those who met Abdullah found him very British in speech, manner and ideas. Indeed, he had been educated at Eton and Oxford (and the University of Paris), and had served in the British Army in the Middle East, India, and China, but he was actually the son of a Russian Grand Duke, the second cousin of Czar Nicholas II. His Russian name was Alexander Nicholayevitch Romanoff (sometimes given as Romanowski). His Muslim name was Achmed Abdullah Nadir Khan el-Durani el-Iddrissyeh. While the byline "Achmed Abdullah" was easy to remember and quite exotic, it wasn't, strictly speaking, a pseudonym, and he came by it legitimately. Admittedly "Achmed Adbullah" was more likely to sell books of Ori-ental adventure than "Alexander Romanoff."

Abdullah/Romanoff was born in 1881 and died in 1945. His birth-place is variously reported as Malta or Russia. What is certain is that after his army service, he embarked on a general literary career, writing novels and stories of mystery and adventure and some fantasy, with much of his work appearing in pulp magazines such as *Munsey's, Argosy,* and *All-Story.* His first novel was *The Swinging Caravan* (1911), followed by *The Red Stain* (1915), *The Blue-Eyed Manchu* (1916), *Bucking the Tiger* (1917), *The Trail of the Beast* (1918), *The Man on Horseback* (1919), *The Mating of the Blades* (1921), and so on, all the way up to *Deliver Us From Evil* (1939). He edited anthologies, including *Stories for Men* (1925), *Lute and Scimitar* (1928), and *Mysteries of Asia* (1935).

Among his fantasy volumes, the story collection *Wings: Tales of the Psychic* (1920) is most recommended by aficionados. His best-remembered and most famous work is the 1924 novelization of Douglas Fairbanks, Sr.'s film, *The Thief of Bagdad.* As it has been reprinted many times over the years, clearly Abdullah's *Thief of Bagdad* is more than a mere typing exercise. It is, after all, the novelization of a *silent* film, which meant the novelist had to be considerably more creative and invent most of the dialogue.

Abdullah's connection with Hollywood did not end with a novelization. He had written plays for Broadway, such as *Toto* (1921) and went on to do a number of screenplays, including *Lives of a Bengal Lancer* (1935), for which he and collaborators John Balderston and Waldemar Young shared an Academy Award. The film was based on the novel by Francis Yeats-Brown, but it is clear that Abdullah was eminently suited to the material.

ACHMED ABDULLAH'S works are the product of another era, when the British Empire was widely seen as a pinnacle of civilized achievement and native peoples were not supposed to aspire to nationhood. His outlook has much in common with that of H. Rider Haggard, Talbot Mundy, or Rudyard Kipling.

Certainly he is an authentic and articulate voice of his era, and a first-rate storyteller. He published his autobiography in 1933, *The Cat Had Nine Lives: Adventures and Reminiscences*, detailing a real life as eventful as his fiction. He also was one of several authors who embodied the ideal of the adventure writer, who was himself expected to be an exotic figure, a world traveler, whose wild yarns were given a sense of reality from having been lived, rather than merely made up.

— Darrell Schweitzer
July 21, 2004

The Charmed Life

FROM A letter dated September the eleventh, 1917, by Captain Achmed Abdullah to the Editor of the *All-Story Weekly*:

... and as to that, you are, of course, perfectly right. Magazine readers want to be entertained — that's what they plunk down their little dimes for — and take them all around, they prefer a story which is full of action, of things daring, with some love and a fair dose of adventure thrown in, and yet, as you put it, they do not want their credulity strained to the breaking point. They like to say to themselves — well, not exactly "This did happen" but rather, "This might have happened"; and as an afterthought, chiefly if they're young (by which I mean the sunny side of seventy-three) they often add the two tiny words "to me."

An adventurous and slightly fantastic love story — yet substantially a true story — that's the dope: and the only thing which remains is to catch your hare, to quote Mrs. Glass's famous Cookery Book. I heard such a story not so very long ago, when on my way home to Afghanistan, I stopped for a few weeks at Calcutta.

The name of the man who told me the story — his own story — was — [name deleted by the editor]. You may known some of his people in Boston. And when you come to the end of the tale, remember one thing, the hero — though I hate the appellation — is happy; and that, perhaps, is the final aim and object of man's life — to achieve happiness without making others unhappy.

I hope your readers will like the tale. At least it is a true tale; as true as all India; as true as the fact that before there was a Europe, India worshiped the Trimurti, the triple deity composed of Brahma the Creator, Vishnu, the Sustainer, Shiva the Destroyer, and — to believe certain Hindus — will continue to worship this triple image long after Europe has ceased to exist; as true, finally as the facts that never there lived, nor will live, American or European who can get below the skin of India without doing what the Boston man did in his little house in Calcutta, not far from the Chitpore

Road

Best Regards,

Achmed Abdullah.

[Note by the editors — Captain Abdullah's manuscript contained the real names of the people and localities whom this story concerns. We changed them — for obvious reasons.]

> *On the day when death will knock at thy door, what wilt thou*
> *offer him?*
> *Oh, I will set before my guest the full vessel of my life — I will*
> *never let him go with empty hands.*
> — Rarindranath Tagore

CHAPTER I.

THE MEETING.

Kiss happiness with lips
That seek beyond the lips.
— from the *Love Song of Yar Ali*

I MET him in that careless, haphazard and thoroughly human way in which one meets people in Calcutta, in all parts of India for that matter. He and I laughed simultaneously at the same street scene. I don't remember if it was the sight of a portly, grey-bearded native dressed incongruously in a brown-and-grey striped camel's-hair dressing-gown, an extravagantly embroidered skull-cap, gorgeous open-work silk socks showing the bulging calves, and cloth-topped patent leather shoes of an ultra-Viennese cut, or if it was perhaps the sight of Donald McIntyre, the Eurasian tobacco merchant in the Sealdah, abusing his Babu partner in a splendid linguistic mixture of his father's broad, twangy Glasgow Scots and of his mother's soft, gliding Behari.

At all events something struck me as funny. I laughed. So did the other man. And there you are.

Nice-looking chap he was — of good length of limbs and width of shoulders, clean-shaven, strong-jawed, and with close-cropped curly brown hair, and eyes the keenest, jolliest shade of blue imaginable. And — he was an American. You could tell by his clothes, chiefly by his neat shoes. They were of a vintage of perhaps two or three years before, but still they bore the national mark; they smacked, somehow, of ice water and clanking overhead trains and hustle and hat-check boys — and his nationality, too, was a point in his favor, since I had spent the preceding three years in New York and America had become home to me, in a way.

So we talked. I forgot who spoke first. It really doesn't matter — in India. Nor did we exchange cards nor names, that not being the custom of negligent India, but we conversed with that easy, we-might-as-well-be-friends familiarity with which strangers talk to each other aboard a transatlantic liner or in a Pullman car — west of Chicago. Presently we decided that we were obstructing the thoroughfare — at least a tiny, white bullock was trying his best to push us out of the way with his soft, ridiculous muzzle — we decided, furthermore, that we had several things to talk over. Quite important things they seemed at the time, and tremendously varied: the home policy of the ancient Peruvians, the truth of the Elohistic theory in the study of the Pentateuch, and the difference between Lahore and Lucknow chutney. In other words, we felt that strange human phenomenon: a sudden warm wave of friendship, of interest, of sympathy for each other.

So we adjourned to a native café which was a mass of violet and gold — slightly fly-specked — of smells honey-sweet and gall-bitter, of carved and painted things supremely beautiful and supremely hideous — since the East goes to the extreme in both cases.

We sipped our coffee and smiled at each other and talked. We discovered that we had likings in common — better still, prejudices and mad theories in common, and presently, since with the bunching, splintering noon heat the shops and the bazaar were clearing of buyers and sellers and since the café was filling with all sorts of strong-scented low-castes, kunjris and sansis and what-not, chewing betel and expectorating vastly after the manner of their kind, he proposed that we should continue our conversation in his house.

I accepted, and leaving the tavern I turned automatically to the left fully expecting him to lead toward Park Street or perhaps, since he was so obviously an American, toward one of the big cosmopolitan hotels on the other side of the Howrah Bridge. But instead he led me to the right, straight toward Chitpore Road, straight into the heart of the ancestral tenements of the Ghoses and Raos and Kumars — the respectable native quarter, in other words.

That was my first surprise. My second came when we reached his home — a two-storied house of typical extravagant bulbous Hindu architecture, surrounded by a flaunting garden, orange and vermilion with peach and pomegranate and peepul trees and with a thousand nodding flowers. For, as soon as he had ushered me into the great reception hall which stretched across the whole ground floor from front to back veranda, he excused himself. He did not wait to see me comfortably seated nor to offer me drink and tobacco, after the pleasant Anglo-Indian, and, for that matter, American habit. But he dropped hat and stick on the first handy chair, left the room with a hurried "be back in a jiffy, old man," and, a moment later I heard somewhere in the upper story of the house his deep mellow voice, quickly followed by a tinkling, silvery burst of laughter — the unmistakable, low-pitched laughter of the native woman which starts on a minor key and is accompanied by strange melodious appoggiatures an infinitesimal sixteenth below the harmonic tones to which the Western ear is attuned.

So I felt surprised, also disappointed and a little disgusted. The usual sordid shop-worn romance — I said to myself — the usual, useless pinchbeck tale of passion of some fool of a young, rich American and a scheming native woman, doubtless aided and abetted by a swarm of scheming, greasy, needy relations — the old story; the sort of thing that used to be notorious in Japan and in the Philippines.

Impatient, rather soured with my new-found friend, I looked about the room — and my surprise grew, but in another direction.

For the room was not furnished in the quick, tawdry, thrown-together manner of a man who lives and loves and nests with the impulses of a bird of passage. That I could have understood. It would have been in keeping with the tinkly laugher which had drifted down the stairs. Too, I could have understood if the appointments had been straight European or American, a sort of cheap, sentimental link with the home self-respect which he had discarded — temporarily — when he started light housekeeping with his native-born wife.

The room, complete from the ceiling to the floor and from window to door, was furnished in the native style; not in the nasty, showy, ornate native style of the bazaars which cater to tourists — and it is in India's favor that the "Oriental wares" sold there are mostly made in Birmingham, Berlin and Newark, New Jersey — but in that solid, heavy, rather somber native style of the well-to-do high-caste Hindu to whom every piece — each chair and table and screen — is somehow fraught with eternal, racial tradition. It was a real home, in other words, and a native home; and there was nothing — if I except a rack of bier pipes and a humidor filled with a certain much-advertised brand of Kentucky burley tobacco — which spoke of America.

A low divan ran around the four sides of the room. There were three carved saj-wood chairs, a Kashmir walnut table of which the surface was deeply undercut with realistic chenar leaves, and a large water-pipe made of splendid Lucknow enamel. A huge, reddish-brown camel's-hair rug covered the floor, and on tabourets distributed here and there were niello boxes filled with the roseleaf-and-honey confections beloved by Hindu women, pitchers and basins of that exquisite damascening called bidri, and a soft-colored silken scarf — coiled and crumpled, as if a woman had dropped it hurriedly.

The walls were covered with blue glazed tiles; and on the one facing the outer door an inscription in inlaid work caught my attention. They were just a few words, in Sanskrit, and, somehow, they affected me strangely. They were the famous words from the Upanishad:

"Recall, O mind, thy deeds — recall, recall!"

The answer was clear. I said to myself, with a little bitter pang for remember that I liked the man — that here was one who had gone fantee, who had gone native; a man who had dropped overboard all the traditions, the customs, and decencies, the virtues, the blessed, saving prejudices of his race and faith to mire himself hopelessly in the slough of a foreign race and faith. For it is true that a man who goes fantee never acquires the good, but only the bad of the alien breed with which he mingles and blends — true, moreover, that such a man can never rise again, that the doors of the house of his birth shall be forever closed to him. He has blackened the crucible of his life and he will never find a single golden bead at the bottom of it; only hatred and despair and disgust, a longing for the irreparably lost, a bitter taste in the mouth of his soul.

I started towards the door. Out into the free, open sunlight, I said to myself. For I knew what would happen. The man would come downstairs, carrying a square bottle and glasses. Presently he would become drunk — maudlin — he would pour his mean, dirty confidences into my ear and weep on my neck and —

I reconsidered, quite suddenly. Why, this young American had not the earmarks of a man who had gone fantee. There was not that look in his eyes — that horrible, unbearable look, a composite of misery and lust, bred of bad thoughts, bad dreams, and worse hashish —

The man — I had seen him in the merciless rays of the Indian sun — was keen-eyed, clean morally and physically. His laughter was fresh. His complexion was healthy — and yes, I continued my thoughts, he seemed happy, supremely, sublimely, enviably happy!

"Sorry I kept you waiting," came his voice from the farther door as he came into the room, dressed in the flowing, comfortable house robe of a wealthy native gentleman.

He must have read my gyrating, unspoken thought. Perhaps I stared a little too inquisitively at his face for the tell-tale sign of the sordid tragedy which I suspect. For he smiled, a fine, thin smile, and he pointed to the Sanskrit inscription, reading the words out loud and with a certain gently exalted inflection as if his tongue, in forming the sonorous words, was tasting a special sort of psychic ambrosia.

"Recall, O Mind, thy deeds — recall, re —"

"Well," I blurted out, brutally, tactlessly, before I realized what I was doing, "What is the answer — to this and that and this?" pointing, in turn, at the Indian furniture, the inscription, his dressing robe, and, though the stone-framed window, at the native houses which crowded the garden on all sides.

He smiled. He was not the least bit angry, but frankly amused, like a typical, decently-bred American who can even relish a joker at his own expense. "You're an inquisitive beggar," he commenced, "but I'll tell you rather than have some gossiping cackling hen of a deputy assistant commissioner's mother-in-law tell you the wrong tale and make me lose your friendship. You see," he continued with an air as if he was telling me a tremendous secret, "I am Stephen Denton."

"Well," I asked, "what of that?" The name meant nothing to me.

"What? Have they already forgotten my name? Gosh, that's bully! In another year they will have forgotten the tale itself! You see," he continued, dropping into one of the divans and waving me down beside him, "I'm the guy whom the kid subalterns over at the British barracks call 'the man with the charmed life.'"

I gave a cry — of surprise, amazement, incredulity. For I had heard tales — vague, fantastic, incredible. "You —" I stammered, "you — are —"

"Yes," he laughed, "I am that same man. Care to hear the story?"

"You bet!" I replied fervently, and that very moment came once more the sound of laughter from upstairs — soft, tinkling, silvery —

CHAPTER II.

THE CALL.

I broke the night's primeval bars
I dared the old abysmal curse
And flashed through ranks of frightened stars
Suddenly on the universe!
                              — Rupert Brooke

STEPHEN DENTON interrupted his tale now and then with shrewd and picturesque sidelights on native life, customs, and characters which proved how deep he had got below the skin of India. But I shall omit them here — doubtless at a future date, he himself will embody them in the great book on India which he is writing — and, in the following, I shall only give the pith of his incredible tale. I only regret that there is no way of reproducing his voice with the printed word — his happy, frank voice, unmistakably American in its intonations, yet once in a while with a quaint inflection which showed that he had begun to think at times in Hindustani.

You see, he commenced, it was all originally Roos-Keppel's doing — fault, if you prefer to call it that. Roos-Keppel — "Tubby" Roos-Keppel — you must have met him over at the Jockey Club, or in the evening, in the Eden Gardens, driving about in his old-fashioned C-spring barouche — big, paunchy, brick-faced Britisher, who won the Calcutta Sweepstakes — in 1900. Why, everybody in India knows the tale, how a sudden, mad prosperity went to his head; how he gave up his job in the Bengal Civil Service and painted Calcutta crimson for three years; how he lost his hold on everything, including himself; everything that is, except his hospitality, his fantastic ideas, his infectious, daredevil madness.

I met him the day after I got here. How did I get here? Why? When?

Well, two years tomorrow, to answer your last question first, and as to why and how, there's a native proverb which says that fate and self-exertion are half and half in power.

I came here on a sight-seeing trip after I'd got through Yale. I had money of my own, my parents were dead, there was nobody to say no — and I had an idea it would do me good to get a nodding acquaintance with the world and its denizens before I settled down in the Back Bay section — yes — you guessed it — originally I'm just that sort of a Bostonian.

Everything back home — with the dear old, white-haired lawyer, who was my guardian, and his little plump spinster sister who kept house for him, and the black walnut furniture and the antimacassars and the bound volumes, of Emerson and Longfellow and Thoreau — it seemed all so confounded safe and sure. Even timid. Respectably, irreproachably timid, if you get the idea.

Stephen Denton smiled reminiscently.

Preordained, too, it seemed. Preordained from the mild cocktail before dinner to the hoary place on the bench I was expected to grace some day. I had every reason to be happy, don't you think? And I was happy. Quite!

And then I smelled a whiff of wanderlust. And so it happened that that red faced Britisher of a Roos-Keppel kicked me, figuratively speaking, in the stomach — and I'm grateful to him — always shall be grateful.

I met him at the Jockey Club. He took to me and invited me to dinner at the Hotel Semiramis, where he had a gorgeous suite of rooms. It was some little dinner — just the two of us — and you know the sort of host he is. We tried every barreled, fermented, and bottled refreshment from Syrian raki to yellow-ribbon Grand Marnier; and it was at the end of the party — I was busy with a large cup of coffee and a small glass of brandy, and he with a small cup of coffee and a large glass of brandy — that he cut loose and told me tales about India — tales in which he had been either principal or witness — and, in half an hour, he had taught me more about the hidden nooks and corners of this land than there is in all the travel books, Murray's government, and missionary reports put together. What's more his tales were true.

So I asked him, like a tactless young cub: "Heavens, man, with your knowledge of India — why did you throw your chance away? Why didn't you stick to it? You would have made a great, big, bouncing, twenty-four carat success!"

"And I would have wound up with a G. C. S. I., a bloody knighthood, a pension of ten thousand rupees a year, and a two-inch space in the obituary column of the *Calcutta Times* — English papers please copy — when I've kicked the bally bucket!" He guffawed, and he hiccuped a little. For he had been hitting the brandy bottle, and all the other assorted bottles, like a cornstalk sailor on a shore spree after two dry months on a lime-juicer without making port. "Success?" he continued, "why, my lad, I am a success. A number one — waterproof — and, damn my eyes, whisky-proof for that matter?"

"You are — what?" I asked, amazed for the man was serious, perfectly serious, mind you; and he kept right on with his philippic monologue, extravagant in diction and gesture, but the core of it — why it was serene, grotesquely serene!

"I am a success, I repeat: don't you believe me?" He lowered a purple-veined eyelid in a fat, Falstaffian leer. "Take a good look at these rooms of mine — best rooms in the Semiramis, in Calcutta, in India, hang it all — in the whole plurry empire!" He pointed at the gorgeous furniture and the silk hangings, "Viceroys by the score have occupied them — and the Prince of Wales — and four assorted Russian grand dukes — and three bloated Yankee plutocrats. And our little supper — look at the bottles and dishes — how much do you think it'll cost? I tell you — five hundred rupees — without the tip! And," he laughed, "I haven't even got enough of the ready to tip the black-lacquered Eurasian majordomo who uncorked our sherry and, doubtless, swiped the first glass."

I made an instinctive gesture toward my pocket-book, but he stopped me with another laugh. "Don't make a silly ass of yourself," he said. "I don't want to borrow any money. All I want to prove to you is that I live and I do as I please — forgetful of the yesterday, careless of the morrow — serene in my belief in my own particular fate. Tonight I am broke — hopelessly, desperately broke, you'd call it. For I haven't got a rupee in the world. My bank account is concave, I owe wages to my servants, I owe for my stable service and horse feed. Everything I have — even my old C-spring barouche, even my old, patched, green bedroom slippers are mortgaged. But what of it? I'll sleep tonight as quiet and untouched as a little babe. Something is sure to happen tomorrow — always does happen. I always kick through — somehow —"

"But — how?" I was beginning to get worried for him — I liked him.

"How? Because I am a success — a success with reverse English. The world? Why, I put it all over this fool of a world. For I believe in myself. That's why I win out. Everybody who believes in himself wins out — in what he wants to win out. You, Denton," he went on after a short pause, "are a nice lad, clean and well-bred and no end proper. But you are too damned smug — no offense meant — you are like a respectable spinster owl with respectable astigmatism. Cut away from it. See life. Make life. Take life by the tail and swing it about your head and force it to disgorge. Take a chance — say to yourself that nothing can happen to you!"

"Pretty little theory," I interrupted.

"Theory — the devil!" he cried. "It's the truth! Don't take me as an example if you don't want to. Take people who have done real things. Take you own adored George Washington — take the Duke of Wellington, take Moltke, Ghengis Khan, U. S. Grant, Attila, Tamerlane, Joffre, or Theodore Roosevelt! They lived through to the end until they had achieved what they wanted to achieve. They made their own fate. The bullet was not run, the sword was not forged which could kill these — for they had willed to live, willed to succeed! They —" a little superstitious hush came into his voice, "they bore the charmed life —"

He poured himself another stiff drink, gulped it down, and pointed through the open window, out at the streets of Calcutta, which lay at our feet, bathed in moonlight.

I looked, and the sight of it, the scent of it, the strange, inexpressible feel of it crept through me — yes, that's it — it crept through me. You know this town — this Calcutta — this melting pot of all India — and remember, that brick-faced reprobate of a Roos-Keppel had been telling me tales of it — grim, fantastic, true tales — and here they were at my feet, the witnesses and actors, the heroes and villains in his tales — hurrying along the street in a never-ending procession — a vast panorama of Asia's uncounted races. There were men from Bengal, black, ungainly, slightly Hebraic shuffling along on their eternal, sissified patent leather pumps. There were some bearded Rajputs — weaponless, that being the law of Calcutta, but carrying about them somehow the scent of naked steel — and next to them their blood enemies — fur-capped, wide shouldered, sneering Afghans, with screaming voices, brushing through the crowds like the bullies they are — doubtless dreaming of loot and rapine and murder. There were furtive Madrases — "monkey men" we call them here — and a few red-faced duffle-clad hillmen from the North — thin, stunted desertmen from Bikaneer, with their lean jaws bandaged after the manner of the land, and Sikhs and Chinamen and Eurasians and what-not.

And, directly below our window, there was a Brahman priest, a slow, fanatic fire in his eyes — the light from our room caught in them — a caste mark of diagonal stripes of white and black on his forehead, chanting in Sanskrit the praises of the hero and demi-god Gandharbasena —

". . . and thus did the great hero persuade the king of Dhara to give to him in marriage his daughter. Ho! Let all men listen to the Jataka for he was the son of Indra. . . ."

Roos-Keppel's thick, alcoholic voice sounded at my elbow. "India," he hiccuped, "and the horror, the beauty, the wonder, the cruelty, the mad color and scent which is India!" He clutched my arm. "My game's played down to the last rubber, Denton, and my score is nearly settled — but you — why, you've got a stack of chips — you are strong and young — your eyes are clear — and — Gad, I wish I had your chance! I'd take this town by the throat — I'd jump into its damned mazes, regardless of consequences. Heavens, man, can't you feel it beckon and wink and smile — and leer? Listen —" momentarily he was silent, and, from the street came a confused mass of sounds — voices in many languages, rising, then decreasing, the shouts of the street-vendors, the tinkle-tinkle of a woman's glass bracelet — the sounds leaped up like gay fragments of some mocking tunes, again like the tragic chorus of some world — old, world — sad tune. "India!" he continued, "can you resist the call of it?"

It was a psychological moment. Yes — it was that often misquoted, decidedly overworked psychological moment — the brandy and champagne fumes were working in my brain — and something tugged at my soul — if I had wings to fly from the window, to launch myself across the purple haze of the town, to alight on the flat roofs and look into the houses, the lives, the gaieties, the mysteries, the sorrows of this colorful, turbaned throng. And then everything I was — racially, traditionally, you understand — the Back Bay of Boston; the old lawyer, my preordained place on the bench, the antimacassars, Phi Beta Kappa, and all the rest of it, made a last rally in my defense.

"But," I said, and I guess my voice was thin, apologetic — just as if Roos-Keppel was the driving master of my destinies, "this is said to be a dangerous place — away from the beaten paths — so what is the of —"

"The use? The use?" he cut in with a bellow of laughter, and then suddenly his voice was low and quiet "Why, just because it's dangerous, that's why you should try your chance — and your life." He pointed again through the window, east, where, on the horizon, a deep-gray smudge lay across the bent of glimmer and glitter. "See that patch of darkness?" he asked, with something of a challenge in his accents which were getting more and more unsteady, "that's the Colootallah Section — cha — charming little bunch of real estate — worst in the world, not even excepting Aden, Naples and all the wickedness and crimes of Port Said. Only two men are safe there, and they aren't quite safe," he laughed, and to my quickly interjected question, he replied, "Why, a fakir — holy man, you know — and a member of the filthy castes who thrive there — you know even criminal have their own castes in India, and they all seem to congregate there — thugs and thieves and murderers and what-not.

"Wait —" he stopped my questions with a gesture — "perhaps, mind you, I say 'perhaps,' an exceptional detective of the Metropolitan Police in Lal Bazaar may be safe there for three minutes, but —" He was silent and leered at me.

"But what?" I asked impatiently.

"I'd tackle it just the same if I were you, young and strong. No white man has done it before. By Jupiter, I'd tackle it if I had a char — char — charmed life —" and quite suddenly he fell into snoring, alcoholic slumber.

I stepped out on the balcony. India was at my feet, cruel, beckoning, mysterious, scented, minatory, fascinating, inexplicable. Right then it got below my skin.

I gave a low laugh. No, I don't know why I laughed.

Stephen Denton was silent for a moment. He was thinking deeply. Then he shook his head.

Honestly, I don't know why I laughed. I don't know why I did any of the things I did that night, until I came to the wall at the other end of Ibrahim Khan's Gully. No, no. I had imbibed quite a little — couldn't help it with Roos-Keppel — but I was not drunk. Not a bit of it.

Well, imagine me there on the balcony of the Semiramis, laughing at India, if you wish; perhaps at the Back Bay, perhaps at myself. I left the balcony, patted the drunken man on the shoulder, and stepped out of the hotel and into the smoky, purple night. The storm which had threatened earlier by the evening was melting into a quiet night of glowing violet, with a pale, sneering, negligent sort of a moon. A low, cool wind was blowing up from the River Hooghli.

I gave a mocking farewell bow in the direction of Park Street, the white man's Calcutta, Government House, green tea and respectability,, and turned east, sharp east, toward the patch of darkness, toward the Colootallah. I walked very steadily, as if I had a definite aim and object, turned on the corner of Park Street, and there a policeman, an English policeman, stopped me.

"Beg pardon, sir," he said with that careful, Anglo-Saxon politeness, "you're goin' the wrong way, I fancy, sir. The hotel is over yonder, sir," pointing in the opposite direction; and I laughed. I pressed a rupee into his ready hand. "Hotel, nothing!" I said. "I am going toward the Street of Charmed Life!"

"Right-o," commented the policeman. "Some of these 'ere native streets do 'ave funny names, don't they? But — beggin' your pardon, sir — better 'ave a care. Those streets ain't safe for a white man, leastways at night."

"Quite safe — for me!" I assured him, and I walked on, on and on, not caring where I went — away from the thoroughfares, through grimy little gardens in the back of opium dens where the brick paths were hollow and slimy with the tread of many naked, unsteady feet; then through a greasy, packed wilderness of three-storied houses, perfectly respectable Babu houses, from which a faint, acrid smell seemed to emanate; on, twisting and turning, through the Burra Bazaar and the Jora Bagan — you know the sections, don't you, and their New York counterpart, the Bowery and Hell's Kitchen — and then up into the crooked mazes of the Machua Bazaar — evil, filthy, packed.

On and on, farther and farther away, and at every corner, in every doorway, there were new faces, new types, new voices, new odors, until I came to the Colootallah.

How did I know I was there? Oh, I asked a native, decent sort he was, though he was a bit unsteady with opium, and, just like the English policeman, he advised me to go back to Park Street.

Perhaps he was right. For a moment I was quite sure that he was right, but I walked on, through streets that grew steadily more narrow. You know how narrow they can be, with a glimpse of smoky sky above the roofs revealing scarcely three yards of breadth, and all sorts of squirmy, squishy things underneath your feet, and shawls, and bit of underwear, and turban clothes hanging from the windows and balconies and flopping unexpectedly into your face, and beggars, and roughs, and lepers slinking and pushing against you, jabbering, quarreling, begging; and the roadway ankle-deep in thick slime, and a fetid stink hanging over it all like a cloud; and the darkness, the bitter darkness — black blotched, compact, except for a haggard moon-ray shooting down occasionally from above and glancing off into the canyon of the street from bulbous roof and crazy, tortured balcony.

By ginger, I was sick for a moment. I said to myself that there was a steamer sailing the next day — home and America via Liverpool — and I was about to turn when —

Wait a second.

Get first where I was, though you'll never find the place. You'll hear the reason why later on. You see, I had meanwhile turned up a narrow street; it was quite lonely there; not a soul, not a footstep, hardly a sound. They called the place then — mind you, I said then — Ibrahim Khan's Gully. It was typical of its sort. Whitewashed walls without windows or doors, mysterious, useless-looking to right and to left; and straight in front of me, at the end of the gully, was another wall. It sat there at the end of that cul-de-sac like a seal of destiny, portentous threatening. The moon was pretty well behaved and bright just then, and so I looked at that wall. It impressed me.

It was perhaps ten feet high, and it seemed to be the support of some roof-top for it was crowned with rather an elaborate balustrade of carved, fretted stone. At a certain distance behind it rose another higher wall, then another, still higher, and so on; as if the whole block was terraced from the center toward the gully. To the left and right the wall stretched, gradually rising into the dark without a break, it seemed, and surmounted here and there by the fantastic outline of some spire or balcony or crazy, twisted roof, the whole thing a confounded muddle of Hindu architecture, with apparently neither end nor beginning — mad, brusk, useless — like a harebrained giant's picture-puzzle.

There I stood and stared. I said to myself, "Back, you fool? Straight home with you to Boston, to the bound volumes of Emerson, to the mild cocktail — and I wonder who'll win the mile at the Intercollegiate —" And then — and I remember it as if it was today, it was just in the middle of that thought about the mile race—I heard a voice directly above me.

It was a woman's voice, singing in that quaint, minor wail of Eastern music. Perhaps you know the words. I have learned them by heart —

You are to me the gleam of sun
That breaks the gloom of wintry rain;
You are to me the flower of time —
O Peacock, cry again!

"Bravo, bravo!" I shouted. For you see I was only a fool of an outsider, looking into this night-wrapped, night-sounding India as I would look at a fantastic play, and then suddenly the song broke off, came another voice, harsh, hissing, spitting, the sound of a hand slapping bare flesh, and then a piercing shriek. A high-pitched, woman's shriek that shivered the night air, that somehow shivered my heart.

I must help that woman, but — "Home you fool, you silly, meddling idiot." said my saner ego "This is no quarrel of yours." "Take a chance," replied another cell in my brain. "Take a chance with chance! See what all this talk about a charmed life is!"

No, no, I decided the next moment it was mad. Impossible. A native house, a native woman — they were sacred. Not even the police would dare enter without a search warrant; and this was the Colootallah, the worst section of Calcutta; and I knew next to nothing about India, about the languages, the customs, the prejudices of the land, except what Roos-Keppel had told me.

"Hai-hai-hai!" came once more the piercing, woman's wail: and right then I consigned Back Bay and safety first to the devil. I made for that wall with a laugh, perhaps a prayer.

A charmed life! By the many hecks, I'd find out presently I said to myself, as I jumped on a narrow ledge a few feet from the ground, from which I could clutch the top of the stone balustrade.

Up!

I swung myself into the unknown, balanced for the fraction of a second on the balustrade, then let myself drop. I struck something soft and bulky that squirmed swiftly away. Came a grunt and a curse — at least, it sounded suspiciously like a curse — then somebody struck a light which blinded me momentarily.

And at that very moment the bell from the Presbyterian Church in Old Court House Street struck the midnight hour.

CHAPTER III.

A FOOL'S HEART.

Oft have I heard that no accident or chance ever mars the march of events here below, and that all moves in accordance with a plan. To take shelter under a common bough or a drink of the same river is alike ordained from ages prior to our birth.

— From the letter of a Japanese Daimio to his
wife before committing *hara-kari*

RAPIDLY my eyes got used to the light. It came from a flickering, insincere oil-lamp held in the hands of an elderly Hindu, evidently the possessor of the soft and bulky body which I had struck when I had let myself drop.

He looked at me, and I looked at him, silently. I am quite sure we didn't like each other. We didn't have to say a single word to convince each other of the fact. He was an old man, but old without the slightest trace of dignity, he wore no turban, and that gave his shiny, shaven head a horribly naked look. On his forehead was a crimson caste mark — nasty-looking thing it was. His eyes were hopelessly bleared, his teeth were blackened with betel juice, his rough, gray beard was quite a stranger to comb or oil. He was a fat, ridiculous old man, with a ridiculous, squeaky little cough.

I burst out laughing, and I laughed louder when I saw the expression which crept into his red-rimmed eyes. Not that the expression was really funny. Rather this opposite. For it was one of beastly hatred, of savage joy, of sinister triumph. But, don't you see, I wasn't the Stephen Denton of half a year, why, of half an hour before. Right then I had forgotten all about America and Boston and regulation respectability. There seemed to be no home tradition to analyze and criticize and I belonged right there — to that flat rooftop, to the purple, choking night down below in Ibrahim Khan's Gully, to India, to Calcutta. One blow of my fist, I said to myself, and that fat, ridiculous old savage would take an involuntary, headlong tumble from the balustrade to the blue, sticky mire of the gully. So I laughed.

But hold on. Don't get the story wrong. I didn't stand there, on that roof-top in the Coolootallah, exactly thinking out all these impressions, detail for detail. They passed over me in a solid wave and in the fraction of a second, and, even as they swept through me, the lamp in the hands of the old man trembled a little and shot its haggard, dirty-white rays a little to the left, toward a short, squat, carved stone pillar quite close to the balustrade.

And there, breathing hard, clutching the pillar with two tiny, narrow hands, I saw a native woman — a young girl rather — doubtless she whom I had heard sing, then scream in pain. Red, cruel finger-marks were still visible on her delicate, pale-golden cheek.

Stephen Denton lit a cigar and blew out a series of rings, attempting to hang them on the chandelier, one by one.

You know (he said this with a certain, ringing, challenging seriousness) I fell in love right then and there. Sounds silly, of course. But it's the truth. I looked at that Hindu girl, and I loved her. Such a — a — why, such a strange, inexpressible sensation came over me. It seemed suddenly that we were alone — she and I — on the roof-top in Calcutta — alone in all the world —

But never mind that I guess you know what love is.

She was hardly more than sixteen years old, and she dressed in the conventional dress of a Hindu dancer, in a sari — you know, the scarf which the Hindu woman drapes about her with a deft art not dreamed of by Fifth Avenue — of pale rose colored silk, shot with orange and violet and bordered with tiny seed-pearls. An edge of the sari hung over one round shoulder and the robe itself came just below the knee. Her face was small and round and exquisitely chiseled. Her hair was parted in the middle. It was of a glossy bluish-black, mingled with flowers and jewels, and the braids came down to her ankles. A perfume, sweet, pungent, mysterious, so faint as to be little more than a suggestion, hovered about her.

Well — I stared at her. Then I remembered my manners and lifted my hand to raise my hat. It wasn't there. I must have dropped it when I negotiated the wall and the girl, seeing my action, understanding it, forgot her pain and laughed. Such a jolly silvery, exquisite little laugh.

Ever think of the psychology of laughter? To me it has always seemed the final proof of sympathy, of humanity, even. And so that laugh, from the crimson lips of this Hindu girl, finally did the trick. I forgot all about the fat old party with the caste mark and the bleary eyes, I walked up to the girl and offered her my hand, American fashion.

"Glad to meet you," I said in English. It was a foolish thing to say, absolutely ridiculous, but just then I couldn't think of anything else. You see, at midnight, on the roof-top of some unknown native house in the heart of the Colootallah, together with people of an unknown race and faith, of alien tradition, alien emotions, even — what would you have said?

I stuck to my native-born form of salutation and held out my hand. She gave me hers — it felt just like some warm, downy little baby bird — and replied in English, with a certain faint nuance of mockery, "Glad to meet you, sir," and I grinned and was about to open up a polite conversation.

You see, momentarily I had really forgotten all about that bleary-eyed old scoundrel. But he recalled himself to me almost immediately — with an exceedingly rude and, considering his age, muscular push which shoved me to one side and the girl to the other.

There he stood between us, like an exageratedly hideous Hindu idol of revenge and hatred and lust and half a dozen other assorted beastly qualities, the lamp trembling in his clawlike hand. He pointed at me, addressing the girl in a mad, jerky, helter-skelter flood of Hindustani — I didn't understand it — which caused the girl to pale and to shake her head vigorously. It was evidence that he was accusing her of something or other, and that she was denying the accusation indignantly. And then he commenced abusing her in English, doubtless for my benefit.

I was stuffing his mouth at once with my fist, but the girl signaled to me, frantically, imploringly, "No, no" — I saw her lips shaping the words and so, temporarily I kept me peace while the old Hindu proceeded to prove that he could translate Hindu abuse into very fair English.

"Ho!" he shouted at her. "Ho! thou daughter of unthinkable begatting! Thou spawn of much filth. Thou especially illegitimate and shameless hyena! Thou this and that and once more this! By Shiva and Shiva — I shall wrench thy wicked hide with the touchstone of pain and affliction! I shall —"

"Look here" I interrupted "you are getting entirely too fresh. Stow your line of talk, or —" and I made a significant gesture with my fist — would have hit him, too, if the girl had not signaled to me again — this time, and I don't know what she wanted by it, pointing at her forehead and then back at the building which terraced toward the center of the block.

The Hindu man was too angry to notice the by-play. "O Calamity!"

he went on. "O crimson shame! May Doorgha, the great goddess, cut out thy heart and feed it to a mangy pig! What shameless doings are these — O thou bazaar woman — to send word to thy lover — to have him come here, to this house, and at night? Didst thou think that I would be asleep? Thy lover —" he spat out, "and he a man of the accused foreign race, an infidel, an eater of unclean food, a cannibal of the holy cow, a swinish derider of the many gods! He — thy lover! Ah! by the Mother of the Elephant's Trunk — thy portion shall be the pain which passeth understanding!" Suddenly he turned and addressed himself to me, "and as for thee — for thee —" He was so choked with fury that the words were gurgled and died in his throat. He positively did not know whom to insult or bully first, the girl or me. Like Balaam's Ass, he stood there, undecided, and finally he made up his mind to attend first to the girl.

"Thou —" came an unmentionable epithet, unmentionable even among Hindus, and you know how extravagant their abuse is inclined to be, then he turned on her. His right hand still held the trembling lamp. He struck out with his left. She tried to evade him — slipped — I was too late to come to her rescue — only a glancing blow, but she fell, bumping her head smartly against the stone pillar.

She gave a pitiful little moan — and was unconscious.

Then I got mad.

I rushed up to him, lunged, and missed. You see, the old beggar danced away from me with a certain sharp, twisting agility which I wouldn't have believed possibly in that aged, obese body of his. Also, I had to be careful — on that confounded roof-top. No use tumbling over the balustrade and breaking my neck. That wouldn't have helped the girl any. The only chance I had was to get him against the wall on the side opposite the gully — a torn-down wall occasionally connecting the roof-top with the next layer on that maze of buildings.

Finally I managed to drive him toward the wall. I had him cornered. He stood there — the lamp still flickering in his right, its ray sharply silhouetting him against the spectral white stucco. I was quite fascinated for a moment, looking at him. The idea flushed into my brain that I was looking into the visage of something monstrous, impossible. The beastly bald skull, the caste mark, the fat, wide-humped shoulders, suggested that which was scarcely human and, struck by a sudden burst of horror, I stared into that dark, inscrutable countenance.

Then he opened his mouth — in a low voice he said something of what was going to happen to me. It had something to do with one of his beastly, many-armed gods — I didn't understand the allusion at the time. At all events, he pointed at the caste mark on his forehead and —

You see, I am a slow, careful sort of fighter. I hate to waste a blow. Furthermore, up to then we had all been comparatively quiet. I didn't care to make too much noise. And I had him cornered. So, instead of rushing up like a noisy avalanche, I poised myself on my toes, squared my shoulders, drew back my right arm — and then I nearly lost the whole game.

For, quite suddenly, he brought his left hand to his mouth. He was about to shout — for help, I suppose. And then I hit him, right between the eyes, By ginger, it was a wallop.

You see, I was quite mad; and even in that fleeting moment, when I had really no time to register sensations, I could feel his skin break beneath my knuckles, the soft, pulped flesh — the blood squirting up — and, darn it, I liked the feeling!

Stephen Denton gave a strange smile.

Rather bestial, don't you think? But then I told you I was a different man — there, on that roof-top, with purple India whispering about me — than I had been half an hour before.

Well, the old Hindu fell, unconscious, by the side of the girl. The lamp dropped from his hand. I tried to catch it, could not, and over the balustrade it went in a fantastic curve of yellow sparks, and down into the blue slime of Ibrahim Khan's Gully where it gave a little protesting *sshissh* and guttered out.

So there I was, on that confounded roof-top, in utter silence, utter darkness — the moon had hidden behind a cloud-bank — and within a few feet of me was the unconscious form of the girl — the Hindu girl — with whom I had fallen in love — and I knew neither her name, nor her faith — nor anything at all about her. An adventure, don't you think? An adventure — to me. Fantastic, twisted, incredible! And, a few hours before, I had imagined that the greatest adventure that could ever happen to me would be to catch a fifty pound salmon and get away with the tale of it!

But, just then, I didn't even consider the whole mad sequence of events in the light of adventure. It seemed all perfectly sane, perfectly possible — preordained, in a way — and I thought and acted with the utmost self-assurance and deliberation.

Was I afraid, you ask? I was not. Honestly! Sounds silly, bragging, doesn't it? But it's the truth. Of course I realized that my position was ugly. You see, there was that blotchy, purple darkness all about me, and a terrific, breathless silence — and what was I to do? Back across the wall? Into Ibrahim Khan's Gully — and a run for the Hotel Semiramis? Sure, I could have jumped down. I had learned the trick in gym work, back at college — to land on my toes, slightly bending my back and my legs.

But I didn't take that chance. I could not. For there was the girl, and I loved her. She was dear to me — very dear — dearer than my life, my salvation — dearer — what's the old saying? — yes, dearer than the dwelling of kings! Carefully, slowly I crept across to her side, for I didn't want to step on the old Hindu. I didn't want to recall him from his trance before I was ready for him, before I had decided exactly what to do.

I stooped down and touched the girl's soft little face. The touch went through me like an electric thrill. What was I to do? She was breathing, but quite unconscious. I had no way, no time to revive her.

Should I take her with me across the balustrade? Impossible. I couldn't drag her into the gully like a bag of flour, nor was it feasible for me to go down first — wouldn't be able to reach and lift her from below.

I was sure of only one thing. I wouldn't leave without her — without her I wouldn't leave that roof-top, the Coolootallah, nor Calcutta, nor India.

I loved her. I wanted her. I would die for her. The source of that rash courage will ever be to me an inexplicable mystery. For, don't you see, I had always lived a perfectly sheltered life back in Boston, with the antimacassars and the walnut furniture and the volumes of Emerson and Thoreau. But I had resolved to take that girl with me. No more, nor less!

So I squatted there, by the side of the girl, considering. It is strange how trivial things impinge on the consciousness in such moments with a shock of something important, immense. There was just a slight noise — a soft *tckk-tckk-tckk* — but, somehow, I knew what it was. It was the noise of a scorpion scuttling across the roof — to the left of me — towards the old Hindu.

I knew just exactly what would happen — tried my best, with a sharp hiss, to prevent it — but it did happen. The little scorpion, if, indeed, it was one — perhaps it was only a mouse — scurried across the old Hindu's face — startled him into consciousness.

He sat up. He gave a shout for help — just one shout. I was one top of him the very next second — but I could not clutch that shout out of the air — it echoed and reverberated among the terraced walls, sharp, metallic. It tore through the gloom like the point of a knife.

I had him down on his back again in the twinkling of an eye, had him gagged securely with my handkerchief and the heavy leather gloves I carried in my pocket. Working feverishly, I tore the silk scarf from the girl's shoulder, tore off my coat, my necktie — and had him tied before he knew what was happening to him.

Then I sat up and listened. With a little gray thrill of horror I realized that the cry for help had been heard, that the crisis was upon me. Far in the bowels of that crazy mass of terrace buildings I heard confused voices — footsteps.

Tap-tap-tap — naked feet stepping gingerly on cold stone slabs.

A dozen questions leaped to my brain. What could I do? How? The old man — myself — the girl — Yes! The girl whom I loved. At that moment I longed for two things, two things of Western civilization: a revolver and a box of matches. But I had neither the one nor the other about me. All I had was a knife, a pretty good knife, too, very much like an old-fashion Bowie. I had bought it the day I left America, in a spirit of jest, rather than with the expectation of using it.

The footsteps came nearer and nearer from the direction of the wall which connected the rooftop with the next building. I looked about me, for a place to hide the girl, to hide myself.

And the old man! Over the wall with him, I decided brutally, and I dragged at his feet — he was heavy, very heavy — and then I desisted. For the footsteps came nearer, ever nearer; also excited voices in an unintelligible language.

For a moment the voices were drowned in a round, metallic burst of sound. *Banng!* came the bell from the Presbyterian Church in Old Court House Street, tolling the quarter after midnight. Then, when the tolling had trembled away, came once again the sounds — nearer, nearer — voices, footsteps, and also a faint crackling of steel, the swish of a scabbard scraping across stone flags.

And the darkness was about me like a heavy, woolen garment.

Stephen Denton smiled, quizzically, incongruously.

Don't you see? He continued when he saw the expression of surprise on my face, the thing was really quite funny. The adventure itself seemed to me — oh, sort of inevitable, like a Greek drama: and as to the darkness — why, old man, that moon there behind the cloud-bank reminded me of some dear old chaperone at a ball at Magnolia. Prime her with a ball of knitting wool, a glass of near-soft punch, and pop her into a nice warm conservatory, and she'll remain there until the band plays "Good Night, Ladies" and not bother the young. Get it? So it was with that moon. Kept away, left everything blotchy, dark side off by itself. Me and the girl, and the old man and the whole damned rooftop.

Yes, I thought of all that at the time. But I acted, even as I thought, as if I had two sets of nerve-controls, working separately from each other. I moved about in the darkness, feverishly, searching for some hiding-place big enough to hold one or all of us — the footsteps and the voices were coming nearer all the time — and finally I discovered that the balustrade, built out towards the roof-top, formed a sort of box for a length of about six feet. Did I put the girl inside? You bet your life I did not! I told you I wasn't going to leave her ever again. I stuck the old man inside, handled him as I would a bundle of useless, dirty rags; and the next moment, with the strength and haste of desperation, I picked up the unconscious girl, and, holding her in my arms, I squeezed myself behind the carved stone pillar against which she had been leaning when I had burst upon the scene. The place was just large enough to hold us — me and her — pressed tight against me.

Of course, the whole thing took less time than it takes me to tell it.

So, there I was, holding that little Hindu girl in my arms — and — why, man, I loved her — unless the repetition of that detail bores you — my arms touched the soft curves of her young shoulders.

It was quite dark, as I told you. But there, resting on my left arm, was her little face, like an opening flower. Only a slip of a girl, her youthful incompleteness just a lovely sketch for something larger, finer, more splendid — just a mass of happy, seductive hints, with the high-lights yet missing.

That's it! You guessed it first time! I kissed her — either my last kiss on this earth I said to myself; or if there was any truth in that charmed life hope, my first kiss — given, taken rather, in real love.

And, as I pressed her closer against me in the ecstasy of the moment — you see, I had forgotten all about the approaching footsteps, I am such a careless fellow — I felt as if something was giving way behind me. Quickly I squirmed, a few inches to the right — there wasn't so very much room, and at the same moment a door opened up in the wall in back of the pillar, leading up from somewhere in that crazy maze of a building.

The swing of the door missed me by a fraction of an inch — I sucked in my breath — and two men came out on the roof-top carrying naked blades.

No! I didn't see the blades, but both, one after the other, scraped against me, cutting through trousers and underwear like razors.

They wounded me slightly, but I made neither motion nor outcry. For there, in my arms, was the girl who was dearest to me in all the world; and so, just for luck, I bent down and kissed her again.

CHAPTER IV.

DEPTHS.

*Vainly the heart on Providence calls, such aid to seek were
    hardly wise
For man must own the pitiless law the sways the globe and
    sevenfold skies*
                    — From the *Kasidah* of Haji Abdu El-Yezdi

WHAT SAVED me then was the Oriental negligence, the Oriental carelessness as to details, which is — and that's my own discovery — the only thing that is keeping India and the rest of Asia in the rear of Western progress.

An American watchman, hearing a cry for help, might possibly have forgotten his gun. But never his lamp! With these two Hindus it was just the opposite; armed to the teeth they were, judging from the swish and crackle of steel which syncopated their movements about the roof-top, but they carried neither lamp, nor candle, nor even a match. They moved about there in the dark, searching, groping, tapping, and were, of course, very much astonished when they didn't find anybody. I was sure that the old ruffian in the cupboard beneath the balustrade nearly caused his eyes to pop out of his head with effort to shout out to them, to tell them where he was. But my gloves were a good gag — with a fine, healthy, tannic acid taste to them, I guess.

Yes, they were astonished and amazed. At least, I gathered as much from the guttural exclamations. They called on a variety of Hindi deities to be witness to their predicament, but the native gods weren't helping much that night. Just then, a little black-and-yellow box of Swedish matches — prosaic, matter-of-fact Occidental matches — would have beaten Shiva, Vishnu, Lakshmi, and Parvati herself into a cocked hat.

But those two steel-rattling fools did not know it. They just groped about, and searched, and cursed a little, and finally they seemed to decide that, though they themselves had come to the roof-top via the only aperture that led out from the building itself, there was only one other way — from Ibrahim Khan's Gully, across the balustrade — the way I had taken. So one of them swung over the wall. I heard him land on his feet, with a little soft plop, like some great cat, and with a metallic, grating noise as the tip of his scabbard bumped against the ground; and a moment later I heard him down below, walking up and down, up and down, as if he was patrolling the Gully.

By this time I was getting decidedly uncomfortable. The front of me was all right, with that little soft, warm bundle of humanity held tight in my arms. But the back of me! Pressed against the confounded stone wall, with about an inch of sharp bronze door-hinge boring into a choice spot of my anatomy! It was that which I minded. Funny, don't you think? There I was, balancing precariously on the edge of the unknown, and it wasn't my ultimate fate which I feared. I didn't even think of it. The only thing that mattered was that one little pang of pain in the small of my back.

A smile flickered on Stephen Denton's lips. It was not exactly a smile of amusement, nor altogether a smile of triumph. Anyway, here's how he continued:

I was pretty good at college football, sort of solid and reliable; I played tackle straight through my lessons — didn't slip and slide and run about the side-lines.

Don't you get me? Well, put it this was, then:

I went in for the sound and heavy and recognized in learning, and didn't care much for apologies. Regular chief in the tribe of the Philistines I was! Psychology? That was a word always on the lips of some of my classmates, as an excuse, an explanation for almost anything. I didn't care for it at all.

I always thought that a psychologist is like a man who is looking for his spectacles and finally finds them on his own nose, after looking on everybody's else's nose — the sort of a man who loses his spectacles — what? By putting them in the wrong place? Why, no! By putting them in the right place! That's how he loses them! Well, I didn't. I wasn't a psychologist, nor any other sort of intellectual, self-analytical jackass. Perhaps I was too stupid — and it turned out to be lucky for me that night, on the flat roof-top in the heart of Coolootallah, with every wickedness and crime and cruelty and superstition in India floating and breathing and bunching somewhere about me in the purple, choking darkness, with my love in my arms! For — as I should and would have done had I been a junior Münsterberg — I did not stop to dissect and label the psychology of fear and apprehension, as exemplified in myself.

Perhaps I didn't have the time. All I meant to do — I had made up my mind to do — was to get rid of the pain in my back, and to get the little girl somewhere where there wouldn't be a witless hairbreadth of destiny between her life and mine.

But how?

Of course, my first inclination was to assault the Hindu who had remained behind — I could hear him breathe, near me, in the gloom — in fact, to kill him. Yes, to kill him! Remember, I told you I was beginning to feel myself part of the Coolootallah scenery, including the — ah! — primeval emotions of that charming neighborhood. But, if I was a caveman in emotions, I was also a caveman in instinctive, safety-first cunning. I said to myself that I could not kill without making a noise — and there was my Hindu's sidekick prowling about in the Gully. What then? I could not stay all night behind the pillar, even supposing the pain in my back should cease. For, in another few hours, it would be morning, and before that old lady Moon might get it into her head almost any time to pop out from behind her banks of clouds and treat us to a silver bath.

No hope in front of me, thus! But in back of me there was a door, the only solid nail on which to hang my plan. If it had been door enough to let the two Hindu out on the roof-top, It was bound to be door enough to let me away from the roof-top.

I acted on that idea as soon as I thought of it. The door was still ajar. Quite noiselessly, the girl in my arms, I squirmed around the edge of it, and I felt steps under my feet.

Right then I drew a good, long breath — the first in about three eternities, it seemed to me — and I eased the strain on my muscles by letting the warm little burden in my arms slip down until the tips of her toes touched the ground.

What — did I lock the door behind me? You bet your life I did — not!

There was a latch, and I could have barred those snooping beggars out, but what possible good would that have done? Sooner or later they were bound to give up their search and to report to whomever had sent them; and their suspicions would only have increased if they had found that somebody had locked them out. No, I left the door open, and, once more pressing the little Hindu girl tight against my chest, I groped my way down the stairs, slowly, carefully, perhaps a couple of dozen steps, worn, slippery and hollow by the tread of naked feet, down, straight down.

There was not even the faintest ray of light. But I held to my course, the burden in my arms getting heavier every second, carefully setting foot before foot, and finally landing dead against the wall. I gave my forehead a terrific bump and jarred my whole body. It was providential that the girl didn't regain consciousness, for just then I should have had a devil of a time explaining to her.

Presently, by groping tentatively here and there, I discovered that I had debouched on a narrow landing which stretched right and left. What now? I had to turn somewhere, and I chose the left, for no particular reason. But I have often since wondered what would have happened, how the whole thing would have ended, had I gone the other way, although a few minutes later I decided that my eventual choice of directions had been singularly unfortunate.

Still, in the end, it didn't turn out that way.

You see (Stephen Denton made a vast, circular gesture) here I am, and — Never mind, old man. Let me resume my muttons.

He laughed at the word.

Muttons with a vengeance! If not muttons, then at least goats; same family of ruminant animals, aren't they? For, as I walked down, the landing a perfectly brutal, goatish smell seemed to drift from the unknown goal toward which I was making. I wondered if on top of all the other sanitary iniquities the Hindus were in the habit of keeping pens in the middle of their living-houses. But I wasn't going to let a smell, any smell, swerve me from my course. Goats or no goats, I walked on, on for several minutes along the outside which twisted and turned, rose and dipped like some crazy stone snake, and all the time I felt the pat-pat-pat of the little girl's heart-beats, softly beating, against my own heart, as if trying to blend, to mix with it.

Once I stopped. For, from a great distance it seemed, the bell of the Presbterian church on Old Court House Street was tolling the half-hour;

and I, don't you see — I was going away from the bell, from the church and all it implied — civilization, Christianity, safety — away from Boston and mild cocktails and Phi Beta Kappa! "Come back!" tolled the bronze-tongued bell, and the sounds of it seemed to pour through the glassy, grooved floor as though from cellars and tunnels where they lay stored beneath the house, beneath the Colootallah, beneath all India. They sang and trembled about me: "Come back, Come back!" But I —

Well, I told the fool bell to go chase itself. I kept on — yes, in the general direction of that brutal odor.

Presently, though the smell increased in intensity, in a certain unspeakable corroding acidity, it seemed to become less goatish; but, too, it seemed to hold some vague horror.

Doesn't seem reasonable, does it, to be afraid of a smell? But I was, in a way; and heretofore I hadn't been afraid at all! Of course, I controlled my nascent fear immediately. Had to, you see, with all the world's treasures to my arms. But I was in a peculiar state of mind. I put my feet down carefully, but mechanically, and my mind seemed suddenly detached from my bodily sensations, as if it was trying to grope ahead of my body into the dark, to warn, to reassure. Somehow I felt that I had stepped into a hollow; not a hollow of the earth, but one of time.

Still I kept on, and all at once it seemed to me that the smell was directly in front of me, coming from below my feet. I groped in the dark — I had come to the end of the corridor — but there was a door set slant-ways into the wall. There was a handle. I gripped it. The door opened easily. I stepped inside, and the door shut behind me with a little dull, soft thud of finality.

A moment later I thought I had been too rash. Holding the girl in my left arm, I tried to open the door with my right; but it was impossible. I could not even budge it.

Stephen Denton smoked for a while in silence, a silence suddenly broken by the strumming of a native guitar which drifted down the stairs. He smiled.

Can you imagine stepping from utter silence and darkness into a room with a bright light? Why, no! What is there to apprehend, to startle you, even in a bright light? You know it comes from somewhere, through some mechanical or natural agency, don't you?

What startled me into stark, breathless immobility was a faint noise — a faint, rasping noise, the like of which I had never heard before.

Not that, with my back against a cold, moist wall, the girl in my left arm with her feet touching the ground, I had time to run in my memory over all the noises I had ever heard. But I knew that was it — I knew that the noise which I heard had a sinister, grim connection with the fetid scent which had drifted down the corridor in front of me, and, too, that it held in itself a terrible menace. It wasn't a hissing, nor a barking, nor a scraping. It seemed more like a tremendous vibration that filled the space about me, that seemed to close in on me; and while I was not afraid — how could I have been with her in my arms? — I felt, sort of dimly, a rushing wonder as to the aspect, the source, the nature, yes as though it may seem silly to you — the all-fired use and necessity of that unknown noise! I want you to feel that noise as I felt it — yes, felt it more than heard it — perhaps a combination of the two sensations. I seemed to both feel and hear somebody, something listening in the dark! Presently the impression grew into positive knowledge, and then — I guess there's some scientific connecting-link between seeing and hearing and smelling — at that very same moment the fetid smell rose against me like a solid wall, and I saw two small, oblong, green lights — and they appeared to be flat.

You know, I wouldn't have minded so much if those two green lights had seemed rounded, globular. What startled me was the fact that they were quite flat. Mad, don't you think? But true, old man!

And the door was shut behind me; and I and the girl who was all the world and all the world's salvation to me were imprisoned with that strange, humming vibration, the terrible, fetid odor, the flat oblong, green lights!

What was I to do? Get my arms free for action, for savage battle, for whatever might happen — that was the first!

I turned a little to the left to let the girl slip gently to the floor.

And then my heart stood still, quite still. The blood in my veins felt exactly like freezing water!

For as I turned I saw two more flat, green lights. But they were less distinct than the others. Sort of vague, wiped-over — that's how they looked; and they were in the wall, like jewels in a deep setting. I raised my right hand to crush them, to pluck them out; and then I laughed.

I am sure I laughed — at myself.

You see, the moment my hand was in one line with them they disappeared; and then I knew the second pair of green lights was only a reflection of the first pair, the slimy, dank wall acting as a mirror; and so I propped the girl against the wall, drew my knife, and turned back to face once more the unknown danger.

The vibrations were increasing in intensity; the green lights swerved and swayed here and there like gigantic fireflies; and I was a little afraid, perhaps because my love was not in my arms any more; and so I commenced whistling to regain my self-confidence. I whistled quite well, very softly. I used to practice it years ago in prep school to annoy my teachers.

Imagine me standing there like a fool in that inky-black room in the heart of the Colootallah, shielding a Hindu girl, a girl whose name I didn't know and whom I had finally decided to take with me to the very end of life — facing I didn't know what unknown horror and iniquity, and whistling — whistling one of those slow, dreamy, peaches-and-cream Hawaiian melodies, the "Waikiki Moonlight," if I remember rightly, with a little drooping sob to every third note.

I am glad that it was dark and that there was no mirror down there in which to behold myself. I am sure I must have cut a laughable figure — I can imagine it with my hair, since I was a little scared, standing out like ruffled feathers, my eyes wide open and staring into those flat, green, ghastly things in front of me, my jaw a trifle dropped, and my lips pointed, whistling that sentimental poppycock about the dear old silvery moonlight on dear old Waikiki beach. Gosh!

But presently the impression grew on me — to become a stony certainty almost immediately — that those swaying green things in front of me were becoming more quiet, more stationary, the longer and softer I whistled. Too, the vibration, while it did not cease, became indifferent, less terrible and minatory; seemed to lose some of its menacing, crouching, intensity.

A few more staves about moonlight and Liliuokalani and Waikiki, and the vibrations had blended completely into a soft, contented — well a mixture between a purr and a hiss.

What did I do? Why I kept right on whistling. You just bet I did! I must have gone through my entire lengthy repertory of sentimental mush — German tunes, American, Hawaiian, Irish and Greaser! And, which is the incredible part of it, the true, inevitable part, that one little accomplishment saved my life that night.

I was beginning at about No. 33 on my musical program — by this time the green things, had become quite stationary and something like a milky veiled film had settled over them when there was a soft rushing noise, but not at all a terrifying noise, the green lights were blotted out altogether, and something hove up out of the dark: it brushed up against me, it poured over my feet and ankles with the soft, pliable weight of a huge steel cable — something mighty and very cold! I stood there like a statue if a statue can tremble a little — and the coiled, steely, thing drew itself up, up the length of my legs, around my waist with a great turn over my shoulders; then, without any apparent effort, still farther up, over my head a foot or so encircling my neck — the next moment one end of it touched my cheek with a soft, gentle, caressing gesture.

A cobra! yes — a cobra!

That huge reptile had heard me whistle — perhaps it was some sob catch in my way of whistling which did the trick, which reminded the snake of the plaintive notes which the snake-charmer produces from his flat reed pipe.

Anyway, there it was, encircling my body, gently touching my cheeks. Fancy though — wasn't it? — to consider that there, in that rabbits' warren of a building with every one's hand against me, a cobra — most hated and feared of animals — was the only living thing which seemed to have a sort of affection for me!

What did I do? Oh, I patted its head, and I have a vague, shameful recollection that I addressed the great, slimy brute as "good old pussy" — but, whatever it was, it pleased her; and if ever a snake purred, that snake purred!

Presently it must have thought that there had been enough caressing for the time being, for, with one final, deep vibrating hiss-purr, it slid down my body, and with a slight wiggle of farewell which nearly knocked me off my feet, it scooted off.

I didn't waste much time in putting two and two together. For a cobra in India in a building meant priests and a temple.

You see, I had done quite a little sight-seeing in Calcutta; I had also studied my guide-book and had talked to several seasoned old Anglo-Indians, Roos-Keppel included; and I remembered what I had seen and read and heard — about the sacred king-cobra which the Hindus keep in stone caves at the feet of some of their idols, how the Brahmans go down and feed them, and how tame the reptiles become.

Don't you see? I was just in such a snake den, and I said to myself that the way of getting out of it was the way by which the priest brought down the food — they can't throw it down, you know, since cobras drink a good deal of milk — a way which must lead, not back to the landing whence I had come, but straight into the temple. So I groped and tapped about the walls and the low ceiling, and finally I found a curved metal handle. A jerk and a twist — and half the ceiling slid to one side, into a well-oiled groove, sending down a flood of haggard, indifferent light. I picked up the little Hindu girl, who was still unconscious, lifted her gently through the hole in the ceiling, and followed after.

The room in which I found myself was lit by the dull-red, scanty glow which came from an open-work silver brazier swinging on chains from the vaulted ceiling — a dull-red glow sadly mingling with a few pale moon-rays breaking through a tiny window high up on the left wall.

For a few seconds I was bewildered — couldn't quite locate myself. Directly in front of the opening — I saw that plain enough — was a huge, bestial Hindu idol — an image of Shiva in his incarnation as Natarajah, "Lord of the Dance." I remembered that from the other temples I had seen.

You can imagine what the idol looked like — its right leg in the air in a fantastic curve, the left pressed upon the figure of a dwarf; in the whirling hair a cobra, a skull, a mermaid figure of the river Ganges, and the crescent moon; in the right ear a man's earring, in the left a woman's; and with four arms — one holding a drum, and another fire, while the third was raised, and the fourth pointed to the lifted foot — and the whole act on a huge lotus pedestal.

From an incense-burner in the farther corner a mass of scented smoke swirled up, darkening the air with a solid, bloated shadow — and everything seemed shapeless, veiled, wreathed in floating vapors.

Presently my eyes got used to the dim half-light. I discovered that the temple was fair-sized, and that it contained no furniture nor ornament — no article of any sort except the statue of Shiva and the incense-burner. The window was too high up to reach, and there was only one door — a low door, directly across from the idol, a door leading — where?

"Say," Stephen Denton interrupted his tale, "are you getting tired of my adventures? Would you rather play a game of cards — dummy bridge? Say the word."

I told him that I abhorred cards. I told him that just then I was only interested in one thing. "How the deuce did you get away from there?" I wound up. "What was behind that door? How did you —"

"Survive?" he completed my halting question with a low laugh. "Why, old man — you forget that I bore a charmed life that night — a charmed life — just like Napoleon, like Tamerlane, like—"

"What was behind that door?" I interrupted him a little heatedly.

"Wait till we get to it." Stephen Denton laughed. "Something else happened in the temple — before I opened that door and found out!"

CHAPTER V.

NERVES.

E gaio il minuetto, ma tavolta piange
(The minuet's lift is merry, but sometimes a song breaks through)
— Fogazzaro

THERE WAS one thing more in the temple — a fine, soft, silk rug — and I rolled it into a tight pillow and slipped it under the head of the little Hindu girl. I had stretched her out on the floor.

You know — Stephen Denton continued, with a curious, hazy note of embarrassment in his pleasant voice — I am afraid that, at that moment, with the girl at my feet and the grinning idol above me — with the scented, whirling wreaths of incense-smoke floating about me — I had a certain revulsion of feeling.

I was not afraid. Nor was I exactly riled at that mad throw of the dice of fate which had chucked me there — into the dim, mysterious heart of the Colootallah, five centuries removed from the Hotel Semiramis, the Presbyterian Church, the English bobbies, and all the rest of trousered, hatted civilization. I didn't mind that. Of course not! For, don't you see, I loved that warm, little, girlish thing of gold and black and crimson at my feet. My love was one of those mighty, heaving, cosmic revolutions which will attempt and accomplish the impossible — it was one of those stony, merciless facts which no arguing and no self-searching can kick out of existence.

But I guess there is such a thing as loving in spite of one's self — of love being a thing, a condition, a fact apart from the rest of one's life.

Don't you get me? Why, old man, remember what I told you of how the girl was dressed — in the costume of a tuwaif, a Hindu dancer — and here, grinning and jeering above my head, was the idol of Shiva in his incarnation as Natarajah, "Lord of the Dance" — and the connection seemed obvious! And, after all, my people did come over in the Mayflower — and there was that reproachful church-bell from Old Court House Street — just then it was tolling the quarter to one.

Nothing shocking in the art and motion of dancing. But you have seen Hindu dances — religious Hindu dances — haven't you? You know the significance of the image of Natarajah, how in the night of Brahma nature is said to be inert and cannot breathe nor move nor dance till Shiva wills it; how Shiva rises from his stillness of meditation, crushes the dwarf of night and inertia, and, dancing on his prostrate body, sends through all matter the pulsing waves of awakening sound, preceding from the drum; how, in the richness of time, still dancing, he destroys all names and all forms by fire; and how then all emotions and a new rest come upon the Earth.

A mad Hindu notion of bringing together the orderly swing of the spheres, the perpetual movement of atoms, the sensation of the human body, and evolution itself — all represented in the dancing figure of Shiva Natarajah — and in the whirling bodies of the nautch, the Hindu dancing-girls who are consecrated to the service of the gods!

You know the nature and meaning and gestures of those dances, don't you? And there was the girl at my feet in her dancing costume, and the grinning idol above us — there was the memory of some of things which Roos-Keppel had told me about the crimes and vices and the unclean castes which center in the Colootallah; and how — as in the rest of the world — it is always woman who is used as the mainspring of intrigue and venal traffic — and I clenched my fists until the knuckles stretched white.

I looked at the girl — the light was dim, trembling, uncertain, but I could see the pale gold of her little face, the dusky, voluminous clouds of hair, the thick net of the eyelashes.

I touched her face, her shoulders — only for a fleeting second — for, don't you see, to me she was holy, and somehow she was to me part of that temple — of the sacredness of that temple — yes — sacredness — and I mean it. A mad, bombastic, fantastic, cruel faith — that Hindu faith! I know it! But faith, religion, just the same somehow trying to make the world better. I guess there isn't a single religion which really tries to do harm.

Yes, sacred and inviolable she was to me — and I thought how she and the love of her had come to me, in the purple Indian night — precious, swift, unexpected, like a break of glimmering sunlight after a leaden gray day — and there leapt into my heart, with the terrific and incalculable aim of lightning, the blinding longing for complete possession — and deliberately I disentangled myself from the jumble of bitter emotions which had come to me through the thought she was a nautch, consecrated to Shiva Natarajah.

The whole revolution of feeling had only lasted a few seconds. I said to myself that love — real love — has no time to consider and weigh the patterned dictates of abstract morality. Mine own life to make or to mar — and I considered that I would rather mar my life through love than make it through clammy indifference!

Temple girl or no temple girl, it was up to me to get her out of that building, out of the Colootallah, out of whatever shame and misery and disgrace life had meant to her before I had seen her for the first time, back there on the rooftop at the end of Ibrahim Khan's Gully.

This time I had no choice of directions, for there was only one door out of the temple. Should I pick her up and step into the unknown? No — I decided the next moment — instead of carrying her, and thus burdening and slowing my progress, it would be better for me to scout ahead, to hunt about until I had discovered an avenue of escape. When I had found that, I would come back to her and carry her to safety.

But there was the chance that the two Hindu watchmen on the rooftop might give up their fruitless search and come into this room. Too, there was the possibility of some Brahman priest entering the temple to attend to some of his sacerdotal duties. I would have to hide the girl. But where? Remember, the room was empty of furniture and ornaments. I went the round of the walls, hunting for a closet, but found none. There was only the incense burner, and the huge idol of Shiva Nataajiht, the latter standing fairly close to the wall.

I walked around it more or less aimlessly, and then I made a discovery — quite an interesting discovery — with which, had I had time to use it for that purpose just then, I could have blown the thaumaturic reputation of that particular Hindu temple sky high.

I found that the lotus pedestal of the statue had an opening in the back, a sort of curved sliding door three feet high and about seven broad, which was partly open. I stooped to investigate, and then I drew back in a hurry.

For sounds came from within. I suppose my nerves tingled a little, but you mustn't forget that — though at the time the thought never entered my head; I was too busy — all the events of that mad night had been so unusual that I had really lost the common standards of judging and of fearing. So I let my nerves tingle all they wanted to, and I stooped down once more to discover the source and nature of those sounds.

The very next moment I knew, and I guess I was foolish enough to laugh. You see, the sounds which came from the inside of the pedestal were really quite peaceful and prosaic; they might have happened in quiet old Boston, for that matter.

Somebody in there was snoring — in a fat, contented, elderly way!

So I pushed the sliding-door to one side just as far as it would go. I looked, and sure enough, there, comfortably curled up on a litter of rugs and pillows and shawls. I saw the dim form of a portly Brahman priest sleeping with his mouth wide open, his curly white beard moving rhythmically up and down with the intake of his breath. Not a bad-looking old gentleman — quite peaceful and dignified. But that didn't help him any just then; for here was the ideal hiding-place for my Daughter of Heaven.

I drew my knife, poised it neatly over his heart, and jerked him awake. "Keep quiet — perfectly quiet!" I whispered to him, very much like a black-mustached villain in an old-fashioned melodrama. At the same moment he stirred, opened his eyes, heard my warning, and saw the Bowie — saw the point of it, if you will forgive my wretched pun — and, obeying my instructions, he rose and came out of the pedestal, a very incarnation of outraged, elderly pomposity

Gosh, but that Brahman looked mad!

So far so good — here was a cozy little nest for my love — but what was I to do with Old Pomposity?

"What shall I do with you?" I finally asked him direct, and he replied with a stream of low-pitched and extremely foul abuse. That did not help any — neither him nor me nor the girl — and so, after considering a few seconds, I narrowed my question down to a choice of two things. I asked him, quite civilly and good-naturedly — I bore him no personal grudge, you see — what he preferred: to be killed outright, or to go down to the snake. Pretty tough on his nibs; but what could I do? I needed the hollow pedestal, and I couldn't afford to leave a live witness behind.

But he couldn't see it my way, naturally. He threatened and cajoled and argued. He cursed me, my ancestors, my posterity, and my cow in the name of a dozen assorted Hindu deities — in the name of Vishnu and Shiva, Indra, Varuna, Agni, Surya, Chandra, Yama, Kamadeva, Ganesha, and what not! He had a surprising knowledge of Puranic theology; but finally he decided in favor of the snake! I could understand his choice; since he doubtless was the priest in charge of the temple, and thus sure to be on more or less friendly terms with the wiggly old reptile at the feet of Natarajah.

"All right — just as you wish," I replied; and just for luck — also to make him a little more easy to handle — I fetched him a good hard blow on the side of the head which stretched him unconscious. Then I gagged and tied him securely with some of the shawls from his couch, shoved him down into the cobra's den, and pushed the stone slab shut.

Then I investigated the interior of the lotus pedestal. It was big enough to afford sitting and sleeping space to an average-sized human being, and — here is the discovery of which I told you, the discovery which would have raised no end of a row in orthodox Hindu theological circles — I saw that the statue was hollow, and that it could be reached by the occupant of the pedestal.

What for? Why? How? Why, old man, the day of miracles may have passed in the West — with biology and motor-cars and aeroplanes, and all that — but not so in the eternal East! For there, handy to the occupant of the pedestal, was an assortment of ropes and levers and handles and pulleys which were connected with the different parts of Shiva Natarajah's sacred anatomy. Push a lever here, pull a rope there — I tried it, you see — and the idol would lift a leg or wave one of his four arms or wag his beastly old head. There was even one bit of machinery — it was rather rusty and hard to move, as though it hadn't been used for a long time — which allowed the whole statue, pedestal included, to move forward across the room — a very ingenious bit of machinery, a combination system of wheels and gliding planes — and the very thing for a smashing, twenty-four-carat miracle!

But the only miracle which mattered to me just then was the fact that, through a twist and jerk of Fate, I had come to Ibrahim Khan's Gully — in a low voice and to the little Hindu girl. I picked her up and put her inside the pedestal, leaving the sliding-door slightly aslant to give her breathing space.

By ginger — Stephen Denton gave an embarrassed little smile —

she looked pretty in there on that soft mass of pillows and shawls, and the dim light about her like a veil. You know those lines by Rabindranath Tagore, don't you?

> *When ruddy lips blossom into smiles, black eyes pass stolen glances,*
> *Then it is the season, my poet, to make a bonfire of your verses.*
> *And weave only heart with heart and hand with hand.*

Oh, well —

I bent down and kissed the little soft mouth — unconscious she was, and her thoughts dream-veiled, but there was something like an answering quiver on her lips as I touched them with mine — I crossed the width of the temple, opened the door, and stepped out on a corridor, bright-lit with swinging yellow lamps. It was really more than a corridor — more like a long hall, very high, with a vaulted ceiling — and, compared to the slime of Ibrahim Khan's Gully, compared to the oppressive gray reek and misery of the Colootallah compared even to the dignified bareness the temple, it seemed incongruous startling in its utter magnificence — as if it had been flung there, in the heart of that drab, twisted maze of buildings, to echo to the footsteps of — of what and whom?

You see, old man, right then I wondered. I was a little disturbed — with the dim terror of something awfully remote from and awfully inimical to my personality, my race, my life as it had been heretofore. For Roos-Keppel had told me — oh, a whole lot. He had told me how, in the days when he was still in the Bengal Civil Service, he had tracked one of the Indian seditionist secret societies — "Hail, Motherland!" it called itself straight down into the caste labyrinth of assassins and thieves and thugs and criminals of all sorts; how, in fact, the Babu gentry of the Hail, Motherland! had made a hard and fast alliance with the criminal castes, had fraternized with them in life, and in worship, and in death, both fighting the same enemy: the established government, the British raj. And this — all this — why, don't you see? The temple of Shiva, god of high castes, here, in the heart of the low-caste Colootallah — the rattle and crackle of naked steel on the roof-top; and remember that the law against carrying and possessing weapons is as strictly enforced in Calcutta as the Sullivan Law in New York; and, then, as a final proof, it seemed to me, the dazzling, extravagant splendor of this corridor, this long, tall hall!

Up to a height of seven feet the walls were covered with stucco, white on white, ivory and snowy enamel skillfully blended with shiny-white lac, and overlaid with a silver-threaded spider's web of arabesques, at exquisite as the finest Mechlin lace, and, of Sanskrit quotations in the deva-nagari script.

I reconstructed all this later on, in my memory, after — Stephen Denton pointed about the room — India had become part of my life, my whole life. The upper part of the walls, above the white stucco, was a procession, a panorama of conventionalized Hindu fresco paintings — an epitome, a résumé of all Hindustan's myths and faiths and legends and superstitions, from the Chadanta Jataka, the birth-story of the Six-tusked Elephant, most beautiful of all Buddhistic legends, to the ancient tale of Kaliya Damana, which tells how Krishna overcame the hydra Kaliya; from color-blazing designs picturing Rama, Sita, and Lakshman meditating in their forest exile, to a representation of Bhagirstha imploring Shiva to permit the Ganges to fall to the Earth from his matted locks.

The tale of a nation's life, a nation's civilization and faith — yes, and crimes and virtues and sufferings, here in front of me, and the thought came over me — a true thought, I discovered afterward — that never white man had seen the like before, and I felt like an intruder. I had a faint feeling of misgiving. But what could I do? It was Hobson's choice! I had to walk on!

So I moved along rapidly, down that everlasting corridor with all India's gods jeering at me from the wall paintings, and looking left and right for a door, a window, or some other avenue of escape, at least of progress — when, very suddenly, I was startled into complete immobility — into a stark immobility of utter horror.

Directly in front of me, the corridor came to an end — or rather it broadened out, swept out into a circular hall — quite an impressive affair, the walls covered with slabs of the delicate, extravagant Indian stone carving that looks like sculptured embroidery, with splendid furniture of carved, black shishan wood, a profusion of enameled silver ornaments, and the floor covered with huge, squares of that white embroidery which the people hereabouts call chikam.

Of course, I didn't see all that at first — took it in more gradually, for I told you that I was — oh — crushed under a sudden weight of gray, breath-clogging horror, and, in such moments of overwhelming emotion, the eyes search too eagerly, too furiously, to see properly at all; too, the light was flickering — shooting in curly, wavering streams from a swinging lamp and sending out shadows which ran about the walls and the ceiling like running water.

Stephen Denton leaned forward in his chair.

Tell me, have you ever felt the fascination of utter horror? Have you ever had a dream in which everything around you — the inanimate objects even — assume shifting, wavering forms and loom about I you — bending and twisting and stretching toward you like cruel, misshapen arms?

Have you ever feared Fear itself?

The thing which stirred me so profoundly? Yes, yes — I am coming to that — and I guess you'll be disappointed.

For it was only a face.

Only a face — and yet — why, if I should try to tell you what I felt, what I really felt, I would involve myself in a maze of contradictions. There are some nervous reactions for which there are no words in our language: and, anyway. I survived it — that as well as what came after. I am sitting here now, across from you, talking to you — and upstairs —

Never mind. You're getting impatient. Let me get back to my tale —

CHAPTER VI.

OUT — AND IN.

Our horses aren't from Tartary, the land of Tamerlane.
They come from river meadows, out beyond the Southern Main
No lynx we bring for foxes,
No cheetahs for the deer;
With brown and while bedappled
Our English hounds are here.
The jackal he may kennel in the fields of sugar-cane.
The pack is in and after him to drive him out again.

— E. D.

ONLY A FACE, he continued, that of an old man, wrinkled, brown, immobile on a scrawny neck which was like the slimy stalk of some poisonous jungle flower, the body, arms, and legs wrapped in layers of thin muslin, sitting upright on a great chair of gray, carved marble.

I wish I could picture that face to you as I saw it — it would take the hand of a Rodin to clout and shape the meaning of it. The taint of death, the flavor of dread tortures which surrounded it, the face of a sensual, perverted, plague-spotted Roman emperor blended with the unhuman, meditating, crushing calm of a Chinese sage.

Why, man, I can see it even now — at times — heavy-jowled, thin-lipped, terribly broad across the temples — and with an expression in his whitish-gray-eyes like the sins of a slaughtered soul.

Compared to that face — to the solitary fact of that face's existence, if you get me — all the little fears and trembling apprehensions which had come over me since I had swung across the wall at the end of Ibrahim Khan's Gully seemed ridiculous — as unimportant as the twittering of sparrows in a street gutter — and my adventures seemed dull and commonplace.

I had an idea that I spoke — some foolish, meaningless words of greeting. I am not sure if I did or not. For, during some moments, I sought in vain to steady my mind and my senses to the point of understanding, of intelligence, of observation. All I could see and feel was the existence of these features in front of the grotesque, monstrous, unhuman — and I wanted to shriek — I wanted to beat them into raw, bleeding pulp!

Perhaps the whole sensation, the whole flash of emotions, lasted only a moment. Perhaps it was contained in the fraction of the second it took me to pass from the corridor, properly speaking, into the hall. At all events, suddenly I was myself again. I remembered the girl — and the wondrous magic, the sweet, wild strength of the love I bore her.

Whatever the meaning of these sinister, immobile features — whatever the dread prophecy in these staring, unblinking, cruel eyes — I'd have to go through with my task — the task of fighting my way out of this house — and to carry the girl with me, unharmed. So I walked — up to that muslin-swathed body — to that horror of a face —

Stephen Denton ashed his cigar. He was silent for perhaps a couple of minutes, and I did not press him to hurry up with his tale. It was so evident that he was trying to collect his thoughts — so evident too, that the remembrance of that moment was not a very pleasant one to him. But presently he looked up, with a return of his old full, jolly, magnetic smile; and he continued.

Yes — I jerked my wits into a fair semblance of nerve control and took a step forward — one step, two, three — slowly and deliberately — until I was within a foot of that face — and then — why, man, I laughed! It wasn't a very cheerful laugh — rather a harsh, ghastly, scraping sort of machination — but it saved, if not my life, then at least my sanity. For, quite suddenly, when I was within a foot of it, I realized that that face — that thing of dread and horror — was harmless. I realized that it was not alive at all!

A statue? No, old man, guess again — you see, it was the face of a mummy — that's why the body was wrapped in layers of muslin — and the eyes were of glass, cunningly painted. I said to myself that it was doubtless the mummified remains of some especially holy Brahman priest — and I felt quite a rush of affection for his deceased holiness — for at least he couldn't hurt me; he couldn't hurt the little girl who was all the world to me. I have an idea that I was about to pat the old mummy familiarly on the brown, wrinkled brow when —

Wait? It's so confoundedly hard to put it into words — you've got to feel it, as I felt it, that night. You see, I heard a whisper — yes — I knew that wrinkled horror was dead, a mummy — and yet — why, I looked about the room — there was nobody there — and the mad thought came to me that the mummy had whispered!

Don't you get me? I knew it was impossible — and — there it was! A whisper — shadowy, fleeting, secretive! Of course it was ridiculous — and yet I was sure, in spite of my positive knowledge and in spite of the dictates of my sanity, that the whisper had come from the mummy. I don't know why I should have thought so — ask a professor of psychology for the correct explanation — but the fact remains that I jumped back about three feet with a quickly suppressed cry of fear.

The whole impression lasted less time than it takes me to tell it. The very next second I had collected myself — had to, you see, since I didn't want to lose my sanity — and with breath sucked in, my whole body tense and bunched, I tried to follow up the low sibilant tone waves — to locate the direction whence the whispering really came.

What? Did they plant a phonograph inside of that mummy? (Stephen Denton laughed at my question.) No! No! Can you imagine such a Western abomination as a phonograph near a Hindu temple — in the mummified body of a Hindu saint?

Of course not! The explanation was a hanged sight easier. The tone waves — the whispers — came, not from the mummy's mouth — but from the mummy's feet!

So I stretched myself full-length on the floor, at the feet of his holiness, pressed my ears against the cold stone flags, and listened intently.

And I heard — two words, at first! They sort of remained with me, and made me feel uncomfortable and creepy all over again. For those whispered words were: "The Sahib!"

They stood out, those two words, in sharp, crass relief. "The Sahib!" Nothing more — and, subconsciously, I guessed — no! I knew, that it was I — Stephen Denton, Esquire, out of Boston — who was meant by that melodious and honorable appellation. For sahibs, at one o'clock in the morning, are a pretty rare article in the midst of the Colootallah!

The whispering continued, and I heard quite well. There was really no mystery to it — for, don't you see, most of those old buildings in the Colootallah were built many years ago, and since Calcutta was a swamp in these days and since wood and stone were rare, they built their houses with hollow tiles imported from Persia via Delhi — and these tiles act very much like telephones — sending tone waves in straight lines and at a considerable distance.

I was grateful for that — and for one more Indian peculiarity — namely the number and diversity of the many Indian languages and dialects which forces Hindus from different parts of the country to speak in English. There were two men whispering — doubtless either thugs or seditionist, at all events men who hated the very name at England and yet they had to speak in English to each other, to make them intelligible. Funny, wasn't it?

I could hear just as plainly as through a telephone — with a perfect connection. The man who spoke first felt evidently peevish about the Sahib — about me. You should have heard the things he called me; not me alone, but also my father, my grandfather, most of my cousins and uncles and my whole family-tree straight down to Adam and Eve, and beyond, even. It seemed that he was appealing to the other man for help.

"Where is she? Where is she?" came the sibilant whisper; and then, with a splendid flow of Oriental imagery, "he — the Sahib — the this-and-that" — more epithets — "has stolen her—the apple of my eyes, the well of my love, the stone of my contentment! Ah!" — and distinctly, through the hollow tiles, I could hear something like a forced, hypocritical sob — "she is a pearl among pearls — with lips like the crimson asoka flower, with teeth as virgin-white as the perfumed madhavi, with a voice like the mating-song of the kokila bird, with a waist as the waist of a she-lion, and with the walk of a king-goose! By Shiva and Shiva — and again by Shiva!" — here he got busy once more about my ancestry and character — "may that white-skinned, cow-eating, and unthinkably begotten foreigner boil slowly and very, very painfully in the everlasting fire which is vomited from the Jwalamukhi! May Garura pick out his eyes — first the left — and then the right! May Bhawani herself suck his filthy heart dry!"

A pause — then the other man's voice: "But whom has the Sahib stolen, brother?" followed by the first man's answer, "the Lady Padmavati!"

"Padmavati?" repeated the second man, in accents of utter, amazed, horrified incredulity, "Padmavati?"

Then silence — thick, heavy, palpable!

Say, continued Stephen Denton, can you imagine what a crash of silence can be like? Sounds paradoxical, don't you think? But that's exactly what followed the mentioning of the little girl's name.

Silence — for one minute — two — three— rhythmically my heartbeats seemed to syncopate each dragging second while I lay there, my ear pressed against the stone flags, at the feet of that beastly old mummy.

I thought finally that the two speakers had perhaps gone away from wherever they were talking. I was about to rise, to continue in my search for an opening, a door or a window which would help my love and me to escape — when once more, insistent, sibilant, whispering, the tone waves glided through the hollow tiles.

It seemed to be the second man who was speaking.

"We must get him — the foreigner — the Christian — the cannibal of the Holy Cow! Quick — by the heavenly light of Chandra!" and he said it in such a deep, flat, strange voice that I felt something like the letting loose of fate — crashing, terrific — I felt an acrid flavor and taint of death and torture — a crimson undercurrent of gigantic, intolerable horrors!

Came the first man's answering whisper: "Yes, for he is dangerous, as dangerous as Prithwi Pala, the servant of Indra the god, of whom the legends speak; and as for Padmavati —" again he was silent — came another flow of words, in Hindustani this time and thus unintelligible to me. But they seemed to be words of command, and they were followed by other voices, other words; then a sharp, ominous hissing and rattling of steel and the faint sound of quick-running feet.

They're off, I said to myself, off and away and after me! I rose and looked to right and left. I guess I felt as a fox must feel when it hears the view-halloo of the chase and the baying of the hounds, with nothing in front but a bare hillside and far in the distance, a spinney which it can never reach.

For where was I to go? Where was I to hide myself?

Only one thing was certain. I could not let myself be caught in this hall nor in the abutting corridor, both bright with light. Back into the temple then — perhaps into the cobra den — a wild thought flashed through my head that I might have time to change clothes with the priest — a thought quickly given up, for what would I do with the priest himself? — other thoughts followed — but clear above them all rose the stony idea that, whatever happened, I must not lead the chase to the idol, the lotus pedestal where I had hidden the girl who was dearer to me than the dwelling of kings.

So I ran, with my thoughts gyrating madly, like swirling fog in the brain of a blind world, faster and faster! There was a noise in my temples like running water, like the wind in the wings of birds; it filled my head with huge, tenoring sound waves, and, as I came within sight of the temple door, the bell from the Presbyterian church boomed out — *bannnng* — a quarter after one — like a gray seal of doom and despair!

Another rushing steps — already my hand was on the doorknob of the temple — already I was trying to subordinate my physical to my mental action, which seemed both muddled and frantic — for, you see, I know that presently I would have to be capable of one supreme effort of wit to save the girl and myself; battle and struggle it would be, and I did not refute the grim challenge of it; I did not blind myself to the balance of odds which would be against me.

Fight, and win or lose! Frenzied heroism? Not a bit of it, old man: Simply the law of equal action and reaction — if I remember anything of my scientific course at college — applied to the dim, cruel heart of the Colootallah.

I had half turned the doorknob — and then —

Stephen Denton leaned forward in his chair and, for the first time since he had commenced the recital of his mad adventures, he gesticulated — his right hand shot out tensely, dramatically.

And then from the walls, as if they had been parts of the walls, two men jumped at me, one from each side.

No, I saw no door, though, of course, there must have been one — two, rather. I only heard the metallic jarring and grating of rusty hinges, and, that same second, they were there, as if a sinister, supernatural power had visualized them from nothing and popped them out at me!

There they were — two men — with a crackle of naked steel — but wait! Get this right!

You see — and it sounds incredible, I know it! — but even in that fraction of a moment's flash my eyes registered what those two men looked like. Strange, isn't It? But I saw — I actually saw every detail of their persons, their costumes, their facial characteristics: their dark skin, their hooked noses, their broad, thin lips, their flashing purple-black, narrow-lidded eyes, their beards, curled and twisted and parted in the dandified Rajput manner, their voluminous white turbans, with clusters of emeralds, falling over their low, broad foreheads, and, high in the right hand of either, a curved scimitar!

Why, man, I even saw the curling, glittering lights on the points of their blades as they seemed to meet above my head like a double-bar-reled, curved guillotine!

All that, every last bit of it, I saw in that fleeting fraction of a moment, and, speak about quickness of perception, about rushing rapidity of wit, why —

Stephen Denton was silent. His right hand was still in the air, as if it were trying to pluck the tense, incredible facts of his narrative from the atmosphere.

Quite suddenly, from upstairs, came once more the twanging of a native guitar; that a soft, silvery woman's voice, singing in Behari:

"... *chare din ke gaile murga Mor ko ke aile* ... "

Stephen Denton laughed. "You know the old song, don't you?" he said. "The cock goes from home for four days only, and returns a pea-cock!" Same with me that night — in the Coolootallah — I left the Hotel Semiramis a plain, prosaic Back Bay Bostonian, and I returned — oh, you'll see — you bet I returned, in spite of those flashing scimitars! Am I not here — in front of your eyes — in the flesh?

And he continued with another laugh.

Yes, the jarring of the doors, the fact of my being able to register what those two bewhiskered ruffians looked like, the ominous crackle of steel as the blades flickered about my head, my own quick-wittedness — all that passed and happened and surged on in a moment. I was too excited, probably to feel ordinary fear. Something flashed through me akin to fear, but, oh, different; there's no word for it in our language; but with it flashed, also, a certain breathless, sullen audacity that's it exactly; a sullen audacity — and I —

Suddenly Stephen Denton burst into a roar of laughter.

Do you know what I did, old man? Can you guess it? No, no! I didn't draw my Bowie-knife and give battle! Of course not! First of all, there wasn't the time — for remember, the whole thing, from the jarring of the unseen door to the end of the little intermezzo, didn't take more than two seconds; and, furthermore, what chance is there for a quiet Bostonian with a Bowie — a Bowie he isn't used to handle, on top of it — against two big, hairy roughs with six yards of curved, razor-sharp steel between them? I'd have had as much chance against them with my Bowie as a regiment of volunteers armed with Civil War pop-guns against a battery armed with French forty-five millimeter guns!

What did I do? But I am coming to that, Don't get impatient —

You see — I ducked!

Yes, sir, I ducked! I threw myself flat on the floor before those two ruffians had a chance to realize what was happening — before they had time to put the brake on their brawny right arms.

Down came the two scimitars, and — yes, this time you guessed it — they hit each other, instead of hitting little me! They split each other's turbaned skulls — *zzzsh!* through the voluminous layers of muslin — with rather a sickening, sharp-crunching noise — and there were two dead Hindus!

Say, man, speak about Tamerlane and George Washington and Napoleon — speak about the Charmed Life — what?

I told you — haven't I? — that from the moment of my swinging across the wall at the end of Ibrahim Khan's Gully — from the moment, rather, when I felt that my life was one with that of the little Hindu girl — my whole self seemed to have separated itself suddenly and completely from all that it had been in the past; it seemed to have lifted itself with a savage, tearing jerk from the pale, flat dumps of my past life and education and tradition — Boston, in other words — to the flashing, crazy limbos of this new, purple, mysterious India! I realized it, even at that moment, with the two dead men at my feet, one with his features, oh, set in an astonished sort of smile, as if wondering at the dark blood which was running lazily from the split skull to the floor; the other dead man's face like a grinning Tibetan devil mask, with the lips drawn back a little over the gleaming, white teeth in an eerie grin, like the fangs of a wolf who sees the victim, jumps, then finds himself in a trap, smells death in the trap in the moment of killing!

Yes, all that I realized; not emotionally, for I seemed able perfectly to decompose the whole situation into a few negligible elements, as I would decompose a force in a question of abstract dynamics, and I was neither shocked nor even disgusted; and, mind you, this was the first time in my life I had seen death!

But, you see, I seemed to belong to India, to the terrible, corroding simplicity of India, and I felt like chanting a chant of victory. I felt a brutal, sublimely unselfconscious joy at the sight of those two sprawling, stark-contoured figures.

Rather beastly, don't you think? But true!

The next moment — for in that respect, too, the crouching, grim-clever instincts of all India had got into my blood — I looked about me, silently, carefully.

I said to myself that there might be more Hindus out after my scalp — for remember, first, I had heard two voices whispering, then a few sharp words of command in Hindustani, and finally several more voices. I had run toward the temple, away from the lights, and I had evidently miscalculated. For if those two dead beggars had located me in the vicinity of the temple it was three to one to assume that the others would reason the same way.

Away from the temple, then! Back in the direction of the circular hall, in spite of the bright lights, as fast as my legs would carry me! So I ran, and as I ran there came to me the madding, paralyzing sensation that quite near me, inside the walls other footsteps were keeping parallel with my own, and I was afraid.

But only for a moment. The very next second the terror in my heart gave way to a feeling of indignation. I was cross, and I forgot all about that great, purple India which had picked me up and was shaping me into a molecule of its own strange, throbbing soul. You see, all my life I had been surrounded by the comfortable, machine-made, wire-drawn safeguards of Western life — police, laws, corporation counsels, prosecuting attorneys, municipal writs, regulation standards, regulation opinions. Fetishes I used to call them in my world-storming undergrad days; but I had relied on them. With all the rest of the Western world — socialists, anarchists, and I. W. W.'s included — I had always been in the position of a man who can demand and receive protection from the duly constituted authorities; and here I was suddenly up against life in the raw — in the bloodstained, quivering raw! I was up against a condition of society to which no law applied, no regulation, no standard known to me.

By ginger, I was mad with utter, impotent fury. Right then I would have liked to have an interview with some of those visionary jackasses who prate against constituted law; and then (Stephen Denton laughed) quite suddenly I quit kicking. Quite suddenly I became convinced once more that I had a charmed life, after all!

For by that time I had arrived again in the great circular hall where his holiness, the mummified Brahman swami, was sitting in sinister state; and there, not too high up, I saw a window!

I made for it immediately, as a frightened cat makes for an open cellar; a running jump with every ounce of strength I possessed, I balanced myself precariously on the sill! I didn't look down. Might have spoiled my nerve. I just closed my eyes and jumped, and I landed on a nice, thick, soft heap of ashes and cinders.

The moon had come from behind the bank of clouds and was drenching everything with tiny flecks of gold. I looked about me. I found myself in a long, narrow courtyard, with the window through which I had come to the left of me, a high wall with a door to the right, another wall, about fifteen feet high, in front, and in back a fantastic, twisted building which towered up in a wilderness of spires and turrets.

I had my choice of three ways, since I had no intention of returning to the hall whence I had jumped, naturally. Too, I discarded the building immediately; it looked, oh, too populous. Remained the two walls. First I examined the one with the door. There was a crack in it and I looked through; it seemed to open out into the street — some street.

Did I try the door? Did I make for the street? You bet I did not! Why?

But, man, there was the girl, back there somewhere in that maze of buildings; the girl who was all the world to me. No! I took the one remaining choice — the fifteen-foot wall in back of me.

At first I failed to discover anything by which I could mount; but at last, walking down the length of it, I came upon a shed with a heavy padlock on its wooden door, with its roof inclined at an angle against the wall. It was my only chance, and there was but one way to do it. I stepped back a few paces and took a running leap for the edge of the roof, jumping for the padlock. I tried three times. The third time I got my foot upon the padlock, and caught the edge of the wall with my hands. Exerting all my strength, I drew myself up, and where do you think I found myself?

I was back on the roof-top at the end of Ibrahim Khan's Gully! Quite alone, for when I groped beneath the balustrade where I had popped the old Hindu, bound and gagged, over an hour and a half before, I found the space empty.

CHAPTER VII.

THE MIRACLE.

Evil is impossible because it is always rising up into Good.
— Saint Augustine

So likewise is Evil the revelation of Good.
— Cardinal Newman

I LOOKED about me. It was a peaceful summer night, with the low hum of a sleeping world, and a froth of yellow stars flung over the crest of the heavens. Over to my right, where the lights of Howrah Station were flickering through the river-mist like dirty candle-dips, lay the great cosmopolitan hotels — the Semiramis, the Great Eastern, the Taj Mahal; there crouched the faint outlines of the Presbyterian church, of the Bengal Club, of Government House — peace and civilization and all the rest of the white man's world. I imagined I could hear them snore across the distance — the commissioners and deputy commissioners, the colonels and adjutants, the big Anglo-Indian merchants, and the American travelers — snoring, peacefully snoring! And I — I was here in the Colootallah, and, yes, I went straight back to my girl.

Did I think much? But what should I have thought about, old man? The only responsibility I had was the girl — since I loved her. My own life? My own fate? Oh, I guess everybody is the weaver of his own life; and if he wants to entangle the woof and warp of it, it's up to him, and to him alone, isn't it? And that isn't Indian philosophy, either. It's plain Yankee, out of Boston; if it wasn't there wouldn't have been any Mayflower in the first place. Would there?

So back to the girl I went the same old way; through the door in back of the pillar, down the staircase and the narrow landing, straight up to the cobra's den. Again I opened the door without much effort; but again, though I tried to keep it open, it slammed shut, and I found it impossible to open it from the inside. There was a bit of hidden machinery there which I could not find, nor had I time to look.

Carefully groping my way, I found the curved handle in the low ceiling. I jerked it, and the ceiling slid to one side, sending down a flood of light from the temple. The Brahman priest was still where I had dumped him, and — would you believe me? — he was peacefully asleep, sawing wood through his nostrils. Speak about Oriental philosophy and submission to fate! Why, that portly, thrice-born Brahman had an over-dose of it. Compared to his plethora of calm, my own quiet Yankee soul seemed to be shrill, noisy, exaggerated.

The cobra? Yes, she, too, was asleep, curled up in the corner like a huge, coiled thing of watered silk.

I swung myself up into the temple, shutting the door behind me, and rushed over to the statue of Shiva Natarajah. The little girl — "the Lady Padmavati" as the Hindus had called her — was still lost to the world; the blow against her temple must have been a terrific one, but her breath came evenly.

Some of the rugs on which she lay had slipped to one side, and I was just about to bend down to fix her up more comfortably, when —

But wait! Let me get this right.

Stephen Denton gave a fleeting, apologetic smile.

You see, it's rather difficult to describe a moment which blends the physical with the psychical.

Well, I had already bent down. Yes, I remember now! My hand was on her soft, narrow shoulder, and, oh, my love seemed to surge upwards with a rush of sweet splendor. That little space in the pedestal seemed charged to the brim with some overpowering loveliness of wild and simple things, like the beauty of stars, and wind, and flowers, with some-thing which all my life, subconsciously, my heart seemed to have craved in vain, beside which my life of yesterday seemed a gray, wretched dream. You know how these thoughts rush through one — suddenly, overwhelmingly — and at the same time music seemed to chime in my ears, rhythmic, glorious music, the music of my heart, of my soul, I thought, and I wasn't ashamed of the winged, poetical flight.

And then, all at once, I realized that the music was not the music of my heart. I realized that it had a much more matter-of-fact origin; that in steadily swelling tone waves it came drifting in from the outside. I straightened up. I listened intently. Then I knew: the music came beating and sobbing down the long, magnificent corridor on toward the temple.

Presently I could make out the different instruments — the clash of the cymbals, the rubbing of tom-toms, the hollow thumping of a drum, the plaintive twanging of native sitars; voices, too, chiming in with a deep, melodious swing, and footsteps, echoing down the length of the corridor — nearer, ever nearer!

Sort of breathless, that night, wasn't it? Never knew what was going to happen next. In again, out again, just like the immortal Irishman, and in again it was into the pedestal of Shiva, by the side of the girl, or rather crouching over her. Believe me, it was a very uncomfortable position.

My heart was pumping heavily, like the heart of a babe in the dark. I didn't know what was going to happen. But I had a shrewd suspicion that Fate was about to fulminate a whole lot of rusty thunder in my direction.

Twang-zumm-bang, droned the music; and then I guessed what was coming — some sort of worshiping procession. You see, I had been in a Hindu temple or two and was more or less familiar with their noisy theological exercises. Nor was I mistaken. For a moment later the door was flung open and I saw — How did I see? Oh, in the part of the pedestal which was straight across from the door were two peep-holes, very much like those in a stage drop, and I had quite a good view.

Came a procession of Hindus, singing, playing on instruments; some carrying swinging lamps, others wreaths of flowers and bowls filled with milk and fruit and sweetmeats. The first half-dozen or so were nice enough looking chaps — bearded, dignified, clean — doubtless gentlemen in their own country. But the rest of them! Of all the wholesale, bunched, culminating, shameless wickedness! Why, man, in Sing Sing they would have electrocuted them on sight! And I thought of what Roos-Keppel had told me about the close, sinister, underground connection between the Hindu secret political societies and the criminal castes — thieves, assassins, and thugs; high-castes and low-castes — praying to the same, blood-gorged god.

It was the dawning ceremony of the Shiva worship, the ceremony which celebrates the victory of day over night.

At the end of the procession stalked a tall, magnificent specimen of Oriental humanity, swinging a flat incense-burner on silver chains. Around and around he swung it, and there rose long, slow streams of perfumed, many-colored smoke — wavering and glimmering like molten gold, blazing with all the deep, transparent yellows of amber and topaz, flaming through a stark, crimson incandescence into a great, metallic blue, then trembling into jasper and opal flames — like a gigantic rainbow forged in the heat of a wondrous furnace. Up swirled the streams of smoke, tearing themselves into floating tatters of half-transparent veil, pouring through the temple and clinging to the corners, the ceiling, with ever new shapes and colors, as endless and as strange and as mad as my life had been — since I had swung over the wall at the end of Ibrahim Khan's Gully, a little over an hour ago.

Straight up to the idol moved the procession, and Heavens, man, I felt qualmy. You see — there I was — I, a doubting Thomas of a Yankee, inside of their favorite deity, and together with Lady Padmavati! A bit indiscreet, wasn't it? But they didn't know it, thank God! They came right up, bowing with outstretched hands, and depositing flowers and fruit and sweetmeats in front of the pedestal — rather an agony, that last one, since I was getting hungry — and chanting their low-pitched litanies. You know India. You can imagine what those chants were like.

First a wail of minor cadences, more fleeting than the shadow of an echo, strangely reminiscent of some ventriloquist's stunt; then a gathering, bloating volume of voices, gradually shaping the words until the full melody, the full meaning beat up like an ocean of eternity, and the whole punctuated by the hollow staccato of the drums:

"... *nor this the weapons pierce; nor this does fire burn; nor this does water wet; nor the wind dry up! This is called unpierceable, unburnable, unwetable, and undriable, O harasser of thy foes eternal; all-pervading, constant thou; changeless, yet ever changing; unmanifest, unrecognizable thou, and unvarying. ...*"

Didn't mean anything to me in those days — all this long-winded chanting about Veda-born action and the exhaustless spirit and the certainty of cause and effect. I was getting frankly bored, and I was glad when the congregation varied the monotony of their chant by a few, choice, bloodcurdling prayers — loud and throaty and decidedly materialistic.

By this time they were getting excited, frenzied. You know how an overdose of religion grips these Hindus, how it affects them, much like strong wine; goes to their heads, to their feet, too. Yes, they danced, and, believe me, there isn't a single musical comedy star on Broadway who wouldn't have given her little-all to learn some of the steps I saw that night. Tango? Samba? Foxtrot? Why, they weren't in it with that Hindu religious dance!

Interesting, doubtless, but I was getting tired of it; tired, too, of my crouching position, with every bone and nerve and muscle strained to the utmost so as not to crush the little girl and — Well, remember those levers and handles I told you about? There was one handy to my right arm, and just for luck I gave it a good, hard pull.

Immediately there was silence. I wondered which one of Shiva's limbs I had caused to move, and the next moment I knew; for there came a ringing, triumphant shout from one of the worshipers:

"Shiva! Shiva Natarajah! See, brothers, he moves his right arm, as in blessing!"

"In blessing — in blessing!" the crowd took up the refrain, and they thanked Shiva for the sign he had given them, sealing and emphasizing their thanks with another long-winded hymn:

"... *from food come creatures; food comes from rain, rain comes from sacrifice, sacrifice is born of action, and action of thy great miracle, O harasser of thy foes.*"

A good enough light was trembling through the peep-holes and a couple of age-worn cracks into the interior of the pedestal, and I looked carefully to discover with which parts of Shiva's sacred anatomy the different levers and handles were connected. You see, I wanted to scare the congregation out of the temple through a real, simon-pure, overwhelming miracle. Presently I located most of the connections and, pushing a lever here and pulling a handle there, I caused the idol to lift his legs and wag his ugly old head in turns, and then to jerk his four arms in one generous, embracing altogether gesture. It was a success. There was no doubt of it. For the Hindus yelled and shrieked and moaned. But they didn't run away. I guess the Brahman had worked that same miracle before, and so they weren't scared of it any more — familiarity breeds contempt, you know, even in orthodox Hindu theological circles.

"Try, try, try again!" I told myself, and a moment later I thought of the intricate apparatus, the combination of wheels and gliding planes, which made the whole statue, including the pedestal, move forward across the floor. There was one master-handle within easy reach, but I was afraid of using it. For, remember, I told you that that particular machinery hadn't been used for a long time, that it was rusty and hard to move.

The fool thing needed a generous dose of Three-in-One oil; and I said to myself that some of those Hindus might smell a rat if they heard the squeaking and grating of the rusty old wheels.

What then?

Finally I thought of a way. You see, at college I held the absolute hors-de-concours record in yelling. I was the pride, in that respect at least, of my fraternity. I used to be proud of the accomplishment myself at the time being, but I would never have guessed that it would ever be of any practical value in life.

But here was a chance to try and find out. And so, at the moment of jerking down the master-handle, I let out a wild yell. I guess it must have sounded rather startling — sort of ghastly — coming, as it did, from that hollow statue; and the more I jerked at the handle, the louder I yelled. Presently the idol moved, I could feel it trembling beneath me. I continued yelling, and the effect was spontaneous. It was immense. It brought down the house!

The whole congregation gave one long, lone, soul-appalling outcry, and then they ran, pushing, kicking, pulling, biting each other in their mad haste to get to the door. Doubtless they imagined that they had offended Shiva, that their last hour had struck. At the door the whole lot of them bunched into one tremendous fighting knot — they fell over each other — and for a moment I was silent, to catch breath, and just then, at that very same moment, the bronze-tongued bell from the Presbyterian Church in Old Court House Street struck the half-hour — half after one — and, believe me, it was dramatic, that sudden tolling!

Just imagine the smoke, the many-colored light, the lesser miracle of Shiva's moving feet and arms, then the great miracle, my mad yelling, and suddenly that deep-toned bell!

Why, man, that fighting, struggling knot on the threshold dissolved itself into its human components inside of half a second, and a moment later the temple was empty. They didn't stop to shut the door nor to pick flowers on the way. I saw them rushing down the corridor — high-castes and low-castes, thrice-borns and thugs — running as fast as they could, with their legs and arms jerking and shooting out fantastically to right and to left, so that they looked like so many gigantic Indian scorpions scurrying for cover and yelling their lungs out as they ran. Gosh, it was comical! And the funniest part of all was the sight of the very last of the lot.

He had had his swathing robe torn off him in the frantic struggle, and there he ran, as naked as on the day he was born, except for the huge turban on his head, his white robe on the threshold, like a splotch of light!

You know, he interrupted his tale, I felt really proud of myself. Here was I — plain Yankee out of Boston, still redolent of pies and Thoreau and the Back Bay — and I had worked a thumping, all-to-the-good miracle which these Hindus would doubtless tell to their children's children. In the course of time it would go down into legend and tradition, as the thing which the Hindu theologians call Jataka, and I felt a sort of kinship, of comradeship, with that many-armed, grinning old idol of Shiva Nata-rajah. Snobbish of me, wasn't it, to be so proud of my own particular little miracle. But then — oh — it was a miracle, and snobbishness is after all only a simplified form of the desire to be mystic, to drown one's own puny personality in a greater self — as I had drowned myself in that of Shiva, had given him my voice in fact — my good old college yells.

I thought of that even as, with the last shrieking straggler scooting out of sight down the corridor, I came out of the pedestal, closed the temple door, and then — well, I was torn between two emotions. You see, I didn't want the Hindus to come back, and I could arrange for that, at least, temporarily, by setting the machinery into motion again and backing the heavy statue up against the door. On the other hand, I would bar my own exit by the same process.

Finally, I decided to risk it. First I picked up the robe which the last of the fleeing Hindus had dropped and put it on my own back; then I got back into the pedestal and pushed the master-handle until Shiva was plumb up against the door, straddling on both sides of it like a great metallic spider and making it impossible to open it.

That road was barred to the Hindus, and to me! There remained thus only one way of escape: back over the roof-top. Back somehow, though I didn't know how, for there was the long drop into the blue slime of Ibrahim Khan's Gully, and how could I do it with the unconscious girl in my arms?

I said to myself that I would have to try it, and I was about to pick up the little girl when another thought assailed me. For, remember, that both times I had passed through the cobra den — the only communication between the temple and the stairs leading to the roof-top — I had found it impossible to open the connecting door from the inside. It was easy enough to get into the cobra den from the stairs, but to get out — why, there seemed to be some intricate, hidden bit of machinery which I did not know.

I would have to ask. Whom? Why, his nibs, of course; the old Brahman priest down in the cobra den. Whom else could I have asked?

So I pushed open the stone slab, shook my priest awake, took the gag from his mouth, and talked to him like a Dutch uncle.

But it wasn't a go. Not a bit of it. That thrice-born mountain of portliness only laughed at me. Yes, by the many hecks, he laughed at me, and then, when I asked him to elucidate, he spoke, very gently, with a sort of regretful sob in his voice — the old hypocrite: "Ah, sahib," he sighed, "it is, alas! impossible to open the door from the inside — as impossible as wings upon a cat, as flowers of air, as rabbits' horns, as ropes made of tortoise hair! Only from the outside can the door be opened!"

I threatened him with voice and with hand and, you know, I have a large, man-size, persuasive sort of hand. But it didn't do a bit of good. "Impossible, sahib!" he repeated, "impossible by the five sacred Pandavas!" and there was that in his voice which convinced me that Old Pomposity, perhaps for the first time in his life, was speaking the truth.

"Look here," I said after a pause, "there's another way out of the temple, isn't there?"

"Assuredly," he replied. "You can pass through the temple, sahib, out of the door, along the corridor —"

"Cut it out! Can it, you old humbug!" I interrupted him. "I know that way — I took it half an hour ago, and I had a devil of a time getting back here. Now, look here. I have an idea that there's yet a third way out of here, and that you know it. Come through at once, or — well, I'll give you a good sound spanking!" And I made a significant gesture.

But that didn't faze him in the least. He stared at me out of his round, onyx eyes, folded his hands over his stomach and said resignedly, "Beat me then, sahib, for — ah — a beating from a master and a step into the mud are not things one should consider." Cute little metaphor, wasn't it? And perhaps not exactly as flattering as it sounded first shot out of the box. "Sahib," he went right on with his eternal Oriental proverbs, "if the man be ugly, what can the mirror do? Can you plaster over the rays of the sun? No? Then why beat me? It would not help you out of the temple, would it?"

I lost my temper then. "Look here," I said, "if you don't get me out of here — me and the girl — I'll kill you: and by ginger I mean it!"

But he continued staring at me without as much as a blink.

"Sahib," he said calmly, "you are a white man, a Christian, afraid of death, of — ah — final destiny. But I, sahib," he purred, "I am a Brahman, a thrice-born indifferent to life and to death — for death is only a passing breath, only a forgotten wind sweeping over the grassy hills of eternity; indifferent to Satva, and Rajas, and Tamas — to pleasure, and pain, and darkness. You believe that man's life is a bundle of qualities which die with death; and I — I know that man's life is a thing without bondage or limit, perpetually active! I, sahib," he shot out with sudden ringing sincerity, "I am not afraid of death!"

Right then an idea came to me — a mingling of what I had read and of what Roos-Keppel had told me about caste and loss of caste. Roughly, I forced the Brahman to swing himself out of the den and into the temple. I followed.

"Look!" I said, pointing at the idol of Shiva Natarajah, straddling the door; and the Brahman turned as pale as a sheet. "You are not afraid of death," I went on, "and that's the truth. But you are afraid of losing caste; you are afraid of losing your priestly influence, aren't you?" He did not reply, just stood there, staring dumbly, despairingly at the statue, and I continued: "You see, I discovered how you work your little miracles, and I worked them myself — every last one of them. I even made your fool idol talk; and the people saw and heard and ran away. Now, either you get me out of this mess, out of this confounded rabbit-warren, or I give myself up to your countrymen, and I tell 'em how you've fooled them in the past. I'll tell 'em how the miracles are accomplished, and then you, I guess, would —"

"Yes, yes," he mumbled, " I would lose caste! For many lives to come would I be born in the form of insects, of —"

"Well," I interrupted harshly, "what's the answer? Come through! Are you going to lead me out of this building or not.?

"Sahib," he said, "you win. But I can not lead you out of the temple!"

"Stop your hedging," I cried. " How the deuce do I win if you can't lead me out of the temple?"

"Forgive your servant, sahib," stammered the priest, "and have patience until I have explained. For I have given a vow never too leave this building, never even to come within sight of the outer walls of it, a sacred vow to Ganesha, the Elephant-Tusked Lord of Incepts! And should I break this vow I would lose caste as assuredly as if you — ah — would give to the people the tale of the miracles."

"Well, what then?" I demanded impatiently.

"Just this, sahib. I can lead you from here to another room and thence, by yourself easily, assuredly, will you be able to find escape in a short time. Listen! Listen to me, sahib," he continued hurriedly, excitedly, "listen to my solemn oath," and he gave the one solemn vow which — I remembered what Roos-Keppel had told me — no Brahman will ever break: "I swear by Shiva the Great Yogi, by Parvati, and the Sacred Bull Nandi — by Ganesha and Karttikeya! I swear by all the Devas who dwell in Svarga! I swear by the heavenly Apsaras, the Gandharvas, and Kinnaras! I swear by Vishnu's Garuda, by Parvati's Tiger, by Ganesha's Rat, and by Indra's Elephant! I swear that I shall lead the sahib into a room whence he shall find a quick and certain way out of danger, a way to eternal peace and release from worry; nor shall he be molested by man or beast! Ay! peace and rest and safety shall be his! I swear it to thee, O Brahm, Supreme Spirit, O Son of Pritha!"

Then he turned to me, speaking with his ordinary voice: "You believe me, sahib?"

"Sure!" I did believe him. He spoke the truth, and there was no doubt of it. "All right," I said, walking over to the pedestal and picking up the little girl. Her head dropped on my shoulder like a precious waxen flower. "Lead on MacDuff!"

"Good, sahib, good!" breathed the priest, turning directly to the wall to the left of the door, and then he continued speaking over his shoulder, "you are not afraid of trees?"

"You bet I am not," I laughed. "Trees are what I want — trees, and sunlight, and the open —"

"Good, good, good!" the priest replied. "Trees shall be your fate — trees and peace and safety forever!" And for a few minutes he groped over the wall panels, seemed to find what he was looking for, gave a violent little jerk, and part of the wall flung open with a great rush of cool air.

"Come, sahib," he said, and I followed him, the girl in my arms, through the opening and down a winding staircase into pitchy darkness. But I wasn't afraid — not the least bit. I knew that the Brahman would not break his solemn vow.

CHAPTER VIII.

BRAHMAN TRUTH.

The vox angelica replied:
"The shadows flee away!
Our house-beams were of cedar.
Come in with boughs of May!"
The diapason deepened it:
"Before the darkness fall,
We tell you He is risen again!
Our God hath burst His prison again!
Christ is risen, is risen again: and Love is Lord of all!"

— ALFRED NOYES.

DOWN the cool, dark staircase we went — and —

Say — Denton turned on me a smile of sheer joy — do you believe there's such a thing as compressing all that is fine and sweet and precious and wild and simple in life into a few golden, pulsing seconds? What? Do I believe it myself?

Why, man, I knew it, as I walked down the stairs with the little Hindu girl in my arms, her soft, warm body pressed against mine, her heart beating through her flimsy draperies, and with the thought that soon she and I would find peace and safety. Just then I didn't even think of the portly old thrice-born who was walking ahead of me, giving warning every once in a while about a broken or slippery step. I felt an utter sense of complete, lasting remoteness from the gray, grinding worries and unhappinesses of all the world — as if the girl and I had, somewhat audaciously, but entirely successfully, come without passport, without asking leave, into a separate little kingdom of wonder and magic and love.

"We have arrived, sahib," the Brahman's voice jarred into my happy reverie, and at the same time the pitchy darkness was cut off as sharp and clean as with a knife, and a bright, silvery light rose in front of me suddenly, as when a series of motion-pictures snaps short a street scene and shifts without warning into the scenery of lake and forest.

In a moment my eyes got used to the blinding dazzle. It was the dazzle of moon-rays coming through a window and mirroring themselves on the shiny white lac walls of a small room into which the stairs abutted. I stepped up to the window and looked out; it gave on a garden which stood out spectrally in the silken moonlight. I could see the dim stir of the leaves and particles of fine dust blown about by some vagabond wind of the night; and the mystery, the mad, amazing stillness of India surged out of the dark and spoke to me.

But the mystery, the throbbing stillness held, too, a message of peace to me and the girl, for there was the garden, the trees, the open, freedom — the fulfillment of my Charmed Life. I completed my groping thoughts with a smile as I turned to the priest with a heart-felt "Thank you," and was about to throw open the window. But he restrained me. "No, no, sahib," he said hurriedly, "no! There is no way out of the garden; it is surrounded by a huge wall and well patrolled. Wait, sahib! I shall keep my solemn oath. I shall give you your heart's desire — safety and peace — no harm from man or beast — and," he smiled, "trees, better, richer, more glorious than those trees yonder," pointing at the waving palm fronds in the garden.

He turned and walked to the opposite side of the room. "As, here we are," he breathed softly, and very suddenly, with such utter quickness that I did not even see his hand as it worked it, he had set some dull-grating machinery into motion, and four feet of stone wall slid to one side with a little thud. "Step inside, sahib," he went on, "and remember the oath of the Brahman — safety and peace. Step inside, sahib, you who love trees!"

You know, Stephen Denton continued after a short pause, for a fleeting moment a certain shapeless, clammy fear seemed to settle down upon me, focusing about my heart. Looking at the Brahman's smiling face, I had very much the sensation a bird may feel when it runs straight into the jaws of the snake that has fascinated it. I seemed to be falling in with a devilish plan of the Brahman's own making — to — oh, my thoughts seemed to be flying about somewhere outside of my brain, beyond control scattering wildly. But I jerked them back into my nerve-control with a stark, savage effort. I told myself that the Brahman would not break his oath. I stepped through the opening, the girl in my arms, while the priest stood to one side, bowing, smiling, like a deferential butler receiving an honored guest.

"I have kept my oath, sahib," he repeated. "Let the Divine Mother of the Elephant's Trunk be witness to the fact that I have kept my oath! You will find trees — you who do not fear trees, you who like trees — sit beneath them for a while and meditate on Life, on Death, on the Seven Great Virtues, and the Seven Black Sins! Think of it all, and remember, too," suddenly he gave a shrill, high-pitched laugh, "that sense is not a courtesan, that it should come to men unasked! Ho, wise sahib among sahibs!" And, with another ringing laugh, he had stepped quickly back — he was about to shoot the door home — when once more fear and suspicion raced through me.

"Wait a moment!" I said, "wait —" I took a step toward him, but the girl was in my arms — very quickly I shifted the soft, warm burden to my left arm, releasing my right — I made a grab at the Brahman. But I had not been quick enough. I only caught the end of his flowing robe — it tore in my hand. He was out and away, and the door shut with a jarring bang of finality. The only thing he left behind him was the yard or two of white robe which got caught in the slamming door, hanging down like a limp, disgusted flag. Again fear rushed through me — "fear as dry and keen as a new-ground sword," as the Hindus say — and my heart was a great, confused turmoil of mingled dread and despair — and of love for the girl in my arms. I pressed her to me more closely than ever.

Was this a trap, a — But no, no! whispered my saner self. The Brahman had sworn the one oath the breaking of which would make him lose caste; and immediately I became reassured. There was a way out of this room, and it wouldn't, couldn't be hard to find; for the priest had promised safety and peace and escape from worry for me and the girl. He had promised that neither man nor beast would harm me.

I needed just a few minutes' rest, for even the sweetest burden becomes heavy in one's arms, and then I would find my way out. So, very gently, I let Padmavati slide to the floor — beneath the trees.

Trees? Yes! For the Brahman had spoken the truth, There were two trees in the center of the room, striving straight up to the tall ceiling. Indian gold-mohur trees they seemed, in full-bursting, dark-green leaf-age, and crowned with masses of flame-colored, fantastically twisted flowers. The branches touched the walls on all four sides, they seemed to fill the whole upper half of the room, and, like willow-branches, they drooped down, coming within about seven feet of the floor. I smiled at the typical Hindu conceit which had caused trees to be planted in a room, and I touched the trunk of one of them — and then I drew my hand back with an exclamation of surprise.

You see, I had touched something cold, ice-cold!

Startling, wasn't it? And my surprise grew into amazement when I looked closer. For the trees were not living trees at all!

They were made of metal, every last detail of them, every leaf and flower — metal, cunningly wrought and embossed and enameled! I remember the Brahman's question; he had asked me first, if I feared trees; then, if I liked them?

What had he meant by it? Well, it made no difference to me either way, I concluded my thought. Doubtless, these two metal trees had some occult religious significance. Perhaps this room was only another temple, the trees represented some incarnation of one or other of the many Hindu deities, after all, the Brahmans had assimilated into their faith a good deal of the nature worship of the black Indian aborigines. I knew that much from what I had read.

So, I sat there, beside the girl and rested myself. I didn't follow the Brahman's advice — Stephen Denton laughed — I didn't meditate on the Seven Great Virtues and the Seven Black Sins, I thought of simpler, sweeter, bigger things — of love — just that! Love.

I rose, a few minutes later, thoroughly refreshed in mind and body. And, I began once more looking for a door through which to escape. But there was neither window nor door. That didn't worry me, for I said to myself that I would presently chance upon some cellar-flap or some cunningly hidden spring which would release part of the wall, since, judging from past experiences, this seemed to be the usual mode of exit in this mad maze of buildings. I would get out somehow. There was the Brahman's solemn oath — peace and safety, and relief from worry!

First of all, I looked for a cellar-flap, and it didn't take me long to give up that particular search. For the floor, jet black as the Gates of Erberus, proved to be fashioned of a single, unjointed sheet of some sort of heavy metal, so highly polished that the tiniest hinge or button would have stood out like a crack in a mirror.

The walls, then!

They seemed covered with a wonderful, intricate, color-shouting embroidery, the very thing to conceal a tapestry door.

Beautiful stuff it was, and I raised my hand to touch it — you know the desire people have to handle precious textures — and then — why, man, the walls, too, were of metal, like the trees, like the floor! What I had taken for embroidery was in reality exquisitely inlaid enamel. It was perfectly wonderful work. I had never seen the like of it, and even at the time I thought that the whole thing — the walls, the trees, the floor, and what came after — could not be of Hindu workmanship; that it must have been made by the wizard hands of some Chinese craftsman. A Hindu wouldn't have had the patience, nor the neatness, for such delicate work. And you know the Persian saying: "God gave cunning to these three: — the brain of the Frank, the tongue of the Arab, the hand of the Chinaman!"

Well, metal or no metal, Hindu or Chinese, it was up to me to find some sort of an opening, and I began to make the round of the walls. Foot by foot, as high as I could reach, I commenced to examine them, groping, feeling, tapping carefully, minutely — and then, suddenly, I stopped. I jumped back a clear two feet, with an exclamation of surprise.

Something had touched me on the shoulder!

I looked. There was nobody — just the girl and I — yes — and the trees! The next moment I knew what had startled me so. I told you about the branches of the trees, how they drooped, like willows; well, one of the branches had drooped a little lower, it had touched me. That was all!

Again I returned to my work. But I felt dizzy. I was on the verge of fainting. I jerked myself up with a will. I said to myself that I would have to hurry, for day breaks early and people rise early in the tropics; and I would have to make my getaway before the night faded from purple into rose and dull orange — and there was my love for the little girl, my love which was like a fine spring rain, unceasing, penetrating.

I did try to continue my search; but I couldn't!

I called myself a weakling and a fool; for terror — red, rank terror beyond death — seized me.

The trees — the branch of the one tree which had drooped a little and touched my shoulder! But how could it droop, since it was not a living branch — since it was made of lifeless metal?

I looked at the trees, at the ceiling. I looked — and I was appalled! Perhaps my eyes were deceiving me — an optical illusion — just my imagination, I told myself, growing, bloating, expanding like a balloon of evil anticipations, my mad imagination whispering to my saner Self, my real thinking Self; until, steadily growing in volume and effect, jumping from cord to cord in that intricate spider-web which is the nervous system, it had persuaded the thinking, recording cells in my brain, that — Stephen Denton half-rose in his chair — that the ceiling was slowly coming down — slowly, slowly — and with it the trees — the metal trees — with the sharp crushing metal branches!

Yes! They seemed to descend — very, very slowly, but as steadily and pitilessly as God's logic — steadily, steadily.

But no! Impossible!

I said to myself that it could not be so; that what I seemed to see must be the result of autosuggestion, of some wretched sort of self-hypnotism, focusing on my mentality, trying to strangle and paralyze my physical activity at the very moment when I had to use both body and brain to find the door in the wall, to escape!

I would have to convince myself that it was only an illusion, and there was one way of doing it. I told you about the intricate pattern with which the metal walls were enameled. I picked out one, a little black-and-red crane standing erect on a lotus-leaf, a beautiful bit of enamel, high up on the wall, quite near the ceiling, and I watched it. I watched it carefully, without taking my eyes away for a single moment — I watched — watched — and I saw! I apologized to myself for having called myself a fool and a coward, and for having accused myself of autosuggestion and an overdose of crazy imagination. I decided that my real Self was still on deck, after all, working, observing, sober, and more or less subliminal. For, within a short time — perhaps three minutes — the edge of the ceiling had touched the head of the little black-and-red crane. Another three minutes, the crane had disappeared, and the ceiling was halfway across the lotus-leaf.

I saw — and immediately I understood! I understood everything — the walls and floor and ceiling of solid metal, the trees, the Brahman's question if I feared trees, and the Brahman's oath!

The Brahman had given a solemn oath, nor would he break it. He had lured me into this room, me and the girl, and he had set some machinery into motion which would kill us, slowly, mercilessly — crushing us, doubtless as sacrifices, human sacrifices, to his bestial, blood-stained gods. Yes, he had kept his oath, for to him death spelled peace and safety and final release from earthly worries; nor were we being harmed by man or beast, but by metal, by crushing weight!

And he had asked me to sit awhile beneath the trees — to rest myself, to meditate!

What should I do, could I do? The bell from the Presbyterian church, tolling the quarter to two, gave answer. Yes, I knelt down, and I prayed — a foolish prayer of my childhood days, back in Boston. It was the only one I could remember:

> *Dear God, I am a growing child;*
> *Each day of living brings*

A hundred puzzling thoughts to me
About a hundred things.
Sometimes it's very hard for me
To tell what I should do,
And so I say this little prayer,
And leave it all to you.

Childish, wasn't it? But it didn't seem so to me at the time — and, yes, it seemed to — oh! — steady my nerves; it seemed to me like the cool, safe breath of God. It gave me resignation, it left no room for fear. Come what may — there was nothing in my heart except love — love for the little Lady Padmavati — and all the tortures in the world, the slowest, cruelest death, would not blot out from my consciousness the fact that I loved her — her only!

There was nothing I could do. I could save neither her life, nor my own. A pistol clapped to my head, a curved saber waved above me — those I could have battled and struggled against. They were real, tangible. But this — why, I was helpless, and I knew it.

Again I watched the ceiling, the trees. They were still coming down, steadily, slowly, the branches drooped lower and lower; one of them, a specially stout branch, was already within a foot of the top of the low door; another touched my head, the sharp metal cut my scalp — I ducked.

There was just one thing I could do for Padmavati. I could protect her with my own body. She, too, would be crushed to death, but at least the sharp metal branches would not tear her flimsy robe to ribbons, dishonoring her in the hour of death, nor would they cut her soft, golden skin.

I crouched above her, and I prayed, again I prayed! Twice I looked up to see if the ceiling, the trees, were still coming down, fully convinced, before I looked, that they were coming down. They were now descending a little faster — the branch near the door was nearly touching the top.

I bent down lower to kiss the girl, a kiss of love and farewell — I felt her soft, warm, intoxicating breath — and —

I did not kiss her after all! For, suddenly, I heard a noise, loud, sharp, jarring. I looked up, startled — again I was afraid. Was this the end? Were the metal trees about to crush us? Or, perhaps, had the door opened to admit the Brahman?

And then — quite suddenly —

STEPHEN DENTON was silent for a moment. He turned to me with a quizzical smile. He pointed at the fine, white ashes of his cigar, curling around the dull-red glow. He blew the ashes away.

"Half a rupee's worth of tobacco," he said, "burned into a smelly stump of no value at all in twenty minutes — that's a cigar, isn't it? And yet — imagine a puff of wind, an open barrel of gunpowder, a conflagration, a wooden building across the street, a town gone up in flames and smoke! Small cause and thumping result, don't you think?"

"Yes, yes," I interrupted impatiently, "but what's that got to do with those metal trees above you — with the horrible death you were facing — you and the girl you loved?"

What has that got to do with the trees — you ask — with my death? Why, everything, old man!

Remember the loud, sharp-jarring noise I told you about a second ago? Remember the Brahman and the Brahman's white robe, how I clutched at it, how it tore and got caught in the slamming of the door at the height of the knob?

Well, I have an idea that bit of flimsy muslin is responsible for the fact that I am sitting here today, across from you, old man. I am not sure how it happened, though later on, when calm reflection came, I said to myself that the Chinese craftsman with the patient, delicate hands, who was doubtless the builder of that torture-chamber, had been a trifle too patient, a trifle too delicate. It was pretty clear to me that the Brahman had set the machinery in motion — most likely it timed itself — so and so many minutes, until the room had contracted to such a degree that the trees crushed whatever living thing was in their vicinity.

You see, the ceiling and the trees had stopped in their slow, pitiless, juggernaut descent, for the simplest reason in the world!

The flimsy bit of torn muslin had prevented the door from closing completely, by the fraction of an inch, no more! But it was enough to cause the top of the door to protrude the least little bit from the upper part of the door-jamb — and there you are! The stout metal branch of the tree, instead of sliding serenely past door-jamb and along the door, had bumped smartly against the protruding top of the door!

Providence, eh? Chance — perhaps that blind Madonna of children and lovers? Or the Charmed Life?

Whatever the psychical reason, the physical was clear. The whole thing had happened and passed in a moment. The jarring noise — the realization that the muslin had saved our lives — then silence.

Again I looked at the ceiling, at the trees. They could not work past the minute obstacle. And I thanked God — and then I bent once more over the girl, to continue my interrupted kiss, and at the same moment she gave a little sob and opened her eyes.

I guess she must have recognized me immediately. She must have remembered the scene on the roof-top. For she wasn't a bit frightened. She just looked at me and smiled, and then, in a few rapid words, I told her what had happened — from the moment the old ruffian on the roof-top had struck her the glancing blow to the moment when I had come to this room, her unconscious form in my arms.

I did not tell her about the trees, about this devil's devising of a room. For I loved her, don't you see, I did not want to worry her, and, momentarily at least, we were safe. Also — and I know you'll think me mad — when I saw her open her eyes — when I saw that soft, sweet expression in her face as she looked at me and recognized me, the idea, the thought — no! — the all-fired, eternal conviction came to me that God was in His Heavens after all — that I bore the Charmed Life — that, somehow, we would get out of this room, this house, this maze of buildings — out of the Colootallah!

So I told her everything up to the moment when I had crossed the threshold when I had stretched her beneath the trees, and I wound up with a few simple words.

Stephen Denton blushed a little.

What were those words? Can't you guess them? They were the same words which are spoken in every known and unknown language, a million times each day, in every country, in every city and village.

I said: "I love you! Will you be my wife?"

And she replied in English, in soft, beautiful English: "Would you marry a dancing-girl, a nautch, sahib?"

"You bet your life!" I replied, with ringing conviction in my voice. "I'd marry you if you were —"

"The Lady Padmavati?" she interrupted me, mockingly, and then I remembered how I had heard that same name whispered through the hollow tiles at the feet of the mummy. I remembered the sensation, the utter amazement, which the mentioning of that name had caused.

Still, "the Lady Padmavati" meant nothing to me, and so I asked her straight out who she was, and she told me.

I guess you know, Stephen Denton continued; you must have read about it in the newspapers, how one of the Hindu revolutionary secret societies had been trying to bully the Raja of Nagapore into joining their ranks, or, at least, contributing a handsome bunch of money: how the Raja — very pro-British he — had refused, and how his only child, a daughter, had been kidnapped. Well, to make a long story short, Padmavati was the daughter of the Raja of Nagapore. Those ruffians had stolen her and were training her for the temple worship of Shiva Natarajah.

"And," she wound up her tale, "I have made a vow that whoever rescues me him I shall —"

The rest of her sentence was drowned in a loud, metallic noise. At the same moment was a rush of cool air. I looked up. The door had been flung wide open, and there round-eyed, utterly amazed, stood — my old friend, the Brahman!

I doubt if it took me more than a hundredth part of a second to collect my thoughts, to realize my position. "Quick," I whispered to the girl. She rose, catching my arm. We jumped across the threshold! He stood there, mute, and I laughed.

"Miscalculated a little, didn't you, you fat Brahman ruffian?" I asked in a low voice. "Told me to sit beneath the trees and meditate on Life and Death — and meanwhile you'd turn a crank and supply the latter, eh? All right —" Suddenly I grabbed him and pushed him into the steel room — he was quite limp — didn't even fight — "now it's your turn to meditate, and mine to move the crank, and I guarantee you there isn't going to be any torn slip of muslin this time — inside of twenty minutes you'll be as flat as a flounder!" And I scooted out of the room and shut the door. Of course, I had no intention of really crushing him to death — crafty, treacherous old beggar though he was — and though he had come back, doubtless, to have a good look at our flattened-out remains — the gory-minded Brahman gray-beard! But, after all, though India had crept into my blood, I was still an American, a Westerner. I could have killed him with knife or bullet, killed him outright, you see, without too much compunction. But to slowly squeeze him to death — oh, I couldn't do it.

And, too, don't you see, old man, the whole thing was a bluff, anyway. How did I know where to go — how to find the crank or whatever it was which set the machinery into motion? I simply figured on the chance that the Brahman would be too badly scared to see through my bluff. And, to make it appear more real, I took out my Bowie-knife and scraped the door on the outside, to make him think the machinery was jarring and snapping into motion.

Faintly, from within, I could hear his agonized moaning and sobbing.

I felt Padmavati's soft little hand on my arm. "But, dearest" — she whispered, and I understood, though she didn't finish her sentence.

"It's all right, darling," I returned. "I am not going to hurt Old Pomposity more than I have to. Don't you worry about him!" and I continued scraping at the steel door until the moaning and sobbing had ceased. Then, very gently, I opened the door. I looked in.

The Brahman had fallen in a dead faint. His light-brown face had turned ashen-gray.

I shook him awake. He came out of his trance with a start. He clutched my legs, he kissed the hem of my robe, my hands, and whatever parts of my anatomy he could reach. "Sahib, Heaven-Born, Protector of the Pitiful!" he groaned. "In the name of the many true gods — do not — do not —"

"All right!" I said, "I won't, you obese fraud — but —"

"Oh, Shining Pearl of Equity and Mercy!" he interrupted me with another outpouring of Oriental imagery. "Oh, Great King! Accept the vow of my gratitude! Hari bol! Krishna bol! Vishnu bol! Let the mighty gods be witnesses to my gratitude! May earth and life be to you as a wide and many-flowered road! May the clay of the holy river Vaiturani be rubbed on your body after your death —"

"That's exactly it!" I cut in. "After my death! And I don't intend to die — and, if you are as grateful as I am inclined to believe from your protestations, show me a way out of here — quick!"

He rose. Three times he bowed. Then he spoke, solemnly, "I will, Heaven-Born! Follow me!" and he turned to go.

"Can I believe you this time?" I asked.

"Courage is tried in war, sahib," replied the Brahman; "integrity in the payment of debt and interest; friendship in distress; the faithfulness of a wife in the day of poverty; and a Brahman's loyalty in the hour of death. Sahib, follow me!"

And I did — arm in arm with the girl — for, somehow, I felt that the old priest was speaking the truth.

So he led us through halls and rooms, up and down stairs worn hollow and slippery with the tread of naked feet, along corridors, on and on, with here and there a stop, a whispered word from the Brahman to keep perfectly quiet, a silken rustling of garments in some nearby room where people were still awake, with once in a while a hushed, distant voice, and twice the steely impact of a scabbard-tip bumping the stone flags as some unseen, prowling watchman of the night passed somewhere on his rounds; on and on we passed, and we never met a single human being. I hardly noticed the direction. For I was talking to Padmavati.

She gave a low, throaty laugh. Just then we were passing through a long, dark hall.

"Remember, sahib," she asked, "what I was saying just before the priest opened the door? I did not finish the sentence. Let me finish it now. I said that I have made a vow that whoever rescues me, him I shall —"

"You shall — marry!" I interrupted her, catching her in my arms and seeking her lips with mine.

I believe, Stephen Denton continued after a short pause, that science holds it impossible to measure eternity. It is the same thing with the great, deep joy — the huge, pulsing, bewildering elation which comes to man once — once in his life — when he loves, and when he feels that his love is returned. It is — oh, well, perhaps you know it yourself, perhaps you can fill in the details from your personal experience — the hot, exquisite knocking of the blood, the whispering rhythm of the dear, soft body you hold pressed against your own, the gigantic sounds of harmony which fill your soul — your sudden new, golden life as it seems to disentangle itself from the bunched, dark whole of humanity into a great, radiant simplicity.

Love — the first minutes of true love — and you can't measure them! At least I couldn't — that night. I pressed Padmavati close against me; mechanically, I set foot before foot, following the priest; and then, a second later, we ascended a staircase which seemed vaguely familiar to me.

The Brahman pushed open a door, we crossed a threshold — and there we were —

Once more on the roof-top, with the moon slowly fading in the distant sky before the faint rose-blush of dawn!

The Brahman walked straight up to the carved stone balustrade and pointed down at Ibrahim Khan's Gully.

"I have kept my word, sahib," he said, "There is the street — a jump — the turning of a street corner or two — and you will find Park Street! You will find your own world, your own people!" He bowed, then he turned to the girl. " And you, Padmavati — great was the injustice done to you. You were carried away from the palace of your father! You were forced here, into this building, to learn how to dance before Shiva Natarajah! Yes, great was the injustice of it; and yet, can you wipe out blood with darkening blood? Will a wrong right a wrong?"

"A wrong?" she asked. "What wrong?"

"The sahib, Padmavati!" he replied. "You are following the sahib, a foreigner, a Christian, and you are —" he halted.

"Yes," she said after a short pause, "I am the Princess Padmavati. I am the daughter of the Maharajah of Nagapore. I am a Rathor of Kanauj, claiming kinship with the flame, and my mother is a Tomara of Delhi, claiming kinship with the sun! I am a descendant of the gods!" She drew up her little figure in a passion of pride. "My people have lived here — they have ruled this great land of Hindustan for over three thousand years! Never have we mixed our blood with the blood of foreigners! And yet —"

"And yet — what?" anxiously asked the priest, and she continued with a low, silvery laugh.

"And yet there is love, wise priest!" And she turned to me. "Jump, beloved," she whispered, "jump — and I shall follow!"

I jumped without waiting for another word — down into Ibrahim Khan's Gully, landing safely on my feet. The next second her little lithe figure was balanced on the edge of the balustrade. I stretched my arms wide — she jumped — I caught her — just as the bell from the Presbyterian church in Old Court House Street tolled — *binng-bunng* — two o'clock!

Yes, mused Stephen Denton, a descendant of the gods, she, the daughter of a race who ruled this land before history dawned on the rest of the world — and I, from Boston, with memories of the antimacassars, mild cocktails, Phi Beta Kappa, and —

Framed at the Benefactors Club

CHAPTER I.

WHERE THINGS HAPPEN.

ACTING ON a headlong impulse, he called on Martyn Spencer. His motive was typical of Blaine Ogilvie's character and life as he had lived it these last ten years, since he had left college. Marie Dillon, Spencer's distant cousin, had told him of the latter's return to New York, a few months back, after a decade spent away from America, and had given him his address.

"Marie," Ogilvie had said, "he's the very man for me."

"To do what?"

"To help me."

"Do you really need help as badly as all that?"

Ogilvie wasn't a very good liar. He tried his best, though.

"Really, dear," he said, "don't you worry. I am all right. I —"

"Please, Blaine! Be truthful with me! That's our agreement, you know — the truth — always — be it pleasant or unpleasant."

Ogilvie sighed. "The truth is always unpleasant! Fact is — I am not starving yet!"

"I don't like that 'yet.'"

"Nor do I, Marie!" Ogilvie laughed. But, deep down, he was serious and just a little frightened. Life, financially, had not been kind to him of late. "That's why I have to do something — something that pays. And, too, after we're married, I don't want you to wear summer hats all during the winter!"

"Of course not," she replied with a smile. "But why appeal to Spencer?"

"Why not? I've tried all the men I know. But there isn't a chance. Business is rotten, and they're discharging people right and left. But Spencer was always a regular whirlwind at getting the coin. And he and I used to be friends."

"All right, dear, ask him. It can't do any harm."

"Indeed not. Press your darling little thumb for me. D'you mind?"

HE FOUND Martyn Spencer much the same man he had known at college: debonair, yet with an undertone of acrid sarcasm, quick of speech and repartée, yet curiously lumbering of gesture, direct in his opinions, yet at times with a queerly footling manner of commenting on life and life's problems. This was the Spencer he had known at college, and this was the Spencer whom he saw again today, in his wainscoted, cigar-flavored office, on top of the Macdonald skyscraper. Now the man was surrounded by a perfect array of steel filing cabinets, safes, noiseless typewriters, switchboards, marceled stenographers, and relays of private secretaries in immaculate, sober, pin-striped worsted, with an almost episcopal unction of voice.

The man's face, too, was as it had always been: massive-jowled, dead white, and with an exaggerated beak of a nose, the smoke-blue eyes set close together beneath hooded, fleshy lids. If there was a change in him, Blaine Ogilvie did not notice it at first. Of course he had heard rumors about Spencer, but he had dismissed them. Not that he disliked gossip, since he had the average healthy male's appetite for the intriguing cross sections and cross currents of conflicting personalities.

But the rumors that had drifted through occasionally, via commercial traveler, returned globe-trotter or explorer, missionary on sabbatical leave, or rust-spotted freighter's skipper, from the exotic lands where Spencer was said to be piling up a shocking total of millions, were both too grim and too fantastic for the prosy twentieth century. Romance in business had died with Dutch patroons and Spanish privateers, Ogilvie used to say, and he would dismiss the tales with an incredulous laugh, as did the rest of New York that had known Martyn Spencer in the old days.

Ogilvie laughed now at the very thought.

Spencer had always been congenitally a money getter, nothing else, even at college. He seemed to have reached the height of his ambition.

The man breathed moneyed success, a very surfeit of it.

Ogilvie, who had announced his coming over the telephone, had been civilly inspected and scrutinized by the private secretary in the outer office, by another private secretary — the first's twin brother as to well-cut clothes, pompadoured hair, and straw-colored mustache — in the inner office, and then Martyn Spencer greeted him with a hearty handshake and a fat, crimson-and-gold banded Havana.

"Ten years since we have seen each other, eh, Blaine?" he asked.

"Every day of it, Martyn!"

A rapid gathering-up of broken threads and college gossip, inquiries, as perfunctorily polite as perfunctorily answered, about the fortunes, marriages, and divorces of Tom "This" and Mabel "That" followed. Then suddenly, characteristically, Ogilvie came to the point.

"Martyn," he said, "I want a job."

"Why?"

"Simplest reason in the world. I need it."

"Broke?"

"Well — bent all out of shape! Don't you need a handsome, industrious, and intelligent junior partner — or office boy?"

"I don't need as much as a scrubwoman."

"I beg your pardon!" Ogilvie said stiffly.

"Come, come. Don't fly off the handle. I am sorry, but honestly I don't need anybody."

"Seem to have a lot of affairs here?" Ogilvie pointed through the glass partition at the humming outside office.

"Affairs is right, but I am winding them up. I am going to retire from business."

"Rather young to do that, aren't you?"

"At times I feel seven years older than the hills!" Spencer passed a pudgy hand across his round, dead-white face. The hand trembled a little.

The other rose. "Sorry I bothered you, old man."

"Don't go yet. Perhaps I can help you."

"I wish you would. Really — I need it."

"What sort of a job do you want?"

"Anything — anywhere — where I can earn a decent living."

"What do you know? What can you do?"

"I've been to war. I can drill a company and —"

"I know, I know!" Spencer interrupted impatiently. "You can kill people according to the most scientific and up-to-date methods. But there's nothing to that. The world is still groggy. That last round lasted too long. What else do you know?"

"I have a smattering of languages — French, German, Spanish —"

"Which means that you can order a dinner without precipitating a riot between the Alsatian chef and the Polish head waiter, and that you can get the point of a joke in a French comic paper. Nothing to that. One can get any number of bright young Europeans at eighteen per, who can stenog and talk fluently in half a dozen languages. What else can you do?" he continued inexorably.

Ogilvie considered for quite a while.

"I am reckless," he replied.

"Hardly a paying quantity. What else?"

"Nothing."

"Well — marry money."

"But —"

"I've an aunt in Chicago who'll introduce you to the right sort of girl. Marrying off people is her particular avocation."

Ogilvie shook his head. "Marry — nothing!" he said with a laugh. "I asked you what I am going to do with myself, not with somebody else's daughter. Besides, I've the girl all picked out."

"Who is she, may I ask?"

"Marie Dillon, your cousin."

"Oh! What the deuce did you want to fall in love with her for? The Dillons haven't a blessed cent!"

"I'm contrary by nature, I guess."

"Ah —"

"Well — what do you advise, Martyn?"

"Serious, are you? Really need the money?"

"Yes."

Martyn Spencer was silent for several minutes. He turned slightly in his swivel chair and looked out of the window. It was winter, with a bitter, hacking north wind that rode a wracked sky and drove harshly across the roofs of New York. Tiny, sharp points of frozen snow rattled the panes and moaned dismally in the chimneys.

Ogilvie gave an involuntary shudder. His overcoat, though fashionably tailored, was a thin spring garment, and his gorgeously striped silk muffler was arrestingly ineffectual. Spencer's heavy ulster, lined with

Russian sable, was tossed carelessly across a chair. He stared at it enviously, and the other noticed it out of the corner of his eyes.

"Peach of a coat, Blaine, isn't it?" he asked.

"I'll say so!"

"Unique coat, too!"

"Oh!"

"Yes. Imperial Russian sable — priceless — not another like it in America."

"Where did you get it?"

"Grand Duchess Anastasia Michailovna gave it to me."

"Know her?" came Ogilvie's casual question.

"Ran across her in Moscow."

"I thought you were in Africa."

"I've kicked around all over."

"I see."

They were both silent. Then Spencer looked up. A vertical wrinkle cleft his forehead sharply and drew apart his close-set eyes as if he had been thinking deeply.

"Blaine," he said rather sententiously, "there are two types of man. One is the type, like myself, which goes after things, and the other the type which waits for things to happen. I think you belong to the latter."

"You do?"

"Right. You see, I've offered you an introduction to my aunt in Chicago — the finest matchmaker in seven counties — who would have shuffled the right girl, the rightly rich girl, out of the marriage deck for you. In other words, I asked you to go after things so that you might be able to achieve man's real object in life — a silk-hatted, patent-leather-shoe state of genteel vagabondage. You tell me that you are engaged to Marie Dillon, who is as poor as a church mouse. Very sentimental and honorable and charming and all that, I grant you, but hopelessly impractical. Very well. I see that you aren't the pushing sort. Therefore you've got to wait for things to happen to you."

Ogilvie rose impatiently.

"Wait!" came the other's smooth voice. "Things — to happen to you!" he repeated with a queer smile. "And — you said you are reckless?"

"You know I am!"

"Yes, yes." Spencer mused, smiled again, and continued: "Now, in all the world, there are exactly three places where a man can wait for things — things to happen. A man of your sort —"

"Meaning a reckless man?"

"Meaning a fool!"

"Sure I am?"

"Positive. I knew you at college."

"Thanks awfully. And where are these three mysterious places?"

"One is a small and very smelly caravansery near the Kabool Gate in the city of Lahore, in India. One is the northern end of the great bridge at Constantinople —"

"Too far away — both of them — particularly for a chap who's broke."

"It'll cost you a nickel, and, perhaps, an extra two cents for a cross-town fare, to reach the third place."

"Oh —"

"Yes. It is right here in New York." Spencer pointed vaguely through the window, where the houses were running together in purple and gray spots beneath the sweep of oncoming evening.

"Really?" Ogilvie looked up, interested.

"Familiar with the slums of New York?"

"Quite. I had money once and used to dine there, eating beans at fancy prices, when we went slumming."

"Know Meeker Street?"

"I've been there — during my years of affluence."

"Know where Meeker and Commerce Streets come nearly together, in a sort of a triangle, pointing toward Seventh Avenue?"

"Yes."

"Remember a crooked little side street, rather an alley, nearer Commerce Street, which runs in the general direction of the river, like a drunken man?"

"I've a shadowy recollection. What's the name of the street?"

"Braddon Street."

"Oh, yes, I recall now. Funny old brick houses, with Georgian columns and deep-set windows!"

"Exactly, Blaine."

"Well — what about this street?"

"Go there — to No. 17."

"What for?"

"If you want things to happen to you!"

"Do I?"

"I don't know, Blaine, I'm sure. But, at No. 17, you'll find a queer, old-fashioned restaurant, dating back to the days when Aaron Burr dreamed largely about empire and made a sorry mess of it. There's the place —" he slurred, stopped, went on — "the place for —"

"Things to happen?"

"Yes."

"Thanks for the tip, Martyn. I am going there."

Spencer smiled lopsidedly. "I repeat," he said, "that you are a fool!"

"Thanks!" the other interjected.

"What I told you about the Braddon Street place is straight. It isn't a very nice place, Blaine."

Ogilvie laughed. "Oh, yes — you told me things happen there, didn't you?"

"To some people."

"Shall I carry a gun?"

"Heavens, no! Even the slums are well policed these decadent days. Only — well, I warn you. The beginnings and the ends of many things have been brewed in that restaurant — things which men do not speak of except in whispers behind closed doors."

Ogilvie looked up sharply. "As you are talking in whispers — right now!" he said, with a purring laugh. "As your door is closed — right now!"

"Exactly!" came the even, passionless reply. Spencer hesitated. "Blaine," he went on, "if I were you I would not go!"

"Why — you've made me quite anxious to see the place, old man. I guess I shall go."

"When?" came the quick question.

"The sooner the better. Tonight's the night!"

Martyn Spencer studied the other's face for a few tense seconds. Then he gave a forced laugh.

"All right," he said. "I see that you have decided." He coughed, mused, looked at Ogilvie from beneath hooded eyelids. "If you get there after ten in the evening," he said very slowly, "you will find the place closed."

"That so?"

"Yes. But you can still get in."

"How?"

"By knocking at the door. Two short knocks — a pause — then a double knock. A pause — then again a short knock."

"Seem to know all about the place and its habits, Martyn?"

"I've never been there in my life."

"Ah — tell it to the marines!"

"Never in all my life," Spencer repeated. "I'm speaking the literal truth."

Again both men were silent; they were studying each other sharply, unwinkingly.

Then Blaine Ogilvie asked a sudden, brutally direct question: "Why do you want me to go there?"

The other gave a start. "Wh-what?" he stammered. "What d-do you mean?"

"Just exactly what I said!"

Spencer flicked his cigar ash. "Go," he said, "and find out!"

Ogilvie smiled. "Don't want to tell me the reason," he said, "but you do want me to go! Is that right? Of course it is, old man! No use denying it!"

"I'm not saying anything."

"Sure you aren't. I know. Didn't we play stud poker at college, and didn't you always have a high pair back to back? Question is — to put it bluntly — how much is it worth to you if I go — tonight — after ten?"

"I believe I told you that you're a fool?"

"And I believe I told you that I'm broke? Well — how much?"

"Name your own price!"

"A thousand dollars?"

Martyn Spencer laughed, "Blaine," he said, "I am a poor business man, for I'll give you more than you asked. Twenty thousand dollars — how'd that strike you?"

"Splendidly!"

"It's a bargain? Tonight after ten, and you go alone — and tell nobody?"

"Right!"

Spencer walked to the safe, opened it, and drew forth a thick sheaf of high-denomination bills. "Here you are!"

"Thanks!" Ogilvie crammed the money into his inside pocket. "So long, Martyn!" He made for the door.

"Wait!"

"What is it now?"

"You'll catch your death of cold with that thin coat of yours."

"I'll invest part of the twenty thousand in a new coat on my way down Broadway."

"It's after six, and the stores are closed. I'll lend you my coat."

"But —"

"I am going to work for an hour or two and then I'll telephone to my valet to bring me another ulster. Better take this. It's terribly cold."

"I may hock it, old man. You told me it's priceless — and didn't you say something about a grand duchess who gave it to you — tender souvenirs, eh?"

"Not quite as tender as you imagine!" Spencer laughed disagreeably. "Come!" He helped the other on with the warm, soft sable-lined coat. "Bring it back when you're through with it."

"Sure — and thanks." He opened the door to the outer office, when he heard Spencer's voice:

"Blaine!"

"Yes?" The latter turned. "What is it?"

"Oh — nothing, nothing — never mind."

"All right. *Au revoir*, Martyn!"

"*Au revoir!*"

And Blaine stepped out of the office into the street, not quite sure if the pleasantly warm feeling that suffused his body was due to the fur coat or to the twenty thousand dollars that nestled in his inside pocket.

IT WAS still snowing hard that night, with a bitter wind piping across the roofs of the city, a little before ten, when he left his modest hotel in the West Forties, after agreeably surprising the desk clerk by calling for his overdue bill and settling it in full.

"Stroke of luck, Mr. Blaine?" asked the clerk, familiar with the ups and downs of the Rialto.

"Luck — or the opposite; I'm not exactly sure yet, Tommy."

He felt a prey to a tremendous, voiceless excitement as he turned down Seventh Avenue. He preferred walking, thinking that the touch of the cold, snow-wet wind on his forehead would clear his mind. He had been reckless all his life, and usually he had come through with flying colors in the occasional small adventures such as he had run across in the streets of New York and in the Adirondacks and the Maine woods. Besides he had come out of the war unscathed. But the unknown adventure upon which he was embarking tonight — and he realized that there was a reason for it all, for Martyn Spencer was not the type of man to give away twenty thousand dollars, nor any part of twenty thousand dollars, without demanding full value — the unknown adventure upon which he was embarking tonight made him uneasy.

As he thought about Spencer, as he reconstructed the scene in the office, he remembered the man's nervous hands, the occasional look of fear which had come into the other's smoke-blue eyes, the suddenly lowered voice, the interrupted sentence when he had left. Doubtless the other had meant to warn him, and had then reconsidered and said nothing. He remembered, too, the vague, fantastic tales as to the origins of Martyn Spencer's wealth that had drifted into New York.

He went unarmed, for Spencer had told him that he would not need a gun. And the very fact that there was thus no prospect of physical danger made him yet more uneasy. He was a very sane and normal man, with sane and normal reactions, preferring physical contest, even physical danger, to the twisting, gliding struggle between soul and soul or intelligence and intelligence.

"I guess I'm a fool," he thought. "But — I am in love."

Obeying the suggestion of the last thought, he stepped into a telephone booth and called up Marie Dillon.

"I saw Spencer."

"Yes?"

"It's all right. He's giving me a chance, Marie!"

"I'm so glad, dear."

Then a few strictly personal remarks which caused listening-in central to make a sentimental aside to the girl at the next switchboard, and the receiver clicked down. The steely sound jarred Ogilvie unpleasantly. It seemed like an ending to a chapter of his life.

He walked down Seventh Avenue, and by short cuts into Meeker Street and toward Braddon, down through the evil, sodden alleys of that part of town, prurient with dirty memories of the past, slimy with refuse stabbing through the mantle of snow. Foul invectives in English, Yiddish, Greek, and Sicilian cut the air, while garish posters outraged the faces of the buildings.

Braddon Street leaped out of the snow with a packed wilderness of secretive, red-brick dwellings, with stealthy, enigmatic back yards, skulking gables, and furtive, reticent side entrances.

No. 17 was just beyond the corner. It assaulted the night with a flare of yellow lights. He consulted his watch. It was twenty-three minutes after ten. He knocked at the closed door, according to Spencer's directions: two short knocks, a pause, a double knock, another pause, then again a short knock.

The door swung open, and he entered.

CHAPTER II.

NO. 17 BRADDON STREET.

A MOMENTARY hush of expectancy fell like a pall over the company gathered at No. 17 as Ogilvie entered. Spencer's sable coat was wrapped about him in loose, luxurious folds, with the light of the swinging kerosene lamp, in the doorless, octagonal outer hall, stabbing tiny points of gold into the russet-black fur as the draft from the entrance door jerked his coat apart and exposed the lining. He noted in passing the man with the bulbous nose, the great hairy hands, and the exotic, spade-shaped red beard behind the cashier's desk, who looked at him and then turned away. Immediately — the hush of expectancy had lasted only a few seconds — the talk that filled the place like the droning of bees broke forth again; it even rose to a higher note as the hat-check boy — a snobbish anomaly for this part of town, Ogilvie reflected — took the ulster and handed it to a brown-eyed, high-colored, sweet-faced girl who presided over the clothes rack that stood beyond the outer hall, with a rapid stream of clipped, metallic Balkan jargon.

Ogilvie did not miss the strange, almost pitying look in the girl's fine brown eyes as she took the coat, seemed to finger it for a moment as if enjoying the soft feel of it, and then said to him in guttural, broken English:

"Check, sir! Yes, sir — right check!"

Ogilvie held out his hand. "All right," he said, "let's have the check!"

"But —" the girl shook her head and glanced over at the man with the red beard as if appealing to him — "you have the check, sir!"

"I have not, my dear!"

The girl seemed flustered.

"S'bog s'bogjie!" she exclaimed, calling on some Slav deity for help; "you have, you have —"

Blaine Ogilvie laughed. He had always been an easy-going man, had always disliked arguments and quarrels.

"All right, all right," he replied, "have it your own way. Anyhow, that coat is valuable, and I want it back, check or no check. I have witnesses, eh?" He smiled at the red-bearded man, who smiled back with a flash of small, even white teeth.

"Yes, sir," said the girl dully, rather hopelessly. "Oh, yes, sir —"

He tried to dovetail these impressions, between the moment he entered and the moment he sat down and asked for a drink — into a compendious whole — tried to riddle out their keynote.

His first reaction was emphatically tame. He felt disappointed. He had been keyed up to expect something, if not thrilling or bloodcurdling, at least startlingly unconventional or intriguing, and all he saw was an old-fashioned restaurant, harking back, as Spencer had told him, to the days of Aaron Burr and the young Republic. It seemed like an archaic "saloon bar" of colonial days, with its two or three dozen oaken, strong-backed chairs that stood against the farther wall, each fitted with an occupant, its black settle near the bar, redolent of a former generation when, doubtless, it had been filled by a pompous landlord holding forth, clay pipe, in hand, on the comparative virtues of king or parliament. There was the neat, sanded floor, the small, round window high up on the wall with a wheel ventilator in one of the panes, a few quaint pictures in flat mahogany frames, a gaily painted Hadley dower chest, and quite a collection of Spode plates and old English flip glasses.

Altogether a charming, peaceful place — redolent, Ogilvie thought smilingly, of lavender and lace and potent rum toddies. As the outer door clicked in the lock he felt as if the New York that he knew, the brassy, hustling New York of motley, cosmopolitan throngs and hooting motor drays and elevated cars booming along their steely spider's web had been shuttered off, had been sucked back into an air pocket of time.

A purse-mouthed, crane-necked waiter — fully as much of an antique as the rest of the place, with his gray Dundreary whiskers and green baize apron and elastic gaiters — hovered about. Ogilvie gave his order and, after he was served, lit a cigar and settled comfortably in his chair. Then, unhurriedly, he turned to study the occupants of the restaurant.

The latter were now paying no attention to him. They seemed the pleasant, bromidic folk of the neighborhood, small tradesmen and chauffeurs and skilled mechanics, talking in undertones unexcitedly, without gestures, sipping their innocuous drinks and puffing at well-blackened brier pipes and ten-cent cheroots. Some were playing checkers.

Among them only a few men stood out as types rather out of the ordinary. Thinking of Martyn Spencer's cryptic remarks, of the twenty thousand dollars, the unknown, mysterious reason for his being here, thinking finally of the signal code of knocks which had opened to him the outer door, Blaine Ogilvie studied these men more closely.

He tried to classify them logically in his coolly observant brain — for future reference, as he put it; although he added to himself that he would give a good half of the twenty thousand dollars to know what exactly this reference might eventually point to — the reference, the explanation, and the end, the solution —

What end? End of what?

As the moments passed he became conscious of a queer, eerie sensation, like a clay-cold hand gently caressing his spine. It was uncomfortable. He tried to convince himself that it was a draft, the wintry wind booming through the cracked old walls. But he knew that he was lying to himself; knew that it was fear — fear of the unknown — the grayest, most tragic fear in the world! He watched his left hand that held the cigar. It trembled. Then he shook the feeling off suddenly, physically, with a jerk and heave of his broad shoulders, as a cat shakes off raindrops. He turned again to study the few people who seemed to stand out from among the rest of the crowd.

There was, of course, the man behind the cashier's desk, with the spade-shaped, flame-colored beard and the bulbous, large-pored nose. He seemed slightly nervous, shuffling with his fingertips the pages of the ledger in front of him, occasionally looking up in the direction of the door as if waiting for somebody to come. There was also the brown-eyed girl — doubtless belonging to some Slav race — who presided over the clothes rack. She gave a little guilty start as her glance crossed Ogilvie's. Then she turned her back on him and slumped down on her stool, facing the door. The boy in the outer hall, too, was staring at the door, standing quite motionless, tense, like a pointer at bay.

For a second or two Blaine Ogilvie felt fascinated by the grouping of the three figures; it seemed both tragic and incongruous, like a tableau out of some cheap melodrama.

Then he looked away from them and toward the other occupants of the room whom he had decided to observe.

Not far from the black settle by the bar a party of three were sitting around one of the oaken tables, framed on either side by other groups, prosy, uninteresting, small tradesmen or mechanics, as Ogilvie had decided. But these three men were of a different stamp. They sat very quietly, very silently. There was something inhuman about their quietude. One seemed like an elderly roué, handsome in a way, yet amorphous, washed over by the pitiless hand of time and vice. He was smoking a straw-colored cigarette in a ten-inch holder of clear green jade. At his left was a tall, thin man with extraordinarily long arms, the cleaverlike sharpness of his face emphasized by the supercilious upsweep of a heavy black mustache. The third was a youth, not over twenty, dressed in an expensive but foppish manner, with his bench-made brogues, buckskin spats, and a hairy, greenish Norfolk jacket opening over a Tattersall waistcoat of an extravagant pattern. The canary diamond in his purple necktie, if genuine, was worth a small fortune.

In the center of the room, paying not the slightest attention to the click of the counters at the next table, where some men were playing checkers, a man sat alone, a little hunchback whose pear-shaped head just protruded above the table rim. His face was distinguished by an immense hooked nose, a grave brow curving over a tragic, portentous gaze — the look of a mad prophet — and his dome was surmounted incongruously, ludicrously, by a cap in a check of violent magenta and pea green, set far back on the perspiring head. There was something about him that reminded Ogilvie of the Old Testament; not racially, but rather civilizationally — something like the bitter, pitiless logic of the ancient Hebrew annals.

And, finally, at Ogilvie's elbow were two men. One was tall, with a bald, pink head; the face itself, through a trick of the flickering shadows of the swinging kerosene lamps, was indistinct, wiped over with brown and ruby and muddy orange, all but the eyes that, beneath curiously straight and heavy brows, stared hard and shiny blue into vacancy arrestingly expressive of a certain contempt, tinged by a certain pity. The other man would have escaped Ogilvie's notice had it not been for his companion. For he seemed just an average New York business man, spotlessly neat from the exact parting in his honey-colored hair to the gray, herring-bone tweeds that fitted him without a wrinkle. His face was round like a baby's, with a nose inclined to be snub, and his fingers, drumming delicately on the table, were plump and excessively well kept.

There appeared to be nobody else in the restaurant worth considering or studying. Ogilvie tried to determine what these men were whom he had picked out, what they represented — socially, financially, or politically — in the vast macrocosm of New York. Presently, as he watched and thought and weighed, it became clear to him that there was between these men, from table to table, an undercurrent of mutual understanding, expressed by an occasional glance, a faint gesture, even the ghost of a cough. And then suddenly — and it was this which caused fear to rush back upon him — he seemed to notice, to feel more than notice, that all the other people in the room, whom he had dismissed as harmless denizens of the neighborhood, were also involved in this baffling, silent network of mutual understanding, of waiting for something to happen — what — and to whom?

What were these people expecting? Why had they admitted him? What was Martyn Spencer's connection with it all? The three thoughts tumbled over each other, then drew together, blended, crystallized into a third: Why was he here? Because Martyn Spencer had paid him twenty thousand dollars. The answer was obvious. But obvious, too, was the fact that he had earned it. For he had come here, and there was nothing in the agreement between him and Spencer that he had to remain here any specific length of time.

Very well, he thought, the next thing for him to do was to leave the place. He got up unhurriedly, and was about to cross to the entrance hall when the little hunchback in the checked cap spoke two words slowly, without the slightest emphasis:

"Don't go!"

"Why not?" Ogilvie turned and stared at the speaker.

"Because it would be so very useless, wouldn't it?"

The words were quite simple, quite gentle. The hunchback had not moved, nor had any of the other occupants of the room, who continued to converse in low undertones, playing checkers, sipping their drinks, puffing at their pipes and cigars.

But, somehow, through the mists of Ogilvie's apprehension, floated down the knowledge that he was standing on the brink of a catastrophe, a catastrophe of which he knew neither the beginning nor the end.

Somehow, he knew that, whatever the reasons for their keeping him here, they would not let him go until their object, whatever it was, had been attained. It seemed inevitable, like fate, and a curious, helpless lassitude swept over him. He realized instinctively that it would do no earthly good to argue with these people. He had never seen them before, nor had they seen him, as far as he knew. And yet they were evidently acting according to a carefully preconceived plan. Too, he sensed that, for all the hunch-back's gentle voice, for all the general air of excessive quietude and peace that pervaded the room like a subtle, insidious perfume, it would be useless to bluff, as useless to show fight.

The odds were against him, and he felt more than ever sure of it when, out of the corner of his eye, he noticed that half a dozen men had risen and were approaching him very quietly, very unobtrusively, one stepping close up to him and asking him in flat, low accents to kindly sit down again.

Ogilvie obeyed. He sat down with a little bow in the direction of the hunchback.

"Very well, sir," he said and lit his second cigar. "I fail to see, how-ever, what —"

"It's really quite useless," said the hunchback.

"Quite, quite useless," echoed the red-bearded man with a curious sigh.

"No use arguing — you mean — asking questions?" suggested Blaine Ogilvie.

"Exactly!" replied the hunchback. "Isn't that so?"

He turned to the company, gathering eyes like a hostess, and there came a rumbling, affirmative chorus:

"Yes — yes —"

Blaine Ogilvie shrugged his shoulders. His thoughts were in a daze. The whole situation seemed unreal and negative. Momentarily he won-dered if it were all a dream, from which he would awaken presently to find himself in bed, with the young sun streaming in through the window.

He smoked on in silence. When, a few seconds later, there was the roar of an automobile outside, followed by the code signal of knocks at the street door, he was more conscious of relief than of heightening fear. He looked up curiously as the door opened and admitted two men. One was short and stocky and rather ordinary, assisting a second man who seemed ill. The sick man was walking with evident effort, leaning heavily on a rubber-tipped stick, the feet dragging haltingly and pain-fully, the bent body huddled in a thick coat, the hat pulled down over the forehead.

He stood still for a second, blinking short-sightedly against the yellow light. A thin smile curled his bloodless lips.

"Is this the place, Hillyer?" he asked, turning to the man who was with him.

"Yes, Monro," replied the other, helping him off with his overcoat.

"And — when — do you suppose —" commenced the first man rather anxiously. "Though I really don't hope that —"

"Now, please! Sit down first, Monro! You need rest," interrupted the other, assisting him into a chair not far from Ogilvie's.

The latter felt completely mystified as well as disappointed. It was all so quiet, so well bred, so unexciting and unhurried. He was steadily becoming less intrigued than frankly bored. A faint suspicion came to him that the whole thing was nothing except a well-staged hoax, a prac-tical joke of sorts.

He turned in his chair and motioned to the green-aproned waiter. The latter approached at a dignified, shuffling run.

"Yes, sir?" he inquired civilly.

"Bring me another —"

Ogilvie did not finish the sentence.

For there came with utter, dramatic suddenness a crimson flash and a grim, cruel roar — a high-pitched cry cut off in mid-air — the dull sound of a falling body.

Instinctively he turned in his chair. Startled, frightened, he rose and stared wide-eyed.

"Oh —"

Through the pall of silence that had dropped over the restaurant, Ogilvie's choked exclamation cut with extraordinary distinctness.

There, curled up like a sleeping dog, in front of his chair, one arm flung wide, the other stretched up and out, with the fingers bent stiffly, convulsively, as if trying to claw at life, to snatch back the breath of it from the black abyss of oblivion, lay the second of the two men who had come in a few moments earlier, the one who had seemed ill. Something trickled slowly from a neatly drilled bullet hole in his left temple, staining his cheek, his chin, his collar a rich crimson. He was dead. There was no doubt of it.

Murder — thought Blaine Ogilvie. And, if premeditated murder, why had they kept him here? What was supposed to be his connection with it, or, if not his personally, Martyn Spencer's?

CHAPTER III.

BLUECOATS AND A CARVING KNIFE.

EVEN AT that tragic moment, Ogilvie could not rid his mind of the incongruous impression that the whole thing was unreal. For there was no such excitement as is generally supposed to follow the witnessing of a violent deed. The majority of the occupants of the restaurant had indeed risen, but there were no cries of horror and indignation, no hysterical exchange of comments and counter-comments. All seemed quiet, orderly, and well bred, as if murder were a commonplace, rather negligible occurrence.

Ogilvie himself had only turned after he had heard the shot fired. He had turned quickly enough, but even so he could not tell who was the assassin. There seemed to be no weapon in evidence, no telltale, guilty attitude.

Still there could be no doubt that some of the other people in the restaurant must have looked in the direction of the newcomers at the time, must have actually witnessed the killing. Yet there was no sign of it: no pointing, accusing hands reached out, nobody gave way to the natural impulse of those who have witnessed a revolting crime — to hurl themselves upon the criminal, to strike him or do him injury.

The short, stocky man who had accompanied the murdered man was still sitting at the table, looking down upon the dead body, his face singularly unexpressive of any emotion whatsoever. He had not even dropped the cigar which he was smoking. The party of three whom Ogilvie had noticed earlier in the evening — the man who looked like an elderly roué, the one with the cleaverlike profile, and the youth in the foppish clothes — had got up, as had the party of two — he with the bald, pink head and the staring, contemptuous eyes, and the one who looked like an average business man. The five had joined and moved forward in a compact group in the direction of the door, talking in undertones to each other and looking not toward the murdered man, but — Ogilvie realized with a start — toward him.

The red-bearded man was still casually shuffling the pages of the ledger with his hairy fingers, while the brown-eyed girl at the clothes rack sat slumped in her chair, perfectly oblivious to everything, apathetic, and the boy in the outer hall leaned against the door jamb, hands in pockets, staring vacantly at nothing in particular.

Subconsciously, yet with the instantaneous fidelity of a photographic lens, all these physical details impressed themselves upon Ogilvie's brain, as did the fact that the hunchback was standing in a clear space, halfway between his and the murdered man's table. For a second, straight through the confusion in his mind, Ogilvie imagined that the latter must have been the assassin, judging from his position. But he dismissed the idea almost immediately, because he recalled that the man had a cigar in his left hand and a glass in his right. He must have risen, just as he was, the moment he had heard the shot or had seen the actual killing.

Presently, very calmly and unhurriedly, the hunchback crossed the room, exchanged a whispered word in passing with the red-bearded man, and stepped into the outer hall. The girl handed him his coat — Ogilvie noticed that it was next to his own, which was swinging from a peg at the near end of the rack — and the man stepped out into the night. The next moment there was the roar of a motorcar gathering speed, then fading into the memory of sound.

And still the people in the restaurant remained as they were, quiet and orderly and unexcited. Only the group of five men had moved a little closer toward Blaine Ogilvie.

The latter was speechless. His thoughts were bunched into too violent a turmoil and commingling for immediate disentanglement. It was the first time in his civil life that he had seen death, and it appeared to him singularly undignified, singularly drab and commonplace. Even war gave it a certain dramatic *mise en scène*. Yet the shock of it had cut deeply into his inner consciousness.

That thing there on the floor — with the crimson stain slowly trickling down and thickening blackly — the stiff, convulsive fingers — useless, hopeless, weakly ineffectual — and it had been alive a few minutes earlier — had smiled, breathed, talked, acted —

It was beginning to affect Ogilvie physically, and he felt slightly ill. The feeling increased, grew to a choking, nauseating sensation, gripped his chest, his throat, caused him to cough violently. Instinctively he turned from the table in the direction of the washroom, whose sign he had noticed on entering at the left of the outer hall.

He had hardly taken a step when quickly, yet without a word, the group of five men advanced toward him in a solid phalanx, threateningly barring his way. The youth in the Norfolk suit gripped his arm, and it was this physical contact which cleared Ogilvie's brain and caused him to act. Whatever the reason for Martyn Spencer's strange bargain with him, whatever the cause of the murder or the personality of the murderer, whatever the beginning and problematical end of it all, it became suddenly clear to him that he must get away as rapidly as possible. Remembering football tactics on the college gridiron, where he had been fully as famous for the almost African power of resistance of his skull as for the sturdy speed of his legs, he bent almost double and made a flying leap in the direction of the door, head well forward and down, like a battering-ram.

The youth tried to stop him. Ogilvie caught him full in the pit of the stomach with his head. The youth dropped, with a funny, squeaky little noise of pain, while, at the same moment, the other four hurled themselves upon Ogilvie, their fists going like flails. Ogilvie kept his presence of mind and gave a short laugh. He had taken part in a few rough-and-tumble fights and knew that when a number of men turn against one they usually interfere more with each other than they hurt the man whom they attack.

He fought well, careful to step back a little, with his back to the wall, at his left a table where, a few moments earlier, the waiter had carved a beefsteak.

He dodged and danced and grappled. His breath came in short, violent bursts. At one and the same time he was trying to land blow, to parry blow, to sidestep kicking feet and crashing elbows, and to make a dash for the door, the night, safety. The odds were against him. A rough knuckle caught him on the left temple, an open palm hit the point of his chin, the man with the bald, pink head dodged within the very crook of Ogilvie's powerful right arm and grappled, while the others, joined by the youth, who had revived, closed in the next moment like hounds pulling down a stag.

Ogilvie felt himself seized about the chest under the armpits by a bearlike grasp. He reached back, his fingers closed, something ripped, tore, like cloth. He had no time to think what it was. For a moment he felt as if his ribs were crushing in his lungs. His temples throbbed. Blue wheels whirled in front of his eyes. The roof of his mouth felt parched.

Straining, cursing, he fell to the floor, one of the attackers on top of him, another booting him in the ribs, a third dancing about on the outskirts of the mêlée, watching his chance for a knockout blow. Bending down, he shot his fist to Ogilvie's jaw, but the latter jerked his head back in the nick of time, and the next second, with a sudden, hard crunching of muscles, he pinioned the arms of the man who was on top of him to both his sides, spread his strong legs, bridged his massive body, and tried desperately to pull himself up. He was succeeding in this when suddenly the first man, with a wolfish snarl, sank his teeth in his ear.

"Curse you!" exclaimed Ogilvie in rage and pain.

Then, with a great jerk and heave, he freed himself, sending the first man crashing into the second, the second into the third. Jumping back, he saw the curved, razor-sharp, old-fashioned carving knife, which the waiter had left on the table, and reached for it.

He did it instinctively, unthinkingly. Hitherto, by the token of his class and training, he had been fighting according to the unwritten code, had still been playing the game. Now his prejudices and inhibitions danced away in a mad whirligig of rage and resentment, and the carving knife leaped to his hand like a sentient thing, catching the rays of the kerosene lamp, so that the point of it glittered like a cresset of evil passions.

He used the knife like a rapier, with carte and tierce, with thrust and counterthrust and quick, staccato riposte, pinking here a leg, there a hand, and ripping through cloth as with the edge of a razor, stiffening or crooking his arm as he lunged to the attack or estrapaded sideways or feinted to parry clumsy, ineffectual blows and kicks. Some of the other people in the room had rushed up and were joining in the attack, but, as before, they only served to interfere with each other. Somebody threw a chair. It failed of its mark — Ogilvie's head — and hit the youth in the Norfolk suit, who dropped, *hors de combat*, this time for good. Another threw a bottle, it jerked high, crashed against the lamp, and the light guttered out. The room was plunged in coiling, trooping shadows, except for the few haggard rays that stole in from the lamp in the outer hall.

"Careful! Careful!" somebody warned. In the semi-darkness friend was hitting friend. At this moment the street door opened, and by the side of the hunchback two policemen entered, nightsticks readily poised. One of them flashed an electric torch, and the hunchback took in the situation at a glance.

"Quick!" he said to the bluecoats. "There he is — trying to get away —"

"Who?"

"The man I told you about — the murderer!" And he pointed straight at Blaine Ogilvie.

The latter's mind worked with the instantaneous precision of a photographic shutter. He saw the trap — he, the murderer — with a dozen witnesses against him! He acted even as he understood. He danced back from the attacking crowd, then forward suddenly, knife in hand. He catapulted himself through the mass with a sort of breathless, sullen audacity. He was too excited probably to feel ordinary fear at that moment. If he had time to think at all, he considered that he had no chance, in spite of his knife, to give battle to the two muscular, solid policemen who stood there on broad-planted feet, sticks ominously raised, ready to fell him.

He ducked very suddenly, before the two policemen had a chance to realize what was happening, before they had time to put the brake on their brawny right arms. Down came the nightsticks, and they hit each other, temporarily putting themselves out of commission instead of hitting Ogilvie.

With a triumphant little laugh he straightened up again, and, before anybody knew exactly what was going on, obeying some subconscious impulse which reminded him that the night was cold and the coat expensive, he tore Martyn Spencer's sable-lined ulster from the rack, flung it about his shoulders, and was out of the door and into the street.

The automobile which had brought the murdered man and which the hunchback had used a few minutes earlier was still in front, purring invitingly. He jumped into the driver's seat, and the chain-protected tires gripped the snow-crusted pavement. Momentarily the machine seemed to pause, to quiver, as if taking in a great lungful of breath, and a deep, expectant whine rose from its steely body. Then it plunged forward enthusiastically, like a being with a heart and a soul, making naught of the grimy, sticky, slushy snow puddles; and Blaine Ogilvie, who belonged to that new generation which is as alive to the personality and the idiosyncrasies of machinery as the older generation were to horseflesh, rode the steering wheel as he had never done before.

Gradually he increased the speed, sucking every ounce of strength and energy from gasoline and engine, as he heard the voices that poured from the restaurant increase, then diminish, and fade away, bending low as a revolver bullet whistled over his head. He made a corner at nearly a right angle, as if he were trying to lift the car along the pavement by sheer strength of muscle. Taking another corner on two wheels, shaving a lamppost, evading gesticulating policemen, twisting past top-heavy motor drays, scattering a crowd of homing theatergoers, he finally turned into the Avenue that rose out of the snow-blotched darkness between parallel curves of warm, lemon lights.

At Fifty-first Street he turned east until he reached a little house that seemed rather out of place, framed as it was on both sides by tall, pretentious apartment buildings. Small it was, compact, almost pagan in its Greek simplicity. Ogilvie stopped the car, jumped out, ran up the steps, and pushed the electric bell.

A moment later a white-haired servant opened the door.

"Yes, sir?" he inquired, blinking short-sightedly. Then a smile overspread his wrinkled old features as he recognized the late visitor. "Why — Mr. Ogilvie — come in, sir! Please come in!"

"Is the big chief at home?" asked the other, stepping past the servant into the vestibule.

"He hasn't come in yet, sir."

"Very annoying."

"Won't you wait, sir?"

"I guess I will." Ogilvie threw off his fur coat "By the way, will you go outside and drive my car into the garage, if you don't mind, Tompkins?"

"Right, sir."

"And — Tompkins —"

"Yes, sir?"

"All the other servants asleep?"

"Yes, sir."

"Good! Don't mention to any of them that I'm here — that you've seen me tonight — I have my reasons."

"Very well, sir."

And Tompkins bowed with the imperturbable calm of a British butler and withdrew, while Ogilvie entered the next room, occupied himself for a few seconds with a bottle of Bourbon and a siphon that were awaiting their master's return, chose a comfortable chair, and stretched himself luxuriously.

Presently he dozed off.

CHAPTER IV.

IN HIS POCKET.

HE WAS awakened — he did not know how much later — by a pleasant, laughing voice at his elbow.

"Hello, old man!"

Ogilvie sat up and yawned and looked at Gadsby, a tall, lean man with a square, angular jaw, thin, sensitive lips that subtended a quixotic nose, and dreamy brown eyes.

"Quite comfortable?" asked Gadsby with a smile.

"Like a bug in a rug, Bob. And —" he paused a little — "quite safe!"

He had given the last word the emphasis of a suddenly lowered voice, and Gadsby frowned perplexedly.

"What do you mean — quite safe?" he inquired.

"Aren't you the police commissioner?" came Ogilvie's counter-question.

"I have that distinction. What about it?"

"Well, I hardly imagine the police will look for me here in your private residence. Nor will they look for the car — which, incidentally, I swiped — in your immaculate garage."

"What are you talking about?"

"Nothing much. Only — well, your flat-footed minions are after me, hot on my trail."

"What have you done?"

"I was just a plain idiotic fool."

"That's nothing new," Gadsby returned ungraciously. "What else have you done?"

"Nothing — I told you, didn't I? But the police have an idea that I committed —"

"What — for the love of Mike?"

"Murder!"

"Good heavens!"

"And that isn't all, Bob. They've a couple of bakers' dozens of witnesses, all cocked and primed to swear to it!"

Ogilvie lit a cigar while the police commissioner collapsed weakly into a chair.

Robert W. Gadsby was that curiously paradoxical and curiously effective combination: a materialistic idealist. He was both a doer and a dreamer; both a politician and an honest man; both a reformer and a sane man who saw people and conditions as they were, without the lying help of rosy-tinted, psychic spectacles.

Of fine old New York stock and immense wealth, and with a slightly provincial civic pride which had its roots in the days when New York was New Amsterdam, when people imported their liquor from Holland, when wild turkeys flopped their drab wings between Broadway and the Bronx, and when the Gadsbys had their country estate in the eventual neighborhood of Sixth Avenue and Twenty-ninth Street, he had gone in for local politics on leaving college as a simple matter of duty, because, as he put it, he was an American, a New Yorker, and a rich man. He had run for various offices, had been elected repeatedly, and when, at the last city election, the swing of the pendulum swept his party into the seats of the mighty, he had been given his choice of several appointments. Unhesitatingly, believing detection and prevention of crime to be the backbone of good city government, he had chosen the office of commissioner of police.

He was making good. Even his political opponents, in their newspapers, found it increasingly difficult to concoct and correlate statistics misleading enough to prove that crime had increased during his administration. Nobody could accuse him of corruption and graft, for he was a millionaire; nobody could ridicule him as an unpractical visionary and congenital reformer, for Scotland Yard had sent over experts to study some of his methods and innovations; nobody could suspect him of too great political ambition, for a higher office than this would have been his for the asking.

He and Blaine Ogilvie were old friends — the sort who do not see each other with mathematical regularity, but who can continue a conversation, even after an absence of half a year, just about at the point where they had broken it off.

Gadsby looked at his friend. "Of course you are only joking?" he asked.

"I wish I were," came Ogilvie's reply.

"B-but —"

"I'm telling you the plain, unvarnished, rock-bottom truth, Bob!"

"Really?"

"Abso-tively!"

"Great Caesar!" Gadsby walked up and down excitedly. "Let's hear the whole story — every detail — omit nothing."

And Ogilvie told him. "What do you make of it?" he wound up.

"That you're in a pretty mess!"

"I am aware of that myself. What else do you make of it?"

Gadsby shook his head. "I don't know," he said slowly, dully. "I don't know!" He slurred, stopped, went on: "Of course you've come here to give yourself up, I suppose?"

"Don't you go supposing things that aren't so, Bob, and you'll save yourself many a disappointment."

"Why — I don't understand!"

"If I had wanted to surrender, I wouldn't have made that rather sensational get-away, would I?"

"But, Blaine —"

"Well?"

"You are suspected of murder. There are witnesses — didn't you tell me?"

"A whole mob of them — they're all hand in glove — I see that now. What's that got to do with —"

"I must arrest you. There is my sworn duty."

"Forget your sworn duty, man! Didn't I hear you give a long spiel during the last campaign that the unwritten duty is fully as important as the written?" Ogilvie smiled. "I voted for your chosen party. Come on! Make good on your election promises!"

"But — my duty —"

"There you go again! You're becoming tiresome. You've duty on the brain. It's your duty — since you insist on arguing about it — to catch the guilty man, not a poor innocent sucker like myself."

"You're under suspicion until you've proved your innocence, Blaine."

"I know. Three cheers for the logic of jurisprudence! But, don't you see, old man, that I can't remove the suspicion until —"

"Well?"

"Until you've found and convicted the guilty party — the real murderer."

"Exactly! That's where I come in. I will —"

"You can't, Bob. First of all, why should the police trouble? Haven't they a number of witnesses to swear to my guilt? Do you want any more direct evidence? Why should the police trouble to look farther afield since they've got me?"

"I'll make them! I am the boss!"

"A fat lot of good that will do you and me. Don't you see? There are no other witnesses except those who will testify against me."

"You had no revolver!"

"They'll swear that I had one. I tell you the whole gang will stick together."

"But why?"

"I don't know why, but I do know they will. The whole thing was a most ingenious trap. Everybody played a part in it — even the girl at the hat rack and the waiter — everybody except myself and —"

"Who?"

"The murdered man! They got him there under some pretense. Bob, if you arrest me the district attorney's office will try me, and I won't have a chance in the world. It's a cinch that I'll decorate the electric chair."

There was a pause. Ogilvie poured himself another drink and tossed it down neat.

"Bob," he continued, "you're up against something brand-new. You will have to let me go — a man accused of murder, guilty by every last particle of direct evidence. You'll have to let the accused go, so that he can play detective and find the real murderer."

"What about Martyn Spencer?"

"I don't know yet. Haven't had time to think. But he must have known why he sent me there. Didn't he give me the twenty thousand dollars? And — that crowd didn't seem to know Spencer personally — otherwise why did they frame me up? No! Whatever his reasons, I don't think that Spencer will say much. Of course, I'll try and make him come through. But I haven't much hope. He's a business man, and he made a bargain with me — paid me — and — well, I lost."

"I'll put my own detective force on the job."

"What clues can they find? I am more liable to find them than they."

"Why, Blaine?"

"Because I am rather vitally interested in the affair."

"But I must arrest you. I'll do anything else I can. I'll hold up the case —"

"You can't for any length of time. The opposition papers will make it hot for you. They'll discover that you and I are friends. They'll influence public opinion. They'll force your hand. They'll make the district attorney try me and convict me in record time. And, if your detectives should find the real murderer — why, by that time I'll be buried in a prison cemetery. Bob, you'll have to forget your sworn duty for once."

Ogilvie turned and walked to the end of the room. Gadsby sat down, and his troubled face betrayed his preoccupation. Finally he looked up. "I'll do it," he said in a low, clear voice.

"Bully for you!"

"On one condition."

"Name it!"

"Any time I want you, you must come in and surrender."

Ogilvie laughed. "No need for that, old man!"

"Why not?"

"Because you'll have me under your personal surveillance all the time."

"How so?"

"You have a spare bedroom, haven't you?"

"You — you mean —"

"Right!" continued Ogilvie with calm effrontery. "You're going to have a guest — oh —" he laughed — "a paying guest — for I still have Spencer's twenty thousand dollars —"

"But — listen —"

"Your house is the only safe place for me. The police won't hunt for me here. Tompkins has known me since I was a kid in knickers — he worked for your father, didn't he? — sort of inherited him, British accent and 'yes, sir,' and 'thank you, sir,' and all. I've already slipped him a word of warning — all you'll have to do is to swear him to secrecy. As to your other servants —"

"Only one — Tompkins' wife. That part's all right — but —" Gadsby shook his head. "It's very unusual," he commented weakly.

"Very!" agreed Ogilvie. "Here am I, accused of murder, guilty by every last bit of direct evidence — playing my own detective and hiding in the private residence of the head of the police department. It's the most unusual thing I have ever run across." He rose. "We'll talk it over tomorrow. I'm too tired tonight, what with all this excitement and that potent Bourbon of yours. Where did you get it, Bob? I thought the country was dry!"

He poured himself a liberal goodnight cap, and fifteen minutes later was comfortably stretched out in one of the police commissioner's best four-poster beds, dressed in a pair of the police commissioner's silk pajamas, and reading the police commissioner's favorite volume of French poetry. Half an hour later he was fast asleep.

TOMPKINS AWAKENED him with an appetizing breakfast tray, a newspaper, and an embarrassed cough.

Ogilvie sat up in bed and laughed. "Don't look like a conspirator, Tompkins," he said.

"But — oh, sir —"

"Mr. Gadsby told you, I take it?"

"Yes, sir," came the despondent reply.

"All right. Forget it. I'm as innocent as a new-born lamb."

"Oh — thank you, sir!"

"Two pieces of sugar — that's right — a little more cream." Ogilvie sipped his coffee. "Want to do me a favor, Tompkins?"

"Yes, sir."

"Call up Miss Marie Dillon — Spring 43789 — and tell her —" He was puzzled. "What are you going to tell her?"

"Leave it to me, sir," replied Tompkins, a wintry smile lighting up his features. "I've been married thirty-nine years."

"Gosh! And I never knew you had a sense of humor!"

"Thank you, sir."

"Don't thank me — thank your Creator. And now, the newspaper, please!"

"Here you are, sir. You'll find the headline quite interesting, sir."

And Ogilvie did. For, smeared across the front page of the *Morning Sentinel* in screaming, extravagant three-inch type, he read:

SENSATIONAL CRIME.

Stranger Kills Well-known Philanthropist Guest
at Benefactors Club. Assassin Makes His Get-away.

"Assassin will have another cup of the police commissioner's excellent coffee," said Blaine Ogilvie, and suited the action to his words.

The newspaper account related that No. 17 Braddon Street was a little restaurant, dating back to pre-Revolutionary days, which closed its doors to the general public at ten p.m. After ten, the article went on, it served as a nightly meeting place for an organization which called itself the "Benefactors Club," which was composed of business and professional men, who met there to discuss art, politics, science, literature, religion, and other live topics.

The report gave a list of the club members. They had simple, prosy names and simple, prosy addresses: from Thomas W. Robinson of 22456 West Seventy-eighth Street to Doctor Jerome McNulty of 44589 Riverside Drive, from J. J. Mulrooney of 15826 East One Hundred and Eighty-third Street to Donald Kayser, somewhere on the French Boulevard — altogether, on the face of it, an apex of Gotham's civic virtues, a very epitome of all the upper West Side's, the Bronx's, and Chelsea's stout, burgess respectability.

It appeared that occasional late visitors, unfamiliar with the early closing hour of the restaurant proper, were usually turned away by the boy at the door or by the proprietor, who presided behind the cashier's desk and who was also a member of the club — the man with the spade-shaped red beard and the bulbous nose, Ogilvie added mentally as he read — but that last night a stranger had made his appearance around half past ten, evidently a well-to-do man about town, judging from his superb, sable-lined ulster.

Here followed an excellent description of Blaine Ogilvie.

This stranger had explained that he had lost his way, that he was tired and cold and hungry, and finally he had been allowed to come in and had been served with food and cigars.

Shortly afterward one of the club members, a certain Doctor Hillyer O. McGrath, of 11921 West Eleventh Street, had driven up in his automobile, accompanied by a friend not a member of the organization, Mr. Monro Clafflin, the well-known retired merchant and philanthropist. A few minutes later, the report continued, without giving either reason or warning — in fact, without saying a word — the stranger had pulled out a revolver, fired point-blank at Mr. Clafflin, killing him instantly, and had made his get-away in Doctor McGrath's car, after a sensational fight.

Here followed a fairly accurate description of Ogilvie's battle and escape. It seemed that he had thrown the revolver away, and that it had afterward been picked up by Mr. Montross D. Clapperton, the president of the Benefactors Club, who — the hunchback, came Ogilvie's silent comment — had run out a few minutes before the stranger's get-away, to fetch the police. Several of the club members had received minor injuries. Mr. Cornelius van Alstyne had been hit by a chair; Mr. Leopold Fischer had a black eye, besides having his clothes torn; while Captain Jeremiah Blount, Mr. Holister Welkin, and Mr. Audley R. Chester — addresses given in each case — had been wounded by a carving knife which the assassin had picked up.

Ogilvie smiled when he considered that here, doubtless, he had a list of the different men whom he had observed and scrutinized shortly after he had entered No. 17; and he smiled again when he read, in the last paragraph of the article, that the police so far had not discovered either the name or the whereabouts of the assassin, but that, given the accurate description, they expected no trouble in putting their hands on him within the next twenty-four hours — "thanks to the marvelously up-to-date and efficient methods of our police commissioner, Mr. Robert W. Gadsby."

"BOB," Ogilvie said to the latter, after he had shaved and bathed and dressed, pointing at the last line, "the newspapers are handing you a bouquet."

"They'll hand me a brick bat," said the other, "when they learn —"

"Please! No more 'duty' stuff! We had all that out last night. Now — for the real murderer."

"How are you going to discover him?"

"By looking for the motives."

"And how are you going to find his motives?"

"By investigation and elimination. First of all, here's a list of names and addresses I culled from the morning paper. These are the people I specially noticed last night. Have your department look them up. See who they are, what they do, their reputation, and all that sort of thing, you know."

"Yes," said the police commissioner as he tucked the list of names away. "What else?"

"Get a general survey of the other members of the club. You'll find their names and addresses in the *Morning Sentinel*. Here —"

"What about Martyn Spencer?" asked Gadsby.

"I haven't much hope there. But get a line on him, whatever you can. See if you can make head or tail of any of the fantastic tales that used to be afloat about him."

"All right. I'll try."

"And — oh, yes — find out about Clafflin, the murdered man, you know, and that Doctor McGrath, who brought him, and —"

"Pardon me, old man," came the police commissioner's ironic inter-jection, "what are you going to do? I had an idea you were going to play detective."

"I can't leave the house — at least not yet — can I, you chump? I am going to do my bit at long distance. I am going to correlate and eliminate and dovetail. Let's have a look at Spencer's ulster now. I told you — didn't I? — how the girl felt the fur and said something about my having the check — 'the right check' — and how she looked over at the red-bearded man as if to appeal to him."

"Are you sure she didn't give you a check?"

"I am positive, Bob."

The police commissioner took out his cigar case. "Care for a smoke?" he asked.

"Thanks. I will."

Ogilvie took the cigar and groped in his left coat pocket for a match. Then he gave a little, startled exclamation.

"Hello! What's that?" He drew his hand from his pocket.

"Well? Found the check after all?" inquired Gadsby.

"No. I found this!"

Ogilvie opened his hand. It held a ragged bit of gray, herringbone tweed, evidently, judging from the buttonhole, torn from a man's coat lapel.

"The gray suit — the fellow with the round, babyish face who looked like a typical business man — what's his name?" Ogilvie con-sulted the morning paper. "Oh, yes — Leopold Fischer — had his eye blackened and his suit torn —"

"What are you saying, Blaine?"

"I remember. I reached back of me in that rough-and-tumble fight. I felt something rip and give. Must have dropped it into my pocket without thinking. Here it is — and — oh — look, Bob!"

And he turned over the torn shred of tweed and pointed at a small, round metal disk which was fastened to it.

"Bob," he said, "the investigation begins right here."

And he bent closely over the little metal disk, while the other entered the next room to telephone to headquarters.

CHAPTER V.

PLAIN FOOLS OR IDEALISTS.

THE DISK was round and flat, a third of an inch in diameter, with a narrow, well-beveled edge, and no marks of any sort on it except a number — 17 — deeply engraved in the center. Ogilvie was still examining it when Gadsby returned from the next room, where he had had a lengthy telephone conversation with headquarters.

"I have sent some of my very best men out on the case," he said. "Detective Sergeant Miller is going to get a line on Martyn Spencer. O'Neale will investigate the murdered man and his connection with Doctor McGrath. And Campbell and Wimpflinger and a couple of others are going to see what they can find out about the different club members."

"That's bully."

"What do you make of that disk?"

"Oh, nothing much. I guess it's the badge of the Benefactors Club."

"Sounds fairly reasonable."

"There's only one thing about it that's puzzling me," continued Ogilvie.

"What?"

"Here!" Ogilvie gave the round bit of metal to the other. "See for yourself, then we'll compare notes. In the meantime I'll take a look at friend Spencer's luxurious ulster."

While the police commissioner examined the club badge, Ogilvie took the sable coat from the rack in the outer hall and scrutinized it narrowly.

Presently he got up and put on the coat.

Gadsby looked up. "Not dreaming of going out, are you?" he asked, alarmed.

"Heavens — no! I'm just going to reconstruct the scene in No. I7 when I entered. Look here a moment, will you?"

"Certainly."

"That's the way I came in. I took off my coat and gave it to the boy — like this. The boy gave it to the girl — this way. Watching?"

"Yes, yes. Go on."

"The girl —" Ogilvie puzzled, then continued: "Wait! I remember! Yes. First she fingered the coat as if she liked the feel of it. And afterward — afterward, Bob — she made that funny remark about my having the check — 'the right check' — and exchanged looks with the red-bearded man."

"Well, I fail to see —"

"Question is," said Ogilvie, "did she feel something which caused her to make that remark? Let me see if I can recall the scene. She took the coat with both hands — this way. No, no — wait — the other way! Her right hand like this — while her left hand slipped beneath the fur collar — here — watch — this way!" He suited the action to the words. "Now, what did she feel? Or what did she find?"

He turned up the fur collar, looked close for several seconds, and smiled.

"Bob," he said, "let's have that badge for a moment."

"Found a clue?"

"I think so."

The police commissioner came nearer. "Another such badge?" he inquired.

"No, but the marks of one. Look here! See where the fur has been rubbed off? Now watch!" He put the disk over the place he had indicated. "The disk fits it exactly — isn't that so?"

"Right. And —"

"It's quite clear. There was a badge fastened here when the girl took the coat. And — by jingo — Spencer knew it when he forced the coat on me!"

"Where is the disk now?"

"I haven't the faintest idea. The girl took it, or I lost it. 'The right check' — the disk she meant! And it was this disk, combined with the signal code of knocks at the door, which gave me the right to enter, or perhaps —" he slurred, then went on, instinctively lowering his voice — "the duty to enter?"

"What do you mean by that?" came the other's puzzled query.

"Just that."

"But —"

"Listen!" said Ogilvie. "Wasn't Spencer afraid of No. 17?"

"Doubtless."

"Would he have been afraid unless it had been his duty to go there? If it had only been his right — why, man — he needn't have gone! That's clear, isn't it?"

"Yes."

"And, furthermore, didn't he slip me twenty thousand dollars of the realm to go in his place? Weren't they expecting —"

"Not Spencer!" interrupted Gadsby. "Otherwise they wouldn't have framed you up, since they didn't know you — had no reason to —"

"Well, they were expecting somebody — somebody who was going to get it in the neck, for some reason or other. That's the knot we'll have to solve."

Ogilvie was silent for a few moments. He walked up and down, thinking deeply, presently turning to answer Gadsby's question what the puzzling thing was which he had noticed about the badge.

"Just this!" he replied. "What metal is it made of?"

The police commissioner looked at it again. "I don't know," he admitted finally.

"Nor do I. Of course I am not an expert metallurgist. But I know enough to tell that it's neither gold nor silver —"

"It isn't platinum, either."

"And it isn't steel or bronze or any other metal I am familiar with. Bob, please send Tompkins over to some jeweler on the Avenue and have him examine the thing."

"We've an expert assayist at headquarters — one of my innovations," said the police commissioner rather proudly. "He'll give us a report by tonight."

"Bully!"

THE DAY crawled on leadenly. Gadsby left to attend to his duties at headquarters, and Ogilvie fell a prey to certain violent reactions from his cheerful, jesting mood. He became nervous, fidgety, even afraid, as he stared out into the street, well hidden by the window curtains.

Day died, with a white, purple-nicked pall of snow, pierced by the crimson and gold lights reflected on innumerable window-panes, and the dull, lemon glow of the street lamps, and melting, farther out, into a drab cosmos where the brown, moist haze from the Hudson drifted up, twisting and turning to the call of the river wind.

Night was coming. Night — thought Ogilvie, with just a trace of bitter self-pity — night, over on Broadway, with food and light phrases, with the festive hooting of motor horns and gaiety and laughter and the tuning-up of the orchestras and the clapping of white-gloved hands! And here he was — suspected of murder — in hiding.

"Mr. Ogilvie! Please, sir!" Tompkins interrupted the other's gray reveries.

"Yes?"

"I telephoned to Miss Dillon, sir. I met her and talked to her."

"Oh — good!" Ogilvie smiled as he regained his poise. "What particular lie did you tell her?"

Tompkins hesitated for a few moments. Then he spoke up straight: "Beg pardon, sir, but I told her the truth."

At first Ogilvie felt enraged. "What the mischief —" Then quite suddenly he smiled and shook the butler's wrinkled hand.

"Tompkins," he said, "you're an A Number One peach, and — take it from me — you do know women. Miss Dillon's the sort of girl one just naturally has to tell the truth to. You were right and I was wrong. How did she take it?"

"Well, sir, she took it very bravely. But then, of course, she had had a sort of a warning —"

"Warning! What do you mean?"

And, urged on by the impatient Ogilvie, the stoical old Englishman told him how he had telephoned to Miss Dillon, how suddenly he had decided not to trust his message to the telephone wires, but had made an appointment with her. He had met her in front of the public library. "Yes, sir," he added with a little smile, "I felt quite like I used to forty years ago; asked her to wear a red rose so I'd recognize her." Then he had related to her what had happened to her fiancé. She, on her side, had given him also some rather startling news to communicate to Ogilvie. For late last night — she was living alone in a tiny flat — a messenger had brought her an envelope. She had found in it a check for a hundred thousand dollars, drawn on the Drovers' National Bank, and made out by Martyn Spencer, with a note which she had given to Tompkins to bring to Ogilvie. The latter read:

DEAR LITTLE MARIE:

I haven't seen you since you were a small girl in short skirts and I quite a big boy, just out of college, up at Grandmother Ryerson's old farm in Vermont. But I haven't exactly forgotten you. I have made a lot of money these last few years, and so — please — accept the enclosed check with all my very best cousinly wishes. Don't be a silly little proud fool and refuse it. After all, we are cousins, and you may need the money; or, if not you, then the man you are engaged to marry, Blaine Ogilvie. And criminal lawyers are expensive. Don't call me up or write to me, as I am leaving the country tonight, and not even my office force has the faintest notion where I am bound for.

Yours very cordially,
Martyn S.

The news of Spencer's having left the country was confirmed a few moments later by the police commissioner, who came in filled to the brim with the different reports he had received from his picked detectives, as well as from his expert assayist.

All the reports, according to the police commissioner's system, were in writing, and Detective Sergeant Miller's was explicit:

Martyn Spencer left last night for an unknown destination. I don't know yet whether by train, boat, or automobile. I questioned some of his employees, the help of the Hotel Stentorian, where he has taken a suite by the year, rent paid in advance, his valet, and the elevator starter in his office building. They are all new people whom he has hired since his return to New York, a few months back. They have orders to carry on the work which he has mapped out for them, mostly the selling of various parcels of real estate in the Bronx, and which will take them easily twelve months. Mr. Anthony Hicks, his private secretary, has been given power of attorney over whatever local business Martyn Spencer has in New York, with orders to transmit all money realized to the credit of Martyn Spencer with the branch of the British Linen Bank in Glasgow, Scotland. He has also been entrusted with a large sum banked with the Drovers' National Bank to pay the salaries of the office force and of Spencer's valet for the next eighteen months, as well as for overhead expenses and incidentals. I have started inquiries as to Spencer's former life and shall make a further report tomorrow.

"Found out quite a lot, didn't he?" complimented Blaine Ogilvie.

"Right," agreed the other. "Miller has a persuasive way and X-ray eyes. Oh — wait —" turning over the typewritten sheet. "Here's a postscript;" and he read:

I have furthermore found out that the Bronx real estate which Martyn Spencer has given orders to sell was only acquired by him during the last few months, after his return to America.

The police commissioner shook his head, "I don't see what good that particular bit of information will do us," he commented.

"Don't you?" asked Ogilvie softly.

"Do you?"

"You bet!" came the other's reply. "In fact, I think that, taken in conjunction with the other business details, it's the most interesting and illuminating part of the whole report. I believe it constitutes that mysterious and romantic thing which you fellows of the police call a clue."

"Mind explaining?"

"Not a bit." Ogilvie leaned forward in his chair. "There's been a sudden and tremendous slump in business these last few months, hasn't there?"

"Yes," admitted the other rather sadly. "All my own investments —"

"Everything," interrupted Ogilvie, "has come tumbling down like a house made of cards, and chiefly real estate. There has been no building going on in Manhattan for over three months, isn't that right?"

"Perfectly. And —"

"Why, then, should Martyn Spencer — who is a business man, a mighty shrewd one and as rich as mud — take, for instance, that hundred thousand dollars he sent to Miss Dillon and the twenty thousand he slipped to me — sell at this moment, when prices are down to bed rock, instead of holding on and waiting for a rise? Furthermore, why does he, the wary, careful, farsighted financier, leave his local affairs in the hands of a recently hired office force and give his power of attorney to a youthful and recently acquired private secretary?"

"Well, why? What's the answer?" asked Gadsby impatiently.

"Spencer got away in such a hurry that he didn't care, hadn't time to care, what happened to his business here. And, by the same token, it's evident that he does not intend to return to New York. On the other hand, when he came here, he took a long lease on his office space and on his suite at the Hotel Stentorian — which proves that originally he did intend to make a lengthy stay, perhaps to settle here for good. Therefore, he made up his mind to leave in a hurry, regardless of everything except —"

"His safety?" interjected Gadsby.

"Exactly! Clue, eh?"

"Clue is right!" said the police commissioner, and turned to the next report, O'Neale's, which dealt with the murdered man, Monro Clafflin, and his connection with Doctor McGrath.

O'Neale, too, had worked with efficiency and dispatch. Via the gliding gossip of the back stairs and the pantry and with the help of his honeyed Irish tongue, he had ascertained that Doctor McGrath — the same McGrath, he added incidentally, who had invented the famous McGrath pulmotor — had been Clafflin's physician for a number of years, that practitioner and patient were intimate personal friends, that the latter had been suffering for a long time from a complication of organic diseases, and that — here O'Neale had attached a verbatim report by Miss Maisie Heinz, nurse — he had not been expected to live the year out. For the last eighteen months Clafflin had been in almost continuous pain. The report wound up:

> For the last few weeks Mr. Clafflin appeared a little more cheerful. Once he mentioned to Josiah Higgins, his butler — whose verbatim report I attach — that there was a possibility of his recuperating, as Doctor McGrath had spoken to him about a remarkable young physician whom he wished to consult about the case. Last night Mr. Clafflin left in the doctor's car, coughing badly and evidently in pain, but cheerful and laughing in spite of it. The butler overheard the last conversation between the two. "Monro, old man," had said the doctor, "there's a pretty good chance that you'll be rid of your sufferings for good and all tonight!" "Rather quick cure?" Clafflin had replied, with a smile. "But possible!" had come the doctor's final words.

The police commissioner put down the report, and Ogilvie looked up.

"Bob," he said, "Doctor McGrath's prophecy came true, didn't it?"

"How so?"

"Well, Monro Clafflin did get rid of his sufferings for good and all last night, didn't he? He died!"

"That's one way of putting it," said the police commissioner, and added that he had met O'Neale coming up the Avenue on his way home, and that the latter, in the meantime, had made further investigations about Doctor Hillyer McGrath.

"Did he find out anything interesting?" asked Ogilvie.

"No. He called on the doctor — under some professional pretext, sore throat or something like that — and found him at home. He tells me the doctor lives in an extremely modest little apartment and seems to be a poor man."

"Funny!" commented Ogilvie.

"You mean — because Clafflin, his friend and patient, was rich?"

"No. But I would have imagined that the pulmotor he invented must have brought him in quite a lot of money."

"Perhaps he didn't have it patented," said Gadsby, and turned to the next report.

Detectives Campbell and Wimpflinger had been sent to investigate the hunchback, as well as the five men whom Ogilvie had particularly noticed at No. 17 and with whom he had had the fight.

It was pithy and succinct, and read as follows:

1. Montross D. Clapperton. *Studied in Boston, Paris, and Freiburg. Forty-three years of age. Excellent reputation. Quiet, kindly, charitable. Engineer by profession. Inventor of the Clapperton automatic cream separator and the Clapperton self-adjusting tube wrench. Lives alone, in a modest two-room flat, without servants.*

2. Cornelius van Alstyne. *College man. Twenty-four years of age. Good reputation in his neighborhood, except that his landlady and the small shops where he trades complain that he is very slow to pay. Chemist by profession. Was instrumental in separating and classifying a new metal, called rhizopodin, which may eventually revolutionize and cheapen the entire manufacture of electric globes.*

3. Leopold Fischer. *Studied at Berlin and Vienna, his native town. Thirty-nine years of age. Engineer by profession. Well liked by his neighbors, though he went into bankruptcy last year. Inventor of the Fischer piston pump, the Fischer water gauge, and said to be at work now on a new gyroscope.*

4. Holister Welkin. *Fifty-seven years of age. A native of England. Earlier life unknown. Came here twenty-odd years ago. Lives at Gordon Hotel, evidently in very straitened circumstances. Is a recluse, and nothing could be found out about him except that — according to the proprietor of a hardware store in his neighborhood — he was quite famous, twenty years ago, as the inventor of Welkin's electric windlass.*

5. Audley P. Chester. *Sixty-four years of age. Belongs to the well-known Chester family of Portland, Maine. Very rich, though he lives in a modest hotel of the west forties. Is said to be a miser. The same Chester who was so viciously attacked a year or two ago by certain newspapers for his refusal to contribute to any of the war charities.*

Gadsby folded the report and gave them to his friend.

"Here you have all of it."

"What about the disk?" queried the other. "Did your assayer examine it?"

"Yes. It's made of rhizopodin —"

"Oh, yes — that new metal, which our friend Van Alstyne of the green Norfolk and the buckskin spats separated. I might have known it. What about the other members of the club?"

"Oh, just a repetition of this special list. A few doctors and business men, but mostly engineers with a sprinkling of skilled mechanics."

"All rather poor?" suggested Ogilvie.

"Yes, with the exception of Chester. And all have excellent reputations. We looked up the records as much as we could, and not a single one of them seems to have ever been convicted of a crime or a misdemeanor, not even suspected or accused. And here they go and commit murder and frame you up."

He stopped, then continued:

"I wonder why they call that organization of theirs the Benefactors Club?"

"I don't wonder," replied Ogilvie. "I am beginning to understand."

"Oh — sort of ghoulish self-irony, you mean?"

"Not a bit of it. They are quite sincere — quite, quite sincere! The Benefactors Club! The very name for it!"

"Why?" asked the police commissioner.

"I'll tell you presently," replied the other, and added with cool arrogance, "just as soon as I have cleared up the rest of the case."

Gadsby gave a crooked smile. "The rest of the case?" he repeated in mockery.

"Exactly!"

"Pretty cocksure, aren't you?"

"Yes," said Ogilvie, "Fact is, after I get out of this pickle —"

"If you get out of this pickle!"

"I repeat — after I get out of this pickle, I shall apply to you for a job with the detective force. My boy, I am finding no fault with your methods, your elaborate system —" He pointed at the voluminous reports.

"Thanks!" the police commissioner said dryly.

"But," Ogilvie continued unabashed, "it takes a man like myself to use the information they contain, through a thing called applied psychology."

"And which," interjected the police commissioner, "might with equal truth be styled applied poetry."

"By the way," said the other, "do you happen to know anybody in Washington, in the patent office, some big bug, I mean?"

"Yes."

"Do you know him well enough to get him on the long-distance telephone this time of night and have him look up certain records?"

"Well, yes. In my capacity as police commissioner I can cut a couple of miles of official red tape. Why do you ask?"

"Because I want you to get your Washington party on the wire as quickly as possible. And I want you to introduce me to him over the wires as your confidential assistant — which, I repeat, I am going to become as soon as I'm out of this mess."

"More clues, I suppose?" asked Gadsby ironically.

"As right as rain!"

"But — in Washington?" queried Gadsby, seeing that his friend was serious.

"Yes. You see, I am curious to find out why all these people —" he pointed at the detectives' reports — "are so poor in spite of all their inventions. I want to find out if all of them neglected taking out patents for their brain-children — if they are all plain fools or —"

"Or?"

"Idealists, Bob," said Ogilvie; "members of the Benefactors Club!"

CHAPTER VI.

OGILVIE STATES HIS CASE.

IT WAS nearly three hours later — night had dropped like a veil, secret, mystical, netted in the delicate silver mist of the drifting snowflakes and with the sleepy voice of the city whispering through the heave and sough of the wind — that Blaine Ogilvie, after three long-distance conversations with Washington, finally slammed back the receiver and announced triumphantly:

"That little matter is settled!"

He entered the next room.

"Good thing," he said, "that Spencer slipped me that twenty thousand. Those toll charges to Washington are going to cost me a pretty penny."

Then he noticed that Gadsby was fast asleep in his winged chair in front of the open fire, and shook him awake.

"Bob," he said, "leave off sawing wood and listen to the words of Baruch, the son of the priest."

"What is it?" asked the police commissioner, sitting up and rubbing his eyes.

"I have found out what I expected to find —"

"Namely?"

"That Doctor McGrath, Mr. Clapperton *et alii* are —"

"What?"

"Are not plain fools — unless you call idealists fools!"

"Would you mind being less philosophical and more explicit?" suggested Gadsby.

"That friend of yours at the patent office did a whole lot of tall hustling and doubtless disturbed the slumbers of half a dozen assorted Uncle Sam servants, working all of five hours a day and five days a week for thirty per of the taxpayers' hard-earned simoleons, but he roused them. He hustled and made them do likewise. He looked up dusty files and ledgers and card indexes and cross-reference books and loose-leaved records — and —"

"For the love of Mike! Come to the point!" exclaimed the police commissioner, exasperated.

"I am at the point! They looked up the records of the patent office. Bob — it's really tremendous news!"

"What, what?"

"Not one of the members of the Benefactors Club — neither McGrath nor Clapperton nor that green-tweed addict — failed to take out patents for their various inventions and discoveries. And they are all poor!"

"All except Chester."

"Right," agreed Ogilvie. "But he didn't invent anything!"

"Don't forget Martyn Spencer!"

"Who disappeared," commented Ogilvie, "but who did belong to their club just the same."

"I can't make head or tail of what you are intending to prove. Blaine."

"Intending to, did you say?" asked the other. "Boy, I have proved —"

"What?"

"That here is an organization of people who all have most excellent reputations —"

"Except, perhaps, Spencer —" suggested the police commissioner.

"Who disappeared. Let me resume. This organization is largely composed of engineers and mechanics, many of whom have invented extraordinary devices, others of whom have doubtless helped with the perfecting and working out of these inventions, still others of whom — here's where I take a shot at the blue — are working at inventions and discoveries. They are not fools. But they seem to be idealists. For they have protected their brain-children by patents — by the way, Bob, it takes money to get the right, waterproof sort of patent — and they have not made money out of their inventions, since they are all poor."

"Except two."

"Exactly — Chester and Spencer! As to the latter, allow me to repeat that he disappeared suddenly, scared to death, sacrificing a mint of money in doing so, while the former — well, Bob, I have an idea on the subject and I am going to find out presently if I am right."

The police commissioner lit a cigar.

"And still I fail to see," he objected, "how all these undoubtedly very interesting details will help you sidestep the electric chair?"

"Don't be so brutally realistic. Also, if you can't see, I can — chiefly after you have called in some of our best New York physicians and have them make another autopsy of Monro Clafflin's body."

"What for? The man was shot. A bullet pierced his brain. There's no doubt of it."

Ogilvie smiled.

"Perfectly correct," he admitted. "The man was shot — and a bullet did pierce his brain."

"Then —"

"Just the same, please do what I tell you, do you mind?"

"Well, if you insist on being mysterious —"

"I don't insist," replied Ogilvie, "But, first of all, there are your professional limitations which would keep you from understanding anything new and a little unorthodox."

"Thanks awfully!" came the dry rejoinder.

"Don't mention it. Secondly, I am dog-tired. I am off to bed." He rose, yawned, stretched himself, "Lend me a book, do you mind?"

The police commissioner crossed over to his bookshelves. "I don't see," he said, "how a man in your predicament can read frivolous French poetry. Why — it's positively uncanny."

"I'm not going to read any French poetry tonight," replied Ogilvie. "You have quite a complete library, haven't you?"

"Fairly representative."

"I want you to find me a book — oh — a sort of encyclopedia, all about inventions and discoveries."

"Going to join the Benefactors Club?"

"Possibly. I want a book about the inventions and devices people used to know centuries ago, but which have been forgotten — like the use of the pyramids and the tempering of copper and that sort of thing."

"More clues?" came the ironic query as Gadsby hunted among the shelves.

"You've guessed it first time, old man."

"Here's the kind of book you mean, I suppose," said Gadsby, taking out two volumes — "*Forgotten Discoveries* and *Valuable Inventions Not Yet Made*."

"That's the dope!" replied Ogilvie, taking both. "By the way, think it'll be safe to telephone to Miss Dillon?"

"Quite. The police haven't yet discovered that the escaped murderer's name is Blaine Ogilvie and that he is engaged to her. Feel in a sentimental mood and want to phone?"

"No — in a scientific mood."

And he went upstairs to bed and read for a while. Finally he seemed to have found what he was after. For he made a note, called up Marie Dillon on the telephone which stood on his night table, talked for quite a while, then switched off the electric light and fell into dreamless, untroubled sleep.

HE CAME down to breakfast fairly late to find the police commissioner impatiently awaiting him. The latter looked up rather angrily as the other entered with a bright "Good morning!" For, like most men of average honesty and average dyspepsia, he had occasional, spasmodic attack of antagonism even against his best friends — chiefly before breakfast.

"Heavens!" he exclaimed. "I could hear you snore clear down here. Detective Sergeant Miller asked me if I had a walrus visiting me."

"Oh! Has he been here?"

"Yes — confound his soul!" came the heated rejoinder. "He came an hour ago — before breakfast! Called me out of bed!"

"What did he want? Anything that bears on my case?"

"Yes. He found out quite a little more about Martyn Spencer,"

"Let's hear it," said Ogilvie, neatly slicing a muffin in two, buttering it generously, and commencing breakfast with a hearty appetite, which Gadsby seemed to take as a personal affront.

Detective Sergeant Miller was the old-fashioned policeman, the sort whose sources of information are diversified, patchy, and often — if the truth be told — slightly muddy. The tale he had told his chief, and which the latter was now relating to Blaine Ogilvie, was a mosaic gathered here and there, partly by bullying and partly by cajoling, from a number of people, including two taxi-cab drivers, a Sicilian fruit vender, a Russian cobbler in a cellar on Charles Street, the head waiter of a Broadway restaurant, three sardonic and elderly reporters, one youthful and enthusiastic cub reporter, and the intoxicated mate of a disreputable Liverpool tramp ship that had just docked, after a smelly and uneventful voyage out of some West African port. The sum total of this information was that a man, closely resembling Martyn Spencer, had been seen going up the gangplank of another, equally smelly and equally disreputable Liverpool freighter, outward bound, dressed in the rough clothes of a deep-sea sailor, that he had been greeted by the captain of the ship with: "So glad to see you, sir. Please, sir, won't you —" And that he had interrupted roughly with; "Cut it out, you poor fool! I am Tom Higgins, able-bodied seaman, and that's all you know —"

"Disguise and change of name," said Ogilvie, a little disappointed. "But nothing new — it really only corroborates my theory that Spencer is scared clear out of his wits."

"Yes," agreed the police commissioner, "but Miller also did a bit of cabling over to London — to Scotland Yard."

"What results?"

"He found out how Martyn Spencer made his money," said the police commissioner with pompous impressiveness.

Ogilvie laughed. "Why," he said, "I know how he made it."

"Oh — you do — you —"

"Yes," Ogilvie cut the other's words short.

"How?" asked Gadsby with satanic suavity. "Let's hear how clever you are."

"I am not clever. I only know that two and two makes four — and, at times, five," he said. "And chiefly in detective work — naturally so. For, since crimes are an extraordinary, and not an ordinary, thing, one must apply extraordinary, and not ordinary, logic and arithmetic."

"After which philosophic interjection —"

"After which philosophic interjection," said Ogilvie with a laugh, "I rise to maintain that Spencer, since he left New York, did a heap of traveling in the wilder places of the Earth — Africa, Central Asia, Western China, South America, certain regions of Russia. Why there? Because, since he was out after new, exotic, and expensive minerals difficult to obtain, he specialized in mineral regions that had not yet been exploited. Why did he need those minerals? Because the gentlemen of the Benefactors Club needed them for their new inventions, discoveries, and devices. So he kicked around a whole lot and bought up mining claims and concessions. Often he had to use a great deal of pull — pull which, on the other hand, cost him a great deal of money. With West African chiefs, for instance, and Manchu mandarins and Tartar Khans — and — oh, yes —" smiling reminiscently — "Russian grand duchesses who, if extra well paid, extra well bribed, might throw in a priceless sable coat as a commission. Isn't that so?"

"Absolutely!" admitted the other just a little grudgingly. "But I fail to see how —"

"I repeat," said Ogilvie, "that two and two make five — and occasionally seven!"

"Don't be so supercilious!"

"Really, Bob, I didn't mean to be. Let's get back to Martyn Spencer. He was well paid for these voyages and these mining claims he accumulated the world over — by whom do you think?"

"Chester?"

"Move to the head of the class, sonny! By the millionaire who did not see fit to contribute to the war charities, but who, according to his own light, is quite a public benefactor. But Martyn Spencer was not rich. You see, you can work out your liver, but you simply can't become really rich on a straight salary — until rather more recently. Am I still right, old man?"

"Quite. That's what they cabled to Miller from Scotland Yard." Something like admiration had crept into Gadsby's accents.

"Perhaps," continued Ogilvie, "our friend only started making real money during the last year or eighteen months. Then he made it hand over fist."

"How?"

"By selling the foreign rights to various patents which were registered in his name."

"What patents?" asked the police commissioner.

"Oh — for instance. Doctor McGrath's pulmotor and the Clapperton automatic cream separator and the Fischer piston pump. He either sold them for cash or took a certain amount in the stock of the new foreign corporations founded for the exploitation of these various patents and devices."

"Perfectly correct," admitted Gadsby, consulting a London cable which Miller had decoded and read:

> Martyn Spencer, chairman of the board of directors of Pulmotor Limited, Rhizopodin Produce Limited, Clapperton —

"Cream Separator Limited," interrupted Ogilvie, "and a few more Limited!"

To the other's question if he thought that the Benefactors Club, angry at having been cheated, had tried to frame up Martyn Spencer, getting Ogilvie into the trap by mistake, the latter replied that it was something like it, but not exactly so.

"That's just what Martyn Spencer thought," he added, "and I have an idea, yet to be proved, that he was a fool for thinking so, a fool for running away scared to death, when all he had to do was to keep his nerve and stand pat, when all he needed was a little knowledge of applied psychology. You see, it is clear that these people did not know him by sight, isn't it?"

"Quite," said the police commissioner, "or they would not have mistaken you for him."

"Yes. I imagine the club has a number of foreign members and corresponding members in Europe."

"Indeed," agreed Gadsby, consulting the cables from Scotland Yard.

"There are half a dozen belonging to it in London —"

"And doubtless in Paris and Rome and other parts of the world. Spencer, though an American, joined abroad. It's easy enough to figure out how. He must have made some small invention. He was poor then. His family, fine old American stock, knows the Chesters. Followed a correspondence between him and Audley Chester, the financial backer of the club. Gradually the correspondence became more intimate. Eventually Chester made him a proposition, and Spencer accepted it and joined. Then, when the club needed a man to pick up mining claims for them here and there, they naturally thought of Spencer. He proved clever and valuable, until in the course of time he became their confidential man, all the foreign rights to the patents being registered in his name. Spencer kicked about from pillar to post these last years, without coming home; and these people never went abroad, because they were too poor and too much wrapped up in their Utopian dreams."

"Utopian?" echoed the police commissioner.

"Exactly! I'll explain all that presently — after I've made quite, quite sure — with the help of —"

"Who?"

"Marie Dillon, I guess. I'll tell you later. Let's get back to Spencer. He and the members of his club here in New York never saw each other, that's quite clear, isn't it?"

"I guess so. But why did he return? Homesickness?"

"Not a bit of it. Indirect, upside down, negative, vicarious fear!"

"I don't get you!"

"Listen, Bob!" Ogilvie went on, "When Spencer first decided to use these patents for the benefit of his own pocketbook — well, he just did it. He was money mad — he made up his mind — and that's all there was to it! He expected a big row, perhaps a civil or criminal action. He had prepared for these eventualities, had retained beforehand the best legal talent in New York and Europe, felt quite safe. But the members of the Benefactors Club did —"

"What?"

"Nothing, Bob! And that's what first made him afraid."

"Why should it?" asked the police commissioner.

"Because Spencer knew them. He knew what sort of people they were — idealists, terribly sincere, of single-track minds — and they did nothing. And, I repeat, he became frightened, nervous, uneasy. Do you know the old adage about the murderer who always returns to the scene of his crime? I guess it applies in Spencer's case, too. He grew more and more fidgety as the club remained silent, and so he decided to come to New York, perhaps to force their hand, to brazen it out, or to get it over with, once and for all. And still, even after he returned here, the club did nothing. They surrounded Spencer with a wall of complete, inhuman silence and inaction, and he became more and more uneasy — he imagined that this wall of silence would presently topple over and crush him. Then, one day — perhaps the very day I called on him or a few days before — he received a notification from the club to come to No. 17.

"By this time he was absolutely scared stiff. He imagined that they would either kill him or make such a scene that somebody would lose his head; in the latter case he thought there would be a fight, he would find himself in a minority of one, battling for his life, and then in self-defense, but with a number of witnesses to deny it, he would draw a weapon. This part of his reasoning —"

"If he reasoned that way," sardonically interrupted the other.

"This part of his reasoning," Ogilvie continued, unheeding, "was remarkably lucid. You see, Spencer is no fool."

"If he isn't, why did he go to No. 17 — make up his mind to go there at all?" demanded the police commissioner.

"Because he was getting crazy with that complicated and illogical emotion called fear. Because he had arrived at that stage where he preferred anything, even death, to waiting for something to happen. All right. I dropped in on him. We talked. He saw that I was stone-broke. Right then, suddenly, he decided not to go, but to send me instead. He must have reasoned very quickly, must have said to himself that the only thing for him to do, now that the club was on his trail and had sent him notification to appear at their meeting, was to disappear under a different name, and there was that Liverpool freighter in port which doubtless belonged to him.

"He argued that the club members would pounce upon me quickly and kill me before I had a chance to explain that they were making a mistake, that I was not he, but an innocent party. Or, if they gave me time to explain, he thought they would calmly point at the club badge — which must have been fastened to the nether side of the lapel of the fur coat, remember — might even point at the sable-lined ulster itself, a quite extraordinary and priceless garment of whose acquisition by Spencer, in the course of some mining deal with the grand duchess, they may have heard — yes — they would have pointed at the club badge and discounted my denial that I was Spencer by a sudden desire on my part to bluff them, to fool them, to get away with a whole skin. Finally, he reasoned, if they did believe me, it would take a long time before they did. Either way, by the time I was killed, or got into the pickle into which I actually did get, or even persuaded them they had made a mistake, he would have escaped. Incidentally let's give the devil his due. He tried to be decent. He warned me against carrying a gun. But, not sure if I would take his advice, he sent that thumping big check to Marie in case she needed money for herself or me.

"At all events, as to the club members, he underestimated their intelligence, or he overestimated their brutality — it comes to the same thing. I repeat, all he needed was a little knowledge of applied psychology —"

Ogilvie interrupted himself.

He said that terribly idealistic people — and in his own mind he was convinced that those of No. 17 belonged in that category, from the hunchback down to the check boy and the brown-eyed girl — were also, when occasion seemed to warrant it, terribly cruel and shrewd and vindictive. It was as if, he added, the Creator did not want human virtues to run to extremes, for fear that they might run amuck. "Nature," he said, "always tries to strike a logical balance between good and bad. If we let our virtues overwhelm us we cease to feel sympathy and pity and tolerance for others less virtuous than ourselves. No, no, Bob," as the other made an impatient exclamation, "I'm not shooting off at a tangent. I am just trying to show you what a confounded fool Martyn Spencer was for being afraid."

"Seems to me, the way it panned out, that he had mighty good cause to be afraid," replied the other. "I agree with you that excessive goodness often leads to cruelty. Aristotle was right, virtue is the mean between two extremes. Witness the cruelty of the medieval reformers."

"But you must not forget that these people at No. 17 are removed from sixteenth-century fanatics by several hundred years of human development — call it increased moral weakness, if you prefer. They are men of the twentieth century who have forgotten the clean, fearless brutalities of the Middle Ages. When their slightly hectic, idealistic virtues turned into the gall of hatred through another's — Spencer's guilt — they were weak enough or careful enough — it comes to the same thing — to stop short of murder. You see, they might have killed Spencer, but they didn't. So why, logically, should I assume that they killed Clafflin?"

"Well — if you didn't kill him, and if they didn't, who did, for the love of Mike?"

"Must, necessarily, anybody have killed him?" came Ogilvie's counter query.

"You don't mean to say suicide?" asked the police commissioner.

"I don't indeed!"

"Or accident?"

"Nor accident!"

"Well, what other possibility —"

"Beg pardon," interrupted Tompkins, who had come in. "Miss Dillon to see Mr. Ogilvie."

CHAPTER VII.

"NEITHER BY MURDER, SUICIDE, NOR ACCIDENT."

DIRECTLY ON the butler's heels Marie Dillon entered.

"Oh — Blaine! Blaine, dear!"

She threw herself into Ogilvie's arms and held him tight, quite disregarding the presence of the police commissioner, who after a moment or two, when a discreet, twice repeated cough had seemed to have made no impression on the girl, moved in the direction of the door with a rambled word that he hated to be in the way.

She turned. "Please, Mr. Gadsby," she said, "forgive me, won't you?" She smiled, and he smiled back at her.

"There is nothing to forgive, Miss Dillon," he replied, "except that instead of falling in love with a perfectly proper and perfectly respectable police commissioner —"

"She wastes her young affections on a reckless idiot who is going to become said police commissioner's chief assistant and confidential clerk," Ogilvie interrupted.

The girl laughed and kissed Ogilvie again.

She was small and strong, with russet, short-cut hair. You could tell by looking at her rather large, firm, well-shaped hands, her short, softly curved nose, and the straight black eyebrows which divided her gray eyes from the broad, low forehead that she had imagination and claims to independent ideas.

"Have you any influence over Blaine?" asked Gadsby in a martyred voice.

"How?"

"To make him less fresh!"

"I'll try to," she said, "after we're married."

The next moment she was serious and turned to Ogilvie. "Blaine," she said, "I did what you asked me to do last night over the telephone."

"Already?"

"Yes, dear. I got up early."

"Succeed?"

"I guess so," she replied.

And, in answer to Gadsby's questions, Ogilvie explained that he had telephoned to Marie Dillon last night, after he had hunted through the two volumes on forgotten and not yet discovered inventions.

"I hesitated a long time," he said, "between the absolute, fool-proof gyroscope, the tempering of copper, and a self-adjusting linotype machine. Finally I decided that no woman takes an interest in that sort of thing, and that it might make the whole thing look fishy. Woman, I thought, housewifely duties — sewing machine! And so, in my poor male brain, I studied it, I decided that what the world needs is a new device which will sew on trouser buttons by a simple twist of the wrist — something like that. I wrote it all down — a lot of stuff — enough to fool a chap who isn't an engineer, but only a rich visionary — prompted Marie across the wires, and she went there this morning — didn't you, honey?"

"Yes," replied the girl.

"Went where?" asked the exasperated police commissioner.

"Where do you think? To Audley Chester! To whom else?"

It appeared that the Chesters and the Dillons were old friends, as were the Chesters and the Dillons' cousins, Martyn Spencer's family. And so, asked Ogilvie, wasn't it perfectly natural that Marie Dillon, being poor, should go to her family's rich friend, Audley Chester, to ask him for advice and help with that marvelous invention of hers; and too, perhaps, though without saying so since she was not supposed to be familiar with Chester's connection with the Benefactors Club, indirectly, by mental suggestion, get the idea into Chester's brain that, as a budding inventress, she might be promising material for a member of the club which, added Ogilvie, had at least one other woman member — the brown-eyed Slav girl who presided over the hat rack at No. 17?

"Good heavens, man!" exclaimed Gadsby. "You certainly drew a long bow! How did you imagine you'd get away with it? Didn't you consider that Chester, chiefly since the Clafflin murder, might suspect a trap?"

"Not in the least," replied Ogilvie. "Marie and I talked it all out over the telephone last night, point for point, logically and psychologically. We figured out the exact part she was going to play. An idealistic young enthusiast — can't you see her, with those wide gray eyes of hers? All for giving the benefit of her brain, her work, her invention, to the public, the world at large, long-suffering, long-overcharged humanity — and not so as to line her own pockets with gold! You see, these last forty-eight hours I've been considering what sort of people the gentry at No. 17 are — chiefly Audley Chester. So I couldn't very well go wrong, could I?"

"And you didn't," said Marie Dillon, "Chester was awfully kind and considerate and patient. He listened to me. Told me he would be glad to back me financially if my invention turned out feasible, that he knew very little, though, about mechanical details, and would therefore find me some expert engineers and skilled mechanics to go over my plans, report on them, and help me, if practicable, with working them out and perfecting them —"

"Don't you see, Bob?" interrupted Ogilvie. "That's where the club members come in."

"Yes, yes," came the other's slightly impatient rejoinder. "You needn't cross all the t's nor dot all the i's. Once in a while, when a thing is as plain as a pikestaff, I can see it — even though I am only the police commissioner."

"Stop your quarreling, both you children!" said the girl. "Chester was delighted when I told him that I wanted to give my idea to the world, that I did not wish for any personal remuneration —"

"Except the satisfaction of a decent thing decently accomplished — did you get in that line, Marie?" asked Ogilvie. "Remember — we rehearsed it last night over the telephone."

"I did," replied Marie Dillon, "and I improved on it on the spur of the moment. I said something to him about poverty not mattering as long as I knew that the rest of the world found life a little more easy to bear through my invention."

"Like the rest of the benefactors," commented Ogilvie, "Their idealism! That's what kept them so poor, and that's just why they are so terribly vindictive against Martyn Spencer. It wasn't really because he cheated them, stole money from them by appropriating their patents for his private use, but because he stole it, as they figured, from the public, the world, humanity at large."

Marie Dillon went on to say that toward the end of the interview Audley Chester, carried away by her carefully rehearsed, girlish enthusiasm, had become even more confidential. He had told her of the existence of an organization composed of people — as he expressed it — trying to do social uplift work not, as usually attempted, by giving money, thus pauperizing those whom they were trying to help, but by using their inventive brains and faculties so as to reduce the cost of living and to make life easier for the masses.

"If somebody invents, for instance, a new mangle," he had explained, "which reduces time and effort of labor by fifty per cent and incidentally does not ruin the linen or cotton which it rolls and smoothes, such an article, ordinarily, would cost the price of manufacture plus the overhead, plus the profit to the company which manufactures it, and plus the royalty to the inventor. We cannot always regulate the profit which the manufacturing company demands. But we can always influence it by giving our invention to a company which is more reasonable, and we always do cut out our own royalties, reducing the cost by just that amount to the poor woman who needs the mangle. We, as an organization, make therefore a gift to the people at large, not of money — no, no, no! We don't believe in that — but of our brains, our talents. We are the world's real benefactors!"

At the next meeting of this organization, he had gone on, he would mention the matter to the other members, and they would talk it over together. He had added that they had to be very strict and careful about whom to admit to their circle, because, on the very face of it, they had to rely absolutely on the honesty of each individual member. "Mutual trust is our motto," he had wound up, "and the moment anybody breaks this trust —"

"What happens then?" Marie Dillon had asked casually, but with enough of a shade of feminine curiosity to make the question appear natural.

And Ogilvie had smiled disagreeably. "We rely on fate to punish him," he had replied. "Fate — possibly helped by — oh — deputy fate!"

"Deputy fate?" she had queried.

"Yes," had come Audley Chester's slow reply, "After all, even fate is more or less man-made. And — don't forget — we have in our organization some very great inventors, some very great physicians and surgeons and biologists!"

"Such as Doctor Hillyer McGrath," commented Blaine Ogilvie, "who had been Clafflin's physician for many, many years and knew all about the state of his health."

"What gets me," said the police commissioner, shaking his head, "is how any member of the Benefactors Club, be he the very cleverest physician, surgeon, inventor, or biologist in the world, can stage manage a death, clearly caused by a revolver bullet, since Clafflin's temples were pierced, which is neither due to murder nor to suicide nor to accident — to believe you," and he turned to Ogilvie.

"You'll believe me all right after your expert doctors at headquarters get through with the autopsy on Clafflin's body," replied the latter, "or I lose my bet."

"What bet?" asked Gadsby.

"Oh — long odds! My life against the district attorney's wits! For, of course, I realize that you can't keep me in hiding forever."

"Oh — please — please — Blaine!" exclaimed the girl, suddenly nervous and frightened.

"Don't worry, honey!" Ogilvie said. "I'm not worrying. Let's see — one hundred thousand bucks Martyn Spencer sent you. That'll get you a peach of a trousseau." He interrupted himself and turned to Gadsby.

"Look here, Bob," he said. "Show a little delicacy and leave the room when an engaged couple talk about intimate details. Too, you might run down to your office and see how that autopsy came out!"

IT WAS quite late in the afternoon when the police commissioner returned, accompanied by two men, whom he introduced as Doctor Elliot and Doctor Griffith, and — "Miss Dillon, and Mr. Blaine Ogilvie, the man who —"

"The commissioner told us about you," said Doctor Elliot, shaking hands with Ogilvie.

"Did he blacken my reputation?" demanded Ogilvie with a twinkle in his eye. "Did he tell you a long sob story of how I, a fugitive from justice, a supposedly crimson-handed assassin, took refuge in his house and caused him to be false to his sworn duty?"

"He did," said Doctor Elliot with a laugh.

"Heavens! I'm surprised he tried to put that one across!" said Ogilvie.

"But he has reformed," interjected the other doctor. "Mr. Ogilvie, let me be the first to tell you the good news. You are a free man. You can come and go where and as you please. You are no longer under suspicion."

"Which means you finished the autopsy and you found out —"

"Well, what did we find out?"

"That the revolver bullet which pierced Clafflin's temples was fired after the man had died," said Ogilvie. "That he died by natural causes, neither by murder, suicide, nor accident!"

"How did you figure it out?" asked the police commissioner with admiration.

"Why, you chump, I was trying to tell you straight along! Simply by figuring out the psychology of the case — the peculiar psychology of the gang of idealists at No. 17 — Clapperton and McGrath and —"

"Incidentally," cut in Doctor Elliot, "it's that same McGrath whom you have to thank for the fact that you are free from all suspicion."

"Oh," asked Marie, "he confessed?"

"We didn't see him," said Doctor Elliot, "nor would he have had anything to confess. But Mr. Ogilvie has to thank McGrath for another of his marvelous medical discoveries, namely an instrument which, used during an autopsy, registers almost automatically to what cause death has been due. If death apparently has been due to more than one cause, it decides between them and points at the right one.

"It's the most delicate instrument you ever saw. You lay people wouldn't understand it. It looks rather like a tiny barometer, with a number of needles composed of a new metal. This metal has a great deal to do with the success of the instrument, since it has a peculiar, almost uncanny, power over blood circulation and blood pressure. It can, so to speak, catch the reflex action of blood even after death. The metal is called rhizopolin.

"We used the instrument," continued the doctor, "and we discovered that death was due to heart failure, while the heart failure, in its turn, was due to a complication of organic troubles which had ravaged poor Clafflin and had sapped his vitality for a number of years."

"Exactly," said Ogilvie. "And McGrath had been Clafflin's physician for a long time. He could read the state of his health — marvelous physician that he is — with the same ease as I can read a simple book. He took him to No. 17 that night. Everything had been minutely prearranged, minutely dovetailed. They were sure that Spencer would come. Perhaps Spencer telephoned or wrote them that he would, and, beforehand, I mean before arranging for the date of Spencer's coming, McGrath had mathematically figured out that Clafflin would die that night — perhaps, though I don't know, kept him alive with powerful drugs until that very night."

"Medically quite possible," commented Doctor Griffith.

"He got Clafflin out of the house," went on Ogilvie, "under the promise — remember the testimony of Clafflin's nurse and butler — that he would meet a remarkable young physician who would cure him. All right; they came. I, whom they supposed to be Spencer, was there. Clafflin died suddenly. McGrath, the great physician, and absolutely, intimately familiar with the man's state of health, saw it at once, gave the signal, when I happened to be looking the other way. Then the shot, either fired by McGrath himself or by somebody else — it makes no difference — and there you are."

"Except," said the police commissioner, "that I believe you have a clear case against the Benefactors Club for trying to frame you up. In fact, I think it is really my duty to —"

"Forget your duty!" interrupted Ogilvie. "After all, they are idealists, public benefactors, and they can't and shouldn't be measured with the ordinary yardstick of police morality. Just you go down there, Bob, to No. 17 some night and throw a good scare into them. By the way, how about that job as assistant something-or-other with your detective force you promised me?"

"I didn't promise," said Gadsby, "but you're on, old man."

"Thanks!" Ogilvie turned to Marie Dillon. "Shake hands with my new boss, honey," he said, "and smile at him. I need all the pull I can get in my new profession. My first job will be to trace Spencer and hand him the accumulated dividends of the Benefactors Club."

The Yellow Wife

A HOT, moist crack of August wind broke through the window, flaring the gas-jet to a forked, yellow flicker, painting bloated, malicious shadows on ceiling and walls and furniture, clattering the unfastened shutters without, and fluttering the plum-blue silk under Chung-hsi's nimble fingers — the plum-blue robe of state embroidered with moonbeams, scarlet butterflies, and chrome-yellow roses, which belonged to Fanny, the daughter of Nag Hong Fah, proprietor of the Great Shanghai Chop Suey Palace, and the second wife of Chung-hsi's husband, Yeh Ming-shen, the wealthy wholesale tea-merchant.

Fanny would wear the robe tomorrow over a fourteen-and-a-half-dollar tailor-made serge bought on Grand Street, and topped by a home-made, sleazy, three-dollar straw-and-maline toque, when the little son she had borne her lord and master four months earlier would be christened in the Baptist Mission Chapel around the corner on Mott Street, with Miss Edith Rutter, the social-settlement investigator, acting as godmother, and Chung-hsi herself as dry-nurse.

For the latter's marriage, performed in Los Angeles nineteen years back, had been Chinese, from the shooting of giant firecrackers to the tossing of the quilt, from the proper obeisances in front of the ancestral tablets to the priest fumigating the bride's finery over a charcoal brazier and chanting the ceremonious words:

"A thousand eyes, ten thousand eyes, I sift out; gold and silver, pearls and diamonds, wealth and precious things, I sift in!"

Complete the wedding had been, in every detail and ancient ritual, but Chinese; while Fanny's marriage to Yeh Ming-shen had been Christian, American — and, by the same token, legal.

All this was unknown to Miss Edith Rutter, who, for nearly three decades, had been groping at the elusive fringes of the Mongol soul; unknown to Bill Devoy, the detective, whose honest Irish feet had become almost furtive walking the padded slime of the Chinatown beat; unknown to all the whites of the neighborhood. They knew Chung-hsi only as the respectable and elderly tea-merchant's respectable and elderly housekeeper.

II.

BUT ALL the yellow boys knew.

They knew that Chung-hsi was the "great" wife of Yeh Ming-shen; that she was still *kuei jen*, the "honorable person," though it was Fanny who was entered on the marriage register as Mrs. Ming-shen. Moreover, they were all familiar with the reason, and approved of it, on moral as well as on sociological grounds.

For Chung-hsi had borne no man-child to her husband, not even a daughter; and it was proper that he should have married again.

"It is your duty," had said Yu Ch'ang, the priest of the joss temple, acting as official spokesman for the Azure Dragon Trading Company, of which Ming-shen was president. "You are the most respectable burgess in Pell Street. You are a shining example for our younger men; and there is nothing quite so unfilial as to have no children."

"It is your duty," had said Nag Hong Fah, the restaurant proprietor, quoting a rude Cantonese river proverb. "For if you have no children, you will have no one to burn sacred paper for you at the Feast of Universal Rescue."

"It is your duty," had said Nag Hop Fat, the soothsayer. "For you need a son to pacify the little devils who follow when your dead body will be buried in its charming retreat, while your soul will be leaping the Dragon Gate."

"It is your duty," had said Quong Mah, his mother-in-law. "For a man without a son is like a finely dressed person walking in the dark, like a learned man without nobility of character, like a cloud without rain."

"It is your duty," had said Yung Long, the wholesale grocer, when Yeh Ming-shen, who loved Chung-hsi with a slow, passive sort of love, had tried to rebel against the Pell Street dictum — epitome of the Chinese creed that the individual is a negligible nothing, while the family, including its unborn children and its dead and buried progenitors, is an unbreakable entity. "Love itself is a shadow. Love, without the fruit of children, is a flattened flower, a breath of wind flitting into the dark, an infidel act, a stinking, spent candle, a diamond fallen into a refuse-heap."

"A diamond fallen into a refuse-heap is nonetheless precious," Yeh Ming-shen had argued.

"But you will muddy your hand to your wrist fishing it out, wise and older brother!" had come the grocer's reply. "Love without children is an indecency and a blasphemy, especially condemned by Tzeng Tzu, the great philosopher. Love without children is like the aim of the archer who misses a hairbreadth at the bow — and a mile at the butt."

"Fate!" Yeh Ming-shen had remonstrated rather weakly. "It is not the fault of the spring-time that the leafless tree does not bring forth leaves. It is not the fault of the sun that the owl cannot see by daylight. It is not the fault of the cloud that the rain does not drop into the mouth of the cuckoo. Who can interfere with what fate has written on the foreheads of all of us?"

Yung Long had smiled.

"Fate?" he had echoed ironically. "When I see you, strong and rich and well-fleshed and not yet fifty; when I look down Pell Street and behold the little buds of plum and lotus that grow and giggle on every painted balcony — then I say that there is no fate as long as a man has his loins and a woman soft lips. Take another wife unto yourself, wise and older brother!"

"'A lack of harmonious subjection spills the tea!'" Yeh Ming-shen had quoted. "The little buds of plum and lotus you speak of are for-eign-born, American-born. Their ideas are curiously independent and immoral. Their perception of what love is is abominable. Such a little bud will not be satisfied with being the pearl-wife. She will want to be the gold-wife. She will demand that I divorce Chung-hsi — whom I love."

"There are still some buds brought up in the good ways, the old ways, the ways of our fathers."

"Perhaps; but who? I spend my life between my office and my home. I know nothing of buds. Who will act as go-between?"

"There is decency and orthodox fastidiousness in such matters, wise and older brother. Ask your wife. It is both her right and her duty to choose the mother of your children. Also, having lived in close intimacy with you for many years, she will know what type of woman is best for your honorable happiness."

III.

WHEN FINALLY, overwhelmed by the massive surge of Pell Street public opinion, Yeh Ming-shen had given in and had told Chung-hsi that he would take a second wife — that he would "sip vinegar," as he had expressed it — she, too, had said that it was his duty.

"I myself shall pick her out," she had added. "A stout, full-breasted, wide-hipped woman. A girl who will bear men children to you."

"And to you, old woman!" Yeh Ming-shen had rejoined.

"To both of us. My withered heart craves for the feel of soft, warm, selfish, helpless little baby hands. I shall love your second wife for the sake of the children she will bear."

And that night, while Chung-hsi was paying observantly ceremonious visits to several Chinese women of her acquaintance who had marriageable daughters, Yeh Ming-shen, speaking to the priest over the spiced cups of the liquor-store which belonged to the Chin Sor Company, and was known as the Place of Sweet Desire and Heavenly Entertainment, had said that a good wife condensed in her soul the wisdom of the three faiths of China — the faith of Buddha, the faith of Confucius, and the faith of *tao*.

"For," he had added, "such a woman's heart holds the essence of the three great sages' teachings: *li*, which is the ultimate law of right action; *chu*, which is the golden rule of tolerance and equity; and *chuntz*, which is good morals."

"Pooh!" had sneered the priest, whose domestic bickerings were a byword in Pell Street. "The titmouse held up its feet so that the sky might not fall upon it and crush it; and the tailless ox attempted to push away the elephant with the strength of its back. Both tried the impossible — as does the fool who prates of the soul of woman. Consider her body, and only her body. Kiss her, or beat her, but do not think about her. Do not thresh straw. Do not paint a picture on running water."

Yeh Ming-shen had smiled, serene in his and Chung-hsi's mutual affection, and after a careful survey, a great deal of close bargaining, and questions asked with that mixture of sudden, brutal directness and flowery, archaic ceremonialism which means good breeding to the Mongol, she had found a second wife for her husband — Fanny, the seventeen-year-old daughter of Nag Hong Fah, who, in spite of the white blood inherited from her mother, had been trained in the Chinese manner.

Fanny had submitted without much argument.

"Betcha sweet life!" she had said to Gwendolyn Wah Yat, her chum, like herself a half-caste with golden hair and slanting eyes, and like herself familiar since early youth with the smug reek, the tame conveniences, the hot, secret passions of the Pell Street world. "I know wot's goin' on. I can hear the fleas cough. But — Gawd! — all men are alike, ain't they? Sure. Po-ly-gam-wotyecallit?" She had learned the word and its meaning in Miss Edith Rutter's sociological classes. "They're all po-ly-gams, white and yeller and polka-dotted — sure Mike! But them Chinks is decent about it, y'understand. They owns up to it like little men — among themselves, that is. They don't do it just out o' beast wickedness as them Bowery toughs do, and give the goil the doity end o' the stick. And then I'm sorta fond of Yeh. He's nice and solid and — oh, smooth, like some piece of Chinee silk, see? And his old goil ain't so bad — and, say, she's a swell cook. You oughta taste the way she fixes up duck cooked sweet and sour! Take it from me, kid, this three-in-one is goin' to pan out all right, all right!"

And it had, from the very first, thought Chung-hsi, as she bent over her work.

Of course, Fanny was young, and had the sweeping sublimity and selfishness of youth. She had done little of the household work; she had run off to the motion-picture theater around the corner on the Bowery, night after night; she had occasionally caused Chung-hsi to lose face by a thoughtless word; she had a vague and sketchy way of washing and dressing — alien to Chung-hsi's meticulous Chinese soul — and a strong perfume followed her wherever she went.

Moreover, at times Chung-hsi had been jealous.

But — had she?

Jealous of that frothy, tinkly, golden-haired little half-caste?

She threaded her needle with twisted gold, looked up, out, into the rushing, wailing silence of the night, punctured by the gliding of slippered feet, an eerie Cantonese song, staccato stammering, a soft clash of crockery from the Great Shanghai Chop Suey Palace across the way, where Pell Street plays follow-the-leader with the Bowery, the singsong of a Chinese voice speaking in English with passionate laboriousness:

"Sure I'll be good to you — damn good — Malie —"

"You better, old yeller-face! You better, you old Chinky sweet-meat!"

A smacking kiss and a policeman's obscene laughter; and Chung-hsi smiled.

Jealous of — *that*?

Voices and laughter slurred into the thick, reeking night. The wind collapsed, beaten by the heat. The padded, slippered feet shuffled away mysteriously, nastily. The silence clogged, choked.

Then, again, clanking, jarring, shrieking, maniacal, the night noises — the Elevated shooting past in its screaming, brassy modernity; a beer-bottle smashing against the pavement; the asthmatic hiss of a pop-corn wagon; a curse — once more voices.

"I'm clazy about you, Malie."

"All right, yeller-face! We'll make it a go, sure."

"Clazy — clazy —"

Again the wind broke, again collapsed. The gas-jet straightened, jerked sidewise, flickered, blue, gold-tipped, and Chung-hsi sighed. She felt the heat like a stabbing pain. It seemed to her that Pell Street, the whole earth, had shrunk to a mote of stardust madly whirling in the moon's immense white dazzle.

But she must finish her work. She had promised Yeh Ming-shen.

"For the sake of the little son whom Fanny has borne — to both of us!" he had said, gently patting her smooth, raven tresses.

To both of them!

Fanny had been in the room at the time, and Chung-hsi remembered the crooked, elusive little smile on her face.

IV.

SHE RETURNED to her work.

Steadily she embroidered the bottom and shoulders of the robe, threading with gold among the moonbeams and scarlet butterflies and chrome-yellow roses words in Mandarin ideographs, copied from the "Book of Ceremonies and Outer Observances" lent her by Yu Ch'ang, the priest — words which would proclaim, amid the cold, alien pomp of the foreigners' church, the Chinese qualifications of the young mother.

Tun she embroidered, and *tuan*; *hung* and *ch'un*; *lung yu* and *fu* and *sung* and *chen* and *yi* — meaning that Fanny, for all the rebel white blood in her veins, was generous and orthodox, respectful and liberal-minded, blessed and prosperous, reverential, sedate, and harmonious.

Kang tu — not jealous — embroidered Chung-hsi, and her hand dropped. Dropped her head.

Not jealous!

Why, there was no reason why Fanny should be jealous, Fanny, who was wrapped in the golden, silken sheen of her arrogant youth! Fanny, who had borne a man-child to her husband!

But she herself — the "great" wife — the old, worn-out wife who cooked and scrubbed and —

She looked out into the hot, violet night with eyes that were less those of an individual than those of a race, an old race. And there is perhaps no more costly and terrible privilege in the world than to belong to an old race. It means the memory of too many pains, too many disillusions — like the church she could see from the roof of her house, gray with years and seamed with sufferings.

She was not a Western woman, given to dissecting her emotions and screwing them into test tubes. She seldom permitted her thoughts to wanton with her fancy. All violent emotions, of love as well as of hate, of joy as well as of sorrow, were repugnant to her — almost physically repugnant. Pity, for herself and for others, was alien to her clear, concise Chinese soul. Such pity she had always dismissed contemptuously, impatiently, as an outgrowth not of good-heartedness but of shrinking, maudlin cowardice.

She had come into the world, as all things come, for an immutable purpose. Hers had been to propagate the honorable name of her husband; and in this she had failed.

Not that she blamed herself for the failure. But, since she had given Yeh Ming-shen no son of her own body to worship him, after his death, with *hiao*, or filial submission, it made it so much more incumbent upon her to look after his earthly happiness. Happiness meant tranquil serenity, and she knew that, as breath stains a mirror and rust a sword, thus anger stains the delicate crystal of the soul, and that there is no anger more corrosive than the anger of the flesh called jealousy.

She did not wish, did not mean, to be jealous; but, meaning to or not, the primitive emotion had been stronger than her ancient racial philosophy, chiefly during those first weeks when it had become known that Fanny would be a mother.

In those days her husband had surrounded his second wife with extra care, extra tenderness. He had brought her a vase of splendid Kiang Hi blue, at which she had sniffed; a quilted silk robe embroidered with black bats — the symbol of happiness — over a shimmering, confused blending of pearly rose, lambent saffron-yellow, and delicate nacreous blue, which, an hour later, in Carlos Garcia's secondhand shop on the Bowery, Fanny had swapped for a ball-gown of arrogant, meretricious scarlet glittering with silver spangles; slippers of pale rose and apple-green, which, to Chung-hsi's slightly malicious but unvoiced amusement, had been too small for her. Finally — acting on the suggestion of Chung-hsi, who had been trying to atone for her gentle malice at the episode of the slippers — he had bought for Fanny a set of white-fox furs which she had folded rapturously to her young bosom. Also, he had spoken to Fanny, softly and at length, in his careful, slightly clipped English, which she preferred to Chinese, and of which Chung-hsi understood little more than a smattering.

But though the English words had been strange to the latter, their meaning had been clear; and then flickers of sudden rage had darted through her calm, bland philosophy, causing her to pray to her painted gods for the eternal and intransmutable *tao*, the changeless principle without labor, without desire, without emotions — without the seething, black passions of the flesh, or the passions, as seething, as black, of the twisting, imagining, lying mind.

V.

HER HUSBAND had seen, had understood, had tried to explain.

"One looks carefully after the new field that is yellow with the glint of kerning corn," he had said. "One looks carefully after the woman about to bear a child."

Then, when Chung-hsi, afraid of losing face, had not replied, he had continued:

"Old woman, an elephant is not afraid of fishes, and it has also been said that if a mouse be as big as a bullock, yet it would be the slave of the cat. You are the wife of my youth, my great wife, my gold wife. The other, the little bud —"

"You love — her?" she had asked, the turmoil in her heart making her breathless.

"No," he had replied very calmly, drawing a tiny fan from his sleeve and clicking open the fretted ivory sticks.

"But — she loves *you!*"

He had inclined his head, without the slightest vanity, without the slightest complacency.

He knew, as all Pell Street knew, that from the first day of their marriage Fanny had loved him with that overpowering, unreasoning passion which once in a while — perhaps to give the lie to the cut-and-dried romantic standards — a young girl brings to a much older man. But, being a Chinaman, thus accepting facts as facts and not as a basis for shifting, harrying speculations, he was innocent of what — again to his purely Oriental mind — seemed the destructive philosophy of the Occident, a mixture of emphasizing trivialities, of cloaking hypocrisy with the mantle of modesty, and obscenity with that of piety.

Moreover, he was without either physical or mental curiosity, and, therefore, the fact that he was loved by the woman whom he had married solely for the sake of propagating his family was as important to him as the fact that the Cantonese lilies which he grew on his balcony, in a square, dragon-painted porcelain pot of glaucous green, were white, gold-flecked, and richly scented.

It was pleasant, but without real consequence. It was a sending of fate, to be accepted as such, to be enjoyed in decent moderation; but hardly to be given thanks for.

He had said so to Chung-hsi; and she had sighed, not altogether convinced.

"She —" this had been after Fanny had given birth to her child — "*she* is the mother of your son!"

"No more than you! For no goal is gained by simple abandonment to action. No child is created by the simple gesture of the body. He who lives by action and gesture alone weaves the boat of his life with withered leaves. The heart and mind, too, help to conceive. And my mind — nearly twenty years have we been married! — is suffused with the flame of yours — and my heart, old woman, touches your feet."

"You kiss her!"

"Yes. And there *is* the child, her child, my child, your child. With every kiss I gave her was the memory of your lips, old woman!"

"You speak to her of love!" she had argued.

"Of course I do, just as I sprinkle the flowers on my balcony; but I only speak to her of love in the language of the white devils — the foreigners —"

"Oh — yes!"

VI.

AND, suddenly, the fact that her husband never spoke to Fanny of love in

Chinese, had seemed all-convincing, all-important, to Chung-hsi. For just as in every terrible memory there is always one moment, often a trivial moment, more poignantly lasting than the rest, thus in every important crisis in a man's or a woman's life it is some negligible detail — negligible only when considered by itself — which at times seems to hold the crux of the matter. It had been so with Chung-hsi, with the groping self-questionings, the perplexities, the mazed, subtle intricacies of her dilemma.

Now she had found the answer. Her husband talked to Fanny of love. Yes — but only in English! That did not matter. There was no meaning, no inner heart, in such words — foreign words — crude, silly, barbarous words — like the hiccupy barking of dogs.

She smiled and bent to her work, embroidering the final word — *kang tu*, not jealous — with steady fingers.

Outside the night rushed. A wind came up from the Hudson and walked across the roofs on slow feet. Pell Street streamed into the east like a fretted, grotesque smudge. The spires of the Baptist Mission Chapel soared up like eager lances. From the joss temple, a short distance away, came the pungent scent of Hung Shu incense-sticks, and the priest's high-pitched words — doubtless for the benefit and the clinking dimes of some goggle-eyed, rubberneck-wagon tourists:

"Strive for meditation, for the purification of the heart, making the mind one-pointed, and reducing to rest the action of the thinking principle as well as of the senses and organs —"

Clear the blessed Lord Buddha's words drifted through the motley, patched symphony of the Pell Street night, and again Chung-hsi smiled.

"Reducing to rest the senses and the organs," she echoed.

Why, she thought, such was her *tao*, her eternal, changeless principle of happiness — reducing to rest the senses and the organs — without labor, without desires, without regret —

She looked at her dollar watch, her one and only surrender to American modernity. It was nearly midnight. Her husband and Fanny and their little son had gone to a Chinese celebration in honor of the child. Soon they would be home, and Yeh Ming-shen would ask for tea and preserves and his pipe.

She folded up the plum robe of ceremony, put it in a camphor-wood chest, and walked to the kitchen. There she prepared the porcelain samovar and returned to the front room and arranged the opium layout — the pot-bellied jar with its treacly, acrid contents, the small silver lamp, brushes, needles, and brass rod. From a black-velvet case she took a smoke-browned bamboo pipe with ivory mouthpiece and scarlet, silken tassels.

A few seconds later she heard a brushing of feet on the door-mat in the hall below, coming up the stairs; a child's fretting, sleepy gurgle — voices.

Momentarily something clutched at her heartstrings. Momentarily jealousy touched her soul, like a clay-cold hand. But she smiled serenely, as the voices came nearer, speaking in English:

"Sure I love you, Fanny."

"Gee, I'm glad, Yeh! You know I'm just plumb nutty about you — you old snoozle-ookums!"

"Yes. And I am — how you say? — yes — nutty about you!" And, as the door to Fanny's room across the hall opened with a creaking of hinges: "I shall take the child. You are tired. Go to bed. Sleep. Tomorrow morning early is the christening."

"Good night, lump o' sweetness!"

"Good night, little Fanny!"

Chung-hsi looked up. Her husband stood on the threshold, holding in his arms a little bundle of silk and linen.

"Look, old woman!" he said, carefully baring the head of the infant. "See the creamy skin, the hooded brow, the high cheek-bones, the long-lobed ears! Our child, old woman! Yours and mine!"

"Yours and mine!" echoed Chung-hsi.

And she added, after a little pause:

"And Fanny's?"

Yeh Ming-shen smiled. He shook his head.

"Oh —" he began; then was silent.

"And Fanny's?" she insisted. "Is not the child Fanny's, too?"

Again he did not know what to reply. Somehow, Chung-hsi's voice made him feel nervous, apprehensive. He seemed to fancy it as an ancient voice of China itself, time itself, echoing down immense corridors of carved, fretted stone, from the depths of vast temples, from the very heart of the black-haired race.

He shook himself together.

"Why," he said, "Fanny is only the instrument — the instrument which we needed, you and I, to bear us this little child."

She looked at him steadily, stonily.

"Only the — *instrument*?" she repeated.

"Yes, old woman. And the instrument has —"

"Done its duty? Served its turn?"

"Yes."

"Ah!" she breathed gently, and left the room.

Came silence.

VII.

AND, a few minutes later, from the direction of Fanny's bedchamber, there rose a high shriek — a shriek that changed, ludicrously, into a choked gurgle.

Again silence; and even as Yeh Ming-shen, the child clutched tightly against his breast, leaped to the door, it opened, and Chung-hsi came in, in her right hand a dagger crimson with blood.

"The instrument has done its duty," she said calmly. "The instrument has served its turn. I have broken the instrument."

Erect she stood, formidable, absolutely in control of the situation, while Yeh Ming-shen shivered, frantically searching his brain how he might be able to dispose of Fanny's lifeless body, how to explain her disappearance when neighbors and the white man's ridiculous law began to ask questions.

Bismillah!

CHAPTER I.

DOUBLE-DEE.

FOR A moment the unexpected sight of Baron Adrien de Roubaix, gold-handled snakewood cane crooked from elbow, dainty boutonnière in his lapel, featherweight Shetland tweeds emphatically outlining his portly Flemish curves, green-lined cork helmet throwing a thick, inky shadow over his bulbous forehead and down the length of his hawkish, predatory nose, monogrammed Turkish cigarette in three-and-a-half inches of jade holder peaking up at a truculent angle from the left corner of his ruddy-mustached lips, and strolling down the main street of this fetid, fever-scabbed West African coast town with the same rather arrogant, rather supercilious ease as he would in his native Brussels on a walk from stock exchange to café or from his cigar-flavored, mahogany-wainscoted counting-house to his pretentious, neo-Gothic residence in the Rue Van Artevelde — for a moment the unexpected sight of Baron Adrien de Roubaix threw Mahmoud Ali Daud off his guard and conquered in him the long habit of outward self-control acquired by a lifetime of special training.

"*Allah kureem!*" he muttered under his breath, rapidly snapping his lean, brown fingers to ward off the little hunch-backed *djinni* of misfortune. Not that he was a superstitious man; but, being a Moslem, he was a Jesuitical opportunist in spiritual as well as in worldly affairs, and while on the one hand he believed neither in the *djinni* nor in this hand-snapping method of protecting one's self against them, he believed on the other hand that there could be no harm in being careful.

So he snapped his fingers again — they cracked through the dull, heat-pregnant air like pistol-shots — and stood still. His keen, dark, aquiline face was marked by a look of almost alarmed inquiry. Then, seeing the glint of oblique, malign amusement in the other's washed-out blue eyes, he greeted him with his usual faintly ironic suavity of manner.

"Good morning, Baron." The Arab's French was faultless.

"Oh — ah — good morning —" came the reply with a negligent

drawl.

It was the opposite of friendly eagerness. Negligent, too, was the man's way of poising himself lightly, for all his well-fleshed bulk, on the ball of his left foot, the toes of the right just brushing the ground, about to walk on, as if he had not noticed Mahmoud Ali Daud until the latter had addressed him; as if even now it bored him to stop and converse.

The Arab flushed. His hands opened and shut spasmodically; they searched, almost automatically, for the jeweled hilt of the short, broad-bladed dagger that was hiding its deadly soul in the crimson, voluminous folds of his waist shawl. He felt hurt in his thin-skinned Semite pride. Rash words of ever ready invective crowded on his lips. But, with an effort, he choked them back.

Business! he thought — thought of James Donachie, his dour Scotch-American partner, with his frequent, monotonous sermon — to the point fully as often as not — that business is business, and not a matter of personal sympathies or antipathies; that business demands the cool hand, the cool head, the cool, purring words —

Mahmoud Ali Daud changed his scowl into a lopsided smile.

"When did you arrive, Baron?" he went on. "I had no idea that the Woermann liner had already —"

He looked out to sea where brilliant wedges of sunlight, filtering through the lacy finials of the palm-trees, misted the waves with golden gauze. There was no ship in the open roadstead except a weather-beaten Norwegian tramp wallowing drunkenly to both sea anchors and, far out, the slim, coquettish silhouette of a French gunboat. "I did not know that the —"

The baron's gurgling, guttural laugh drowned the tail end of the question and rumbled into words that, indeed, the Woermann liner would not show her house flag for at least another week.

"We passed her six hundred miles north," he continued, "down the Moroccan coast — and she's taking off and putting on freight at every stinking little port. Don't be impatient, Daud. She'll lurch in some day. What's the matter? Expecting important mail?"

"No. But how did you —"

"Inquisitive beggar, aren't you? Well — curiosity is one of your racial characteristics. Look yonder!" And he took the Arab by the arm and flung a thumb to the southwest, where the sun laid a shining ribbon from point to point of a land-locked bay, not big enough nor deep enough to give anchorage to the large liners and tramps, but providing plenty of snug, safe harbor for the little white-painted craft that etched its trim gear and graceful, crimson-rimmed smoke-stacks and ventilators against the dazzling, amethyst-colored cliffs.

"Oh —" the Arab drew in his breath — "you —"

"Right, I came down in the company's yacht."

"In a hurry, were you?"

"Perhaps."

The Belgian smiled softly, and the Arab looked at him, worried, intrigued, rather nervous.

"Why didn't you cable us?" he demanded. "I might not have been here — nor Donachie. Not that our terms have changed the least little bit," he added, "but —"

"I didn't come here to see you or your partner."

"No? On a pleasure trip, are you?"

"Why — yes. Business is pleasure, my friend," laughed the baron. "Big business! The biggest pleasure in the world! You know that, don't you?" And he went on, with sharp, sudden emphasis, "Special business! Business dealing with — oh — shall we say a plum-colored, heathenish African king's ransom in gold dust and rubber and ivory? A goodish section of this sweating, miasmic continent begging for the wares and the protection of the Chartered Company?"

"Or of Donachie & Daud!" suggested the other.

Baron de Roubaix smiled.

"Dead men tell no tales," he said, "and dead men cannot trade."

"You —" the Arab was excited — "you have heard —"

"Who hasn't by this time? Why — there isn't a kraal in the whole of Africa that hasn't heard the news. My very office boys, back home in Brussels, whisper about it, and speculate. Oh — but you are ingenuous, my little Daud!"

The baron talked in a flat, drawling voice — a voice, thought the Arab, different from the hectic, chopped, hacked, imploring accents with which he had spoken to him a few months earlier when he had faced the Belgian in the Brussels headquarters of the Continental Chartered Company, behind the ground-glass door with the gold-stenciled legend:

Somehow, that day in the baron's office had marked the apex of Mahmoud Ali Daud's career. Twenty years back, at the time when the Chartered Company had tremendously expanded with the help of French and Belgian capital and had begun to throw its gold-baited nets all the way from Morocco to the Cape, north to Timbuktu and southeast to the giant swirl of the Murchison Falls, the Arab, then a trade-station inspector for the company, had been dismissed to make room for some younger son whose father had invested twenty thousand pounds in the company stock.

Almost immediately a toss of the dice of Fate had thrown together — in some stinking Congo settlement — him and his future partner: the latter, James Donachie, whose dour Scots blood had been but imperfectly tempered by the fact that he had been born and bred in Chicago, and himself, Mahmoud Ali Daud, the grave, dark, sloe-eyed Arab from Damascus.

Strange bedfellows!

For the one was a Scot of the Scots, rigidly Presbyterian, hardheaded and hard-souled, but suffused with an incongruous, sentimental Celtic mysticism that often caused him to look below the practical surface of practical things and conditions and to stay the weight of his hand even at a loss to himself. Narrow where his own and broad where other people's morals were concerned, demanding each penny in the pound less for avarice than because of the principle involved, and, furthermore, a man whose Glasgow ancestors had contributed innumerable divines to the Kirk since the days of John Knox; while the other, a purebred son of the al-Ansari tribe, a noble race, kin to the Prophet Mohammed, who for over twelve hundred years had been the hereditary keepers of the keys of the sacred Kaba Mosque, was Arab in everything: greedy, and yet generous; well-mannered, and yet overbearing; sincere, and yet sneering; sympathetic to his friends, and incredibly cruel to his enemies; austere, and yet passionate; simple, and yet complex.

And — partners!

"Donachie & Daud" — shortened generally into Double-Dee —

their firm, from small beginnings, was now known from the Cape to the Congo, and up through the brooding hinterland, the length of the great, sluggish river, even as far as the black felt tents of the Touaregs. It had made history in African commerce. It was respected in Paris and London and New York, feared in Brussels and Amsterdam, envied in Hamburg and Berlin.

Donachie & Daud traded in ivory and ostrich feathers and rubber, in gold and beads, in calico and gum-copral and quinine and orchilla roots, in Canadian canoes and tiny, tight American motor launches, in cotton and oil and tobacco, and — if the truth be told — in grinning, heathenish *juju* idols manufactured in Birmingham by a firm of devout Baptists, cases of cheap Liverpool gin, and the sort of rifles guaranteed to explode at the first discharge which the Congolese Arabs call the "mothers of bellowing."

Two decades of hard, hard uphill pull and work — work in this black, fetid land of Africa which gives riotously of its treasure, and which maims and squeezes and kills even while it gives! Two decades, apart occasional business trips to England, France, Morocco, or the Cape, spent on the west coast and up the miasmic hinterland where, to quote Sir Charles Lane-Fox, governor of the colony, the cemeteries were the only thriving white settlements!

Two decades of grueling, heart-breaking competition against the great Chartered Company that had a king for main shareholder, a prime minister for chief counsel, a bishop for secretary, a Hebrew banker with a historical name for treasurer, and whose agents and factors and explorers were the picked and reckless spirits of all the seven seas, keen, clever, unscrupulous down-East Yankees, north-country Englishmen, Brazilian Jews, Portuguese half-breeds, Arabs, Welshmen, Sicilians, Armenians, and Glasgow Scots.

But Double-Dee had succeeded against tremendous odds.

Today, all the way up the river, their factories and wharves, their stations and warehouses, proclaimed their insolent wealth. They ran their own line of paddle-steamers as far as the Falls; they had their own dry-docks and repair-shops; twice a year they chartered fast, expensive turbine boats to carry precious cargo to Liverpool and Antwerp and even direct to New York. They had their fingers in every African financial or commercial pie.

Years earlier they could have retired from business; Donachie to a brick-and-stone realization of the Chicago Lake Shore Drive palace about which his imagination wove nostalgic dreams on those choking days when, outside, the sun-rays dropped down like crackling spears while, inside, behind closed rattan shutters and the velvet punkah going at top speed, the heat was like a woolen blanket; and Mahmoud Ali Daud to his pleasant Damascus villa gleaming like a jewel in its setting of rose-bushes and the flaunting garden with the ten varieties of date-trees of which he talked so much.

They spoke of it — retirement from business, home — with longing in their voices. They quarreled about it, cursed each other about it, year after year.

But they remained, year after year. For this was Africa. The cloying, subtle poison of it had entered their souls. It was like a drug. They could not do without it.

There was always something new waiting for them, behind the ranges, the rivers, the whirling, swirling falls, the jungles, and the forests; something new to be discovered, explored, tamed, exploited, colonized —

"Africa," the Arab would say and thereby greatly shock his Scotch partner, "a passionate mistress she, but clever — Allah! Allahu! — as clever as Shaitan, the cursed, the stoned, the father of lies and fleas! Always withholding the full sweetness of her kiss, the full thrill of her embrace — always luring on, on!"

One day there would be a clicking, grunting whisper in the kraals of a virgin ground of ivory caches above the last bush station of the Grand L'Popo Basin; another day there would be florid, metaphorical talk brought by an Arab runner, drunk with hemp, of an incredible store of gold-dust, the plunder of the swinging, heathen centuries, in some jungly village near the Bight; or, perhaps, the night drums would throb forth the tale of a new find of rubber beyond Kimbedi.

Then the Chartered Company would be after it, and so of course — "wolf running side by side with gray wolf," was Mahmoud Ali Daud's comment — would be Double-Dee. Victory swinging her ironic pendulum — throwing the flash and thrall of the red gold into the lap of the one or the other; today causing the frock-coated, silk-hatted gentry in Brussels to smile and rub their palms, and tomorrow causing the Arab to give sonorous thanks to Allah and the Prophet while his Presbyterian partner would look on with a strange, but typical mixture of financial satisfaction and spiritual disapproval.

Then finally some months earlier, had come the apex of Donachie & Daud's career — a double apex and, by the same token, a double triumph, conceived — logically, properly, since this was Africa — in the lap of hazard and mad chance and leering, hiccupping coincidence.

CHAPTER II.

THE MAN FROM THE FAR PLACES.

FOR, ONE sultry night, out of the jungle, naked but for a crimson-fringed Galla blanket, his face and body burnt the color of age-darkened mahogany, bearded to below his chest with a thick, ruddy-gold, matted beard, a grisly collection of voodoo charms about his ankles, had come a white man — rather the fantastic semblance of a white man.

He had walked stealthily, with the suspicious tread of the jungle-bred, slinking like a dingo-dog past the few, scattered residences of the European settlers, avoiding the pretentious double row of electric lights that swept up to the governor's corrugated-iron mansion, passing at a run the red brick church of the Jesuit Fathers, hugging close the coiling, trooping shadows of a clump of carob trees as, suddenly, a square, yellow glare cleft the darkness, and subaltern Johnny Mortimer of the Haussa Gunners swaggered out of the officers' mess-room, and finally coming to rest in the back parlor of the Grand Hotel, owned by Leopoldo de Lisboa de Sousa, a west coast Portuguese, whose presence in the colony was a continuous thorn in the side of all the respectable whites and most of the respectable blacks in the little port settlement.

It was an open secret that De Sousa had committed every crime on the rather comprehensive African calendar, from slave-dealing to gun-running, from illicit diamond-buying to other less mentionable felonies closely connected with the Quartier St. Jacques of Marseilles. But he was as slippery as an eel. He had never been caught; and the standing reward of a thousand pounds, offered by Sir Charles Lane-Fox, the governor of the colony, from his large, private fortune for any information sufficient to jail De Sousa for a term of not less than five years, still remained un-claimed, though many were the traps laid for the hotel-keeper's wary feet.

The night was heavy and thick; the sour smell of fever was in the air, keeping all the world within the snug shelter of wall and roof; and nobody had seen the blanketed, bearded figure creep out of the jungle. Nobody had seen him enter the back parlor of the Grand Hotel, nor there heard him buy food and drink and opium *and* silence from De Sousa with a couple of large, uncut diamonds drawn from a leopard-skin pouch, except one M'Kindi.

He was a wizen, tattooed, flat-faced Balolo from beyond the Yellala Falls, an outcast from his tribe, who, for decidedly unsavory reasons, for reasons the tale of which has not yet been written, for reasons furthermore, which James Donachie, so as to save his peculiar Scotch conscience, refused to know, was bound hand and foot to the latter's partner and used by him as a spy, a listener, a gatherer of subterranean information.

Three minutes after the jungle man had entered the hotel, M'Kindi bowed low, with outstretched hands, before Mahmoud Ali Daud in his great living-room which was as typically Arab as if he had never left his native town of Damascus. For there was a polished expanse of mosaic marble under foot, cut everywhere by small, silken, yielding Persian rugs; in the corners stood tall candlesticks of gilded wood with huge candles of saffron-colored, spikenard-perfumed wax; the high dado of tiles on the walls was softly luminous with nacreous-blue and peacock-green and dull, burnt orange; the dwarf windows, high up, were darkened by reed blinds; and there was no furniture except a *mastabha*, a long, low, carpeted platform heaped with pillows and shadowed by a brattice screen of ancient Moorish stucco work, an immense, turquoise-studded waterpipe, and a carved, inlaid palm wood table with the more intimate of the Arab's belongings: a basketed bottle of holy Zemzem water, coffee-cups in engraved brass holders, perfumery-bottles, a stray book or two, a traveling Koran in crimson, pliant Bokhara leather, and a magnificent, black-and-gold turban cloth which coiled about the table like a snake.

Daud raised his eyelids that were slightly reddened with hasheesh, as M'Kindi slid through the room on silent, unclean feet, then squatted on his flat heels, lifting one withered, plum-colored paw and giving ceremonious greetings:

"My life is in the hollow of thine hand, O Inkos! Thy heart is indeed my aim and my contentment!" — a salutation which usually tended to precede a maudlin demand for money, tobacco, or drugs.

Thus small blame to the Arab that, instead of returning greetings, he snarled blood-curling threats of the many and extremely painful things that would happen to the Balolo if he did not immediately remove his "abominable and most odorous shadow" from the room and indicated, significantly, the sjambok of pickled hippo-hide which lay convenient to his hand; but he sat up straight and a gleam came into his eyes when the other neither fawned nor asked for money, but poured forth a stream of clicking, grunting Bantu words, winding up with:

"Even now, O Inkos, he is with the Portuguese, eating opium as a goat licks salt — and a great fear is in his bones — and the diamonds —"

"Is it the truth, great and uncouth cockroach?" asked Daud.

"It is! By my mother's honor!"

"Bah — thy mother's honor — which was, belike, thy father's dishonor! Thy mother's — *aughrr* —" Daud spat — "may pigs defile her grave!" His lean, brown, steely hand gripped the Balolo's bony shoulder and squeezed unmercifully. "*Is* it the truth — tell me, O whelp of thy mother's breeding — and not a dog's trick to —"

"It is the truth — the truth!" came the negro's agonized protest, and something in the man's accents, in the flash and roll of his popping white eyeballs, convinced the Arab who released his grip and pointed to the door with his thumb, on which shone a great star sapphire in a hammered lead setting.

"Go back to the hotel," he said, "and watch. I shall follow presently."

"But — Inkos!" wheedled the Balolo.

"Well?"

"Thou knowest — I am a poor man — my children are starving —"

"*Ya Malhut*! Have I ever forgotten to pay — in friendship or in hatred — in reward or revenge — in good deed or bad? Go, thou M'Kindi! Go in peace. Thine shall be a shining reward if, belike, thy tale be true."

And the Balolo was out of the house and away into the sweating, purple night, while Mahmoud Ali Daud slipped a Webley automatic into his waist-shawl, fastened the thong of the sjambok about his wrist, twisted the turban around his shaven head with a few rapid turns, and wrapped himself in the earth-brown folds of his voluminous, woolen burnoose. He seemed to hesitate a moment, then entered the next room, his partner's, which the latter had made as homelike as possible with the help of Grand Rapids furniture, a large square — to the Arab's never-ending, sardonic amusement, since frequently he had offered him the pick of his own collection of choice Persian and Turkoman rugs — of blue-and-gray, machine-made Axminster carpet, a map of the United States, a framed picture of Theodore Roosevelt, with months-old numbers of American magazines lying about and a few tattered volumes of Robert Burns's and Lady Nairn's poems to give a Scots tang to the atmosphere.

He looked up as the other entered, and smiled.

They were as far apart as the poles, these two men, in race and education, in ambitions and aspirations, in ideals and morals, in religion and ethics. But they were the best of friends, the most loyal of partners, even though, at times, the language they used to each other seemed to give the lie to the statement.

James Donachie surveyed his friend from head to foot and winked a chilly blue eye.

"Where are you off to this time o' night," he asked, "arrayed like Solomon, the King of the Jews, in all his glory?"

The Arab smiled. His friend's Presbyterian fear of beauty and luxury, in the abstract or the concrete, had never ceased to amuse him, and he used every opportunity to lead him on.

"I am off to see somebody who —" he coughed gently — "ah — somebody who has come back from the far places. And my heart is tight at the thought."

"That's just what I imagined," came Donachie's ironic grumble. "King Solomon indeed! What does it say in the Song of Songs? 'Thou art black but comely!' Mahmoud, my lad, your morals are wretched and heathen — and some day you'll get five inches of steel between your ribs — and then I'll have to look round for a new partner, and I'll be careful to pick someone who isn't as fond of the ladies as —"

"*Aywah!*" cut in the Arab with a hooting bellow of laughter. "It is your imagination, O great Scotch buffalo, which is at fault, and not my morals — which are the whitest this side of Mecca! It is a man who has come back from the far places, and not a woman! It is a man at whose thought my heart is tight. And his name is —" he paused, then, sure of the sensation he was going to cause, gave to his words the emphasis of a suddenly lowered voice — "his name is Darwaysh Ukkhab!"

"Darwaysh Uk —" Donachie jumped up. "You don't mean to say that — it isn't possible — it isn't credible — oh —"

"Everything is possible to Fate the which is Allah's immutable will!" came the Arab's slightly hypocritical rejoinder; then, a practical man of the world once more: "M'Kindi told me. He saw him enter the back parlor of the Grand Hotel, heard him hold whispered converse with that Portuguese father of piglings, saw him take great diamonds from his pouch — diamonds — you know the old tale, little brother!"

"Yes, yes. But M'Kindi may have lied."

"He had no reason to."

"But — why should he have told you, instead of turning the information to his personal benefit?"

"Because it meant nothing to him. He does not even know the Darwaysh's name."

"Then — how —"

"How do I know?" smiled Mahmoud Ali Daud. "M'Kindi described him. There is no mistaking Darwaysh Ukkhab. M'Kindi saw him — saw the diamonds — and brought me his report. After all, that dog of a Balolo is on Double-Dee's pay-roll —"

"Aye! But under the rubric marked 'Mahmoud Ali Daud — private account.'"

The Arab laughed good-naturedly.

"Careful man!" he said. "But, anyway, the Darwaysh is here, for a reason yet to be discovered, yet to be twisted to the benefit of our purses, partner mine, and to be made to smell most evilly in the nostrils of the Chartered Company. You know that the Darwaysh —"

"You believe the tales are true?"

"Believe? How can I doubt the stony fact of it, heart of my heart? There was never one, these many years, of our own men nor of the Chartered Company, could get the proper twist and password of the trade up in the Waranga country, though our wares are good and honestly priced, though there is rubber up there and the warm, red trickle of gold-dust and enough ivory to fill seventeen times seventeen laps of greed."

"I know," cut in the other, disagreeably. "But to whose profit?"

"The Darwaysh's and half a dozen stinking Waranga chiefs', and never an attempt at proper organization and proper trade! It is Darwaysh Ukkhab rules up there — always the Darwaysh, for some hidden reason — and it is his matted, yellow beard which is the great *juju* of the outer kraals — *Allah kureem!*"

"But — why does he — how —"

"How am I to know, little brother? Only the fact of it remains — the fact that, up yonder, his word is law and his gesture a command. And now it seems that he is here, slinking into town in the thick of night like a dog that has been well beaten with thorn-sticks — and afraid of —"

"What?"

"What indeed? I tell you, heart o' me, here is the final chance of Double-Dee — a sweeping expanse of virgin soil to be exploited — and as for the Chartered Company — *wah!*" He snapped his fingers derisively.

"Maybe you're right." The other rose. "No harm in trying at all events. I'll come with you, Mahmoud."

"No. I shall go alone. Remember, there are certain bonds that hold Darwaysh Ukkhab tight and fast to the sweep of my sword-arm and the clear ringing metal of my soul — certain bonds whose strength I would have tested before, had I ever had the opportunity of coming face to face with him up there in the Waranga country. And as to Leopoldo de Sousa —" he paused, chuckled reminiscently, and went on — "he, too —"

"I don't care to know, Mahmoud, what unholy bond there is between you and that Portuguese rogue. I do not altogether approve of some of your methods, you know."

"Then stay here, O man blessed in the sweet scent of your own righteousness!"

And the Arab smiled affectionately at the Scot, who smiled back.

CHAPTER III.

NAVARRO D'ALBANI.

TEN MINUTES later, in his stockinged feet, his yellow leather *babouche* slippers in his hand, Mahmoud Ali Daud stepped noiselessly on the back veranda of the Grand Hotel; then, as the great steel hilt of his dagger scraped crackingly against the stucco wall, he raised his sjambok and brought it down, with the full strength of his lean, muscular arm, on the kinky head of the Galla houseboy, the night watchman, who had loomed up from somewhere out of the dark at the sound. The man dropped with a guttural sob of pain, immediately scotched into breathless silence, as he heard the Arab's low, even, passionless voice:

"Be quiet, dog and son of many dogs. Be quiet, nameless thing without morals or pedigree. Or —"

Faintly the answering whisper brushed up from the ground as the Galla kissed the Arab's foot:

"My life in thy hand, O Inkos!"

"It is indeed! Here — lest thou forget it!" And even Donachie, who knew Africa, who knew the Arabs, and who especially knew his partner, would have been shocked could he have seen the latter again raise his sjambok and bring it down on the negro's unprotected head.

Without paying any further attention to the groveling houseboy, Mahmoud Ali Daud walked up to the locked back door and knocked at it imperiously. Twice he knocked; and, when no answer came, when there was no sound, no movement, no sign of life, nothing except the thick African night that folded about him like the slimy tentacles of some evil, half-fluid monster of the swamps and, far in the distance, the staccato thumping of a signal drum sending the coast gossip to the outer kraals, he drew his dagger, calmly inserted the broad blade between the door and the jamb, pushed, pressed, forced open — and jumped rapidly back as, out of the sudden orange glare from within, a knife whizzed past his right ear and buried itself inch-deep in the door.

The Arab smiled quizzically, and bowed with an ironic "*Salaam aleykhum.*"

"Is that the way to greet a friend?" he went on, his hand reaching neither for dagger nor automatic. "Chiefly —" and there was a minatory, feline purr in his words — "a friend such as I who holds your life by the string of his tongue? And, remember, it has been said that we Arabs are blessed with leaky, clever, twisting tongues, that we are babblers of babblings. And, perhaps, a little word of mine — flying on winged feet to the ear of the governor of the colony —" He paused, and continued, "*Wah*, friend of my soul, you are rash and wanting in caution — and —"

"Peace, Mahmoud!" cut in the Portuguese whose right hand, which had thrown the knife, was still drawn back across the shoulder with the fingers crooked and slightly apart as if petrified in the act of speeding its sharp message that quivered in the door.

"Peace, indeed, Leopoldo of my soul!" replied the other; and he drew the door shut, stepped fully into the room and surveyed the scene in front of him with bright, mocking eyes — nor did it need a detective trained in analytical ratiocination to interpret it.

For, sprawled across the table, his bearded face buried in his arms, breathing stertorously, his lungs working with a heavy, staccato thump that caused the shoulders, from which the Galla blanket had slipped, to move rhythmically up and down, lay the stranger from the jungle whom

M'Kindi had described. The acrid, sickening odor that filled the room gave silent testimony to the nature of the influence that had sent the man into such heavy slumber.

"You do not know how to prepare a proper opium pill, my Leopoldo," smiled the Arab sarcastically. "You mix the poppy-juice too thoroughly, far too thoroughly, with the deadening juice of the asclepias plant."

"Well —" The Portuguese gave a short, shameless laugh. "I —"

"I know!" Daud indicated a pouch of leopard-skin with a handful, dozens and dozens of uncut, large-sized diamonds rolling from it, that must have dropped to the floor as the hotel-keeper, at the sound of the door bursting open, had thrown the knife.

"You are right," agreed the other, again smiling shamelessly, "there is the reason. And —" a greedy glint eddied up in his blue-black eyes — "they are mine — mine — I —"

"Wait!" Mahmoud Ali Daud picked up the stones, took two, gave them to De Sousa, returned the others to the pouch which he put back on the table. "That is enough for you."

"No, no, no! We split even! I was the first to —"

"Silence, dog!" broke in the Arab contemptuously. "I do not want any of these diamonds. I am stalking for bigger game — silence!" he thundered as the Portuguese tried to expostulate. "And —" suddenly he stared straight at the other — "remember, I am a babbler of babblings and the governor's very good friend. And so — tell me — the truth!"

"What?" The word came like the snarl of a wildcat, afraid of the trainer's whip, more afraid of the trainer's stony, merciless, compelling eye.

"Do you know this man?"

"No."

The Arab took a step nearer. His eyes contracted to narrow slits. He thrust out his chin so that the short, well-cropped beard jutted out like a battering ram. His nervous fingers toyed with the thong of the sjambok.

"Are you telling the truth?" he demanded.

"Yes, yes, yes!" There was no doubt now of the man's sincerity.

"How then," came the next rapid question, "did he happen to come to you?"

"I don't know. I only know that — he told me so! — he had heard of me —"

"Who hasn't — on the west coast?" came the sarcastic rejoinder.

"And —" continued De Sousa with rather a pleased smile at the Arab's interruption — "he offered me some of these stones if I would hide him here, get him clothes, and then smuggle him, unbeknown to all, aboard the first ship that made port. And — well —"

"I understand. You, being a dog without honor or faith or morals, thought it more profitable to drug the little, little opium pills with which he wanted to sooth his frayed nerves, and to rob him of all he has!"

"Naturally!" came the callous rejoinder.

"Naturally, indeed! A vulture back to the reek of carrion, and a dog back to the dung-heap! Go, now. This man is a friend of mine. I shall talk with him and attend to his wants. And — once more — remember my so distressingly leaky tongue. Remember that the governor is my friend. Remember that once, when the English fought the Bayakas, in the interior, I ran across a certain Portuguese pig selling stolen rifles and ammunition to — "

"Yes, yes! I remember!" said the hotel-keeper with a crooked, nervous smile and left, while Mahmoud Ali Daud stood still for several minutes, listened close, opened the door suddenly to find out if De Sousa was eavesdropping, then returned to the table, where he busied himself over the drugged man with skilled hands, pressing the glassy eyeballs, rubbing the throat and neck, massaging the sinewy arms, pulling the fingers one by one, and working up and down the spine; until finally the man gave a deep, gurgling sob, sat up with a jerky start, blinked against the light, and, at once, burst into laughter and shook the other's hands with every indication of pleased surprise.

"Daud!" he cried. "Mahmoud Ali Daud!"

"Heart of my heart!"

The two embraced each other after the exaggerated manner of the Orient, hugging like wrestlers, blowing kisses into the air with the tips of their fingers, pressing cheek daintily against cheek and flat palm against flat palm, then holding each other at arm's length and beginning the whole process all over again, with evidently a great deal of relish; and, finally, they sat down, and the Arab having produced tobacco and cigarette-papers, they talked at length, reminiscently, with the little incongruous pauses, the little chokings of voice and heavy pulsings of heart, the sudden, queer, groping gestures of two men who read in each other the tale — the swing, the drama, the comedy, the splendid, shining, never-to-be-realized ambitions — of their past youth.

Nor, straight through, was it by the name of Darwaysh Ukkhab that the Arab addressed his friend, but by another name — limpid, soft, metallic, Latin — "Navarro d'Albani! Heart of my dead youth! Navarro d'Albani!"

The other, smoothing his yellow, matted beard with his hand, laughed in his throat. "Twenty years," he said, "since I've heard the name!"

"Thirty — thirty-one or two!" gently corrected Mahmoud.

"What difference? Years enough to have forgotten the very sound of it! But — by the God of Abraham and of Jacob — it does sound sweet!"

"*Ahee*!" sighed the Arab. "Sweet in the nostrils of memory!"

CHAPTER IV.

SHADOWS FROM THE PAST.

AND AGAIN reminiscences — the talk of the dead years — of the days when Navarro d'Albani, a Turkish Jew of ancient Moorish-Spanish descent, whose ancestors had occupied high seats of honor at Granada during the days of the Abencerrage Caliphs, had followed the call of adventure in his own wild heart, and had gone to Egypt, thence to Tunis, the Sahara, the Sudan, deeper and deeper into the brooding heart of the Black Continent, keen and flushed with the enthusiasm of youth, thirsting for the spoil and color and thrill of the far places.

His life had been a fantastic, incredible odyssey, a twisted, scrolled page torn out of Africa's unwritten, never-to-be-written annals, and it had peaked acridly into blood and torture and slavery when the Mahdi swept out of the south to the gates of Egypt and blazed a crimson trail across the Sudan, with flame and torch and hangman's noose — *and* the Moslem priests' nasal incantations.

It was then that Navarro d'Albani, being an opportunist, had for safety's sake embraced Islam — little difference to him if he called his god Jehovah or Allah — including the brand-new name of Darwaysh Ukkhab. Even so, the Mahdi had never quite trusted that great, yellow beard of his and that coldly ironic eye and, for years, his life had swung by a gossamer thread.

Once he had been sentenced to death, the scarlet-cloaked Nubian executioner had already bared the two-handed sword graved with the name of Allah the All-Merciful — the which was not Moslem sarcasm, but Moslem piety — when, dressed rather foppishly in a pistache-and-lavender silk *djebaa*, a voluminous *dulband* of orange-colored gauze twisted coquettishly about his head, a sprig of wild basil stuck above his right ear, Mahmoud Ali Daud, then a youth of twenty who had but recently bidden farewell to his family in Damascus, had ridden into camp atop a slim, creamy-white dromedary, and followed by some ruffianly servant-retainers.

For some vague reason, psychological or — for Allah alone knows how, in the swing of the centuries, families that once were friends, have drifted apart to the far lands — perhaps atavistic, hereditary, reaching back to the days when the d'Albanis and the Dauds were both sitting beside the lion fountain in Granada's Alhambra and sipping their musk-scented coffee, Mahmoud had taken an immediate fancy to the other youth, and, secure in his spiritual position and privileges as a kinsman of the Prophet, had given imperious orders that his life be spared.

Hereafter, for years, the two had traded and fought and laughed and ridden and swaggered together, throughout north and Central Africa, until, one year, Navarro d'Albani had gone on a visit to his home in Smyrna. He had gone with a laugh on his lips. But he had returned to Africa, three months later, a changed man, weary, bitter, sardonic, hard, a confirmed cynic and misanthrope.

The rich sweetness of his soul had turned to vinegar, the honey of his words to gall, his love of mankind to brooding hatred. He had not vouch-safed an explanation, nor had the Arab, with the delicacy, perhaps the intuitive, almost feminine knowledge of the race of Shem, asked for one.

And then one day — and well Mahmoud Ali Daud remembered the scene, the house in Tunis where they lived at the time, with the covered portico of small Moorish arches, round like the horn of the crescent moon, upheld by slender pillars of rose marble, the tinkling fountain, the flaunting rose garden, and his friend jumping to his feet from his couch, the precious, jade-tipped pipe splintering on the ground, his great hands stabbing up and out, his yellow beard flinging to the breeze like a battle-flag — then one day his friend had cried out, suddenly, without warning or cause, that he was going away, into the heart of Central Africa, that — he had sworn it, by the God of Abraham and of Jacob — never again did he want to see a white face, of Arab or European, of man or woman or child, that he would hereafter throw in his lot with the blacks.

"*Fantee*! I shall go, *Fantee*! I shall turn native!"

Deliberately! Not because of drugs or drink! There had been no arguing with him, no reasoning. And he had gone that same night, Africa had swallowed him — to appear, years later, in the reports that filtered through occasionally to the coast, as a legendary figure, a yellow-bearded white man whose word in the Waranga country was law, whose gesture was a command, whom the natives obeyed with superstitious awe, and who would let no white man enter the country which he ruled — France and England had not yet divided the whole hinterland into spheres of interest — though it was rich in gold and ivory and rubber and though many were the indirect offers made him both by independent traders and by the Chartered Company —

"NOT EVEN ME," said the Arab with gentle reproach, "me, thy friend, wouldst thou allow to come face to face with thee these many years."

D'Albani smiled.

"Tell me," he asked. "Was it the memory of thy old friendship which made thee send messages to me back yonder, or perhaps — for thou art an Arab — thy greed for trade and the profit of trade?"

"I am an Arab and thou art a Jew," replied the other. "We understand each other. And" — with sweeping honesty — "it was both! Greed — and friendship. But, by Allah and by Allah, it was chiefly and foremost the latter, my friendship. I did want to see thee!"

"Remember — I had given an oath that —"

"That — yes, yes — that thou wouldst never want to see again a white face, of man or woman or child. But — now — here —" and the Arab's lean hand shot out eloquently.

"Now," replied the other, "it appears that my oath is broken and shivered, and perhaps the God of Abraham and of Jacob will understand — and forgive. Now I am back among the whites. And —" his voice dropped, and he leaned across the table so that his face jutted into the full radiance of the lamp — "there is in my soul a great fear — and a great, sweet hope."

"Tell me!"

"The hope is —"

The Arab's hand cut mockingly through the sentence, and he laughed.

"I know the hope," he said. "A woman! The same woman who,

years back, when thou hadst been home on a visit, changed thy heart and sent thee to the far places. That I guessed — long ago. A woman who —"

"Who trampled on my heart!"

"And who now again, somehow, across the dead years and the great distance, has called thee to her —"

"How dost thou know?"

"Am I a prattling babe *not* to know? Have there not been many soft, henna-stained feet that used my soul for a tasseled rug to step on — many little hands that twined about my foolish heart — Zoleikha and Ayesha and Nadja and Soltana and Zorah and — I have forgotten the names — but never the words. They were always the same — soft, silken, gliding, lying —"

He paused, smiled reminiscently, and went on:

"But the fear? What, little brother, is the fear which has sent thee here, slinking, furtive, in the dead of night, like a dog that has been well beaten with thorn sticks?"

"Mahmoud!" came the counter query. "Dost thou believe in —" d'Albani's voice trembled, shivered, peaked to a strange, eerie note — "in evil influences — in witchcraft — in devils —"

The Arab did not look up. Nervously he fingered his amber rosary.

"My friend," he replied Jesuitically, "there are indeed — so the learned doctors of the Faith have told me — certain references, in the Koran as well as in the sacred Hadith, to devils — *djinni*. Even the great king of the Jews, Solomon the Magnificent, is said to have —"

"None of thy twisted Moslem hypocrisies! None of thy theological playings with words and thoughts! I am speaking — and well thou knowest that I do — of heathen devils — negro — oh — fetishes —" the voice dropped flatly — "*juju* —"

He was silent. So was the other. The mad, amazing stillness of Africa was all about them, like a sodden blanket, like a red mist, like a knife that cut through to their very hearts. Presently a rattan window screen flapped loose and whispered sardonically, startling them, and the tropical heat brushed in and touched them with a stabbing touch as salt as tears, and it seemed that Africa — the whole earth — had suddenly shrunk to a mote of stardust crazily whirling in the moon's immense, white dazzle.

A night hawk was sounding his grim, melancholy cry from an isolated tree in the back yard. A signal drum sobbed in the distance, broke off in mid air. Far off, a hyena laughed in its obscene, staccato dirge.

"Dost thou believe in — *them*?" repeated d'Albani, through clenched teeth.

"Yes — and no!"

The other laughed.

"The which means yes?" came his comment, "and —"

"Well?"

"Hast thou ever heard of Mohammed Bello, the Emir of the Fulahs?"

"He has been dead these two hundred years or so."

Again d'Albani laughed, disagreeably.

"Has he?" he asked.

"Go on — go on!"

And, after a moment's hesitation, Navarro d'Albani bent his head and spoke in whispers, at length, tensely, hectically, while the Arab listened, asking an occasional, pertinent question, and finally demanding in a hushed, slightly awed voice:

"Thou — thou hast it here — with thee — the — the thing?"

"Yes."

D'Albani's hand disappeared beneath the Galla blanket and came out holding a small, round, compact bundle wrapped tightly in layers of discolored silk and exhaling a pungent aroma of myrrh and spikenard.

"Give it to me," said Mahmoud Ali Daud.

"But —" the other looked up, and an expression came into his eyes of relief and, too, of fear — "but thee — I told thee and — Thou dost believe?"

"I do," came the low reply.

"Then — why —"

The Arab took the little round bundle from between d'Albani's fingers and fastened it carefully into a fold of his waistband.

"I shall do it," he said. "I shall bear its burden of good things and of evil — because of our old friendship and —" he smiled — "a little, too, because of my greed for profitable trade. As to thee —" he drew a purse from his shawl and passed it across the table — "there are about fifty guineas in here. Enough to see thee to London and thence to Stamboul; once there, thou wilt go to my friend Hussain Mabrouk, the jewel merchant, in the quarter of Eyyoub, near the Mosque of El-Hajji Othman, and thou wilt mention my name, and he will give thee an honest price for the diamonds —"

"But — the medicine men of the Warangas — they will know — in a few days — and —"

"I or my partner shall be there before they know. And as to thee — have no fear. One of the ships we have chartered sails from here tomorrow morning on the early tide. Thus thou art safe if even — though I doubt it — the medicine men should find out about thy disappearance and the disappearance of — ah — the thing before I or Donachie should be able to get there. The captain will keep his mouth shut and, doubtless, for a few guineas, will let thee have a suit of European clothes. Come."

A minute later another diamond sped the Portuguese hotel-keeper into immediate action. Turning to the hut where his houseboys slept, with curses and cuffs he recruited a dozen strong young men. Silently but rapidly, they went to the water's edge and launched a boat. Eight bells had just sounded when it was propelled up to the side of the turbiner *Dalziell Castle*. Navarro d'Albani, followed by the Arab, came up by the pilot's ladder and —

"Right-o!" said the russet-bearded Liverpool skipper. "I'll keep my bloomin' trap shut. Clothes? Another right-o. I got my Sunday-go-to-meeting kickin' about my locker somewhere. It's yours for four quid. A bargain? Good. Goin', goin', gone!"

An hour later, with the young sun of the tropics shredding the night mists into ragged scarves and skeins and a staccato breeze flickering out of the west like the wind of a gaily flirted fan, Mahmoud Ali Daud entered his partner's room, shook him awake, and rolled the little bundle d'Albani had given him on the bed.

"Here, heart of my heart," he said, "is the key to the Waranga country. Here is the 'Open Sesame' to its locked treasure-house of gold and ivory and diamonds."

CHAPTER V.

THE *JUJU* OF THE WARANGAS.

"ER — OH — what?" Donachie sat up and rubbed his heavy eyelids.

Then, seeing the package, he unwrapped it and, at once, dropped it back with a grunt of disgust and nausea. For, blotchy brown against the white of the bed linen, stared at him out of empty, grinning sockets, the head of a man, mummified and shriveled to one-fifth its original size by the secret method known only to certain African tribes and to the Malay pirates of the Straits, though, in former centuries, it was also known to the South American Indians.

"God!" Donachie shivered. His lips and jaw worked as if he had swallowed a loathsome drug.

But his disgust did not last for long. He had lived in Africa for too many years; had been, if not exactly marred, yet tainted by its scabbed, cruel hand; had felt, too closely, the bunched, brutal enormity of this acrid land of lies and darkness and bloody superstitions. So, smiling grimly, he touched the shriveled head with second finger and thumb.

"What's the little gentleman's name?" he inquired. "And what's he supposed to be good for?"

"His name," replied the Arab, gravely, almost reverentially, "was Mohammed Bello. Dead he has been these two hundred years. But still his great Arab soul — may it rest in the sweet shadow of Paradise — rules the hinterland where, once, as Emir of the Fulahs, he ruled when he was alive, when he was a man of craft and pluck and strength upon the blue hills and in the green, steaming jungles."

"And now he is rather considerably dead," commented the other, his dour Scots soul rubbed the wrong way by his friend's Arab mellifluence. "Now there isn't even enough pickin's on his head to satisfy a gorged carrion-hawk."

"Indeed!" Mahmoud Ali Daud inclined his head. "But — I repeat — his great soul still rules the land of the Warangas, the outlying province of that huge Fulah Empire of which he was Emir during his lifetime. Still the Warangas look up to him. His shriveled head is the fetish, the all-powerful *juju* of the outer kraals. And he who possesses this head —" He made an eloquent gesture.

And, in answer to his friend's questions, he repeated the conversation he had had with Navarro d'Albani, winding up with:

"He did not tell me how — by bullying or bribing the medicine men, or by playing hand in hand with them and killing off the more dangerous of them later on, after they had served their turn — he possessed himself of the *juju*-head. But he did, somehow! And you know — Double-Dee knows — all the independent traders know — the Chartered Company knows — how he succeeded —"

"You mean that — really — it was this *juju* which helped him to —"

"Of course. There was nothing else. He was a white man, in the heart of the jungle, alone. Then — and this is another tale — a tale of his youth and of a woman and of the love which passeth understanding —"

"A tale which you might spare me!"

"A tale which I have no intention of telling you — he decided to return to his own land. He took along a fortune. In diamonds. As to the chiefs and the medicine men —"

"He told them some cock-and-bull story, I guess?"

"Yes. That he had to go away, by himself, into the deep jungle, to commune with the spirit of Mohammed Bello, for all I know. For you know what these savage blacks are like — half children and half monkeys. And superstitious — may Allah protect me against the craftiness of the idolaters!"

"It'd be fairer to ask Allah to protect the idolaters against the wiles of the Moslems," Donachie interrupted dryly.

But Mahmoud Ali Daud continued, unheeding:

"They depended on him, the possessor of the *juju*-head. They believed that the spirit of the dead Emir had entered his soul. He himself, the better to keep out the other traders, had spread the legend that possession of the head meant mastery and dominion; that the head must never leave the Waranga country, otherwise a bitter blight would descend upon the land, killing the cattle, drying up the rivers, causing the fields to die and the women to become sterile. And the Warangas believed the legend thoroughly. Perhaps too thoroughly."

"*Too* thoroughly?"

"Yes. For, at the last, obeying some perverse streak in his nature, perhaps resolved that, even after his return to his own land, no white man should enter the Waranga country or, if a white man did succeed, that the road should be made as hard and thorny as possible for him, he decided to take along the *juju*-head. He did. He left. And —" the Arab made a great, sweeping gesture — "three days later, after he had crossed the border, fear came to him in the watches of the night, squatting on his soul like a black devil of misfortune. Fear of the unseen! Superstitious fear! Fear that — perhaps — the legend had become true to the clouting — that really the spirit of the dead Emir protected the Warangas. And, too, actual, physical fear. For, he thought, the medicine men and the chiefs would begin to worry about his protracted absence, they might enter the *juju* lodge and find that the head had been stolen. And then —"

"Well, what then?"

"You know these Warangas. They never forget, never forgive. Let Navarro d'Albani hide where he please — they will find — and kill — and —"

"Yes —"

"It will be our work, brother mine, to go to the Waranga country and put the head back in its secret place in the jungle lodge before the medicine men find out. And then — with the help of Allah — will come the shining apex of Double-Dee! And as for the Chartered Company — *wah* — they shall chew the bitter kernel of disappointment and envy, and they shall not like the taste of it!"

ThE SHINING APEX of Double-Dee!

Mastery of the hinterland trade! Dominion of the Waranga country! The Chartered Company humbled in the dust! A shimmering, rainbow dream — but it had materialized!

For, the next morning, without servants or bearers or guides lest their secret mission become known and be gossiped about from kraal to kraal with the droning and the thumping of the drums, James Donachie and Mahmoud Ali Daud had set out from the coast and gone up-country; and never, to their dying day, did either of them forget the bitter, long wilderness pull: the steady, heartbreaking trek through the miasmic hinterland of the colony, a blistering two days through a yellow-and-purple wedge of desert with the sun poised high like a coppery-red balloon, and on into a density of virgin forest where the blackish green of the giant trees and the huge, bloated creepers refreshed them after the pitiless open spaces and the blanched sands; the plunge across the border, using unbeaten paths so that nobody might know or suspect and bring word to the ever-watchful spies of the Chartered Company, into the deep jungles of the interior; the trail for many days that was nothing but a few fugitive tracks in the undergrowth where every second step squished down to thick, smelly water; occasionally a clearing where the sun struck like the fires of purgatory and where flashing white and green things rustled out of their way — day after day, night after night — nearly two weeks of travel through a dense forest.

But they had succeeded. They had found the jungle temple, squatting by the side of a far, nameless river like a great toadstool. The medicine men had not yet become worried over Navarro d'Albani's protracted absence, and so the two partners — the Scotchman disapproving of the action with every cell and fiber of his rigid Presbyterian soul, and the Arab clicking his rosary beads and mumbling ceaseless prayers of forgiveness to Allah — had put the *juju*-head back where it belonged, its sightless eyes once more, sardonically, surveying the grisly collections of voodoo charms that the worshipers had spread below it on the ground.

Then, through the forcefully recruited services of a couple of bush dwarfs, they had sent for the chiefs and the medicine men. They had met them in full, solemn conclave. And it was here that the Arab had been in his element — "the crackingest bit o' bluff ever pulled in Africa," Donachie used to call it afterward.

For, with all his sweeping Semite eloquence, with all his remarkable knowledge of savage psychology, embroidering the legend which d'Albani had started, adding to it, toying with it, weaving new superstitions into the old, and shamelessly twisting to heathen purpose certain quotations from his favorite esoteric tome, Al-Bayzawi's "*'Ilm al-Tajsir*" or Exegesis of the Koran, he had convinced them that Navarro d'Albani, *alias* Darwaysh Ukkhab, had left his "beloved Warangas" in the keeping of Double-Dee, that to Double-Dee had descended the keeping of the *juju*-head — they had it, proof supreme, since even in the wilderness possession is nine points of the law — that into the soul of Double-Dee had now entered the dead Emir's worth and spirit.

Trade, then!

Trade, systematic, constructive, thorough, perfectly dovetailed in every step from steamer's wharf to overland porter, from loom to jobber, from jobber to factory agent, from factory agent to the chief's obese wife bullying her plum-colored, ocher-painted, plumed warrior-husband into the purchase of twenty yards of American cloth blending an unlikely sunset of purple and sulfur-yellow and pink and glaucous green.

Gold dust and rubber, tusks and hides and orchilla roots; and — flitting back across the overland trail, with a thousand per cent profit on the investment and, perhaps, occasionally, when beyond the white man's coast law, salted down with the swish and pain of the sjambok — beads and knives and trinkets.

Trade!

Trade that had made the independent merchants gasp with impotent envy and — after Double-Dee, the Waranga country fully organized, had appointed Hendrick Van Plaaten, the expatriate Vaal Boer, as their chief agent there and, in a way, given the sanctity of the *juju*-head which was their spiritual and financial trade-mark, their semi-divine viceroy — that had finally caused the Chartered Company to make certain overtures to them, at last cabling them to come to Brussels for a business conference.

CHAPTER VI.

WEDDED TO FATE.

AT THE TIME, Donachie had been down with fever, and so it was his partner who had gone to Europe, and there had been that memorable interview — the second apex of Double-Dee's career — with Baron Adrien de Roubaix.

The Chartered Company suing for peace! The Chartered Company asking for terms! The Chartered Company *begging* to be allowed to share the rich plums of the Waranga country.

At first, of course, the baron had been slightly sarcastic, rather patronizing. He had attempted to cheapen the price by cheapening the quality of the ware. Then, seeing the sardonic, mocking look in the Arab's hooded eyes, seeing, furthermore, the handful of uncut diamonds, Waranga diamonds, which the other had drawn from his pocket with studied carelessness, he had become friendly and somewhat confidential; then he had cajoled; at last wheedled and implored.

And, always, Mahmoud Ali Daud's stony reply that — yes — Double-Dee was willing to sell, would turn over their assets and good-will, including their mysterious hold on the Waranga country — for fifty-one per cent of the stock, common as well as preferred, of the Chartered Company. Control, in other words. Mastery.

"No, no!" the baron, had exclaimed, fluttering his white, beringed hands. "Forty per cent!"

"Fifty-one!"

"Forty-two!"

"Fifty-one!"

"Forty-three!"

"Fifty-one!"

Up to forty-nine the baron had raised the price, to find himself confronted by the same stone wall, the same wearisome, maddening repetition:

"Fifty-one!"

There the matter had rested, the baron, at the very last, so far forgetting his usual good breeding as to make a threat against Double-Dee; and, flushed with triumph, Mahmoud Ali had returned to the west coast, to be greeted there by bitter news; news that Double-Dee, suddenly, overnight, finding themselves in a fight for their very existence, had tried to keep secret from everybody except their most confidential agents, Gonzelez, and Kinsella, and DuPlessis, and Shareef Ansar, formerly the Arab's pipe-wallah, a half-breed Zanzibaree, who had recently been raised to the position of sub-agent, because of his loyal services and his great knowledge of the hinterland.

There had been no reason to suspect that the secret had not been kept. Otherwise there would have been a change in the slightly servile manners of the independent traders to the two partners when they met on the street, at the Grand Hotel over a cup of coffee and a game of matador-dominoes, or at the Double-Dee go down to bargain over discounts, an obligatory glass of gin conveniently at their elbows. There would have been desertions from the ranks of their blacks, and their credit in London, Manchester, and Liverpool would have tumbled.

No, thought the Arab; their secret had been well guarded, and yet, here, today, a few months later, was Baron Adrian de Roubaix, and he was not the same man who had spoken to him, in Brussels, with hectic, imploring accents. Arrogant he was now, and haughty, *and* — he had made certain sneering, slurring allusions.

"Dead men tell no tales," he had said, "and dead men cannot trade."

And he had added that the very office boys in Brussels were whispering about what was happening up-country.

The last was doubtless a lie. For — slim consolation — the manners of the independent traders were unchangedly suave, and, only two days earlier, the London & Union Bank had cabled their assent to a three-months, unsecured loan of thirty thousand pounds sterling at bank rate. But there was no denying the fact that the baron knew what had befallen Double-Dee in the Waranga country. There was no sidestepping the fact that the baron, who, a sharp businessman, was also a pleasure-loving man about town, had made a hurried trip to the west coast, in the hottest season of the year, aboard the Chartered Company yacht. He had said that it was "special business" which had brought him here.

What did it portend?

What was in the wind?

"FI AMAN 'ILLAH!" piously mumbled the Arab, looking after the Belgian's truculent back, and, a few minutes later, he faced his partner in his private office.

Donachie, a cigar between his teeth, his feet elevated to the heat-gangrened table which was littered with correspondence and stray bits of riding-gear, looked up as the Arab entered, and the latter sensed at once, instinctively, that if his own news were unfavorable, Mahmoud Ali Daud, too, had some to communicate that were not exactly roseate.

For they knew each other. Their partnership, through the hot, stinking, yellow African years, had grown into a thing finer and stronger than a mere business combination for the sake of profit.

A real affection had sprung up between these two men from the ends of the Earth; and though, when alone in their wattle-and-daub living house which overlooked the rush-fringed river, they quarreled freely and frequently — never about their decisions, but rather about their divergent methods of arriving at the selfsame decisions — they could read each other's mind like an open book.

Thus it was with a lop-sided smile that James Donachie said he was willing to wager dollars to doughnuts that his own news were fully as bad as his friend's, and he pointed at a blue cable-slip.

"Came shortly after you left, Mahmoud," he said, "I've decoded it."

The other read.

It said, courteously, lyingly, and expensively, at four and sixpence a word, that the London & Union Bank regretted exceedingly, *et cetera*; but that in the matter of the three months' unsecured loan of thirty thousand pounds sterling, though they knew that they agreed to it three days back, though they realized the un-businesslike methods, *et cetera*, still, given certain unforeseen conditions of the market, *et cetera*, they would be greatly obliged if, *et cetera*. If Double-Dee had already drawn on the loan, such amounts would be transferred to the current account — and then a few more hypocritical and expensive *et ceteras*.

"Rats leaving the sinking ship," commented the Scot.

"Yes," agreed the Arab, "and sharks waiting below in the black, swirling waters, for the ship to turn turtle — to gorge themselves with flesh. One sharp especially! Blunt-nosed! Cruel! Most evil! A Belgian shark!" — and he told his friend about the meeting with Baron Adrien de Roubaix.

"In other words," said Donachie, "the gentry of the Chartered Company have found out about what's been going on up there in the Waranga country" — he pointed through the window, to the east, where the land rose slowly, then, suddenly, curved fantastically and raced away to a tight, pigeon-blue sky — "and they are at the back of this" — indicating the cablegram.

"Perhaps not exactly at the back of it," replied the Arab.

"No?"

"No. Rather" — Mahmoud Ali Daud lowered his voice — "in front of it!"

"Which — translated into less metaphorical English — is s'posed to mean what?"

"Just an idea of mine thrown out! Just a soft-footed, groping suspicion — a feeling — an instinct — that the Chartered Company did not have to *hear* about what happened to us in the hinterland."

"What do you mean?"

"I mean that it was the company which caused the — ah — accidents — call them what you wish — which, in their turn, caused the news and led to the curtailing of our credit in London — which may lead, if Fate be harsh and our own flesh not strong enough, to the end of Double-Dee."

Donachie shook his head.

"No, no," he said. "I have no call to break a lance for that Chartered gang. Still — it's impossible — impossible, man!"

"Nothing is impossible in the eye of Allah," said the Arab. "When the impossible happens, it is seen — a stone swims in the water — a feather breaks the back of a full-grown man — an ape sings a love song — and once I met an honest Greek!"

The other made a weary gesture.

"Yes, yes," he said. "Very pretty little metaphors. But — why — we carried right on with Navarro d'Albani's scheme — we've stopped every hole — sealed the whole darned hinterland up as hermetically as —"

"We *thought* we had. And yet the facts of the case remain — three graves up yonder in the bush, heart of my heart — and the baron knows — and smiles!"

"Even so — even suppose he found out, somehow — why — what you accuse him of —"

"I do not accuse. I suspect."

"I know your way of suspecting. And — no — the Chartered Company — they would not stoop to —"

"Murder — since, doubtless, it was murder?"

"Exactly!"

"And why not, little brother? *Wah*!" And there was in the Arab's words all the sordid heart of the scabbed, festering Black Lands — "this is Africa, Africa! The graveyard of the white man's decencies! The land of the cursed, thin-shanked, flat-footed seed of Ham! Why not murder then? You yourself — look back into your own life as Africa made you live it. And I — when I think of the past years and the past sins — of — oh — things — May the Prophet intercede for me on the Day of Judgment!"

"Yes," admitted Donachie. "I — I have taken life — but — not for gain — for the sake of profit —"

And the next moment, not with clean-cut suddenness, high-stepping, sharply silhouetted, but matter-of-fact, drab, not as the unexpected but as the ever-to-be-expected — bitter, startling news drifted in, on the lips of a short, bow-legged Zanzibaree half-breed, Shareef Ansar, still white as a leper with the dust of the long trek, his eyes burning deep in their sockets with the fatigues of the wilderness pull, his thatch of rough, bristly hair bleached blotchy-red by the merciless sun of the hinterland.

"DuPlessis!" Shareef Ansar whispered, as he stumbled across the threshold. And he shivered and stopped, and took breath deeply, painfully trying to speak, choking — "Allah."

Mahmoud Ali Daud caught the fainting man in his arms and bent close. He read more than heard the next words from Shareef Ansar's blanching lips.

"Dead — DuPlessis — same way — ears — nailed to chest —"

And then Donachie raised his hairy fists to heaven and broke into curses, while the Arab, having lifted the unconscious man into a chair, opened his shirt, and set the electric punka into motion, walked over to the wall and studied closely the back pages of the calendar where tiny black crosses, accompanied by names, marked certain dates.

"McDonald," he read, "Alvensleben, Moustaffa el-Touati. Three of our best — of Double-Dee's best. And each lasted less than a week. And now — now DuPlessis — 'Afrikander' DuPlessis —"

He turned, looked at his partner, and put his hand on his shoulder. It was a steady, strong, soothing hand, caressing the heaving shoulder with a deliberate rhythmic motion. For he could feel for the other; could read the seething, maddening rage in the other's heart, and he remembered moments in his own life, in the past, when suddenly the madness of the tropics, following bitter disappointment, had seemed to creep out of the jungle, out of the pitiless heart of the bloated noonday sun and touch his brain with a pricking, sardonic, red-hot needle.

"Friend," he said; "old friend — come —"

Donachie did not reply. His feet tapped the floor with rapid beats in a paroxysm of nervous restlessness. He was staring straight in front of him with unwinking, dull eyes, thinking of the past, the killing, heartbreaking work, the years of uphill fighting, the shining hopes, the promises, the great ambitions, clouted together, finally, into high achievement, into a solid burgess building cemented with blood and sweat and the enthusiasm of their youth, the steady strength of their manhood: Double-Dee, respected, envied.

And then he thought of the future — stretching before him like a gray, leprous sunset, without hopes or promises — the future of Double-Dee — a pitiful memory on the lips of the west coast traders — a leering, sneering mockery on the lips of the very riffraff, the genteel species of beachcombers, the driftwood of the outer seas who met night after night in the bar of the Grand Hotel and cadged for drinks.

He felt a strange moisture in his eyes. His words came thick, halting, enormously sincere.

"God — help, O God!"

"God *will* help," gently said the Arab. "But He will only help if we help ourselves!"

And then calmness returned to James Donachie on the backwash of his pawky Scots humor.

"You're all to the good for a Moslem fatalist, Mahmoud my lad," he said; and he gave a short laugh. "Double-Dee —"

"Double-Dee is wedded to Fate itself, heart of my heart!" came the Arab's magnificent boast.

"Maybe. All I hope is that Fate will stick to her lawfully wedded husband." And they both laughed.

CHAPTER VII.

THE CLEMENCY OF MAHMOUD ALI DAUD.

YET THE NEWS, culminating in the baron's mocking allusions and the

London & Union Bank's refusal to grant the loan, were bad; had been bad for months now.

It had started within two days after Mahmoud Ali Daud had refused Baron de Roubaix's offer with his stolid counter offer of fifty-one per cent of the stock of the Chartered Company.

At first the Waranga country had been a veritable treasure house. Under the ministry of Hendrick Van Plaaten, their chief agent, the *juju* of Mohammed Bello's head had worked like a charm. Trade had been smooth and tremendously profitable. Ivory, rubber, gold, and — diamonds. Diamonds had trickled down to the coast in an incessant, precious stream, so steadily that already the great DeBeers Company of Kimberly, the Diamond Trust, had begun to make diplomatic overtures to Double-Dee with a view of keeping the market from becoming glutted and the prices from tumbling.

The Warangas had seemed unspoiled and friendly, serene in their heathenish superstition that the spirit of the dead Emir Mohammed Bello had entered into Double-Dee, and that, as long as the grisly *juju*-head was enthroned in the jungle lodge and received certain nameless periodical sacrifices — to the fact of which Double-Dee's agents casuistically closed their eyes — no harm would come to their kraals and their cattle.

"Nor had harm come — *to them!*" as James Donachie would comment ruefully.

Of course, Van Plaaten's death had been an accident or, rather, his own fault.

A big, hairy Vaal Boer, solid, trustworthy, fearless, shrewd, he had had but one failing: whenever he came out of the wilderness and reached the comparative civilization and plenty of the coast, he had rioted and debauched for three weeks, never more nor less, on a pompous, magnificent scale.

Returning from the Waranga country one day with a very fine eighty-five carat steel-blue diamond which he had not wished to entrust to the native bearers — a diamond known afterward to the trade and to the world at large as the *Double-Dee Apex*, and which, after many romantic, blood-stained adventures and vicissitudes, the telling of which is another story as yet unwritten, sparkles today in the tiara of Mrs. Jackson Oberhuber, the widow of the famous Chicago packer — he had gone on his usual spree, and an overdose of *dop* and brandy had killed him, after his dying imagination had peopled the back room of Leopoldo de Sousa's hotel with a splendid collection of pea-green elephants and crocodiles in a delicate shade of rose-madder.

McDonald had been sent in his stead, then Alvensleben, and then Moustaffa el-Touati. Three men of different races and temperaments: Ulster-Scot, Dane, and Arab, but all three African born and bred, familiar with the country, its customs, prejudices, and superstitions, and a diversity of its clicking languages, and all trusted employees of Double-Dee who had made good at other important bush stations before they had been sent to the Waranga country.

And, one after the other, each lasting less than a week, they had met the identical cruel, incredible, rather sardonic death. They had been found with their eyes gouged out, their tongues and ears cut off, the ears nailed to their chests with the help of spiky elephant thorns — as if, commented Mahmoud Ali Daud, the unknown assassin or assassins had meant to convey some sinister message, perhaps a warning, by the very method of killing.

It had been the fact of this method, of the three bodies having been thus mutilated, which had immediately exonerated the Warangas. For, as Sigismondo Mercado, a clever and trustworthy half-breed Portuguese bush detective who had been sent up by Double-Dee under pledge of secrecy to investigate the cases, had pointed out: the Warangas never mutilate, not even the bodies of their most hated enemies, considering such a deed blasphemy unspeakable.

Mercado had made an exhaustive examination, but had found no trace of the criminals. The natives had been fully as shocked and grieved as Double-Dee and very willing to answer all questions.

In the first case, that of Angus McDonald, his houseboys, living in a hut a stone's throw away from the agency building, remembered having heard voices the night of the murder, McDonald's voice, and another man's. They had seen McDonald leave the house, still talking animatedly to someone by his side.

"Did they talk in English?" Mercado had asked.

And the answer had been that — yes — it had been English or some other European language — the Warangas did not know the difference, but were sure it had not been any of the African dialects of the neighboring countryside. Nor had they been able to recognize the stranger — it had been a dark and moonless night — not even to see if he wore the dress of a white man or of a native. They had found the mutilated body the next morning, a mile from the agency post, in the jungle undergrowth, led there by the barking of the jackals.

The news had been sent by private drum code to Double-Dee, who, knowing the jealousy of the independent traders and of the Chartered Company, and how the latter might use the murder as the thin end of the wedge wherewith to spread uneasiness among the negroes and open their campaign for commercial penetration of the Waranga country, had kept it secret and had sent Alvensleben to the interior.

Shortly afterward he had met his death when he had gone out hunting warthog, alone; and Moustaffa el-Touati, forewarned by the fate of his two predecessors, had been unable to escape it. Always, day and night, he had been protected by files of armed blacks. Yet one day, out of the thick jungle, an assegai had sobbed and pierced his heart, and two days later, in the dead of night, the grave had been opened and the corpse mutilated as the others had been.

Now, finally, it had been the turn of DuPlessis, "Afrikander" Du-Plessis, the best man of his kind in Africa, just as conversant with jungle and forest lore and with savage psychology as Mahmoud Ali Daud himself. He had left with a laugh on his lips, with calm words that echoed a serene belief in his own power.

"No, no!" he had said to the two partners. "Don't you worry on my account. I can take care of myself. If any obbligato ear-slicing has got to be done, it's going to be little me who's going to do the slicing."

He had been accompanied by Shareef Ansar, the half-breed Zanzi-baree, one of Double-Dee's most loyal servants.

"I give DuPlessis effendi into thy keeping!" Mahmoud Ali Daud had said, on parting, to his former pipe-wallah. "It shall be thy honorable duty to protect him with thy life!"

The other had salaamed deeply.

"Indeed!" he had given reply. "The sword which is meant for the heart of DuPlessis effendi will have to pierce first mine own heart. I swear it on the Koran, O Sheykh!"

Everything had gone well. Another package of diamonds — two hundred odd carat in fair-sized stones — had reached the coast under DuPlessis's seal. Word had come of a king's ransom in first-class ivory that had been discovered. The production of rubber had taken an imme-diate upward leap. Peace and plenty was in the kraals. Then DuPlessis had drum-coded that he was proceeding to the coast, with Shareef Ansar, to bring important news.

And now —

Mahmoud Ali Daud bent over Shareef Ansar who was opening his eyes.

"Tell me what has happened — exactly, little brother," he said.

And, the next moment, Shareef Ansar sat up, tried to speak, could not, and fell back at once with a choked gurgle, a thick, blackish whip of blood staining his tattered burnoose.

"God — what —"

Donachie rose, as white as chalk, while the Arab tore the burnoose apart and saw, below Shareef Ansar's first rib, a ragged wound that had slipped its clumsy, impromptu bandage of rags and palm leaves. He snapped his lean fingers rapidly to ward off the hunchbacked *djinni* of misfortune.

Then he straightened up.

"Donachie," he said to his friend. "Shareef Ansar has kept his oath — partly!"

"Partly!"

"Yes. For he swore that the sword meant for DuPlessis would have to pierce first his own brave heart — and it appears that it was DuPlessis who was killed first. Shareef Ansar came here — with his last, dying strength — to bring the bitter message. And now —"

"What?" James Donachie hit the table with his clenched fist. "What'll we do? Sell out to the Chartered Company — at their own terms — for a beggar's pittance — shall we — shall we —"

He was silent. From the compound outside, at the river's edge, came the incessant, uncouth babble of native voices, high-pitched, clicking, grunting, half-articulate, and every once in a while breaking into shrill, meaningless cackles and hooting laughter — the staccato, night-and-day undercurrent of all Africa's symphony —

Donachie looked up, suddenly, sharply alert. A native voice had pronounced a name:

"DuPlessis!"

Answering clicks — uncouth grunts — excited babblings — laughter — then again:

"DuPlessis! Bad *juju* —"

Click-click-click — a great, sobbing grunt — more babblings —

Donachie turned to his partner.

"They also —" he began. "They seem to know — already — and —"
a bitter smile curled his lips — "when the jackals howl —"

"The jackals howl indeed," interrupted the Arab, sententiously.
"But, even thus, will my old buffalo die therefore? Allah!" he went on,
picking up his sjambok and making a significant gesture. "A stick to tan
the jackal's stinking hide! And, as for the old buffalo of Double-Dee —"

"Well?"

"He still has the pride and strength of his horns — to rend and
gore — and kill, if need be!"

He rose and left the room with unhurried step; and, a few minutes
later, James Donachie could hear his partner's voice brushing in from the
compound near the river's edge, talking in gently purring accents; then,
suddenly, a wicked curse in Arabic; the swish of the sjambok as it cut
through the air and raised welts on naked, plum-colored backs, and the
command, in clicking Galla:

"It is thus then —" down came the sjambok — "and thus — and
again thus, O ye evil-mouthed grandsons of great filth, that I argue with
you — aye — plead with you, belike, to remain loyal to the house of
Double-Dee that has been your father and mother these many years! A
covenant — This is the covenant —" another sharp swish-swish-swish
and answering howls of pain and imploring voices — "between ye dogs
and Double-Dee! A most secret covenant which ye will keep faithfully!
A covenant of silence — and no questions answered, whoever may ask
them — and no desertions — and all of ye held responsible for every
single one among ye — do ye understand, O ye sons of burnt fathers?"

"Yes, yes, O greatness, O clemency!" came the sobbing chorus.

And then the Arab's final:

"Great I am indeed! Clement to all the world — but most clement to
ye, dogs, though ye do not deserve it!"

And once more the acrid swash of the sjambok.

CHAPTER VIII.

SIR CHARLES LANE-FOX.

HALF AN HOUR later Mahmoud Ali Daud exchanged the usual grave
and elaborate oriental salutations with Sir Charles Lane-Fox, the governor of the colony and an old friend of his, in the latter's office. Sir
Charles Lane-Fox, ruling a land of many races, prided himself on being

all things to all men — British to the British, Portuguese to the Portuguese, and Arab to the Arabs. Thus it was classic Arabic he talked to his visitor, and Arabic, too, was the manner in which the Galla servant appeared, poured thick, burning, musk-flavored coffee into tiny cups, and placed on the low, inlaid taborets orange-flower water, cigarettes, rose-scented fruit-pastes cut in small squares, and honey-balls made of ground almonds and pistache-nuts.

Slowly Mahmoud Ali Daud sipped the aromatic and nearly scalding liquid, uttered a polite *"Bismillah,"* replied to in kind by the Englishman, wiped his fingers daintily on the embroidered napkin, and then remarked, with studied carelessness, that soul speaks closely to soul, but that the head and the hand answer for both.

"In other words," smiled Sir Charles, "you want my help?"

"Yes, old friend," said Mahmoud Ali Daud, slipping easily into English. "I want your help. I need it. There is nobody like you in the whole of Africa. Guide, philosopher, and friend — is not this the English saying — you are not only to Europeans and Arabs, but also — the which is salt to the impossible — to the natives themselves!"

Salt to the impossible, indeed! And it was the truth.

For it is known to all the world that Sir Charles Lane-Fox is the only man who understands the Africans — not only their virtues and their vices, which is nothing — but their mysteries — mysteries of which the Royal British Society for the Advancement of Science is completely and jeeringly ignorant, mysteries, the telling of which does not look well in an official, red-taped report to the Colonial Office.

He had lived up — is still living up — to the extraordinary theory that, as the governor of an Imperial Crown Colony, it is his duty to know more about the Dark Continent than the natives themselves — more even than the Congolese Arabs; and intent on such knowledge, he has dabbled in many unsavory places of that festering, gangrened, brooding land where he is serving his country because of his pride of race and class.

Withal, a lifetime in Africa had not scotched his sense of humor; and it was with humor — dry, slightly mischievous, slightly ironic — that he looked at the Arab and thanked him for the compliment, adding:

"Haven't I read something somewhere or other about looking out when an Arab becomes too eloquent? And, too, didn't a little bird whisper words to me a while back about an Arab's greed?"

"Possibly," came the unruffled reply, "and it is indeed greed which has sent me here. For, through recent events, the very existence of Double-Dee has become threatened."

The governor laughed.

"Joshing me, aren't you?" he asked. "Double-Dee threatened? Why — might as well threaten the Old Lady of Threadneedle Street!"

"True, though. The dagger of bankruptcy is at our throat."

The words carried utter conviction, and Sir Charles looked serious. Double-Dee, apart certain lapses, the result of climate more than anything else, to which a wise governor did well to close his official eyes, had been a steady influence for law and order in the colony.

"Surely not as bad as all that, Mahmoud," said the Englishman.

"Absolutely. You know that African trade depends on long credit with the banks —"

"Of course. Well?"

"The banks have stopped our credit —" the Arab's voice broke slightly — "the credit of Double-Dee —"

"No — no — impossible —"

"But a fact!"

"Spite work — perhaps of the Chartered Company?"

"That — and more — and worse —"

"But — why — why?"

"Because of something that has happened to us up in the interior — in the Waranga country. And we need your help, Sir Charles."

The latter was a rich man and a generous man.

"How much money do you need?" he asked. "I fancy I can —"

"No, no. Many thanks. But it isn't that. Money — even a large amount — would only help us temporarily. How do you say in English — a drop in —"

"A drop in the bucket?"

"Yes. Big trade needs continuous support, continuous, almost automatic credit. You see — it is the foundation of our building which is shaking."

"Been over-speculating?"

"No. We have not speculated at all. We have seen and grasped the greatest commercial opportunity in the whole of Africa — the Waranga country — a country twice the size of France, and rich — Allah — choking with riches! We have devoted all our influence and time and money to its development — and — now —" Mahmoud Ali Daud made a great gesture.

The governor inclined his head. Of late he had heard a great deal about the Waranga country, and there was at that moment, in his safe, a code message from the Colonial Office, marked secret and confidential, which spoke of it, spoke of British Imperial ambitions and interests and demands, of an all-British railway from the west to the east of Africa; spoke finally of a former treaty with a certain Continental power, that delineated the frontiers of future colonies and spheres of interests to be carved out of the huge African carcass. The certain Continental power was friendly. And still — there were the British Imperial interests; there was the old treaty gone into by a careless ambassador when the wine had been red and the little glasses of liqueur many and varicolored.

The Waranga country — thought Sir Charles — and Double-Dee's mysterious, potent influence up there — the old, foolish treaty — and, perhaps, since even the best are ambitious, dreams of a peerage —

Sir Charles was silent. He considered. Tried to develop and dovetail half-formed thoughts. Momentarily, the friend was lost in the shrewd diplomat.

"Yes, yes," he said finally, with the suspicion of a drawl that might have stood for many things. "Very interesting, I am sure, my dear Mahmoud —"

He was still suave, courtly, friendly. But there was a subtle, psychic change in the atmosphere, and the other, a Semite, sensitive to the core of him, noticed it, thought rapidly, then hid a smile. For years he had followed Europe's shifting, gliding game on the African chessboard, and — to quote his own metaphorical boast — when it came to African politics he could "hear the fleas cough."

Thus, for all the good it did in that particular quarter, the code message sent Sir Charles by the Colonial Office might as well have been written in plain English and lie on the table in full view. He lit a cigarette, sipped his coffee; then, with crafty ingenuousness, he told the other exactly what had happened in the Waranga country, winding up with:

"Therefore I repeat, we need your help — to discover the murderers — to bring them to justice. If we fail, the natives will lose confidence — might be won over by —"

"The Chartered Company?"

"You have said it. Will you help us?"

He was fully prepared for Sir Charles's reply that, in his official capacity, he had no right to interfere.

"Of course you can't," Daud agreed. "The Waranga country is independent — the property of the native chiefs —"

"Under the — ah — protection of Double-Dee?" gently suggested Sir Charles.

The Arab gave a tiny wink, and the governor smiled.

"Suppose — well —" he began, stopped, stroked his honey-colored, silken mustache, and smiled again; and, at once, the Arab knew that the psychological moment had arrived, and put his cards on the table, face up.

"You have wondered about Double-Dee's influence among the Warangas?" he asked.

"Yes."

"Ah —" the Arab lowered his voice — "there is a head — a shriveled, human *juju* head — a very great fetish!"

"The possession of —"

"Yes. Of Double-Dee. But, supposing Double-Dee should prefer to paint this shriveled old fetish head with the Union Jack?"

"Splendid idea! Only — there happens to be an old treaty, Mahmoud, of which you know nothing —"

"Of which I know everything!" calmly interrupted the Arab. "A treaty with a certain Continental power — a power which also, incidentally, is the sovereign lord of the Chartered Company!"

"Right," admitted Sir Charles.

And again the Arab winked slowly and meaningly.

"Tell me," he asked. "Is it not the immortal principle of Great Britain to protect weak and independent countries against foreign aggression — too, against the ruthless inroads of corporate interests — such as" — he purred — "the Chartered Company?"

"Quite so. Only — such weak and independent nations, to rely on Britain's strong arm, must show — well — a reason for existence, stability, a measure of civilization, certain political stamina — a something, in other words, hardly ever obtained by savage African chiefs."

Came a pause. Then the Arab's casual:

"How about the men of my own race? Are *they* savages — without civilization — without stamina and political stability?"

"No."

"Ah —" gently breathed the Arab, and they looked at each other as

Greek is said to look at Greek, and for many minutes they conversed in a flat, cozy undertone.

Half an hour later Mahmoud Ali Daud left the governor's residence with a mocking salaam in the direction of the Chartered Company's corrugated building that looked like a gray stain upon the yellow nakedness of the square near the Chapel of the Jesuit Fathers, while Sir Charles Lane-Fox sent for his aide-de-camp and caused a certain amount of relief to that festively inclined young Briton by announcing that he had decided to take a leave of absence.

"How long, sir?"

"Don't know yet. I am leaving tomorrow, Molyneux."

"Going to England, sir?" inquired the aide-de-camp, dreams in his heart of shorter work hours, longer play hours, and a special gymkhana to be arranged in honor of a rosy-cheeked, violet-eyed Sussex maiden recently arrived in the colony on a visit to her uncle, Major Patterson of the Haussa Gunners.

"No. I am chevying up the interior for a bit, on *safari* — big game hunting —"

"Hope you'll have jolly good sport. Any special instructions, sir?"

"Come back in an hour. Cable to go to the Colonial Office."

"Code, sir?"

"Yes. But I'll attend to the coding myself, Molyneux."

"Thank you, sir."

AND, LATE THE next afternoon, the purse-necked, red-faced Yorkshire knight who presided over the destinies of the Colonial Office, in Downing Street, London, read a cable slip, whistled through his teeth, and remarked in the direction of a framed portrait of Disraeli — Lord Beaconsfield — that "by gad! there are still a few constructive imperialists left in the bally old empire"; while, far out on the fringes of the little West African coast town where it merges, with the dramatic suddenness of the tropics, into a purple-gray welter of jungle and forest and thorny bush, the governor was stepping out with the easy, hip-swinging step of a man used to the long trek.

He was alone, nor had this created comment or curiosity. For years it had been a habit of his to roam through the hinterland unaccompanied by as much as a porter or a gun-bearer.

The second day out, late in the afternoon, he met an ash-smeared, wild-locked, fierce-eyed Moslem dervish — a sort of Islamic hedge-priest — who popped out at him from a clump of odorous cinnamon palms with a sonorous:

"*Salaam aleykhum!*"

"*Yah aleykhum salaam!*" came the courtly retort.

Then a low-voiced inquiry, an answer; and the governor disappeared in a small palm-leaf hut that blended perfectly into the thick under-growth, to reappear, not long afterward, the first dervish's brother-in-the-craft in sacred unkemptness.

"Sir Charles —" began the first dervish.

"Sir Charles no more! I am the Hajji Othman ibn Othman el-Yezdi, and a most learned man, well versed in the Koran and the Hadith, a disciple of the great Saint Abu Hanifyieh, and your lodge brother, Mahmoud!"

"Oh — Mahmoud?" smiled the other.

"Yes. No reason why you should change your name. It's as common among you Arabs as Campbell is in the Highlands of Scotland. Come — lodge brother — together we two shall bring the blessed lessons of the Koran to the naked savages of the outer kraals!"

And, with correct, nasal, guttural intonation, thereby slightly scandalizing the Arab, the Englishman chanted the Moslem declaration of faith — the "*Allah il'ulah Mohammed rasul 'ilah —*" and "*Allah il'ulah Mohammed rasul 'ilah,*" he chanted again, with hierarchic, pontifical unction, a day or two later as, well beyond the northeastern frontier of the Crown colony, he entered the hut of a Waranga tribal chief who bowed before the two dervishes with courtly greetings and a barbarous clanking and jingling of copper ornaments.

For to savages — they being perhaps the most tolerant people on earth — a holy man is a holy man, be he Moslem or Christian or Jew or Buddhist or fetish medicine man; and so the Waranga chief treated his guests with respect, gave them food and drink, and replied to their questions to the best of his ability.

CHAPTER IX.

THE WORD FROM NOWHERE.

AND IT seemed that the two wandering dervishes had many questions to ask, that they were leaky-tongued gossips even when measured with the garrulous Arab yardstick. The news of the villages they wanted to know, of the pasture lands, of the desert and the town, the forests and the jungles and the swamps, of kraals and compounds and voodoo huts; gossip of white man and black and half-breed.

Everything appeared to interest them, everything they asked, of chief and medicine man and villager and shepherd, day after day, the farther they penetrated into the hinterland. The natives gave answer readily, unsuspecting, even a little amused; for, of old, since the days of the Congolese Arab conquerors, did they know that curiosity and greed for information are the besetting sins of the tribe of Shem.

It was thus, by gradual elimination, never pushing a point too far for all their insatiable curiosity, that Arab and Englishman — working the one for his and his partner's private interests, the other for imperial glory, yet, both, somehow, for civilization and peace — discovered a certain thin trail that, while proving nothing exactly startling or altogether new, yet corroborated Mahmoud Ali Daud's instinctive suspicion that the Chartered Company was at the back of the whole trouble.

Their first discovery was of the negative variety. For they found out that nobody had attempted to interfere with the *juju* head by fief of which Double-Dee held spiritual, political, and commercial sway over the country.

On the other hand, since the unknown assassins had plied their deadly trade almost within sight of the fetish temple, they must surely have known of its existence and powerful significance.

Why then had they not tried to steal it, to do away with it, to duplicate, to all intents and purposes, the trick by which Double-Dee had gained possession?

Here Arab and Englishman differed radically as to the reason.

The former opined that the *juju* head's sacro-sanctity was entirely due to physical causes, to the armed show of force by which he had surrounded it, since he had strengthened the Waranga guard of honor about the lodge temple by picked and trustworthy blacks from among his own followers, Bakotos and Bagaweles and Banonogos, chief of them M'Kindi, the outcast Balolo, who had first brought him word about the mysterious coming of Darwaysh Ukkhab, *alias* Navarro d'Albani; while Sir Charles Lane-Fox explained the continued state of inviolability in which the *juju* head was held as really a master stroke on the part of the

Chartered Company.

"For," he said, "a savage is a simple human nature. He understands force, but is quite blind to intrigue, to subterranean underhandedness. To obtain the *juju* head by force, or theft, since theft *is* force would — oh — rather cheapen its spiritual value. But, if it should get under the control of the Chartered Company by clever, invisible manipulations, by intrigues — why, my dear Mahmoud, that would be rather a tremendous point gained by the Continental gentry — what?"

At all events, whatever the reasons, the fact remained the *juju* head seemed inviolate in its place of honor in the jungle temple, its sightless eyes, as before, surveying the grisly collection of voodoo charms that the worshipers had spread below it on the ground.

The other discovery was that a certain dissatisfaction was spreading like powder under spark among the Warangas. It was not exactly directed against Double-Dee themselves, but rather an uneasiness — even a sort of affectionate worry since both partners were popular with the native population — as to the firm's spiritual standing and salvation.

"Yes! —" to quote the words of M'pwa, a great Waranga chief, whom they interviewed — "pumped" would be the more correct expression — one night over tobacco and palm wine. "There is no doubt of Double-Dee's kindness and justice and fairness to all our people. Father and mother they have been to us and the morning dews and the ripening sun and the soft, soft rain of the wet season —"

He slurred, paused, sobbed, looked away from the two strangers, stirred the fire with the naked, callous sole of his foot till it blazed bright and hard and clear. He shivered a little and glanced rapidly over his shoulder, and, at once, the Arab winked significantly at the Englishman and whispered:

"Here comes the beginning of the end of the mystery whose slippery tail we have been chasing these many days!"

And it came, with a few words, short, broken, hacked, pronounced with a voice that was low, and yet pregnant with an unexpected, rather bitter strength:

"And — *yet* —"

Again the chief slurred and paused, again shivered, again glanced over his shoulders into the dark corners of the hut where the flickering flames were painting shadows among the black shadows, then grinning out with yellow eyes like mischievous hobgoblins.

"And yet — what?" softly echoed Mahmoud Ali Daud.

M'pwa shrugged his massive shoulders. He looked away from the compelling Arab eyes, felt drawn toward them as a bird is said to be fascinated by a snake's flat, filmy eyes, sobbed with all a savage's congenital melancholia, then, suddenly, as if to get through with an unpleasant task that had to be performed, made up his mind and spoke.

"I will tell you —" he said. "Perhaps you two can help and advise — you two — being holy men —"

"Very holy!" interrupted Sir Charles Lane-Fox, with never a smile.

"In league," commented Mahmoud Ali Daud, not to be outdone, jealous of his eloquence as only an Arab can be, "with the forces of good — but also with Musboot, the Devil, the Great Devil, the Father of Lies and Confusion, the Lord of Black-Black Darkness! Thus —" and the feline purr of his voice was marred by a threat — "tell us truthfully, O chief!"

"I will. Peace was in the land and plenty and satisfaction. And then — word came —"

"From where?" sharply cut in the Arab.

M'pwa made a vague, hopeless gesture.

"Out of the nowhere," he replied — "out of the bush — the swamps — the forests — the jungles —"

"Word by the sob of the drum, belike? By the gossip of the kraals —"

"Word from all over —" again the vague, hopeless gesture, and a flash of white, frightened eyeballs — "word from all over, all at once. Wherever men talked in council hut and women gossiped over the cooking fires and *umlinos* brewed medicine, the word came — was there — grew and stretched and bloated — like a snake of fire, burning, burning —"

"Like a snake of fire, burning, burning," he repeated, and the Arab remembered that this was a Waranga synonym for the supernatural, while the Englishman became a little impatient.

"Are you an old woman," he asked, "belike a barren spinster, fit only to wipe the children's noses and clean the household pots, that you babble babblings like the east wind, the wind without sense? 'Word came,' you say, '*came!*' You say that word was all over, all at once. But — whence and why and whither? Give us straight talk, chief!"

The Waranga rose, crossed the hut, and pulled aside the crimson, woolen blanket that covered the entrance. With a great deal of dignity, he pointed out into the night where, suddenly, the amazing stillness of the tropics was broken by the sounds of jungle and forest: the sardonic hooting of some great, dog-faced ape, the growl of a feeding lioness peaking from a rumbling, guttural bass to a shrill, incongruous treble, the mocking chirp and whistle of innumerable monkeys, the vicious, staccato barking of a fetid, spotted hyena sniffling for the reek of carrion, the crash of a warthog breaking uncouthly through the undergrowth, the frightened flutter of soft-winged birds before the murderous pounce of the hawk.

"Ask — *them*!" he said. "*I* do not know!"

He spoke with a sort of tense simplicity, enormously tragic in a way, throbbing with all the ever-present drama, the nameless fear and melancholia of the tropics, and the others realized that he was giving them the truth.

"No!" he repeated. "I do not know. I only know that word came, that word was here and there and all over — at once — wherever people foregathered! There was no escaping the word! There was no shutting one's ear or one's soul to its meaning! It was whispered everywhere — aye! — everywhere —"

And he went on to say that this word, which was all over, all at once, brushing out of the nowhere, the jungle, the forest, the pasture, and the sky, had spoken strange things; strange things — though this was not the way he put it — that, challenging, menacing, incomprehensible to the savage mind, had frightened the Warangas the more through the very pageantry of their obscure and ominous possibilities, the presentiment of a nameless doom that, once the theory was partly established in their minds, seemed to lurk ill-concealed behind every detail of what was going on in the hinterland —

Things that caused Sir Charles Lane-Fox to look up sharply, and Mahmoud Ali Daud, as was his superstitious wont, to snap his fingers rapidly and to touch the string of blue lapis beads about his neck.

For, it appeared, the word which was "all over, all at once," had declared and was declaring everywhere that the spirit of Mohammed Bello, the dead Fulah Emir whose shriveled head was the fetish of the land, was dissatisfied with its psychic abiding-place in Double-Dee; that it was seeking for a new home, in somebody else's body; that, in fact, it was transmigrating, ready — said the Englishman in a whisper to the Arab — to reincarnate itself very much like the soul of the Gautama Buddha or the Sakhyamuna Buddha which never dies, but chronically seeks and finds a new flesh envelope in which to work the many miracles.

"But —" Mahmoud Ali Daud turned to the Waranga — "why — tell me — why? The Warangas are in the keeping of the sacred *juju* head, aren't they?"

"Assuredly!" The answer came with a thump of utter sincerity.

"And —" was the next question — "the Warangas are not complaining of Double-Dee?"

"What reason is there for complaint? Father and mother are Double-Dee to the people of the kraals! Never an unjust action, never a bad deed! Merciful they are — and —"

"Exactly! So I was told before. Therefore — why should the spirit of Mohammed Bello be dissatisfied with Double-Dee? It is unreasonable, unjust, and —"

"Yes, yes! But that, too, has been explained by the word that is everywhere, all at once! For —" the Waranga was trying hard to put strange, unaccustomed ideas into the uncomplex native dialect which had no words even for the germs of these ideas — "you have heard of —" he paused, puzzled, wrinkled his forehead in strong endeavor, went on hesitatingly — "former lives? Former lives of — oh — same people — in other bodies — often, often, years ago, as many times as them are rays in the noon sun?"

"What do you mean, M'pwa?" asked the Arab a little angrily, to be immediately interrupted by the Englishman's soft:

"Go on, M'pwa. I understand!"

"Former lives! Other bodies! *Ahn'kwa!*" he clicked. "*Ahn'kwa!*" Again the puzzled, childlike expression on his face in rather ludicrous contrast with the ocher-and-white tribal smear across his flat nose and the waving plumes fastened by some mysterious methods in his short, kinky poll; again the vague, helpless gesturing.

His toes stirred the nearly extinct fire, kicking up a gray dust of warm ashes.

Another sobbing pause — and:

"Sayeth the word that is everywhere, all at once, that there is reward for merits of former lives — rewards in this life — ah —"

Yet another pause — the Arab's impatient grunt — the English-man's whisper: "Ssstt! Hold your horses!" and the Waranga continued, struggling on wearily in his endeavor or to give expression to unfamiliar thoughts, almost physical pain in the set, distressed look of his eyes:

"Punishment for sins committed in former lives — punishment in this life! A — ah — a cycle that never ends — like a snake swallowing its tail — a —" He slurred, stopped, moved his sinewy arms up and down, woodenly, clumsily.

"Perhaps," gently suggested Sir Charles — "a wheel of lives — a great wheel of good deeds and bad, M'pwa?"

"Yes, yes, yes!"

There was relief in the negro's accents; too, surprise, and boundless respect and admiration.

"You are indeed a most holy man," he continued, "learned and wise. Nothing is hidden from the mirror of your eyes. A wheel of lives — in an eternal accounting and reckoning of good and bad deeds! Thus — even thus — sayeth the word that is everywhere, everywhere, all at once! Pun-ishment for sins in former lives — committed in former lives by Double-Dee! Now, for these, in this life, the bitter price —"

And, while M'pwa droned on, with frequent sighs and pauses and vaguely helpless gestures, telling how the "word that was everywhere" accounted for it all, how the mysterious murders of Double-Dee's agents and the mutilations of their corpses dovetailed to make the "word" rea-sonable, how, finally, the Warangas, though they loved and respected Double-Dee, were becoming afraid that they, too, might have to share their fate and, therefore, eagerly awaiting another "word" that had been promised them and that would explain how the spirit of the great *juju* head had left Double-Dee's body to enter somebody else's; while the Arab listened impatiently, and with occasional, deep-throated ejaculations of "*Bismillah!*" and "*Aywah!*" and "*Allah kureem!*" and "*Insh'allah!*" — Sir Charles Lane-Fox was perfecting a certain theory.

He put it into words, an hour later, when he and Mahmoud Ali Daud were once more on the trek, on the last lap toward the jungle lodge. The moon squinted down sardonically, hostilely, with a red, bleary eye. The forest was about them like a living thing, possessed by the masterful con-sciousness of its strength, reaching up from below the two men's feet with a somber, tangled mass of undergrowth — seething like evil thoughts, like a nest full of venomous snakes — closing in on them like an implacable foe in a serried mob of immense trees that towered above in a great spread of twisted boughs and extravagant, fantastic creepers —

"Hateful, severe, pitiless!" murmured the Arab as he brushed aside a spiky liana. He felt lonely and small and crushed.

The Englishman laughed a mirthless laugh.

"Not exactly the proper background, it seems to me, for a successful preaching of the Buddhist sages' esoteric thoughts!" he drawled.

The Arab stopped in his tracks — they had come to a sudden clearing where the moon mirrored in a ragged expanse of black slime, caused by recent rainfalls, with, far in the silent west, the afterglow of an incongruously tender sunset.

"Meaning — what, brother-in-the-craft?" he asked, cool, alert, once more the hard-headed, materialistic Semite, the man of affairs who made his imagination subservient to his common sense.

CHAPTER X.

THE EMISSARY.

SIR CHARLES-FOX smiled. "You Moslems," he began, with that maddeningly academic precision of his which the other knew of old, "are rather a utilitarian lot — even in matters of religion. You are practical, hard-bitten, four-square —"

Mahmoud Ali Daud made an impatient gesture and spoke an impatient word.

But the Englishman continued serenely that — quite so! — all Moslems were alike, brothers under their skin.

"It makes no difference," he said, "if you are soldiers or sailors or priests or explorers or merchants or what-not. You are, every blessed one of you, missionaries, congenital proselytizers. And, as I said, you attend to your converting in a practical, hard-bitten way. You preach a simple, easily digested creed to these Africans. You give them no difficult theological nuts to crack, no extraordinary miracles and all that thaumaturgical bosh to believe in. All you ask them to do, so as to become fitly prepared for Islam, is to stop child murder, to cease worshiping idols, and to regulate divorce in a decent manner."

"I give salaams for the compliment," replied the Arab ironically, "But —" He lifted his eyebrows questioningly.

"We Christians," went on the other, in an even voice, "are also a fairly practical lot. Our missionaries, just like yours, preach a something that can be digested by these savages. Perhaps — unlike you — we are a trifle *too* spiritual, *too* ethical. Still — Christianity can be and has been successfully preached in Africa. Like Islam, it does not attempt to interfere too crassly with the negroes' basic, tribal ethics and their inherited ideas of right and wrong, and —"

"*Bismillah-lah-lah*!" came Mahmoud Ali Daud's deep-throated interruption. He threw up both his hands. "I admire your wisdom! I dote on your learning! I acknowledge you sage among the many sages. But —"

"But," said the Englishman, unruffled, "speaking about yet a third creed — the creed of the Lord Gautama Buddha —"

"Who is speaking of it?"

"*I* am, my impatient friend! I said that this —" he pointed into the great jungly silence that closed about the clearing like a remorseless wall — "that this is hardly a logical or promising background for the esoteric teachings of the Buddha —"

"Of course not! Who is preaching Buddhism here?"

"Who? Why — the man, or men — or shall we say the Chartered Company — who are trying to instill in the minds of the Warangas the theory of Buddhist incarnation and transmigration of souls, of sins committed in former lives to be punished in this life, of the wheel of things — the pitiless, eternal wheel to which all human lives are tied! The theory which even now is undermining the great firm of Double-Dee, which explains why your agents were murdered, which ultimately will cause the *juju* head of Mohammed Bello to seek a new abiding-place — ah — perhaps in the pompous, well-fed body of Baron Adrien de Roubaix.

"Why," he went on, a little more excited, "it's clear, isn't it? All that we heard tonight — and which the Waranga chief had such a deuce of a time expressing in his clumsy dialect — why, man, it's Buddhism — pure, unadulterated — and preached for a purpose. Don't you see, Mahmoud?"

"I do. But —"

"But?"

"Baron de Roubaix is a good Catholic!" exclaimed the Arab. "And — the Chartered Company people — there are Protestants among them, and Moslems — and Greek Orthodox — and Jews. Even — may Allah curse them most especially — atheists! But — Buddhists —

impossible! Buddhists — in Africa — working for the Chartered Company? As well look for fish on top of a mountain, or drag for the moon reflected in the water!"

"No faith except Buddhism believes in the theory of transmigration, of metempsychosis," insisted the Englishman, "in the wheel of things! The man at the back of all your trouble, the man who, by underground intrigues, by spreading whispers and rumors wherever he went, perhaps by a wholesale bribing of the medicine men, has sent forth the word — how did that Waranga chief put it? — yes! — the 'word that is everywhere, all at once,' he —"

"He was a clever man! But not a Buddhist! No!" The Arab shook his stubborn head. "A Buddhist — why — that means a Chinaman, or a Japanese, or possibly a Siamese. And I know all the employees of the Chartered Company. There is not a single yellow man among them —"

"Mahmoud!" smiled the Englishman. "At times I am disappointed in you. Chinaman — you say? Jap? Yellow man?"

"What else?"

"Rot! Why — he might be a white man, a Scot or Englishman or American, for all I know —"

"How — then —"

"The Chartered have recruited their people from all the four corners of the Earth, from all the seven seas, haven't they?"

"Yes. The Chartered people are freelances!"

"Exactly. Freelances. Buccaneers. Wanderers upon the face of the Earth. Surely there may be among their number one who has lived in the Far East a long time — in China, let us say — one who has become familiar with the Buddha's transcendental wisdom —"

And then the Arab's sharp interruption:

"There is — by Allah! There is! Witherspoon! 'Gloucester' Witherspoon they call him at the coast!"

"Oh — the old chap with the white goatee who curses so picturesquely — has been with the Chartered Company about three years — came up from the south after some incredible adventures of sorts?"

"The same," said the Arab. "He used to be — how do you say in English? — a Yankee skipper — used to be in the China trade — then in the service of the Chinese government —"

"How do you know?" asked Sir Charles.

"From his own lips," replied Mahmoud Ali Daud. "Down at

De Sousa's place, he has told me many a story of the Far East. Too —" and his thin, sensitive lips curled in a lopsided smile — "it appears that there are other tales. African tales. True tales, belike, about 'Gloucester' Witherspoon himself. Tales he did *not* tell me —"

"Of course not!" said Sir Charles. "I know. Bitter, reckless, blood-stained tales. Tales of crime and rapine and murder — the dregs of a white man's passions under southern stars — oh," he sighed, "tales hard to prove, and —"

He was silent.

At heart he was a simple man who, deep within himself, put the ordinary decencies of life above Magna Charta, above the demands and duties and tangled interests of ever-growing empire. Yet, in the past, there had been many instances when, for reasons of the latter, he had been forced to scotch the former, when the pride and whip of national, racial ambition had compelled him to be deaf to what, with slightly saturnine pathos, he called his "private conscience away from Downing Street's shadow."

Thus it had been with the Chartered Company, with their agents — with men like 'Gloucester' Witherspoon.

They had committed, were committing, every crime on the rather comprehensive African calendar — nor were these crimes always impossible to prove. But there was the pulling of international wires hither and thither. There was the dread of international misunderstandings and complications. There was the power of foreign chancelleries — *and* reigning houses — *and* stock exchanges.

Witherspoon! Sir Charles Lane-Fox had that honest, homespun New England name on several secret files in his private safe — with dates and names and little, dramatic black crosses.

And yet —

Mahmoud Ali Daud read the Englishman's heart like an open book.

"Perhaps this time —" he said very gently, "if Witherspoon be indeed the man who —"

"*If?* Heavens! There isn't even the margin of doubt. I happen to remember that, through the Chartered Company, he asked me for a special trade permit for the French Congo shortly after you went to Brussels to talk business with Baron de Roubaix. The French Congo runs around the north and northwest of the Waranga country like an arm crooked at the elbow, and the Chartered people are as thick as thieves with all the chiefs up there. It would be a losing game, commercially, to tap the Waranga treasures via the French Congo. The road is too long, too round-about.

"There is a stretch of jungle three hundred miles across that is nearly impassable, and there are three great rivers to cross. But it's a handy enough jumping-off place to start rotten propaganda among the blacks, to disseminate the 'word that is everywhere, all at once.' Well — don't you see? — the whole trouble started the very moment you refused the offer of the baron. He cabled to the coast and — it dovetails, Mahmoud!"

"Then — why — if we can prove it —"

"Even so —" again Sir Charles sighed — "perhaps once more the interests of empire will —"

He slurred, stopped, then went on with unexpected bitterness;

"Compromise! Always compromise! There you have the slogan of Britain! Compromise! Bargain!"

"But a profitable bargain," smiled the Arab, "for the empire!"

"Not to forget Double-Dee!" chimed in the governor with a return to his usual good humor.

CHAPTER XI.
WHAT THE DRUMS TOLD.

FOR A long time the two walked, considering the situation from every possible angle.

"Strike while the iron is hot," finally said the Englishman.

"Aye!" rejoined the other, in Oriental metaphor. "A good head has a thousand hands! And two good heads — yours and mine — *wah*!"

And, when the morning sun rose, golden and scarlet, netting the jungle in delicate reddish mist, painting tiny shadows of somber, crushed rose-pink among the tufted grass in the clearing, and sweeping up to the feathery tree-tops with a wild purple saraband of high-lights, they opened the bundles they had carried on their shoulders, plied scissors and razors, handled collapsible mirrors and other toilet accessories that seemed strangely out of place here in the gangrened heart of the Dark Continent, stripped, buried the ragged dervish clothes they had been wearing, washed, then dressed themselves in the clothes they had taken from the bundles: Mahmoud All Daud in loose cotton shirt and trousers and a light, volumi-nous woolen burnoose, fitting the large, fringed kerchief, the *kufiyah*, close to his head with the help of the *aakal*, the twisted rope of camel hair, and projecting it well over the forehead, thus both body and face thoroughly protected against the rays of the sun; Sir Charles Lane-Fox in the creamy, snug uniform laced with gold braid which he wore by right of office — and which he cursed roundly.

"Damn it!" he said, as he hooked the belt with perspiring fingers, "I s'pose it is all right to work for the empire — even to die for it on the field of battle. But why, in the name of all that's holy, should I have to court apoplexy and a heat stroke and all the plagues of ancient Egypt simply because my forefathers have decreed that tight trousers and tunic are the correct thing regardless of the climate?"

Mahmoud Ali Daud laughed, and the two trudged on, the Englishman still swearing and perspiring and nervously fingering his gold-braided collar, the Arab cool and comfortable in the swathing garb of Shem.

*   *   *

A few hours later, in the Waranga kraal on the outskirts of the sacred jungle temple enclosure, half a mile below Double-Dee's chief up-country agency post, the African drums boomed an odd tale into the glaring west, from village to village, spanning river and forest and jungle, on to the coast— where the sounds were caught and interpreted by a native drum-code specialist in the employ of the Chartered Company, and having been communicated to Baron Adrien de Roubaix, who was at breakfast, caused him to rise suddenly and upset the cup of steaming coffee at his elbow over his immaculate white linen trousers.

"Nom d'un nom d'un nom!"

The baron used decidedly bad language in French and Flemish and English, severely cuffed an unoffending Galla houseboy, who happened to be near, and rushed, hatless, coatless, to the main office of the Chartered Company, where he called the department managers into immediate, confidential conclave:

"Baker! Maillerand! OToole! Ali Othman! Lubersac! Van Raalte!"

They came on a run, listened — and remained speechless with chagrin and astonishment, Van Raalte finally crystallizing the prevailing sentiment into one sound Anglo-Saxon syllable:

"Damn!"

For the gossiping drums had boomed forth the news that Sir Charles Lane-Fox had once more done the impossible. While local rumor, aided and abetted by the governor's aide-de-camp acting under final instructions, had him hunting big game not far from the frontier, he had made a sudden and impressive appearance, in the steaming heart of Africa, at the kraal of the sacred *juju* head.

Like a shooting star sizzling out of the upper ether, he had dropped among the astounded Warangas, not as a footsore traveler, but as a British diplomat, gorgeous in creamy linen and gold braid, embodying in himself all the pomp and glory and circumstance of the empire which he served; accompanied — throbbed the drums — by Mahmoud Ali Daud — and saying that he had come because the "word that was everywhere, all at once," had commanded him, and —

Here, although the drum-code specialist listened close to the sound waves that separated themselves, like the taps of a Morse code, from the accompanying African symphony, the barking of the dogs, the shrill cackling of the houseboys, and the querulous falsetto of the women bending over their cooking pots, the tale of the drum had shut off in mid air.

"What the devil does it mean?" stormed the baron. "Here, Witherspoon!" as the white-bearded Gloucester skipper, who had recently returned from the interior with reports of splendid progress, came into the room. "What *does* it mean, you —"

He turned to Lubersac, who had given up an honorable berth in the Paris Foreign Office to become the Chartered Company's special adviser on international affairs.

"What do you make of it?" he asked.

Lubersac stroked his silken beard.

"Sir Charles has no right up there —"

"Why not?"

"There's the old treaty between England and —"

"Sir Charles has not double-crossed that treaty yet —"

"No — not *yet*!" chimed in Maillerand, the ironic Parisian expatriate.

"But — *enfin*," cried the baron; "there is no trouble between England and — we would have heard —"

Bannng! the drums commenced again; mentioned with thump and thump and double thump that the tale was not yet ended; that even greater things were brewing up-country. For Sir Charles Lane-Fox, even now, was assembling the chiefs and medicine men in solemn audience. He was taking — said the drums — a small silken flag from his pocket — was holding it high — it was the Union Jack!

Again the drums ceased throbbing, and the baron clenched his fists till the knuckles stretched white.

"No, no!" he cried. "Sir Charles can't get away with that!"

"Crude, isn't it?" smiled Van Raalte.

"Yes. The old treaty holds — and holds tight. The Waranga country is within our sphere of interests —"

"But," suggested Lubersac, "it's still an independent country, you know —"

"Yes. But the old treaty says distinctly that, if ever it should be annexed — by any European power — it's we who have the first right, the first refusal —" He lowered his voice. "Here, Lubersac! A cable to Paris — send it in duplicate to Amsterdam and Brussels — I'll show Sir Charles a thing or two!"

And he dictated for several minutes while, at the same time, a thousand miles inland, Sir Charles Lane-Fox, standing below the grinning *juju* head of Mohammed Bello, Mahmoud Ali Daud by his side, was finishing his harangue to the Waranga chiefs and medicine men who surged about him like a plum-colored sea, in all the barbarous regalia of their caste and craft, their bodies smeared with ocher, their faces plastered thickly with white and striped with crimson, their hair carefully trained into fantastic shapes, their forearms clanking with broad brass bracelets, their legs covered from foot to ankle with coils upon coils of copper wire.

"Thus," he said, "O ye chiefs and *umlinos* of the Waranga nation, the word that is everywhere, all at once, has once more spoken the truth. For there is no doubt that Mahmoud Ali Daud has committed the many sins in his former lives —"

"Let us not mention this life!" mumbled the irrepressible Arab.

"Nor," went on the Englishman, "is there a doubt that, tied to the inexorable wheel of things, he must atone for these sins in his present span of life. First came there punishment — harsh, destructive punishment — the killing and mutilating of Double-Dee's agents, the ruining of Double-Dee's business. Now the word that is everywhere, all at once, has spoken to one in the watches of the night, saying that there shall be yet another punishment, that Mahmoud Ali Daud must atone with the deed, too; that he must carry, in the future, that most crushing burden, that most galling of all the chains of slavery called Sovereignty.

"Yes — thus sayeth the word that is everywhere — he must bow his proud neck to the yoke! He must become your Sultan, your Emir, your highest servant, O you men of the Waranga nation! All wrongs he will right. Justice and mercy and prosperity he will bring. Never ceasing shall be his toil. He will serve you well and faithfully as did, centuries ago, Mohammed Bello, the great Emir, whose sacred head is your powerful *juju*. Yes! The spirit of Mohammed Bello has left the soul of Double-Dee. It has entered the soul of Mahmoud Ali Daud. And —" again he waved the small, silken Union Jack — "as representative of the British Empire I give most solemn oath that my country will faithfully protect the rights of this new country, this new Sultanate, ruled by Mahmoud Ali Daud, Emir!"

It was over six weeks later that Sir Charles Lane-Fox was closeted with the two partners of Double-Dee and Baron Adrien de Roubaix.

"Baron," he said, "I don't care how you make your peace with your people at home, how you straighten out that mess you got yourself into with your Foreign Office and your Colonial Office and all the rest of them. I repeat — I shall not recede from my position —"

"But — Sir Charles — the treaty!"

"The treaty says that, in the final division of the African spoils, England gives up all claims to the Waranga country —"

"Well?"

"There *is* no division of any spoils! England has not annexed one square inch of Waranga territory. The Warangas, out of their own free will, have united their tribes into a Sultanate, have appointed an Arab, a civilized man, as their Emir. We simply were asked by the new Emir —" he bowed to Mahmoud Ali Daud, who bowed in return — "to protect the country against foreign aggression. Loyal to the traditions of empire, of justice, we could not say no!"

"I — I —" blustered the baron.

"Wait!" Sir Charles continued. "If, by any chance, you should feel inclined to pull wires right and left, to make trouble for the new Emir, for Britain, for me — why — I, personally, should be glad —"

"Glad?" Baron de Roubaix was utterly astonished. "Why?"

"Because, for once, I should then be able to disregard the interests of the empire — to follow the call of my own conscience — to —" his voice dropped to a very gentle whisper — "to bring to justice, which means the gallows, one 'Gloucester' Witherspoon, agent of the Chartered Company. And perhaps, Baron, perhaps it might also come out during the trial that you yourself — oh — murder of several of Double-Dee's agents — accessory before the fact — all that sort of thing. *Good* morning, Baron! You leaving, too, Mahmoud — and you, Donachie? All right. Drop in again — any time."

Out on the street, the Arab touched the baron's arm.

"Baron," he said, "I am a man of few words. I detest bargaining. My first offer still stands. My partner and I — we are still willing to sell all our African interests —"

"Mahmoud — what —" interrupted Donachie.

"For fifty-one per cent of the Chartered Company stock — for control —"

"Control? Why, man —" said the baron, who at times had a certain sardonic sense of humor, even when directed against himself, "you have control now! Complete control! Control over all the trade of Africa! All right, though. Come along to the office and we'll sign up."

"*Bismillah*!" said the Arab piously.

Light

BENEATH the sooty velvet of the New York night, Tompkins Square was a blotch of lonely, mean sadness.

No light loungers there waiting for a bluecoat's hickory to tickle their thin, patched soles; no wizened news vendor spreading the remnants of his printed wares about him and figuring out the difference between gain on papers sold and discount on those returned unsold; no Greek hawker considering the advisability of beating the high cost of living by supping on those figs which he had not been able to sell because of their antiquity; no maudlin drunk mistaking the blur in his whisky-soaked brain for the happy twilight of the foggy green isle.

For Tompkins Square is both the soul and the stomach — possibly interchangeable terms — of those who work with cloth and silk and shoddy worsted, with needle and thread, with thimble and sewing-machine, those who out of their starved, haggard East-Side brains make the American women — the native-born — the best dressed in all the world. Sweatshop workers they are: men from Russia and Poland, men from the Balkans, from Sicily, Calabria, and Asia Minor; men who set out on their splendid American adventure, not for liberty, but for a chance to earn enough to keep body and soul together — and let the ward boss and the ward association attend to the voting, including the more or less honest counting of votes.

Work — eat — sleep — and lights out at ten! Such is the maxim of the neighborhood, since lights cost money, and money buys food.

Thus Tompkins Square on that night, as on all nights, was sad and dark and tired and asleep. Just the scraggly, dusty trees, the empty benches, and a shy gleam of the half-veiled moon where it struck the fantastic, twisted angle of a battered municipal waste-paper receptacle, or a bit of broken bottle glass that was trying to drown its despair in a murky puddle.

On the north side of the square stood the tenement house with the lighted window — like a winking eye — directly beneath the roof, high up. The house was gray and pallid; incongruously baroque in spots, distributed irregularly over its warty façade, where the contractor had got rid of some art balconies and carved near-stone struts left over from a bankrupt Bronx job. It towered over the smug red-brick dwellings — remnants of an age when English and German were still spoken thereabouts — with thin, anemic arrogance, like a tubercular giant among a lot of short, stocky, well-fleshed people; sick, yet conscious of his height and the dignity that goes with it.

HE SAW the lighted window as he crossed the square from the south side, and sat down on one of the benches and stared at it.

Steadily he stared, until his eyes smarted and burned and his neck muscles bunched painfully.

For that glimmering light, gilding the fly-specked pane, meant to him the things he hated, the things he had cheated and cursed and ridiculed — and, by the same token, longed for and loved.

It meant, to him, life — and the reasons of life.

It meant to him humanity and the faith of humanity: which is happiness. The right to happiness! The eternal, sacerdotal duty of happiness!

Happiness?

He laughed. Why — damn it! — happiness was a lie. Happiness was hypocrisy. It meant the dieting of man's smoldering, natural passions into an artificial, pinchneck, thin-blooded Puritanism. It spelled the mumming of the thinking mind — the mind that was *trying* to think — into the speciosities of childish fairy-tales. It was a sniveling reminder of pap-fed infancy.

The only thing worthwhile in life was success — which is selfishness. Selfishness sprawling stark-contoured and unashamed, sublimely unself-conscious, serenely brutal — a five-plied Nietzscheism on a modern business basis which acknowledged neither codified laws nor principles.

It had been the measure and route of his life, and — he whipped out the thought like something shameful and nasty, like a nauseating drug which his mind refused to swallow — it had cheated him.

Yes, by God! It had cheated him, cheated him!

For, first, it had given him gold and power and the envy of men, which was sweet.

Then, as a jest of Fate's own black brewing, it had taken everything away from him overnight, in one huge financial crash, and had made of him what he was tonight: gray, middle-aged, bitter, joyless — and a pauper. It had brought him here, to Tompkins Square, and had chucked him, like a worn-out, useless rag, into this dusty, sticky bench whence he was staring at the lighted window, high up.

He wondered what was behind it, and who?

Three days earlier he had come to New York with ten dollars — his last ten dollars — in his pocket. He had taken a room in this tenement-house, and every night he had sat on the bench and had stared at the warty, baroque façade.

Always it had been dark. Always the tenants, the hard-working people who lived there, had turned out their lights around ten o'clock with an almost military regularity that reminded him of barracks and a well-disciplined boarding-school.

He knew most of them. For they had talked to him, on stairs and landings and leaning from windows, with the easy garrulousness of the very poor who can't be snobs since they are familiar with each other's incomes and flesh-pots. They had lifted the crude-meshed veils of their hearts and hearths and had bidden him look — and all he had seen had been misery.

He checked the thought.

No! That wasn't true!

He had also seen love and friendship, and fine, sweet faith — and that was why he hated them — why he pitied and despised them.

Faith — love — friendship! To the devil with the sniveling, weak-kneed lot of 'em! They spelled happiness — and happiness did not exist — and —

Happiness!

The thought, the word, recurred to his brain with maddening persistency. It would not budge.

Happiness.

"Why, happiness is behind that lighted window!" The idea came to him — almost the conviction.

But what happiness? And whose?

He speculated who might be up there, in the garret room squeezed by the flat roof. He tried to picture to himself what might be shimmering behind that golden flash.

Perhaps it was Fedor Davidoff, the little hunchbacked Russian tailor, with the fat, golden-haired, sloe-eyed wife. He might be cele-brating the coming of freedom to his beloved Russia. Or he might be sitting up late to finish some piece of work — to earn extra money. For his wife was expecting a child. He had three already, curly-haired, straight-backed. But he wanted more —

"Children make happiness, eh?" he used to say.

Or — wait! Perhaps it was Peter Macdonald, the artist, dreaming over his lamp and his rank, blackened pipe, and deliberating with himself where he would live — upper West Side or lower Fifth — when the world should have acknowledged his genius and backed up the opinion with solid cash. Peter had lived now for over three months in the tenement-house. "Like the neighborhood — bully atmosphere — marvelous greens and browns," was the reason he gave. But the other tenants smiled. They knew that Peter lived there because his room cost him only two dollars a week, and because he took his meals with the Leibl Finkelsteins on the first floor for three dollars more.

Perhaps a pair of lovers. Enrique Tassetti, the squat, laughing Sicilian, who had taken to himself a bride of his own people. They would have spent fifty cents for a bottle of Chianti, another fifty for bread and mushrooms and oil and pepper to turn into a dish worthy of a Sicilian — or a king.

Again it might be Donchian, the Armenian, burning the midnight oil over the perfection of the mysterious invention of which he spoke at times, after having worked with needle and thread since six o'clock in the morning; or old Mrs. Sarah Kempinsky, reading and rereading the letter which her soldier son had sent her from France; or —

What did it matter?

Whoever was sitting behind that lighted window was happy — happy — and the man's imagination choked, his mind became flushed and congested.

He was quite unconscious of his surroundings. The stillness of the streets seemed magical, the loneliness absolute. Only from very far came sounds: the Elevated rattling with a steely, throaty sob; a surface-car clanking and wheezing; a hoarse Klaxon blaring snobbishly; a stammering, alcoholic voice throwing the tail-end of a gutter song to the moist purple veils of the night.

But he did not hear.

He was conscious only of the lighted window, high up. It seemed to glitter nervously, to call to him, to stretch out, as if trying to communicate to him an emotion it had borrowed by contact with something — with somebody.

That was just the trouble. He wondered who that somebody was, what that something might be. Whoever it was, it seemed urgent, clamorous. Silently clamorous. His subconsciousness grew thick with amazement and wonder and doubt. It surged up — crowded, choking, tumultuous.

The lighted window!

What was behind it? What was its riddle?

HE KNEW that he must find out, and so he rose, crossed the street, entered the house, and was up the stairs three steps at the time.

He found the room without any trouble, and opened the door. He did not knock.

He stepped inside; and there, on the bed, he saw a motionless figure, faintly outlined beneath a plain white sheet, a tall candle burning yellow at the foot of the bed, another at the head.

He crossed over, lifted a corner of the sheet, and looked. And he saw the face of a dead man. It was calm and serene and unutterably happy.

Then it dawned upon him:

The man on the bed was himself.

A Yarkand Survey

AND IBRAHIM said: Power is a dangerous weapon, my dear. The many use it only to their own advantage and to split the noses of their enemies. But the few who use it for the good of the many, their names shall be exalted and their memory kept ever green through lasting monuments of stone and brass, cunningly carved and ornamented, so that unborn generations may see and admire.

You, Abdullah, you read my heart as an open book, and you know how I dislike to speak about myself. But still—let me tell you what happened when Yakoob Beg the Wise, the Fount of the Just Law, ruled the land beyond the snows of the north.

I had come in the glittering retinue of the Beg who, quick to read talent and to appreciate devotion, looked at me with favor and appointed me Governor of the Province of Yarkand, and not only governor, but also assessor and collector of taxes, high judge, and commander of the local contingent.

I had come up from the passes with seven annas in my waistband, and accompanied by a woman whom I had found in the harem of a Yuszufai mollah who had given me hospitality. But once Governor of Yarkand, I invested my scanty fortune most judiciously, and I prospered exceedingly, both in money and wives.

Allah Kureem! How I prospered!

Eh? through iniquity and oppression? No, no. Am I an Armenian that I should grip fangs of cruelty in the bowels of the land which the All-Merciful has given into my keeping? No, no.

First of all I made a personal inspection of the district under my command. There was hardly a merchant, cultivator, or horse-dealer, rich or poor, powerful or weak, Orthodox or Soofi, whose lands and belongings I did not scrutinize with eyes of honest discernment, until finally, after comparing and studying and figuring, I had acquired exact knowledge of the personal affairs of every householder within my jurisdiction. And assisted by my faithful Hindu clerk, the pandit Rakhal Chandar Tawari, I used this knowledge with miraculous results.

How? How?

Are you a little lisping babe that you should ask me how?

Heart of my heart, was I not the governor, the assessor, and collector of taxes, the commander of the local contingent, the power-clothed representative of Yakoob Beg the Wise, the Fount of the Just Law?

And though I say it who should not, I was always willing to pour forth the broad stream of benevolence and to assist the struggling peasants with personal loans, so that they could pay their taxes and keep out of prison.

And Fate had endowed me with such miraculous skill in the making out of accounts, that a man to whom I had loaned fifty rupees might go on making monthly payments of twenty rupees for three years without reducing his debt by a single anna!

Great are the virtues of compound interest, and indeed, my books proved beyond the shadow of a doubt that the debt, instead of being reduced, had grown with each successive payment, until in the course of a few years the original loan of fifty rupees had become half a lakh — thanks be to Allah the Compassionate!

In good years, when abundant rain watered the smiling fields, when the crops were green and bounteous, the fish swarming in the river, and the trees heavy with fruit, I would reap a goodish share of Allah's gifts, and, loyal servant of the Beg, I would increase the taxes a little, just a little.

And in bad years, when black famine stalked through the fields, when the sun burnt as do the eternal fires in the Seventh Hall of Perdition, when the smoky, yellow haze rose from the ground and suffocated the parching crops, when the fish perished of thirst in the drying streams, when Yarkand was dying of hunger, and the call to prayer gave way to the chant of despair — when my tortured heart bled with the pity of it all — even then I would prosper exceedingly.

For look you: I am a follower of the True Prophet — whose name be praised — charitable to a fault, and quite unlike the Armenian pigs who suck the heart-blood of this unhappy land: again I would loosen the strings of my compassionate purse and advance thousands of rupees to the men of Yarkand.

Never would I accept more than three hundred and twelve per cent a month, and I would be contented, as only security, with a mortgage on every bullock and goat, every cart-wheel and fishing-net, every tree and well in my blessed province.

My eyes filled with tears of gratitude when I beheld the righteous growth of my treasures. I said that I prospered— and indeed, there was never cart-wheel tired, there was never net anchored, tree planted or grain sown, but I received a fair share of the profits.

I was the Corporation of Yarkand.

But the border mountains of my domain were inhabited by savage Kanjuti tribesmen who recognized no ruler and respected no law, who fought among themselves and believed that Allah had created their neighbor weaker than themselves, so that they could safely steal his cattle and carry off his female relatives. They looked down from their round tower houses and beheld the broad acres of Yarkand smiling at their feet, verily a heaven-sent invitation to loot and kill and be happy.

They saw fat Turki cattle grazing in the pastures. They saw lithe Turki women prepare rich food for their masters. They saw ample-girded bankers count their gain.

So the *jirgahs* met, and the priests went among the rock-perched villages preaching war, Holy War, in the name of Allah, the king of swords and men. They descended into the trembling plains, smashed my regiments as the whirling mill-stones smash the dry grains of the field, and raided the land for many miles. And they returned to their rocky fastnesses well pleased with themselves and the bounty of Allah's gifts.

Yakoob Beg the Wise, on hearing of this outrage, decided to send a punitive expedition against the robbers and to recover the stolen cattle and women. He proclaimed that he would carry the flames of revenge into the remotest villages of the Kanjutis.

And one day a messenger hastened to my palace and delivered into my hands a letter from the Beg.

I opened it and trembled.

For, behold—the Beg commanded me to proceed on a journey up the Yarkand River, from my capital as far as the mountains, and to survey the main stream and its principal tributaries.

It had been decided, he wrote, that the army, so as to save them the long march across the sun-scorched, man-killing plains, should travel on boats to the head of navigation, thus using its undiminished strength in climbing and conquering the steep Kanjuti strongholds.

I should therefore make an exact *personal* survey of the river and exert especial care in measuring the breadth of it, that it might be known to the war-chiefs how many boats could travel upstream, shoulder on shoulder, without danger of collision.

The Beg's letter wound up with recommending me to the mercy of Almighty Allah, the King of the Day of Judgment, and the detailed account of the many cheerful things which would happen to me in case of mistakes.

I said that I trembled when I read the letter, the Beg's written orders.

And indeed — though mine was a miraculous skill in the raising of the many taxes, the making out of accounts, and the intricacies of compound interest, I possessed scarcely any knowledge in the art of surveying treacherous streams.

Gladly would I have commissioned some ancient and learned sheik to do the work for me. But I thought of the Beg's implicit orders, I thought of the Beg's many spies, and then I thought of the Beg's skilled executioners, those red-robed gentry who hold the Central-Asian record in the swift removing of perfectly healthy heads.

I increased the taxes on fishing-nets and water-rights, and I administered a severe bodily chastisement to my favorite slave. But it failed to make me feel any happier.

So I sent word to my confidential adviser, the pandit Rakhal Chandar Tawari, and told him of my bitter plight.

We put our heads together and talked earnestly and long, the Hindu quoting the Vedas and the Upanishads, and the laws of Manu, and I referring to the Koran, as well as to the Lila-Shastra and other more worldly books. Finally we evolved a plan of judging distances which combined the merits of facility with the charm of novelty.

Early next morning, after ceremonious prayers, we proceeded up the stream on a comfortable native craft, and I took up a commanding position on top-deck, cross-legged, calm, and dignified. By my side sat my faithful Hindu clerk, in front of me stood a large jewel-incrusted hubble-bubble, and across my knees lay a carefully-sighted rifle which had fetched its weight in silver north of the Khaibar.

Slowly we sailed for a few miles, and presently the river broadened, and we came within sight of a village. The Hindu looked up, smiling his oily Babu smile, and gravely I winked at him and asked in accents of disinterested serenity:

"Tell me, Chandar. What wouldst thou judge to be the distance from here to yonder village?"

The Hindu replied timorously:

"Protector of the poor, mayest thou look with favor on thy undeserving slave. I judge the distance to be about three hundred yards, oh, thou pilgrim."

And I said:

"Curse thee for a blind owl. Thy ancestry is rotten, thy manners deplorable, and thou hast been fed on the flesh of a yellow dog. Verily do I declare that thy female progenitors have been noseless, shameless, and disreputable since the day of the Hegira. Thou doest lie to me, thy benefactor and master. For indeed do I proclaim that the distance is nearer six hundred yards."

Again I winked a grave wink, and, bringing the rifle to my shoulders, I opened fire on the village. The bullets took effect, and crowds of shrieking Turkis rushed out of their huts to see what all the trouble was about, while the groans of a wounded man drifted across the water.

Then I turned again to my faithful pandit and said:

"Did I not tell thee so? The distance is indeed six hundred yards. My rifle spoke the truth, and thou art as blind as that new-born, objectionable, and particularly illegitimate mongrel-pup, thy unclean female ancestor, which justly ashamed of having given birth to thee, committed suicide, thus losing its chances of paradise."

Thus, beloved one, did we journey up the river, exchanging pleasant converse and measuring with bullets from shore to shore, in obedience to the orders of Yakoob Beg, and to the greater glory of myself.

And I, to commemorate the successful survey, caused the following inscription to be engraved on a copper tablet which to this day can be seen in the great bazaar of Yarkand's capital:

> During the just and equitable rule of Ibrahim Fadlallah, the Egyptian, that accomplished and charitable governor who, faithful servant of Yakoob Beg the Wise, the Fount of the Just Law, brought law and order into this province, whose generosity like clouds showered blessings everywhere, and at whose door fortune attended as an insignificant slave, this monument was erected to commemorate the survey of the great river which waters Yarkand, and as a feeble testimonial of a nation's gratitude.

Fear

THE FACT that the man whom he feared had died ten years earlier did not in the least lessen Stuart McGregor's obsession of horror, of a certain grim expectancy, every time he recalled that final scene, just before Farragut Hutchison disappeared in the African jungle that stood, spectrally motionless as if forged out of some blackish-green metal, in the haggard moonlight.

As he reconstructed it, the whole scene seemed unreal, almost oppressively, ludicrously theatrical. The pall of sodden, stygian darkness all around; the night sounds of soft-winged, obscene things flapping lazily overhead or brushing against the furry trees that held the woolly heat of the tropical day like boiler pipes in a factory; the slimy, swishy things that glided and crawled and wiggled underfoot; the vibrant growl of a hunting lioness that began in a deep basso and peaked to a shrill, high-pitched, ridiculously inadequate treble; a spotted hyena's vicious, bluffing bark; the chirp and whistle of innumerable monkeys; a warthog breaking through the undergrowth with a clumsy, clownish crash — and somewhere, very far away, the staccato thumping of a signal drum, and more faintly yet the answer from the next in line.

He had seen many such drums, made from fire-hollowed palm trees and covered with tightly-stretched skin — often the skin of a human enemy.

Yes. He remembered it all. He remembered the night jungle creeping in on their camp like a sentient, malign being — and then that ghastly, ironic moon squinting down, just as Farragut Hutchison walked away between the six giant, plumed, ochre-smeared Bakoto warriors, and bringing into crass relief the tattoo mark on the man's back where the shirt had been torn to tatters by camel thorns and wait-a-bit spikes and saber-shaped palm leaves.

He recalled the occasion when Farragut Hutchison had had himself tattooed after a crimson, drunken spree at Madam Celeste's place in Port Said, the other side of the Red Sea traders' bazaar, to please a half-caste Swahili dancing girl who looked like a golden Madonna of evil, familiar with all the seven sins. Doubtless the girl had gone shares with the

Levantine craftsman who had done the work — an eagle, in bold red and blue, surmounted by a lop-sided crown, and surrounded by a wavy design. The eagle was in profile, and its single eye had a disconcerting trick of winking sardonically whenever Farragut Hutchison moved his back muscles or twitched his shoulder blades.

Always, in his memory, Stuart McGregor saw that tattoo mark.

Always did he see the wicked, leering squint in the eagle's eye — and then he would scream, wherever he happened to be, in a theatre, a Broadway restaurant, or across some good friend's mahogany and beef.

Thinking back, he remembered that, for all their bravado, for all their showing off to each other, both he and Farragut Hutchinson had been afraid since that day, up the hinterland, when, drunk with fermented palm wine, they had insulted the fetish of the Bakotos, while the men were away hunting and none left to guard the village except the women and children and a few feeble old men whose curses and high-pitched maledictions were picturesque, but hardly effectual enough to stop him and his partner from doing a vulgar, intoxicated dance in front of the idol, from grinding burning cigar ends into its squat, repulsive features, and from generally polluting the *juju* hut — not to mention the thorough and profitable looting of the place.

They had got away with the plunder, gold dust and a handful of splendid canary diamonds, before the Bakoto warriors had returned. But fear had followed them, stalked them, trailed them; a fear different from any they had ever experienced before. And be it mentioned that their path of life had been crimson and twisted and fantastic, that they had followed the little squinting swarth-headed, hunchbacked *djinni* of adventure wherever man's primitive lawlessness rules above the law, from Nome to Timbuktu, from Peru to the black felt tents of Outer Mongolia, from the Australian bush to the absinth-sodden apache haunts of Paris. Be it mentioned, furthermore, that thus, often, they had stared death in the face and, not being fools, had found the staring distasteful and shivery.

But what they had felt on that journey, back to the security of the coast and the ragged Union Jack flapping disconsolately above the British governor's official corrugated iron mansion, had been something worse than mere physical fear; it had been a nameless, brooding, sinister apprehension which had crept through their souls, a harshly discordant note that had pealed through the hidden recesses of their beings.

Everything had seemed to mock them — the crawling, sour-miasmic jungle; the slippery roots and timber falls; the sun of the tropics, brown, decayed, like the sun on the Day of Judgment; the very flowers, spiky, odorous, waxen, unhealthy, lascivious.

At night, when they had rested in some clearing, they had even feared their own campfire — flaring up, twinkling, flickering, then coiling into a ruby ball. It had seemed completely isolated in the purple night.

Isolated!

And they had longed for human companionship — white companionship.

White faces. *White* slang. *White* curses. *White* odors. *White* obscenities.

Why — they would have welcomed a decent, square, honest *white* murder; a knife flashing in some yellow-haired Norse sailor's brawny fist; a belaying pin in the hand of some bullying Liverpool tramp-ship skipper; some Nome gambler's six-gun splattering leaden death; some apache of the Rue de Venise garroting a passerby.

But here, in the African jungle — and how Stuart McGregor remembered it — the fear of death had seemed pregnant with unmentionable horror. There had been no sounds except the buzzing of the tsetse flies and a faint rubbing of drums, whispering through the desert and jungle like the voices of disembodied souls, astray on the outer rim of creation.

And, overhead, the stars. Always, at night, three stars, glittering, leering; and Stuart McGregor, who had gone through college and had once written his college measure of limping, anemic verse, had pointed at them.

"The three stars of Africa!" he had said, "The star of violence! The star of lust! And the little stinking star of greed!"

And he had broken into staccato laughter which had struck Farragut Hutchinson as singularly out of place and had caused him to blurt forth with a wicked curse:

"Shut your trap, you —"

For already they had begun to quarrel, those two pals of a dozen tight, riotous adventures. Already, imperceptibly, gradually, like the shadow of a leaf through summer dusk, a mutual hatred had grown up between them.

But they had controlled themselves. The diamonds were good, could be sold at a big figure; and, even split in two, would mean a comfortable stake.

Then, quite suddenly, had come the end — the end for them.

And the twisting, gliding skill of Stuart McGregor's fingers had made sure that Farragut Hutchison should be that one.

Years after, when Africa as a whole had faded to a memory of coiling, unclean shadows, Stuart McGregor used to say, with that rather plaintive, monotonous drawl of his, that the end of this phantasmal African adventure had been different from what he had expected it to be.

In a way, he had found it disappointing.

Not that it had lacked in purely dramatic thrills and blood-curdling trimmings. That wasn't it. On the contrary, it had had a plethora of thrills.

But, rather, he must have been keyed up to too high a pitch; must have expected too much, feared too much during that journey from the Bakoto village back through the hinterland.

Thus when, one night, the Bakoto warriors had come from nowhere, out of the jungle, hundreds of them, silent, as if the wilderness had spewed them forth, it had seemed quite prosy.

Prosy, too, had been the expectation of death. It had even seemed a welcome relief from the straining fatigues of the jungle pull, the recurrent fits of fever, the flying and crawling pests, the gnawing moroseness which is so typically African.

"An explosion of life and hatred," Stuart McGregor used to say, "that's what I had expected, don't you see? Quick and merciless. And it wasn't. For the end came — slow and inevitable. Solid. Greek in a way. And *so* courtly! *So* polite! That was the worst of it!"

For the leader of the Bakotos, a tall, broad, frizzy, odorous warrior, with a face like a black Nero with a dash of Manchu emperor, had bowed before them with a great clanking of barbarous ornaments. There had been no marring taint of hatred in his voice as he told them that they must pay for their insults to the fetish. He had not even mentioned the theft of the gold dust and diamonds.

"My heart is heavy at the thought, white chiefs," he said. "But — you must pay!"

Stuart McGregor had stammered ineffectual, foolish apologies:

"We — we were drunk. We didn't know what — oh — what we —"

"What you were doing!" the Bakoto had finished the sentence for him, with a little melancholy sigh. "And there is forgiveness in my heart —"

"You — you mean to say —" Farragut Hutchison had jumped up, with extended hand, blurting out hectic thanks.

"Forgiveness in *my* heart, not the *juju*'s," gently continued the negro. "For the *juju* never forgives. On the other hand, the *juju* is fair. He wants his just measure of blood. Not an ounce more. Therefore," the Bakoto had gone on, and his face had been as stony and as passionless as that of the Buddha who meditates in the shade of the cobra's hood, "the choice will be yours."

"Choice?" Farragut Hutchison had looked up, a gleam of hope in his eyes.

"Yes. Choice which one of you will die." The Bakoto had smiled, with the same suave courtliness which had, somehow, increased the utter horror of the scene. "Die — oh — a slow death, befitting the insult to the *juju*, befitting the *juju*'s great holiness!"

Suddenly, Stuart McGregor had understood that there would be no arguing, no bargaining whatsoever; and, quickly, had come his hysterical question:

"Who? I — or —"

He had slurred and stopped, somehow ashamed, and the Bakoto had finished the interrupted question with gentle, gliding, inhuman laughter: "Your friend? White chief, that is for you two to decide. I only know that the *juju* has spoken to the priest, and that he is satisfied with the life of one of you two; the life — and the death. A slow death."

He had paused; then had continued gently, so very, very gently: "Yes. A slow death, depending entirely upon the vitality of the one of you two who will be sacrificed to the *juju*. There will be little knives. There will be the flying insects which follow the smell of blood and festering flesh. Too, there will be many crimson-headed ants, many, ants — and a thin river of honey to show them the trail."

He had yawned. Then he had gone on: "Consider. The *juju* is just. He only wants the sacrifice of one of you, and you yourselves must decide which one shall go, and which one shall stay. And — remember the little, little knives. Be pleased to remember the many ants which follow the honey trail. I shall return shortly and hear your choice."

He had bowed and, with his silent warriors, had stepped back into the jungle that had closed behind them like a curtain.

Even in that moment of stark, enormous horror, horror too great to be grasped, horror that swept over and beyond the barriers of fear — even in that moment Stuart McGregor had realized that, by leaving the choice to them, the Bakoto had committed a refined cruelty worthy of a more civilized race, and had added a psychic torture fully as dreadful as the physical torture of the little knives.

Too, in that moment of ghastly, lecherous expectancy, he had known that it was Farragut Hutchison who would be sacrificed to the *juju* — Farragut Hutchison who sat there, staring into the camp fire, making queer little, funny noises in his throat.

Suddenly, Stuart McGregor had laughed — he remembered that laugh to his dying day — and had thrown a greasy pack of playing cards into the circle of meager, indifferent light.

"Let the cards decide, old boy," he had shouted. "One hand of poker — and no drawing to your hand. Showdown! That's square, isn't it?"

"Sure!" the other had replied, still staring straight ahead of him. "Go ahead and deal —"

His voice had drifted into a mumble while Stuart McGregor had picked up the deck, had shuffled, slowly, mechanically.

As he shuffled, it had seemed to him as if his brain was frantically telegraphing to his fingers, as if all those delicate little nerves that ran from the back of his skull down to his fingertips were throbbing a clicking little chorus:

"Do — it — Mac! Do — it — Mac! Do — it — Mac!" with a maddening, syncopated rhythm.

And he had kept on shuffling, had kept on watching the motions of his fingers — and had seen that his thumb and second finger had shuffled the ace of hearts to the bottom of the deck.

Had he done it on purpose? He did not know then. He never found out — though, in his memory, he lived through the scene a thousand times.

But there were the little knives. There were the ants. There was the honey trail. There was his own, hard decision to live. And, years earlier, he had been a professional faro dealer at Silver City.

Another ace had joined the first at the bottom of the deck. The third. The fourth.

And then Farragut Hutchison's violent: "Deal, man, deal! You're driving me crazy. Get it over with."

The sweat had been pouring from Stuart McGregor's face. His

blood had throbbed in his veins. Something like a sledgehammer had drummed at the base of his skull.

"Cut, won't you?" he had said, his voice coming as if from very far away.

The other had waved a trembling hand, "No, no! Deal 'em as they lie. You won't cheat me."

Stuart McGregor had cleared a little space on the ground with the point of his shoe.

He remembered the motion. He remembered how the dead leaves had stirred with a dry, rasping, tragic sound, how something slimy and phosphorous-green had squirmed through the tufted jungle grass, how a little furry scorpion had scurried away with a clicking *tchk-tchk-tchk*.

He had dealt.

Mechanically, even as he was watching them, his fingers had given himself five cards from the bottom of the deck. Four aces — and the queen of diamonds. And, the next second, in answer to Farragut Hutchison's choked: "Show-down! I have two pair — kings — and jacks!" his own well simulated shriek of joy and triumph:

"I win! I've four aces! Every ace in the pack!"

And then Farragut Hutchison's weak, ridiculous exclamation — ridiculous considering the dreadful fate that awaited him:

"Geewhittaker! You're some lucky guy, aren't you, Mac?"

At the same moment, the Bakoto chief had stepped out of the jungle, followed by half a dozen warriors.

Then the final scene — that ghastly, ironic moon squinting down, just as Farragut Hutchison had walked away between the giant, plumed, ochre-smeared Bakoto negroes, and bringing into stark relief the tattoo mark on his back where the shirt had been torn to tatters — and the leering, evil wink in the eagle's eye as Farragut Hutchison twitched his shoulder blades with absurd, nervous resignation.

Stuart McGregor remembered it every day of his life.

He spoke of it to many. But only to Father Aloysius O'Donnell, the priest who officiated in the little Gothic church around the corner, on Ninth Avenue, did he tell the whole truth — did he confess that he had cheated.

"Of course I cheated!" he said. "Of course!" And, with a sort of mocking bravado: "What would you have done, padre?"

The priest, who was old and wise and gentle, thus not at all sure of himself, shook his head.

"I don't know," he replied. "I don't know."

"Well — I *do* know. You would have done what I did. You wouldn't have been able to help yourself." Then, in a low voice: "And you would have paid! As I pay — every day, every minute, every second of my life."

"Regret, repentance," murmured the priest, but the other cut him short.

"Repentance — nothing. I regret nothing! I repent nothing! I'd do the same tomorrow. It isn't that — oh — that — what d'ye call it — sting of conscience, that's driving me crazy. It's fear!"

"Fear of what?" asked Father O'Donnell.

"Fear of Farragut Hutchison — who is dead!"

TEN YEARS AGO!

And he knew that Farragut Hutchison had died. For not long afterward a British trader had come upon certain gruesome but unmistakable remains and had brought the tale to the coast. Yet was there fear in Stuart McGregor's soul, fear worse than the fear of the little knives. Fear of Farragut Hutchison, who was dead?

No. He did not believe that the man was dead. He did not believe it, could not believe it.

"And even suppose he's dead," he used to say to the priest, "he'll get me. He'll get me as sure as you're born. I saw it in the eye of that eagle — the squinting eye of that infernal, tattooed eagle!"

Then he would turn a grayish yellow, his whole body would tremble with a terrible palsy and, in a sort of whine, which was both ridiculous and pathetic, given his size and bulk, given the crimson, twisted adventures through which he had passed, he would exclaim:

"He'll get me. He'll get me. He'll get me even from beyond the grave."

And then Father O'Donnell would cross himself rapidly, just a little guiltily.

It is said that there is a morbid curiosity which forces the murderer to view the place of his crime.

Some psychic reason of the same kind may have caused Stuart McGregor to decorate the walls and corners of his sitting room with the memories of that Africa which he feared and hated, and which, daily, he was trying to forget — with a shimmering, cruel mass of jungle curios, sjamboks and assegais, signal drums and daggers, knobkerries and rhino shields and what not.

Steadily, he added to his collection, buying in auction rooms, in little shops on the waterfront, from sailors and ship pursers and collectors who had duplicates for sale.

He became a well-known figure in the row of antique stores in back of Madison Square Garden, and was so liberal when it came to payment that Morris Newman, who specialized in African curios, would send the pick of all the new stuff he bought to his house.

IT WAS on a day in August — one of those tropical New York days when the very birds gasp for air, when orange-flaming sun rays drop from the brazen sky like crackling spears and the melting asphalt picks them up again and tosses them high — that Stuart McGregor, returning from a short walk, found a large, round package in his sitting room.

"Mr. Newman sent it," his servant explained. "He said it's a rare curio, and he's sure you'll like it."

"All right."

The servant bowed, left, and closed the door, while Stuart McGregor cut the twine, unwrapped the paper, looked.

And then, suddenly, he screamed with fear; and, just as suddenly, the scream of fear turned into a scream of maniacal joy.

For the thing which Newman had sent him was an African signal drum, covered with tightly stretched skin-human skin — white skin! And square in the center there was a tattoo mark — an eagle in red and blue, surmounted by a lopsided crown, and surrounded by a wavy design.

Here was the final proof that Farragut Hutchison was dead, that, for-ever, he was rid of his fear. In a paroxysm of joy, he picked up the drum and clutched it to his heart.

And then he gave a cry of pain. His lips quivered, frothed. His hands dropped the drum and fanned the air, and he looked at the thing that had fastened itself to his right wrist.

It seemed like a short length of rope, grayish in color, spotted with dull red. Even as Stuart McGregor dropped to the floor, dying, he knew what had happened.

A little venomous snake, an African fer-de-lance, that had been curled up in the inside of the drum, been numbed by the cold, and had been revived by the splintering heat of New York.

Yes — even as he died he knew what had happened. Even as he died, he saw that malign, obscene squint in the eagle's eye. Even as he died, he knew that Farragut Hutchison had killed him — from beyond the grave!

www.ingramcontent.com/pod-product-compliance
Lightning Source LLC
Chambersburg PA
CBHW030516020726
47494CB00004B/1123